I0771269

Mischief

at

Middle Wallop

Marel Brady

Lomondvale International Publications
Phoenix

Cover design by JUST INK

Library of Congress Control Number: 2009904325

ISBN-13   978-0-9824541-0-7
ISBN-10   0-9824541-0-4

Printed in the United States of America

THE ANNUAL MEETING

"Ladies, our annual meeting will commence in five minutes." The shrill voice of Cathy Crow pierced the comforting cushion of excited chatter and the aroma of coffee. Cathy's brown eyes were beautiful, but the cool distance disappointed admirers; her voice had a strained quality as if she were using all the muscles in her throat to prevent a scream. Cathy should have been attractive; everything about her was neat and trim, but her skin had a sallow hue which did not seem to match her professionally colored auburn hair. Something about Cathy made you conscious of her bones; her hands, her feet her ankles, her shoulders and elbows seemed oddly prominent. Cathy had been reluctant to become Lady Captain of Middle Wallop Golf Club, feeling she had insufficient support for her nomination, but she had soldiered on throughout the year. Cathy's husband, Rodney, was a morose character who didn't like spending money; he seemed content within their marriage but Cathy was unhappy and had crafted a lifestyle where they spent very little time alone; their life together was like a business arrangement around their only son. Cathy came across as sharp, hard and cold, but used all her emotional strength to keep up appearances; most days, it was all she could do to keep from sobbing. Rodney's marriage proposal was her only offer; the prospect of a wedding was very appealing, so she had taken a chance. Would life have been better if she had the courage to turn down his proposal? Who knows! Too late now!

"Come on, ladies! We need to start promptly." Cathy's job as a driving instructor had imbued her with a keen sense of punctuality; she gazed down at her oversized wrist watch and noted, with annoyance, that she had forgotten to manicure her nails.

"Oh, the crow has cackled," muttered Lynn Harper, under her breath, to Robina Restler. In a louder voice, she continued, "Better get moving, girls. Hope this doesn't go on too long. Got my body pump class tonight. Need to get into my LBD for the Valentines' dance." She gazed fondly around.

"LBD?" Robina queried."

"Little black dress!" Lynn announced, as she noted the attention of several other ladies. Lynn was quite large, big boned, well covered with plenty of flesh; her eyes, under flyaway light brown hair, were a curious kaleidoscope of aquamarine flecked with gold, giving the impression that the pattern might change whenever she looked away.

"Well," said Robina, "I've never had a little black dress. Mine are all large black dresses. Anyway, we have to wear either red or pink for the Valentines' dance."

Robina was bordering on obese; her small grey eyes had an intense look, as if to send a message that she was doing her very best but was a little disappointed that she couldn't do better; her grey hair was straight, quite short but rather badly cut by the traveling hairdresser who had been coming to her home for many years. Robina lumbered along merrily. She loved being a mother to her four daughters. Mind you, Hugo did not hide his disappointment that they had no son. Each pregnancy had been demanding, each birth had been complicated and Robina had never regained her figure. Robina's relationship with Hugo had gradually changed, with the arrival of each daughter creating a little more distance between them. Hugo had turned to food for comfort and was now quite enormous; his face was huge with several double chins underneath milky blue, impenetrable eyes; his torso was vast but, oddly, he was swift on his feet and his legs were quite adept at shifting his great weight. Truly, he looked a little like Humpty Dumpty. Hugo no longer enjoyed working at the bank – all those staff cuts, commuting to London got worse all the time and business lunches were a thing of the past, so Hugo now suppressed all the stresses and strains of his life with food. He often closed his eyes at night, dreaming of a table groaning with large quantities of every imaginable delicacy, which he could wash down with significant quantities of wine. Both Robina and Hugo loved cruising; their next cruise was a few weeks hence, but they wouldn't bother to get off at the ports; they had seen them all before; they would just rest in their cabin, working up an appetite, while the other passengers trudged around, getting footsore and weary, having to suffer the cuisine of some questionable local restaurant. Yes, Hugo often closed his eyes at night, dreaming of being on board ship, seeing the colorful platters of food inviting him to tempt his palate.

Robina could be trusted; she had been Lady Captain last year and done a good job; she wasn't gifted with any creativity, but she stuck to the rules and followed the format from the previous year, so nothing had gone too far adrift. Robina didn't have a great amount of self esteem, but her role at the club was as confidante and advisor to anyone who needed her. Robina was straight-forward and uncomplicated; you knew where you stood with her; she was kind hearted and undemanding.

"I don't want to be too late, either, Lynn," added Robina, "I have to cook Hugo's dinner when I get home."

Around fifty women, dressed to show off their latest outfits, surged into the meeting room, with a lot of fuss and chattering about where to sit, moving over to allow space for a friend, ignoring the lonely stragglers who, like full stops on a page, created little walls of punctuation between groups of people.

Those destined for the top table took their places. It suddenly became apparent that they were dressed differently from the others. No colorful suits or dresses. All were in somber business attire to denote a serious approach to the meeting.

Cathy, performing her final official duty as outgoing Lady Captain, directed the format of the meeting which was the same as previous years. The minutes of last year's meeting were read aloud, the content of so little interest that everyone's mind was wandering. The winners of every competition during the year were read out, interspersed with polite applause, followed by weaker handclapping as a wearisome list of handicap changes were announced. Nobody was listening for anything except the sound of their own name, which gave them a jolt of adrenalin and a rush of pride. Eventually, the real excitement took place.

"And I now have pleasure in announcing this year's committee." Cathy allowed a significant pause after she announced each name, looking up from her notes each time. "Secretary – Alice Tolkein. Handicap Secretary – Primrose Pretorius. Bronze Division Captain – Madeleine Minehead. Silver Division Captain – Barbara Blunt. Vice Captain – Nancy Ruff. Captain – Lynn Harper."

On hearing their names, the newly appointed office bearers feigned shyness, then focused on the faces gazing in their direction. Different faces showed different reactions; some admiring, some surprised, some inquisitive, some disinterested, some resentful. Past Captains, who had been consulted on all the appointments and been 'in the know' beforehand, smugly surveyed the scene.

The announcement of Captain and committee members ended twelve months of speculation. The year ahead would unfold much as any other; power politics would emerge, existing relationships would come under strain and new alliances would be forged. However, tension and discord had been mounting in Middle Wallop Golf Club during recent years. A sense of foreboding was almost tangible. Several members could not shake off the feeling that undercurrents were growing stronger and more dangerous.

"Since we have nothing listed under 'Any Other Business', I declare the meeting closed. I wish Lynn and the new committee good luck in their appointments," concluded Cathy.

A burst of chatter erupted. Some figures moved towards the new office bearers to offer congratulations. Other figures turned their backs, whispering in huddles to share negative views with like-minded ladies. The wave of chatter moved on to discussion of future events and, gradually, the farewells.

"See you for coffee tomorrow."

"Look forward to our match on Tuesday."

"See you Monday night."

"See you at the Valentine's dance."

The members swarmed in groups towards the heavy exit doors; some small groups dashed off into the night, others moved slowly to catch a farewell here and there, a few hung back, wanting a word with someone in particular. Lastly, the newly appointed committee members straggled outside, feeling an increased sense of importance.

"Just look at those stars!" exclaimed Madeleine Minehead, the new Bronze Division Captain. "We're so lucky. Eighty percent of the population of England can't see the stars. All they can see is an orange glow from neon lights." Waving goodbye, she started the car engine, driving home uncertainly along the country lanes from Middle Wallop Golf Club.

THE VALENTINES' DANCE

Seated at the top table on Saturday evening, the new committee and respective husbands were resplendent in their best gear. The Valentines' dance promised to be a fun evening. Robina was dressed sensibly in a long sleeved black dress, a scarf draped around her shoulders which showed a touch of red as a token to Valentines' Day. Hugo, sweating profusely, was wearing a red bow tie with his dinner suit. All the men had opted for a similar variation, some with matching red cummerbunds or silk handkerchiefs, or even a red carnation or red rose in their lapel. Lynn was wearing a short, pink, knitted dress which emphasized the girth of her thighs. The other ladies looked neat and smart in cocktail dresses in various shades of red and pink.

Madeleine looked quite special. Her long dress was styled in a crepe fabric in the shade of a ripe tomato. A broad halter neck flattered her shoulders and arms, displaying her bare back but covering the classic curves of her breasts. Two layers of wide frills started below the knee, parting to reveal her shapely legs. The frills tapered towards the back, eventually reaching the floor in a tantalizing flourish of ruffled fabric. Short unruly dark blonde waves and curls framed her face, her elegant hands moving expressively in tune with her animated conversation.

Sweeping an eye around the ballroom, a vista of red and pink greeted the eye. Soft, romantic music floated in the background. The perfect setting for a most pleasant evening. The men were content to sit back and relax, shaking off the stresses and strains of their working world; they had no need to put in any effort; their wives kept the conversation going over dinner; all they had to do was smile contentedly, and say very little. Alice and Primrose were engrossed in a discussion about the flower arrangements for the next function. Barbara and Cathy were exchanging concerns at the increase in membership fees. Robina and Lynn pondered the merits of various brands of golf balls.

The appetizer of asparagus mousse was served in glass goblets. The entrée of prime beef au jus was served on individual plates. The vegetables were presented to the table in large dishes, with serving spoons. Cathy's husband, Rodney, took it upon himself to serve everyone with vegetables, leaving himself until last. All eyes were on him as he scooped more than his fair share of vegetables onto his plate, scraping the dish with a serving spoon while making screeching sounds of metal on metal. As their ears rebelled against this high-pitched sound invasion, fellow diners' eyes narrowed, their lips stretched out in a grimace. Rodney had become hard of hearing lately and did not realize he was making such a discordant sound; he looked up to find a sea of faces gazing at him with excessive distaste. "I'll never be accepted at this club," he thought. "You would think I just farted the way this lot are looking at me. I'll get them back for this." Cathy was looking at Rodney with pity and embarrassment; little did she know, that her husband was adding each person, at the table, to his list of obscene phone calls.

Madeleine was tense this evening. Adam, her husband, had one of his rages a few days ago and they were not on speaking terms; he was a successful businessman, the chairman of an oil company based in London; he loved Madeleine and his family more than anyone in the world. One thing Adam loved, above all else, was money; he was happy for Madeleine to possess anything she wanted; she had everything money could buy – lovely clothes and jewelry, a luxury car, a large house in the country; but all this was just a showcase for Adam's success. Madeleine managed the household particularly well, dealing with all the maintenance and administration as well as the routine finances. They never argued about money or possessions, everything they owned was in joint names; after a lifetime together, they trusted each other not to spend foolishly; their financial portfolio was considerable at this point in their lives. Adam's rage was engendered by Madeleine's suggestion that they sell some of their shares and spend the profit on a buy-to-let property. In 2004, with lack of confidence in the stock market, this was the way lots of people were moving with their investments. Adam's view was that this was a foolish time to sell shares; he had called her stupid, confounded her by saying that the shares belonged to him since he had earned them, and demanded she give an account of herself on what she did in return for his efforts. Madeleine had been dealing with Adam's rages all their married life; his fury had the power of a tornado, whipping up without warning, crushing everyone in sight, leaving a scorched and barren landscape from which, gradually, without apology, the hopeful green shoots of reconciliation ventured. Surprisingly, Madeleine had managed to stay relatively calm on this occasion; she simply informed Adam that she did not need to justify herself; the law stated that half of all of his wealth belonged to her, regardless of whether or not he found her to be poor value for money. A cold icy grip had taken hold of Madeleine's heart and she had moved into one of the spare bedrooms two days ago.

Trying to push the strain of the last few days into the background, Madeleine felt she should make some effort at conversation. Hugo was seated on her right and, apart from an initial greeting, had not spoken to her this evening. "So, how was your day, Hugo?" she asked.

"Yes, fine," Hugo replied.

"Pretty cold. Apparently, we might get snow," she ventured. Madeleine's voice was soft and pure, like water cascading into a crystal glass.

"Yes, seems like it," Hugo responded, without interest.

Dessert was served – two heart shaped chocolate shells filled with strawberry mousse; the plate was decorated with swirls of chocolate sauce, occasional raspberries were delicately positioned and dusted with icing sugar.

"Are you enjoying your golf, Hugo?" Madeleine tried another subject.

"No," was the reply.

Madeleine wasn't getting very far, so she tried another tack, "There are some wonderful exhibitions in London at the moment. I was at the Faberge exhibition in the Queen's gallery yesterday." Hugo smiled vaguely. Lynn, who had been quiet all evening, was watching now.

"I would love to go to the Orchid exhibition at Kew Gardens," Madeleine continued, "but I don't know how long it's running." Hugo's eyebrows raised a little, but he said nothing. "Have you been up to the theater lately, Hugo? We went to see the Lion King last week."

"No, not been to the theater for a while." Hugo's voice was flat. A long pause ensued.

Preventing the pause from developing into silence, Madeleine changed the subject. "Your last trip was to South America. I would love to make that trip. Would you recommend it?"

"Yes, all their trips are pretty good," replied Hugo, without enthusiasm.

"Don't suppose Robina goes up to London much," Madeleine backtracked. "I know she likes to spend a lot of time in the garden. Even at this time of year, there's so much to do."

"Yes, there is." Hugo gestured to Rodney, saying, "Some more wine here." He filled up his glass, without offering the same courtesy to others at the table. Madeleine and Lynn rolled their eyes at each other.

"Your office is quite close to Oxford Street, Hugo. I wouldn't mind being so close to Selfridges or Bond Street," Madeleine continued the one sided conversation.

"Hmmmph."

"How are things in the banking world?" Madeleine introduced another topic.

"Yes, OK."

"Do you.....?" She didn't get to finish the sentence.

"No more questions!" roared Hugo, thumping the table. His newly filled wine glass fell over, spreading the red wine onto the white tablecloth.

Everyone round the table stared at the scarlet stain and quickly rose to their feet to avoid contact with the creeping cause of confusion. Several chairs toppled backwards. As Madeleine turned with amazement towards Hugo, Robina swiftly managed to stand between them, her back shielding Hugo from Madeleine's view, her eyes giving out a beseeching message. "Things are not good at the bank," she whispered. Madeleine's deep blue eyes were pools of consternation. Everyone became statues. After a moment of reading Robina's gaze, Madeleine simply nodded and sat down. The others followed her lead.

Thankfully, the band started playing loud swing music. The diners dispersed onto the dance floor to escape the tension at the table. Robina was still standing, protecting Hugo with her back. Madeleine and Adam looked at each other across the table; they moved towards the dance floor together and took their accustomed pose for dancing. Swaying gently to the music and finding Adam's hand fitting into hers, Madeleine relaxed a little and the icy chill she felt towards him thawed a fraction. Holding her slim body in his arms, Adam felt a fiercely protective urge grip his soul. The revelers from the top table spent the remainder of the evening avoiding each other. Everyone stayed on the dance floor or mingled with groups at other tables. Relief was felt at the announcement of the last dance. The couples said brief goodbyes to each other, eager to escape the embarrassment of the evening. Robina and Hugo were nowhere to be seen.

Adam and Madeleine drove home in silence. Adam had a wholesome looking, chap next door appearance; fair complexion, close cropped hair, chubby build; just a little taller than his wife, he wore gold-rimmed spectacles which hid the intensity of his hazel eyes. On reaching home, the silence continued. At the top of the stairs, as they were about to part company, Madeleine questioned, "Is this how we're going to continue?"

Adam replied dully, "I don't feel any differently."

"Neither do I," she answered.

"You started the separate living arrangements," Adam stated, reflecting that he had to make his own bed and go to the village shop this morning to buy lunch because Madeleine had done no grocery shopping.

"You made me feel worthless, demanding what I do for you in return for your earnings." Madeleine recalled how she had cleaned the bathrooms and the kitchen floor this morning, making as much noise as possible while Adam watched TV; she wordlessly make the point to him about her more menial existence, compared to his ivory tower at the office as well as his 'off duty' attitude at weekends; she had spent the afternoon in the garden, in full view of the house, trimming ivy from the hedge, trusting that her industrious image would make Adam feel uncomfortable; she felt satisfaction that she had not provided any meals for him for several days. Perhaps Adam would begin to notice the things she did for him, only if they were either done in his presence or not done at all.

"That's not what I meant," countered Adam.

"Well, what did you mean?" Madeleine wanted to know.

"I deal in billions. You deal in pennies. That's not to say that your contribution is any less than mine. Look, I'm an honorable man. I don't see why I have to be treated like this."

"Because you turn into a different person. At times, a demon enters this house."

"A demon! So, that's what I am?"

"Listen here, I didn't marry you for your money; you didn't have any when we first met. I simply find it chilling that I'm not permitted to raise the subject of disposing of shares."

They both stood in silence for several minutes, still at the top of the stairs.

"Do you want a cup of coffee?" Madeleine asked.

"OK."

They slowly descended the stairs to the kitchen. The lemon scent from the morning floor washing session lingered. Madeleine flicked the kettle to boil, hearing the energy surge pushing through the silence. Rapidly, the turbulent water bubbled to a crescendo, simmering down with an exhausted sigh.

"I love you, really." Madeleine said, as she stood at the kitchen sink, with her back to him.

"I love you too."

Madeleine made instant coffee in heavy stoneware cups, and sat down on the hard kitchen chair. Adam moved to stand at the sink, viewing her sideways; he stared at the clock. After several minutes of silence, Madeleine caught his eye and pulled a face. Adam mimicked the childish grimace.

As the echo of silence lingered, Madeleine pondered the country cottage image on the coffee cup, her index finger pressed against the saucer. Keeping her gaze downwards, she ventured, "So...what about the shares, then?"

LADIES' MEDAL DAY

Ladies' Medal day was the week after the Valentines' dance. Most of the ladies dreaded this event since they were sure to play badly and end up with their handicap increasing, yet again. The day dawned crisp, clear and sunny. A perfect winter's day in Hampshire. The weather was not quite so perfect for golf. The temperature was just above freezing, so lots of layers had to be worn which hampered the golf swing, somewhat. A stiff wind wildly swayed the tops of trees, so each well judged shot was caught by gusts and taken off target. The wind was blustering, so a new assessment had to be made with each shot to compensate.

The English countryside looked wonderful at this time of year. You could see far and wide since the trees and hedges were bare; a vista of rolling green hills, interspersed with plowed fields. Country houses dating back several centuries, mostly hidden throughout the year, could be glimpsed in passing. Ponds and streams, shallow and silent in the summer, were skimmed by the wind or gurgled on their urgent journey. After battling the wind for almost four hours, the ladies were glad to reach the clubhouse. Most faces showed exhilaration from the fresh air and exercise; there were lots of rosy cheeks; a few delighted grins beamed out; other faces were expressionless; some looked irritated; others were glowering with annoyance.

"Did you see the snowdrops alongside the fourteenth fairway?" Robina enquired from the gathering in the locker room.

"Yes, weren't they gorgeous?" Lynn responded.

"Just hope we don't get any more frost," continued Robina.

"That'll be a relief," came a voice from round a corner.

"The birds are so busy. You can hear mating calls. It's all happening much too early," said Robina, looking perplexed; she was really a country person at heart.

"Yes. Global warming. I have daffodils in my garden and the crocuses are peeping through," Lynn continued. "The buds on my camellias are bursting to bloom. There's even a daphne in flower at my front gate."

"I wonder when the primroses will come to life?" called out Primrose Pretorius. A general chuckle rippled through the locker room.

Golf shoes were being removed with sighs of relief. Thick socks were being replaced by fifteen denier knee highs. Feet were slipping into smart loafers. Windproof jackets were peeled off and stored in lockers. Warm soapy water brought freezing hands back to life. Hair was brushed. Lipstick was applied. Eager eyes checked the notice-board for forthcoming fixtures. Fingers fumbled in handbags. Pockets were checked for keys and small change.

En route to the stud bar, lots of comments could be heard.

"I couldn't use my woods today."

"My putting lets me down."

"That wind gets in my head."

"I couldn't swing wearing all those clothes."

"I couldn't stay out of bunkers."

"I'm thinking of giving up this game."

In the ladies' lounge, an air of expectation hummed. Sandwiches of every imaginable combination were being delivered to tables along with pots of tea and coffee. Score cards were being handed to committee members. Those who had played well leaned close to adjacent tables to learn the scores of other players. Performing her first duty as Captain, Lynn took the floor. "I would like to thank the ladies for playing on such a cold winter's day. I think the course is in marvelous condition and I hope you enjoyed your game. I am pleased to announce the winners of the February Medal competition. In third place Carol Brown. In second place Jean Hunt. In first place...me!"

A few sour faces greeted this latest announcement. Lukewarm applause followed. The atmosphere changed to a disgruntled buzz.

"Hmmmph, would be nice for someone else to win for a change."

"Of course, she practices all the time."

"Without that lost ball, I would have won."

A restlessness took over the room. Some members took their leave, others remained. There was much to-ing and fro-ing between tables. Members slotted dates into their calendars.

"We need to fix a date for the winter league."

"Are you still free to play in the away match next week?"

"Are you coming to the roll up?"

"Do you need a partner for the spring meeting?"

Gradually, the room emptied leaving behind only a small nucleus. "Another coffee, Robina?" asked Lynn.

"Oh, all right, then."

Lynn wandered off and returned with the coffees. "I don't know how I managed to put up with Alice today. All that talking drives me mad,

Lynn confided to Robina. "She just never lets up. I'm trying to concentrate on my shots and she just keeps gabbling on. And she never says anything interesting! There's not a thought comes into her head that doesn't come out of her mouth. How her poor husband puts up with it, I'll never know – he must be a saint."

"But, Lynn, you did win!" countered Robina.

"Yes, but I could have had a much better score if Alice hadn't spoiled my concentration."

"Oh, well, there we go. How was your body pump class the other evening?" countered Robina, changing the subject.

"Yea, really good. It's the best exercise to keep osteoporosis at bay. Also helps the posture and tones up those arms. You should see my arms, they're so flabby. It's horrible. Occasionally, I catch the reflection of various body parts in the mirror and it's quite alarming."

Robina's eyebrows rose. "What about your holiday, Lynn?" Have you booked it yet?"

"Oh, yes. All done and dusted. Costa del Sol. Just love that area around Marbella. Spain is hard to beat. Great weather, great food, wonderful golf courses and lots of shopping. What more could you ask? Mind you, golf has become really expensive there now. Some courses are charging eighty pounds a round! You know Cathy and Rodney are coming with us? Yes, we talked about it at the end of last year. Confirmed it with the travel agent on the day of the Valentines' dance."

"Hi ladies! Congratulations on your win today, Lynn," said Cathy Crow, as she approached the table.

"I better get moving," sighed Robina. "I need to walk the dog."

"Didn't know you had a dog," said Cathy, with surprise.

"Just got him at the weekend. He's a retired greyhound. His racing name was Prince Rupert of Raithin, but we've renamed him. We call him Spindleshanks – Spindle for short. But he doesn't like being left alone in the house. Seems to get the idea that he's been abandoned. He's OK being left in the car because he can see and hear people. He's quite happy sleeping on a blanket on the back seat."

"A retired greyhound!" said Cathy, incredulously.

"Yes, he's ever so gentle," enthused Robina. "Doesn't bark. He's never been in a house before, so he has to investigate everything. Sticks his nose in the dishwasher, just everywhere, to check out the scents."

"So, where do you walk him?" Cathy wanted to know.

"Oh, we go through the lanes in the village, ending up at the pond. I can't let him off the lead yet and I have to keep him muzzled. He would run after anything that moved. The Rescue Center did say he kept running away from his previous owners. This is a second attempt to find him a suitable home. Hopefully, through time, he'll settle down. But he's ever so sweet and gentle. Actually, he doesn't walk for long. Twenty minutes and he's tired out. He's a racer, you see, so only goes in short sprints."

"What about the garden, Robina? You have lots of wildlife. Won't he chase everything there?" enquired Cathy.

"Poor thing. He gazes out of the window. Sees all the wonderful birds. We have lots of ground feeders – woodpeckers, magpies, doves, jays, blackbirds, robins. Their movement tantalizes him. And the squirrels have him mesmerized. Heaven knows what he'll do when the rabbits and deer pay us a visit." Robina smiled fondly.

"What are you going to do with him when you go on your cruises?" Cathy wondered.

"Actually, that's no problem because we don't, in fact, own him. We just foster him. So, at anytime, he can go back for holidays."

"So, are you going to put him into races?" Cathy looked perplexed at the thought of Robina and Hugo frequenting dog tracks.

"Oh, no! He's retired. He was very well known in the racing world. And he sired over two thousand pups! He deserves a rest!" chuckled Robina.

Suddenly, the door to the ladies' lounge opened. Anastasia, the proprietor of the golf club, moved through the lounge towards the locker room. Anastasia was tall, medium build with dark hair, dark brown eyes and large, bland features; her expression was one of dazed concentration; she looked neither to right nor to left, keeping her head slightly in front of her body, almost like a turtle. Indeed, as she moved, the air around her seemed to part as if she were wading through water. Conversation froze as all heads turned to follow her passage through the ladies' lounge. Once she had exited into the corridor, there was a considerable pause, allowing Anastasia's spirit to be expelled before normal chatter could continue.

"Must go then!" sighed Robina, raising her heavy frame from the coffee table, hitching her bulging handbag onto her shoulder.

"I'll walk to the car with you," chimed Madeleine. "I need to get going, as well. I've got time booked at the learning center today for my computer course."

"Have you almost finished the course, Madeleine?" queried Robina.

"Yes, just one more module to go. I've done Word, Email, Internet, Excel and PowerPoint. Just got Database to do and then I'm done. That'll leave more time for golf with the better weather coming in.

We're off on our skiing holiday tomorrow. So I hope the temperatures are milder here when we get back," responded Madeleine.

"Where are you going skiing?" asked Lynn.

"The French Alps. Need to fix up some travel insurance before we go," Madeleine remembered. "That's the last on my list of things to do, before I close the suitcases."

"You should open an account at my bank. They give free travel insurance," interjected Cathy.

At the mention of a bank, they all thought of Hugo and his amazing outburst at the Valentines' dance. An uncomfortable silence settled. Alice walked towards the group.

"You off home then, Alice?" demanded Lynn, willing her to leave.

"Yes, got my line dancing class this afternoon. So, I need to get going."

"Bye, Alice," the others chorused, leaving her no invitation to stay.

Robina, Madeleine and Alice moved through the doors of the ladies' lounge into the outside corridor, towards the main exit doors.

"Well!" exclaimed Barbara, who had been alertly witnessing the previous conversations. "A retired greyhound! They must have taken leave of their senses. Such a working class accessory." The others tried to hide their alarm at such a politically incorrect statement. "Can you just see the two of them?" Barbara continued. "Hugo and Robina lumbering along like two great oafs, with that skinny mutt slinking between them?" She gave an exasperated sigh of despair, as if she might somehow be associated with this unacceptable vision. A few wry smiles followed this outburst. One or two sniggers escaped.

Primrose moved towards the table. "What am I missing?" she enquired.

"Oh, nothing," answered Lynn. Not being allowed into the secret, Primrose sat down, keeping her face a mask of impassivity.

"So, how's business, Primrose?" asked Nancy Ruff.

"Quiet, really, but it always is this time of year. People get stuff done for Christmas, then take advantage of special offers in January. Won't see much activity till the clocks change." Primrose and her husband, Marius, operated a dry cleaning business in nearby Andover. Primrose was a meticulous person; petite and fragile build, with hair colored to platinum blonde; nails shaped and polished to perfection; make-up always flawless; clothes always neat and well coordinated but never chic or stylish; her face was well proportioned with regular features; the look in her green eyes never changed, always a pleasant smile within an expressionless mask. Primrose changed the subject to committee business. "Do we need to be thinking about the spring meeting? Should we be buying prizes or asking for raffle donations?"

Looking surprised, Lynn answered, "We don't need to worry about that just yet. We'll discuss it at the committee meeting. What about handicap changes? Have you been working on that?"

"Yes, all taken care of," Primrose answered.

"And how did you play today?" Lynn continued.

"Well...thirteen over handicap," was the answer. Lynn looked unimpressed.

"So, I better be going." Primrose's petite feet took her swiftly to the door. "Bye, folks."

"Do you know," said Lynn, once Primrose was out of earshot. "If this was a members' club, she would never get in. There would be a handicap limit." All eyes widened at Lynn's criticism.

"Hopefully, she'll make a good committee member," countered Nancy Ruff. "She's a very conscientious person."

"Bit too conscientious," answered Lynn. "What's she doing interfering with the spring meeting prizes?"

"That's what you get from these foreigners!" Barbara spluttered. "They arrive here and get all the benefits. Free health care and education, and the government gives them a free house with a television and a computer."

"She's not a foreigner, Barbara," responded Nancy. "Primrose has a British passport."

"But she's only lived here a few years!" retorted Barbara.

An uncomfortable silence descended. Breaking the tension, Cathy, still feeling the responsibility of her role as Immediate Past Captain, called out breezily, "Anyone want to play in an open competition?" Let's have a look at the book. It's in the locker room."

Barbara, Nancy and Cathy moved out of the ladies' lounge back into the locker room, leaving Lynn, their new Captain, lagging behind. Madeleine and Robina had already left the clubhouse building, walking together towards their cars.

"Hope Spindle's OK." Robina looked worried. "Haven't left him this long before," she said, opening the rear door behind the passenger seat. A canine head, with gentle eyes, showed mild interest as the door opened. Madeleine moved forward to inspect the new arrival; his necked stretched out to sniff her at close quarters. "What a handsome fellow!" Madeleine said, politely, backing away.

"Actually, I wanted to talk to you," said Robina, opening the driver's door. "Have you got a minute?"

"OK," answered Madeleine. Robina was now seated in the driver's seat and had opened the passenger door. Taking the invitation, Madeleine sat in the passenger seat and waited for Robina to close the driver's door before quietly closing the door at her own side.

"What's up?" Madeleine took the initiative.

"I just wanted to apologize for Hugo's behavior at the Valentines' dance."

"Oh!" said Madeleine, casting her eyes down with embarrassment.

"Things are not good. Hugo is spending more time at home than he is at the bank. He's very irritable. To be quite honest, he's under investigation – lots of questions to be answered. That's why he lost his temper. It's just unfortunate that you got the brunt of it. I'm sorry, Madeleine."

"Well, perhaps I shouldn't have kept the conversation going when he wasn't responding. Asking him questions was the only way I could get him to talk. But you shouldn't be apologizing for him, Robina. I don't think he sees the situation like you do."

"OK, I'll speak to him. I'll ask him to apologize to you next time he sees you." Madeleine nodded, wondering how Hugo might deal with this entreaty from his wife.

"Hey, look, it's starting to snow," exclaimed Madeleine, as a few white flakes melted on the windscreen. "I better get going." She opened the car door, ready to move round to her own vehicle, parked nearby.

"I'm making pancakes tonight," called out Robina, as Madeleine climbed out of the passenger seat.

Cathy, Nancy, Barbara and Lynn had moved out of the clubhouse and were walking together towards their cars. "Can I come to your house tonight?" called out Nancy. "If you're making pancakes, Robina, I want to be there."

TWO MINUTES

No-one was quite sure how Rodney Crow earned a living; something to do with engineering parts; he traveled a lot, sometimes to the Middle East, sometimes to Europe, often to Italy, mostly by air. The only time Rodney traveled by road was when he crossed the channel to France: he always hired a white van. Cathy wondered why Rodney didn't take his car, but he said the van was useful for bringing back duty free items; he seldom filled the van, although, occasionally, he would bring back large quantities of beer. Cathy admired Rodney's uncharacteristic generosity, as he gave the beer to business friends who called round next day to collect the cans; she wanted to meet his friends, invite them in for a drink but Rodney wasn't too sociable and not keen on the idea. Cathy always gave Rodney her duty free shopping list – some wine, some perfume, coffee and cheese; he never failed to deliver her list of goodies. Cathy loved when Rodney went to France – these were the rare occasions when he stepped out of his usual morose character: he always returned with excitement in his eyes, so she hoped he was planning another trip soon. Picking up her car keys from the hall table, Cathy called out goodbye to Rodney and made her way out to the driveway; she had a nine o'clock lesson with one of her pupils. During half term, lots of teenagers wanted driving lessons.

Opening the front door, Cathy was surprised again by the fog; she had been taken aback by it first thing this morning as she opened the curtains. Now, she would have to consider whether a lesson was feasible in these weather conditions; she would decide once she had assessed the conditions in Stockbridge, where she was picking up her pupil. Maybe she would cancel the lesson and come back home and do some ironing instead.

It was unusual. Fog. Seldom happened in the south of England. Most infrequent in Hampshire. Mid morning and it still hung around. Early this morning, just as it was getting light, Rodney looked out of the window to see the black silhouettes of naked trees advancing towards him out of their grey shrouds. He knew he would do it today. He took time, getting himself ready; giving himself the treat of a leisurely wet shave, he scrutinized his face in the mirror which reflected dark wavy hair and smooth, pale skin; his pale blue eyes, the whites streaked with red veins, were curiously bulbous and wide giving the impression of peripheral vision. A calm expression compelled comparison with some cold blooded creature ... perhaps a lizard or other species of the reptile family. Rodney slowly descended the stairs, the reflection of his partly dressed thin body gliding across the glass doors of the dining room, as he made his way into the study. He carefully turned over the pages of Cathy's address book. Who would it be today? As the names floated past his eyes, he conjured up visions of how they looked in the flesh and what their reactions might be. Each night, over dinner at the kitchen table, he would get Cathy to talk about her pupils. If a pupil sounded like a possibility, he would ask for a physical description. Now, he had a database of potential victims in his head. Cathy was delighted that Rodney took an interest in her work, as he chatted with her each evening: little did she know what he got up to when she wasn't around. Enjoying the delicious anticipation, Rodney looked for other addresses. What about the golf club? He picked up the Middle Wallop Golf Club telephone list. "Yes, those smug cows!" he thought. "One of them will hear from me today." Adrenalin rushed through his veins. "Which one? Which one?" He picked up the phone, dialed 141 to withhold his identity, and entered Nancy Ruff's number into the keypad. Excitement leapt from his eyes.

"Hello, Nancy, it's Edward Braithwaite, general manager at the golf club."

"Oh, yes, Edward. What can I do for you?"

"I'm phoning about your membership renewal at the golf club."

"You don't sound right, Edward ... it doesn't sound like you."

"I'm a bit stressed out."

"Oh ... so it's about membership renewal?" Nancy repeated.

"Well, things have changed. You need to do something else to renew your membership."

"Oh, what's that?"

"You need to suck my cock!"

"Whhhhhhaaaaaatt!!!!"

"You heard me. You need to suck my cock."

"Who the hell is this?" Nancy thought if she could keep him talking the police would be able to trace the call.

"Just suck my cock."

"Who the hell are you? You're just a cowardly creep! A vile creature!" Nancy shouted at the top of her voice.

"I want you to suck my cock."

Nancy wanted to vent her anger on him. Anger at the invasion of her peaceful world. "He must know who I am," she thought. "He knows I'm a golf club member ... I must know him ... keep him talking ... keep him talking ... listen to his voice ... listen to his voice." She recognized the voice but couldn't place it. She was timing the call on her wristwatch. Nancy wanted to attack him; her blood was boiling now; her only defense was words. "You're a perverted pig!" she yelled. She seemed to remember that a call needs to be two minutes long to be traced by the police.

"But you must suck my cock."

"You're mentally deranged. You need to crawl back into the dirt you came from."

"I just want you to suck my cock."

"Go to hell." Enough! Nancy slammed down the phone. "Who was it ... who was it?" His voice was so familiar; it kept ringing round her head. "I know him ... I know him." Fury flooding her veins, she dialed 999.

"Emergency. Which service, please?"

"Police." Nancy's call was swiftly directed. "I've just had an obscene phone call."

"Do you know who it was?" the police officer asked, his voice sounding so calm and civilized.

"No. He tried to impersonate someone I know. I want the call traced. I kept him talking for two minutes, so it should be possible." Nancy's heard started to ache.

"I'm very sorry, Madam. We are unable to trace calls, no matter how long. And, unless the caller can be identified, we cannot report it as a crime."

"I recognized his voice. If I think about it long enough, I might work out who it was." Nancy felt the tears prick her eyes now.

"Yes, contact us if you can identify the caller."

"I want this phone monitored," Nancy demanded. "What if he phones again?"

"Yes, Madam, we can put a six month monitor on your phone. All numbers phoning your residence will be recorded. You just need to let us know the date and time and we will trace the call."

"What should I say if he phones again? Should I keep him talking for two minutes?" asked Nancy.

"No, that won't be necessary," advised the police officer.

"So, I don't need to talk to him?"

"What did he actually say?"

"I'm not going to repeat it!" Nancy was resolute.

"No, Madam."

"What do I say if he phones again? I just kept shouting at him to keep him talking."

"Unfortunately, Madam, you just played into his hands. People like that want a reaction. That's what gives them a thrill. He'll be satisfied that he upset you."

"Oh, I see. OK. So, I let you know if he phones again. And I tell you the date and time. And you'll be monitoring the line as of now. OK. Thank you."

Nancy sat down; she knew that voice; she had a good ear for music; she sang in Stockbridge choral society; she couldn't read music, never had the training, but she could hear a song and remember the notes quite clearly; she knew that voice; she would probably hear that voice in person soon.

Nancy Ruff had been married to Colin for thirty years; they were both seventeen years old when they met, messing about with the village hall dance scene and getting their first taste of vodka; he was just one of many boys with whom she had become familiar; he went further; he had been so insistent; grabbing her like a devil; she couldn't fight him off; she didn't try too hard; she was curious and foolish but her hormones fired her on; she had lost her virginity; it felt like a loss; she had fought against lust but she had been conquered. Funny how people talked about losing your virginity; nobody talked about gaining anything when you allowed a man to claim you; now she was his; she had lost choices in life; word got around; other local boys kept clear. Colin had power; he didn't say much but his physical strength kept other males out of his arena. When Nancy got home that night, her mother gave her a look that lasted a lifetime; a hard investigative look which took in all the details of her appearance – her muddied and crumpled cotton dress and labored breathing; a look which traveled to her flushed cheeks and her swollen lips, finally colliding with her eyes in a knowing reproach. Nancy had allowed Colin to mark his territory again; before long, she was pregnant and, after a hasty marriage, installed in one of the farmhouses with her newborn; the course of her life was forged. Nancy thought of life in farming terms – birth, weaning, shelter, breeding, survival of the fittest, and eventually sickness and death; she didn't think about love, she just got on with life as best she could. Twenty years ago, Colin bought the Old Dairy in the nearby village of Nether Wallop; it was a sound structure, but the roof had collapsed many years before. Colin was a worker, that's for sure; every spare minute, he labored on that place, built it up to double story, putting on a new roof, creating rooms, installing the kitchen and bathrooms; anything he came across second hand, he used: so, they had quite a unique and spacious dwelling with amazing fireplaces and quirky bathrooms. Reaching the house was tricky in bad weather since the Old Dairy was situated up a mile long cart track from the main road but, undaunted, they gradually bought and developed the fields alongside. Initially, they permitted campers to pitch their tents; over the years, by scrimping and scraping, saving and mending, they had managed to buy caravans which were now forty in number; they ran a shop on the site which was used by villagers, as well as those who, attracted by the trout fishing on the River Test, rented the caravans.

"... that voice ... that voice...," it was ringing in her head. "...need to get going ... due at the caravan site at eleven o'clock ..." Nancy looked in the mirror, catching sight of her plump figure; she sighed, watching her hand shake with delayed shock, as she put on her caramel colored lipstick; she stared into the depths of her bright blue eyes and ran a broad hand through her hair, noting the dry texture and promising herself a visit to the hairdresser for a conditioning treatment and another copper color rinse to cover the increasing grey hairs. Nancy had gained a bounce in her step since becoming a red head, making her feel a little bolder in her outlook; thinking about the forthcoming hairdresser visit cheered her up, but her legs started to tremble now; he really had shaken her up "... that voice ... that voice ..."

SATURDAY COMPETITION

"Those guys asked me to play with them in the Saturday competition," Adam commented to Madeleine over breakfast, a few days later.

"So, will you do it?"

"Yes, I put my name up."

"So, who are you playing with?" asked Madeleine.

"Hugo Restler, Percy Blunt and Colin Ruff."

Saturday morning dawned; another frosty winter's day, clear blue skies and sunshine. The wind, of previous days, had died down. Adam had set his alarm clock for seven o'clock; he hated an alarm clock at the weekend preferring to wake up naturally, so he was a little irritable. Madeleine was fixing him a protein breakfast of bacon and eggs and had filled his golf bag with cereal bars to keep the hunger at bay on the way round the course. Adam had showered and dressed and was heading downstairs as Madeleine looked up. "Oh, God! No!" she shrieked.

Alarmed, Adam shouted, "What???"

"Your clothes. You can't go out like that!"

"What are you talking about?"

"Nothing matches."

"Well, who cares!"

"Look, you can't wear that striped shirt under that sweater. You have two patterns together that don't work. You need to wear a plain black or plain beige collar under that sweater. What about a vest – are you wearing one? No? Well, you'll have to change. I'll leave out a black polo neck. And you need to wear a vest underneath. And those socks don't work either. I'll leave out black ones, then everything will be coordinated and you'll be warm enough." Madeleine was exasperated.

"I thought we'd been invaded by aliens the way you shrieked!" mocked Adam. With a sigh, he turned around making his way back upstairs to the bedroom. A few minutes later, he emerged having changed into the clothes which pleased his wife. Coming back downstairs, Adam checked he had everything he needed – locker key, spare socks, golf gloves, bar card, tee pegs, balls, markers, pitch repairer, and small change for entry fee.

Reaching the entrance hall, Madeleine was there to send him on his way. "Have a lovely day, darling. Doesn't matter how you play. Just enjoy." She gave him a brief hug and kiss as she opened the door.

Adam's car was covered with frost. While Madeleine stood at the window, waiting to wave him goodbye, he scraped the frost from the windscreen, his expression one of mild irritation that he hadn't bothered to use the garage last night. Reaching into the car, he found the can of de-icer and sprayed the windscreen, watching the liquid quickly change from artistic splodges into clear rivers spreading across the landscape of his world. If only all problems could be solved so easily, he thought!

Reaching the clubhouse, only a few miles away, Adam entered the pro shop to sign up and pay his entry fee. There were lots of witty comments and snorts of laughter flying between the various groups of men who were moving around outside. Golf bags were hauled out of cars. Golf shoes thudded towards the clubhouse in the frosty air. The atmosphere was like a stable yard of restless horses, eager to taste the freedom of a morning gallop.

Hugo, Percy and Colin had already arrived. Along with Adam, the foursome made their way towards the first tee. Adam reflected how the clubhouse looked like a Tesco supermarket, the red tiled roof with little turrets and dormer windows defiantly guarding the white washed walls. On the expanse of rough grass, a hundred yards behind the tee, some men were swinging their clubs to loosen up their muscles, some were fiddling with the contents of golf bags, some were zipping up windproof jackets, some were standing back relaxed and chatting, others were already 'in the zone' with a faraway look of concentration. The tension mounted as Adam's group were next to tee off. "Handicap or ready golf?" asked Hugo. They agreed that ready golf was fine. Colin, who never had much to say, teed off first; his shot was splendid – a high trajectory, which looked like it might be a few degrees off target but, at the highest point, the ball swerved into position like an aircraft banking to land; the ball dropped to earth, rolling on the fairway until it came to rest with a wisely judged view of the green.

"Hey, what a shot!" commented Adam; he was a fairly new golfer and would have been thrilled with such an accomplished drive.

"Yea, you're lucky the frost has thawed on the fairway. A few more yards to the right and you would have had a nasty bounce on that icy patch," announced Percy, almost gleeful at the vision of Colin being at a disadvantage.

Colin said nothing; he was 'in the zone'; his lips were parted, his breath wisping upwards as it collided with the cold air; his eyes were vacant. Colin was tall and sinewy with straight, dark hair streaked with lots of grey; at first glance, he had the look of the man next door; his clothes were always unremarkable in color and style but his face, which might have been handsome, was rather too thin: he never smiled, but often grinned, displaying dark yellow teeth which seemed too small for his head. Colin had lived in Hampshire all his life; his family had farmed here for generations; he knew every footpath and right of way through the fields for miles around. Colin was proud of himself; he had dragged himself up from nothing to become a member of this golf club; as a kid, he and his friends often sneaked onto nearby Leckford golf course after school; possessing just one club, he taught himself how to master the game. Colin had very little back swing but a powerful follow through which took the ball quite an amazing distance; accuracy was his problem; too often a wayward shot would reach the adjacent fairway. But, hey, that first shot of his, just now, was a joy.

Hugo was next to tee off; he sported a fixed grin which said, "I know I should be enjoying this, but I would rather be somewhere else!" His enormous frame swiped at the ball and produced a very poor shot which landed in a bush, well into the rough. He muttered about not being able to concentrate with so much on his mind.

Percy was next on the tee; with his muscular build and pure white bushy hair, he was actually quite handsome for a man in his fifties: no amount of money had been spared on his appearance; perfect teeth, whiter than seemed possible; muscular build produced from daily workouts at the gym; year round suntan from ultraviolet light, either natural or artificial; clothes from the most expensive designer range: today, he was togged out in coordinating navy and yellow. Percy withdrew his Callaway driver from a pristine cover, marched to the tee and took several practice shots; with a stylish but unaccomplished swing, he landed the ball on the fairway, but failed to achieve much distance; his confident approach to the tee dissipated a little as he replaced the club in his bag.

Adam took the last shot. Wearing an unbecoming blue thermal hat atop the black and beige ensemble chosen by Madeleine, and a look of determined concentration, he produced a decent drive which achieved an acceptable distance.

The foursome moved off towards their balls; they stood back while Hugo retrieved his Topflite from the bushes and took a penalty drop. Hugo hacked at the ball producing an air shot, but managed to follow this by a good connection with his five iron, placing the ball at the one hundred and fifty yard post. The game continued in similar fashion. Colin produced magnificent shots, occasionally somewhat wild, but always managed to recover from a bad position to play below his handicap. Hugo made a mess of each hole. Percy failed to achieve many points. Adam produced acceptable shots most of the time, without much fuss.

After a somewhat grueling four hours and twenty five minutes, the group returned to the clubhouse; there was a distinct lack of camaraderie as they changed their shoes in the locker room. Colin could well turn out to be the winner of the competition. Hugo had a disastrous round. Percy was not pleased with his mediocre score. Adam was content, but not thrilled, that he played one over handicap.

No-one had much to say as they moved into the stud bur. Adam bought a round of drinks and the foursome installed themselves in soft seats. The atmosphere cheered up a little once the conversation moved away from golf into rugby, football and motor racing. Once the drinks were finished, Adam wasted no time in bidding farewell with the intention of spending the rest of the day in front of the television.

Hearing Adam's car crunch on the pebble driveway, Madeleine made her way to the door to greet him; she always hoped he might play well enough to bring his handicap down a little and called out, "How did it go, darling?" as he opened the car door.

"Bloody nightmare!" was the answer.

"Oh dear," Madeleine sighed, as she stood in the hallway, ready to give consolation to this disappointing news. Adam brushed past her into the family room, threw himself on the sofa and used the remote control to turn the TV to Sky News.

"Want a cup of tea?" she ventured.

"Yep," was the response.

Bringing tea in Adam's favorite pot, the tray set with two cups and saucers from the Wedgewood tea set they had inherited from his mother, Madeleine gently enquired, "So what went wrong?"

"Those guys are a nightmare. I never want to play with them again."

"What happened?"

"Well, Hugo ate his way round the golf course – he couldn't hit a decent shot so he slowed us all up, and every time I looked back he was stuffing his mouth with chocolate bars and littering the golf course with wrapping papers. Colin was OK, didn't interfere with anyone but not good company – nothing much to say, but he uses a carry bag and doesn't keep covers on his clubs, so every time he walks, as you're trying to concentrate on your shot, all you can hear is clank, clank, clank as he strolls up the fairway. As for that guy, Percy, he cheated his way round.”

“Cheated?” echoed Madeleine. “How?”

“Well, he was miscounting his score. Unfortunately, I had to mark his card. He kept claiming his score was less than it actually was, so I had to argue with him and count back his shots. Then he lost his ball a few times, which slowed us all up looking for it. At one point, he claimed he found his ball, but Colin remembered it was a Wilson and this was a Pinnacle. He was about to play the wrong ball, but Colin intervened. Then, whenever, we were on the green, he kept jingling coins in his pocket while we were trying to putt. He just drove me absolutely mental!”

“Oh, well. Enjoy your tea and try to forget all about Percy. We’re going to see ‘Cold Mountain’ tonight. On the cinema at Festival Place in Basingstoke. Let’s go early and grab a bite to eat.”

“Can’t we just stay home?” entreated Adam.

“It’ll do you good to have a change of scene. You can keep on the clothes you’re wearing and pull on your leather jacket. Just relax now and enjoy the TV.”

Meanwhile, Robina was waiting for Hugo to return; she needed help in moving some furniture, ready for the decorator on Monday morning. The door slammed. He was back. “How was it, dear?” she called from the kitchen.

“Terrible!”

“You didn’t play well?”

“No. Got too much on my mind. I’m hungry.”

“Oh, well, I’ve got some freshly baked cherry scones and some caramel shortbread for you,” Robina called through the hallway.

“Where are they? How many did you make? Let me feast my eyes on the little darlings.” Robina could hear Hugo’s footsteps on the hardwood floor, as he made his way into her domain. “Ah, yes!” he sighed, gazing fondly at the black granite countertop, which was the perfect backdrop for the display of Robina’s talents. Munching his way through a scone, rolling the cherries round his tongue, immensely more cheerful, he volunteered, “Oh, we saw a deer running across the fairway on the fifth hole. And there was a flock of siskins on the seventeenth hole.”

“Feeling better now, dear?” Robina smiled. “That’s good. When you’re ready, I need some help moving furniture in the sitting room so the decorator can start on Monday.”

Turning back into the hall with a scone in one hand and caramel shortbread in the other, Hugo called back, “Oh, get someone else to sort that out for you. I need to concentrate on some work in the study. Tea would be nice."

Not tea, but coffee, was the drink of the day at Percy Blunt's house. When Barbara first met him, she was impressed; she was fond of the name, Percy; he often visited the store in New Bond Street, London, where she worked; he was very attractive, always sporting a suntan and dressed in clothing purchased from nearby designer shops. Percy was a diamond merchant, so had contacts with all the jewelers in London and Europe, as well as the mining houses in Africa. Barbara's only regret was Percy's surname; she had gone through life until the age of twenty nine with the name of Barbara Bellington Calcot-Fford; her mother's maiden name was Calcot; her father's surname was Ford; her parents had asked the minister who christened her if she could adopt his last name of Bellington. Before he met her mother, Barbara's father had added the second 'f' to his surname to give himself more style in the City; her mother had inserted the hyphen, feeling it lifted them from middle class into upper middle class. Barbara had used all three of her surnames throughout her school days into her adult social life, but Percy had been firm that she must drop her former surnames and become Barbara Blunt after their marriage; she had never quite swallowed the disappointment at the loss of her identity, but Percy felt satisfied that she had become his property. Using her maiden names, Barbara had developed a consciousness of style which reflected her apparent privileged background but, somehow, a door had slammed shut when she took the name of Blunt and she felt compelled to develop a new persona. Blunt, Blunt, Blunt ... how often she heard that name every day ... constantly at the golf club, regularly when making purchases, often when making dinner reservations and occasionally when making appointments ... Blunt, Blunt, Blunt ... so blunt she became, more and more outspoken with each year passing; now she was proud of her characteristic; she was up-front, told it like it was, courageous in voicing her opinions.

Barbara heard Percy's key in the lock, followed by a cheerful whistling. "You're back. How did it go?" she called from the sitting room, her dark eyes dancing with anticipation. Percy entered the room, enjoying the vision of tasteful surroundings, in which Barbara sat relaxing with a magazine in her hands. The walls of the room were a golden yellow, a perfect backdrop for the white paintwork on the regency windows, pilasters and cornices. The room was a showcase of expensive porcelain, all of which would have fetched a pretty penny at auction. Indeed, the impression of good taste went far beyond a graceful home to reach the proportions of a vault of carefully invested valuables ready to be converted into cash with a willing buyer. Barbara complemented her surroundings perfectly; not an aspect of her appearance escaped careful management; dark hair, short and waved in a sporty style; a black cashmere polo neck sweater and narrow black slacks encased her trim figure; neat black shoes with a gilt designer buckle held her feet; her neck was adorned with an intricate heavy gold necklace, elegantly complemented by a silk scarf in black and gold.

"Yea, it was good. Enjoyed it. Played quite well. Won't be placed but Colin should probably win the competition. But that guy, Adam, none of us like him, he's a cheat." Percy's brown eyes wavered as he spoke.

"What ... how do you mean?" Barbara's pose changed from relaxed to alert.

"He can't count his score. You have to keep arguing with him because he tries to make it less. He also tried to play a ball in the rough which wasn't his. And he keeps trying to distract you when you're taking your shot. Tries to put you off your game. Didn't work with me, though."

"But, Percy, people like that shouldn't be allowed in the club. You need to bring this to the attention of the main committee."

"Don't make a fuss. You might just mention it quietly to your close friends. Word will get around." was Percy's nonchalant reply.

Meanwhile, Colin drove home to find Nancy cleaning the oven; she was bent over, rinsing the solution from the open glass door; she continued with her task but looked up, turning her head round, as she heard him come in. He took several large strides towards her and grabbed her buttocks hard. "Back away from the oven," he commanded. Outside, in a nearby field, a sparrowhawk swooped in a mid air attack on a woodpigeon, bringing it to earth with a swift dive towards a tree stump. Once plucked, the predator consumed its prey.

Snow. Falling thick. Melting on impact. Early evening. A pause. Later a fine flurry of sleet, disappearing into the dryness of the earth. Bedtime. Four households looked out from the windows of dark unlit rooms to see thick chunks of white, as if torn from a freshly baked loaf, descending in a free fall vertical dive to merge with the fluffy coverlet already engulfing the outside world. Four households sharing the same experience and feelings; a sense of shock at how the environment could change so rapidly and silently; a sense of anxiety about how the world would look in the morning; a sense of fear that traveling could be difficult. The power of nature asserting a superior force. A gathering of wits to face the challenge of survival.

THING A THONG

The first day of March brought rain. Great splodges. The streets black. The skies grey. Heavy, broken rods of water mesmerizing the eyes. Windscreen wipers waving back and forth, the discordant sound bruising the ears. Everyone running, caught by surprise. Thousands of miniature puddles sliding on the waxed metal of passing cars, like opals displayed on a glass shelf escaping into disarray. Since the regular ladies' competition on Wednesday was cancelled due to bad weather, a small relaxed group gathered in the ladies' lounge with coffee and sandwiches. The conversation had swirled around and was currently focused on the need for regular exercise. Membership at a gymnasium was the current topic.

"You should see those girls in the changing room at my gym." said Lynn Harper, the newly elected Lady Captain. "Shapely bodies, all over suntan, tattoos on their midriffs. And they all wear thongs."

"Oh, I couldn't imagine wearing one of those," responded Alice Tolkein. "They look so uncomfortable!" Her fleshy upper lip quivered as she spoke; her hand moved nervously touching her light brown, permed hair; her thoughts, as newly appointed Secretary, were dwelling on the responsibility of producing minutes of the Annual Meeting from her handwritten notes.

"Have you never tried them?" asked Vice Captain, Nancy Ruff.

"No!" the group of ladies chorused, looking at her with interest.

"Yep, just wonderful," Nancy affirmed.

"How do you mean?" questioned Alice, the normally dull expression in her hazel eyes brightening as she lifted her eyebrows in wonder.

"Well, I tell you, when you put them on, the world takes on a whole new meaning," answered Nancy.

"How's that?" Alice's eyebrows rose further.

"Well, they're sexy, Alice!" Nancy slapped her thigh and grinned wickedly. "Done my marriage the power of good!"

"But you can't wear a thong playing golf?" quizzed Madeleine.

"Oh no, dear. The last thing on your mind would be your golf swing. You need well washed and comfy knickers for golf." Nancy confided.

The others looked shocked. Madeleine confessed, "You know, I bought a thong once, because I didn't want a panty line showing. It was so uncomfortable, I had to go out the next day and buy Preparation H."

The group collapsed into fits of laughter. When the laughter died down, Alice maintaining her usual serious expression, asked, "Where do you get them? Mail order?"

"Oh no, girls. Marks & Spencer," Nancy informed the gathering.

"Right, I'm going there tomorrow," said Alice, imagining her petite frame rejuvenated by the intended purchase. There had been no physical side to Alice's marriage for many years – not since she discovered Don was having an affair. Their relationship during the early years of marriage had been acceptable; she supposed Don had married her because he wanted to settle down and have children, but now their relationship was dead. Yes, he had ended the affair; yes, they went out socially together, mostly to the golf club, but the fabric of their life was held together by routine. Alice and Don both worked in the family garden center with Don's four brothers and their wives. A routine existence: meals were taken at the same time each day; breakfast was at six o'clock, sandwich lunch, dinner at seven o'clock. Every week, Alice did her housework on Monday, visited her mother on Tuesday, played golf on Wednesday, visited her daughter on Thursday, did her grocery shopping on Friday, and worked in the garden center on Saturday. Sundays would be either a family lunch or taking part in mixed golf competitions. Same hours, same days of the week, same routine for over thirty years. Now Alice wanted to rebel; she wanted to reclaim the fragments of her marriage. Although it was probably a hopeless desire, she wanted to forgive Don now – odd, that it had taken all these years of punishing him to make her feel better. The space between them had been like sterile soil. Suddenly, today, Alice experienced an awakening; perhaps the ground was now free of toxins and ready to germinate. Ridiculous for a woman of her age? Well, some sexy underwear could be the first step.

The door opened. Anastasia waded past on her way to the administration office. As usual, all heads followed her progress. Not a word was spoken until she passed through the exit door.

"I wonder if she wears a thong?" pondered Lynn. The room erupted into fits of giggles at this cheeky comment from their newly elected Lady Captain.

"I hear she's looking for a boyfriend," Lynn continued. "Apparently, she's been meeting some guys through a dating agency. And she's in contact with men on the internet. Seems a bit scary to me, but I suppose she's been widowed for some time now."

"I would never go out looking for another man in my life," stated Madeleine, her heart breaking at the thought of losing Adam. "I would much prefer to be on my own. I mean, who wants to get used to another man's health and hygiene?"

"Oh, I couldn't bear to live alone," replied Lynn.

"I would prefer to live alone than put up with all that dating," responded Madeleine. "Much better to be independent than make yourself vulnerable to the danger of strange men. Even with someone you already know, you just have no idea what they would be like to live with."

"Oh, but I couldn't bear not to be loved," stated Lynn.

"But, what do you mean by loved?" asked Madeleine.

"Well, spending evenings together. Going out to dinner. Going on holidays," answered Lynn.

"You can do that with women," Madeleine responded. "There are loads of single ladies who are great company and do lots of things together. Why would you need a man?"

"It's just not the same with women," insisted Lynn.

Madeleine continued, "The only way I would consider marrying again is if I fell in love, by accident. I just wouldn't go out looking for someone. It would have to be someone I admired. Someone I really cared about and who cared about me. Someone to share my life."

"Actually, my neighbor's husband died and she's much happier now than before," intervened Cathy, glancing at her watch and thinking about the driving hazards on wet roads with her next pupil. Everyone stared at her as she continued, "He didn't like her spending money. Now, he's gone, she's had the whole house renovated – new windows, new carpets, new kitchen. He didn't like going places. Now, she goes on holidays with a group of ladies. And, she looks so nice, too. She now has the money to go the hairdresser every week and wear nice clothes. Her husband is probably turning in his grave at her spending all his money. She says she would never consider taking another man in her life." A reflective paused followed, everyone inwardly concluding that Cathy could see herself blossoming in a state of widowhood without her morose husband, Rodney.

Madeleine broke the silence, "Actually, one in four people in this country now live alone. Not just those who are widowed. There are lots of people who are choosing this way of life. Whether we plan it or not, statistically that's how we're going to end up, so we might as well get used to the idea."

"What would you do if you were left on your own, Robina?" questioned Silver Division Captain, Barbara Blunt.

"I think I share Madeleine's view," replied Robina, with a far away look in her eyes, inwardly shuddering at the prospect of life without Hugo. "It would take time getting used to living alone, but I would never go out looking for someone. And, you know, men get a lot grumpier as they get older."

"They certainly do get grumpier," interjected Lynn. "They never stop complaining. At every meal, there's something wrong ... too much lettuce in the salad, the soup is too hot, the cheese is too strong. Barry gets grumpier every day. And I'm not allowed to buy his clothes anymore. And he complains every time I play golf. I don't know what else I'm supposed to do with my time. After all, I'm fifty six years old, I've brought up his children, kept his house clean all these years, gone out to work when we needed the money." Lynn's husband, Barry, was a man who appealed to all tastes; he could share a joke with a group of men; he was respectful and courteous with ladies; he was never vulgar, loud or rude; he was easy on the eye with a regular build, regular features and light brown hair, skin and eyes; his demeanor was pleasant and relaxed. Barry had always worked long hours in his small printing company to provide the very best for his family. Of course, the printing business had suffered in recent years with the upsurge of small computers, but he was managing to struggle through. All these years, while business had been good, Lynn had led the good life: now that times were tough, she had no understanding or empathy with the struggles Barry was facing; she assumed that his irritability was a resentment of her lifestyle. It was widely acknowledged that Barry's relationship with Lynn had moved, over the years, from tolerant indulgence to controlled hatred.

"Nancy, what would you do?" questioned Barbara, ignoring Lynn's outburst.

"I would take a lover," responded Nancy. In fact, I might take several lovers. There may be one or two men I would use as companions for social events. I wouldn't marry again, but I might take a live-in boyfriend. Just for a bit of fun." Nancy wondered how her husband, Colin, would react if he could overhear this conversation. Nancy's statement was met with blank looks, the others unable to imagine themselves leading such a life, although perhaps secretly wishing they had the nerve to be so unconventional.

"And you, Alice. What would you do?" Barbara posed the question to Alice Tolkein.

Startled, Alice replied, "Oh … if I happened to meet someone, that would be OK. Or if I got along all right with a man I already knew, and he was also single, I wouldn't mind. But not to go out looking. What about you, Barbara?"

"I would be right out there looking as hard as I could. No way, would I want to live alone. I'm not going to do all the hard jobs – taking out the rubbish and looking after the garden. No thanks. I want to be pampered. I would definitely look for another husband." Barbara replied firmly. The group of ladies silently digested this information.

Robina sighed, "My eldest daughter is thirty years old. She's intelligent and attractive, sophisticated and good company, but she's very unhappy because she hasn't got a man in her life."

"Yes, but that's different," answered Madeleine. "She wants a home and children. She's not already established like our age group."

"My daughter is struggling with the mating game," Barbara interjected. "She's so fed up with the men in this country that she's decided to go to Canada. She's twenty four years old, an easy girl to get along with, but she finds the men here so boorish, all they want to do is go to the pub and get drunk."

"Or else, all they want is sex," said Madeleine. "A friend of mine has a daughter in her forties. She's divorced and hates being on her own, but all the men she meets expect to have sex on the first date. She doesn't believe in throwing herself away; she has standards and values, but she can't seem to meet a nice, decent man."

"I know. It's awfully difficult," commented Alice, looking worried.

"You know," said Madeleine, "I caught a discussion on my car radio the other day about a commune of women. They're all around retirement age and they bought a large property which they run themselves. Each person has to take responsibility for something whether it's maintenance, gardens, finance, whatever. Everyone has their own apartment, but there's a communal social space so they can get involved with each other if they want to. I think that sort of set-up would work very well. They can have men visiting in the communal areas, but they're not allowed to take men into the private apartments."

Primrose ventured her view, "You know, you're so lucky. Women, on their own can live safely in this country. There are many places in the world where women are scared to live alone. You can go out for the evening here with a group of ladies and no-one will bother you. You can drive at night without fear. You can go home to an empty house without being terrified. And there are many social activities going on where it doesn't matter if you're single or not." Primrose Pretorius was reflecting on the life she left behind ten years ago. Primrose and Marius were born in South Africa; her parents were originally from England, Marius was third generation Afrikaans; they led a charmed life – year round sunshine, business was good, a circle of fine friends, wonderful property, lots of space. No-one questioned that political change was morally the right way forward, but the surge of emotions and lifting of restrictions allowed criminal elements to get out of control. Primrose and Marius decided they had to leave. Their dry cleaning business was shared ownership with Marius's father and two brothers; dismantling their share of the business and transferring funds out of the country had been too difficult to contemplate, so they became dormant partners. Heartbroken but with a grim determination and minimal funds, Primrose and Marius left for England to set up a dry cleaning business. Living in grubby bedsits, all luxuries were a thing of the past. Using up their capital more swiftly than seemed possible, they took four months to find suitable premises and ended up in Andover, quite by chance. Every waking moment was channeled into establishing a new way of life. Eventually, they could afford to lease a house and their three children followed them to England at the end of the school year.

"Yea, guess we are lucky from that point of view," answered Alice.

"Hey, but you don't even need a man to have a baby now!" Madeleine moved the conversation along. "There's a company called 'Man Not Included.' They deliver fresh sperm to your door, within an hour of it being produced."

"Gosh, quicker than the milk man," quipped Nancy. A few impish smiles followed Nancy's remark, other faces remained impassive.

Madeleine continued, "A motorbike delivers it to your door."

"Oooo, all that leather!" sighed Barbara.

"But where does it come from? A sperm bank?" questioned Alice.

"Sounds like artificial insemination on the farm," said Nancy.

"Well, no. Actually, the sperm comes from an agency," answered Madeleine. "The agency checks out the donors, you choose one through the internet and, hey presto, the sperm is delivered to your door with 'do it yourself' instructions."

"Seems you can accomplish a lot on the internet. Precisely why are you doing this computer course, Madeleine?" asked Lynn, smiling broadly.

Madeleine laughed. "Well, you never know what I might get up to. Which reminds me, I must get going. I do need to get to the learning center. I'm having a blip with PowerPoint."

"As one does," answered Lynn.

Madeleine gathered her belongings together and, car keys in hand, moved briskly towards the exit door.

"I gotta go, too. I need to do the handicapping," said Primrose, reaching for her folder.

"Me too. I'm going to Marks & Spencer," said Alice.

"I need to give Spindle a walk," stated Robina, getting to her feet.

As they reached the door, Alice whispered to Primrose, "I hate it when that four are left on their own." Her normally dull hazel eyes, held a tinge of fear as her petite frame slipped through the door. "No telling who they'll be talking about," she added.

After ordering coffee and once the coast was clear, Lynn remarked, "You know, that Madeleine Minehead is always doing something other than golf. She's Bronze Captain now. She should be devoting herself to the club."

"In fact, she's a bit of a smarty pants, don't you think?" added Barbara Blunt.

"Yea, a bit of a know-all. Tries to make us feel inadequate because we're not improving our minds. Well, my mind doesn't need improving," continued Lynn.

"What was she? A lawyer of some kind?" queried Barbara.

"Yea. Apparently, she handled criminal cases up in London. Thinks she's above us all, if you ask me," answered Lynn.

"Ooops, I better get going. I've got a lesson with Darren," said Nancy, glancing at her watch.

"Ahhh, talking of lessons, I've got a pupil in half an hour. She's taking her driving test tomorrow. Better get moving. Bye, folks," said Cathy, checking her watch as she walked away.

"Another coffee?" asked Lynn.

"Why not?" answered Barbara, settling further into the soft armchair.

"You know, she has a lot of lessons with Darren, don't you think?" commented Lynn.

"Who ... Nancy?" answered Barbara.

"Yep, you just watch what's going on there. Something, if you ask me," continued Lynn.

"Well, I'll take particular note. We've got a group lesson with Darren tomorrow."

"Why so we have. What fun!"

HEART ATTACK

"Barry's had a heart attack!" shouted Madeleine from the kitchen.

"What?" called back Adam.

"He's in Andover Hospital."

"Oh my God!"

"He's OK. He's OK. It was a mild attack. He's in an observation unit."

"Poor chap. That's terrible. I should go visit him."

"You could do that on your way home this evening. I'll check that it's OK to visit. If you don't hear from me, just go ahead. I'll hold dinner till you get back home."

That evening, Adam made his way along Charlton Road to Andover Hospital; he enquired at the front desk and was directed to an area with eight beds, all occupied by men either recovering from heart attacks or waiting for pacemaker surgery.

"Hey, man. How ya doin'?" Adam called to Barry as he approached his bed.

"Oh, I'm gettin' there ... gettin' there," came the faltering reply, as Barry shifted himself up on the pillows.

"You been in the wars then?" continued Adam, playfully.

"Well, kinda."

"Guess you're overdoing things. You'll need to take it easy." Once the words were out of his mouth, Adam realized this was the last thing he should have said; he wished he could swallow his amateur medical advice, so he took another tack.

"So, what's the food like?"

"It's OK, actually."

"Managing to catch up on your sleep?"

"You must be kidding. There's never a minute's peace. Don't know how they expect anyone to get better," sighed Barry.

"So, what's the problem?"

"Well, there's always new patients being admitted. So, you might be dozing off nicely and then a bunch of medical equipment comes clanking in ... all kinds of commotion transferring some poor bloke to a bed. Then round the clock, everyone needs medication, so you've got that going on. Then it's meal times, so the food gets delivered and cleared up an hour later. Then if it's not tea time, it's visiting time. Or else, the doctor's doing his rounds, or they're checking your vital signs to see if you're still alive, or there's someone needs a drip changing, or oxygen needs renewed. It's like Piccadilly Circus."

"Oh, dear. What are the other chaps in for?"

"Similar things. We all need round the clock observation. Glad I'm not shipwrecked or I'd be up for murder."

"How's that?" asked Adam, smiling.

"Well, just not a minute's peace. It's doin' my head in. Look at this four across there. See this one opposite? He needs a pacemaker. He's picking up unemployment benefit. He's only been in the country a few months. British passport – never lived here but came to get free medical treatment. He got a free house, too. His wife and kids seem to have nothing to do but hang around visiting all day long, so the kids are running in and out. He seems to have the money for phone calls to all his relatives overseas, though. We have to listen to him yelling down the phone with a blow by blow account of his medical condition."

"Oh, dear," Adam sympathized.

"Then this fat one next to him. He gets double meals."

"How come?"

"He fills in two menu choice cards each time. They must know what he's doing but nobody questions him. He just loads both meals onto one plate and demolishes the lot. I mean, look at the size of him! He should be on a diet. Can't be good for his heart. And the noise he makes eating – must be quieter in a zoo!"

"Oh, dear. And the one next to him?"

"Actually, he's OK, but his visitors are a pain. His wife, daughter and son-in-law are here all the time. None of them get on. The two women arrive at the same time while the son-in-law is parking the car. He obviously uses the excuse to stay out of the way, because it seems to take him half an hour to find a parking space. In the meantime, the daughter is agitating about him. She starts off moaning about where on earth is he. Then, she carries on about how much time he spends watching football on the television. Then, she complains about how he never helps with household chores. By the time the bloke gets here, she's sitting in a sulk on the end of the bed and won't speak to anyone. Then the mother tries to bring her out of the sulk, but she waits till the son-in-law gets here, making him out to be the bad boy treating her daughter like this. She doesn't say anything to him. Just keeps her back to him. Consoles the daughter and keeps throwing him sideways looks over her shoulder. The daughter is encouraged by an audience and gives speeches about how she doesn't need to put up with any of this. The son-in-law seems OK. Smartly dressed. He just stands there and looks at them carrying on. He tries to have a sensible conversation with the old man. The women seem to forget they've come to visit a patient. The mother has these discussions with the nurses about how much she wanted to be a nurse but her father stood in her way. You should see her expression when she says that. She seems so satisfied letting everyone think she would have been a great success if some man hadn't held her back."

"And the one at the end?"

"Oh, the alcoholic? He gets his wife to bring in booze and they have a party late at night. Right here, where we're supposed to be recovering from a life threatening experience. And the one opposite has a drink problem, too, so they're well matched."

"What about the others on this side?"

"Well, the one next to me thinks he's sexy. So, what he does is wait till there's a female visitor and then he parades about, wearing only pajama bottoms. You'll see him in a minute. He's a scrawny thing, but I'm sure he thinks he's mister muscle."

"And next to him?"

"Nice old man, but we had an incident in the middle of the night. Last night, he switched on his light, leapt out of bed and yelled, 'I must get the first flight back to England.' The staff came rushing in to find out what was wrong and he said, 'They're threatening to close the show. I need to get backstage.' They calmed him down and got him back to bed. In the morning, the bare-chested one approached the old fella and asked if he could buy some chocolate from him since he had run out of snacks. He gave the old boy the money, but he looked very puzzled, so he asked him to count the money and tell him how much there was. The old fella put his hand in his pocket, brought out some coins, some buttons and some hard mints, counted them all and said, 'It comes to forty degrees.' So the bare-chested one then said, 'Are you OK with this?' The old fella answered, 'No, it's the fine detail of this transaction I don't understand.'"

"Oh, no. Poor old soul. He's obviously lost the plot." Adam's gaze scanned the ward. "I see you've each got your own TV."

"Yea, but they all watch these quiz shows and shout out the answers. One of them even phoned his wife during the program to ask her what was the capital of Slovakia. Oh, and they all watch these comedy shows and laugh out loud at different times. They don't realize how loud they're laughing because they're wearing earphones."

"Sounds like hell."

"But the worst is the farting. All these blokes farting in the middle of the night. The smell is horrendous."

"Oh, dear. What about the staff? Can't they do anything?"

"I've spoken to them about it. The problem is patients can become violent. So, their attitude is that as long as they're only harming themselves, they just let them get on with it."

"Can't they give you a sleeping pill?"

"Nope. They need to monitor me constantly. That's why I'm cooped up with this lot. Can't give me any medication which might interfere with the drugs for the heart."

"What about a private room, Barry?"

"Can't have one. Need to be under observation twenty four seven."

"Well, you *are* having a fun time. Anything we can do for you?"

"Not really. Just spring me out of here."

"Well, I'll think of a plan," answered Adam, smiling. "When do they say they'll let you out?"

"At the weekend. If I haven't strangled someone before then."

"How's Lynn?"

"She's OK, but she doesn't know."

"Doesn't know you're in hospital?"

"Doesn't know about our daughter."

"What's happened?"

"Well, she got married on Saturday. Bogus wedding to an asylum seeker. She got paid five thousand pounds. Arranged by some guy she met in a pub. Don't suppose it's actually illegal. The whole thing frightens the shit out of me. I suppose that's what brought on the heart attack ... when she told me ... that and the struggles with the business."

"I expect Lynn needs lots of support. I'll ask Madeleine to get in touch."

"She'll need a lot of sympathy, that's for sure. She was here this morning. Moaning that the washing machine has broken down ... and how having me in hospital is interfering with her being Lady Captain at the golf club."

"What?"

"Oh, yes. Some big event coming up. Husband expected to be there. So embarrassing if she doesn't have an escort. The only place I would like to escort her to, right now, is the gates of hell!" exclaimed Barry, unaware that he would soon be living alone and bitterly regretting these words.

Adam looked embarrassed. "Chin up, old boy. I expect she's just stressed."

Barry took no notice. "You can imagine the drama there's going to be when she finds out about this bogus wedding. Best tell Madeleine to keep well away from her. Anyway, how's business with you, Adam?"

Barry was getting himself worked up, so Adam took the invitation to change the subject. "Bit frantic. We're dashing to recover oil properties. Need to get heads of agreement signed to allow exploration concessions. So ... lots to think about."

"I guess there is," Barry answered. He felt difficulty in focusing on business issues; his head was full of irritation at his environment, confusion at the shock of his medical situation and bitterness towards Lynn. Shifting his mind with effort, he followed up with "Doing much traveling?"

"Yea, just had the flight from hell," Adam sighed. "Got back from Jakarta, yesterday. Not a wink of sleep."

"Thought you went first class?"

"Yea, I do, but the other passengers were a nightmare. An enormous guy from Hawaii snored liked a beached whale all night. A couple from Hollywood had a loud argument and demanded to change seats; he then phoned his secretary to insist the girlfriend be transferred back to Los Angeles on the first flight out of Heathrow. An Arabic woman in a headscarf clicked prayer beads all night. There wasn't a minute's peace. And yet, a baby in the cabin slept quietly throughout the entire flight."

Barry shook his head, "You know, Adam, you and I would be just fine if the rest of the world behaved."

"Too true." Adam rose from the chair. "Well, I better get home for dinner, old chap. I'll keep tabs on your progress. Don't let the buggers get you down."

Adam gave a handshake to Barry and made his way to the door. Turning back to wave farewell, their eyes met: his heart went out to Barry, alone in a hospital bed, fighting for his health, worried about his business, shocked at his daughter and bitter towards his wife. Traversing long corridors on the way to the exit, Adam pondered the situation he had just left: he drove home, thankful for his good fortune – good health, a good income, a wonderful wife and sensible children; he wondered whether he was just lucky or whether there was more to it than that. Feeling that he wanted time to think, he decided to take the long way home, using the A303 to pick up the B3084, past the curiously named village of Palestine, on through Over Wallop and Middle Wallop, reaching home in Nether Wallop.

Getting out of the car into bright moonlight, Adam admired the country cottage which Madeleine loved so dearly – thatched roof, cob walls, eyebrow windows; the peacefulness enveloped him and he breathed deeply of the night air. An owl hooted to acknowledge his presence, their spirits merged in a moment of peace and joy.

The eye on the world stared down, blankly, seeing all, knowing all, responding not at all, illuminating the darkness with brilliant, wondrous light, surrounded by silent servants, mischievously twinkling. A quiet presence to be acknowledged and dismissed, or a powerful force to be reckoned with awe.

HAPPY ANNIVERSARY

"It's my wedding anniversary today," concluded Lynn, after announcing the winners of the Better Ball competition. "I'm just sorry my dear husband, Barry, is in hospital and we can't celebrate the day together," she continued, looking sorrowful. The members dutifully sang 'Happy Anniversary' to their Captain while, at the same time, wondering why their own wedding anniversaries were never announced. Within a few minutes the room was almost empty, leaving a void which Robina felt obliged to fill.

"Let's go back to my house and we'll open a bottle of wine," said Robina to the remaining members.

Around a dozen ladies responded with murmurs of, "Oh, that would be nice ... what a lovely idea ... yes, let's celebrate." Belongings were gathered. Discussions of car sharing and directions to Robina's house followed. The group filtered outside; doors slammed and four cars holding twelve people swung out into the main road. Lots of chatter filled the vehicles as they bowled along. Comments about the surrounding countryside, speculation about seeing Robina's house and anticipation of a glass of wine created a festive merriment.

Leading the way and driving alone, Robina was surprised to find Hugo's car in the driveway when she reached home. Entering the hallway and leaving the door open, she found Hugo waiting to meet her; he was about to speak when the other cars arrived and eleven ladies spilled out.

"Oh, isn't it grand," exclaimed Primrose with awe, admiring the patterning on the gateposts created from local handmade brickwork, as the electric gates remained open to allow visitors to enter. "It's hard to believe it's quite new," she continued, gazing up at the ornamental chimney stacks which towered above the arched windows on the second floor. Her gaze scanned over the semi-circular wrought iron balustrade which encompassed the balcony on the first floor; her eyes returned to earth to focus on the paneled oak double entry doors which were open, revealing pale colored parquet flooring, graced by a contemporary design in darker wood.

"Makes you wonder how easy it is to come by money in the banking world," Barbara commented in a low voice, as the group entered the hallway.

"Make your way into the sitting room," announced Robina, ushering the ladies in that direction.

Hugo turned his back and walked into the kitchen. Robina followed and looked at him expectantly as he faced her. "I've had a bust up at work," he announced.

"What?"

"Told them I was leaving and would be seeking legal advice."

"What?"

"An employee has blown the whistle."

"What about?"

"A transaction."

"What do you mean?"

"A thirty million problem. Depends how you interpret it ... how it's presented to the auditors and shareholders."

"I've got this bunch of ladies here. It's Lynn's wedding anniversary. I invited them back for a glass of wine."

"Give them tea."

Robina entered the sitting room where the gathering of ladies had made themselves comfortable and were admiring their surroundings. "Wine cellar needs replenishing," she announced. "Tea all right, girls?"

The chatter stopped. A few sensed that Hugo's presence was the reason for the change of plan; some simply thought it was odd that you could suddenly find your wine cellar empty; others considered Robina to have failed in her offer of hospitality.

"Yes, lovely," Madeleine agreed.

"Any chance of coffee?" enquired Barbara.

"Need some help in the kitchen?" asked Alice.

"Won't take jiffy. Be with you in a minute. Make yourselves comfortable," encouraged Robina. She swiftly returned to the kitchen and focused on producing a tray containing twelve china cups and saucers, a silver tea service and a plate of sliced fruitcake. Returning to the sitting room, she felt strained and worried; she also felt uncomfortable about disappointing the party revelers. Conversation was flat and focused on the various golf games of the day.

Thankfully, once tea was finished, Madeleine said, "You're tired. We must go."

Robina answered, "Yes, I am tired." She couldn't remember any of the farewells; she was just relieved when everyone had gone, so that she could focus on the sudden appearance of her husband.

"What's happening?" Robina asked Hugo, as she entered the study, feeling her stomach lurch.

Oddly, Hugo seemed relaxed. "I have nothing to fear. All the corporate people know about the thirty million problem. I've been under investigation for weeks by internal audit. It's just that one of my junior staff has resigned due to work pressure, and has sited my handling of this transaction as part of the pressure. Unfortunately, it reflects on me, so the situation has become more serious."

"So, you're taking legal advice?"

"Let's see what happens over the next few days. I'll be taking some lengthy phone calls at home to discuss my position. You know, what really gets me is that I have supported this employee through some of his most difficult times. He lives with another man. Very few people know that. I've kept it confidential. They've managed to adopt two children. I approved paternity leave on both occasions. I've always been sympathetic to his circumstances, including when his mother died recently. And now, he's stabbed me in the back. He can't cope with the job pressures and is using this transaction as an excuse."

Robina stretched out her arms to give Hugo a comforting hug. After a few minutes of sharing his despair, she ventured brightly, "Why don't I make some banana bread? You'd like that, wouldn't you, dear?"

Meanwhile, the ladies were out in the driveway, discussing their curtailed celebrations.

"Bit odd, him being home at this time of day," commented Nancy.

"Suddenly run out of wine. Seems a bit strange," Cathy endorsed.

"What should we do now?" Primrose wondered, looking disappointed.

Lynn called out, "Let's go into Stockbridge. Meet you all at the White Hart Inn. I need a drink."

The despondent mood lifted at the prospect of a new venue. The group piled back into three cars and sped towards Stockbridge, without noticing the hazel fences, the eleventh century Saxon church, small groups of ponies, a lone stallion, a few sheep in a field, an enclosure of hens and geese gathered around an overturned wheelbarrow. On reaching Meon Hill Farm and the Museum of Army Flying, they began to focus on the downhill approach to their destination.

In Stockbridge, a busy market town dating back to the Iron Age, parking spaces in the High Street were plentiful but some distance apart. Getting out of their cars, the group called to each other to meet in half an hour which allowed time for errands. Eleven ladies in party mood cheered the shopkeepers of Stockbridge during the next thirty minutes. Robjents sold a pair of thick socks with Dizzy embroidered on one sock and Dame on the other – a good birthday present for a younger sister who loved hiking. Orvis sold a traditional waxed Barbour jacket as a birthday present for an unsuspecting husband. Lillie Langtry's bakery, named after the mistress of King Edward VII who regularly accompanied him during the local horseracing season, sold a sponge cake filled with cream from a local herd. Chatterbox Flowers sold some yellow roses as a hostess gift. Penyards Properties were delighted to hand out details of a thatched cottage for sale at over six hundred thousand pounds. The Post Mistress was agitated at a customer counting out small change to purchase a few postage stamps. Stokes Garage was pleased to fill up the tank of a Land Rover. For Goodness Sake Delicatessen took pride in selling four jars of chutney. John Robinson butchers sharpened their knives to provide a succulent leg of lamb. A cauliflower, some carrots and a head of celery were purchased from Sykes Fresh Fruit and Veg. The Bakhtiyar Gallery was thrilled to discuss the merits of an oriental carpet displayed in the window.

Only Madeleine bought nothing; she wandered past the stores, admiring the contents, smiling at the graceful ambience. She stood staring into the water of the River Test, which ran under the main road across the town, emerging outside the Town Hall, which modestly proclaimed its origins as AD1810 on a small stone plaque. Madeleine always stopped, whenever she visited Stockbridge, to admire the numerous large trout which wriggled in the clear water. She enjoyed watching the ducks waddle around, hoping for some tidbits. She backtracked to Lillie Langtry's to pick up some stale bread, which was usually heaped in a basket at the doorway. She threw morsels of a poppyseed roll into the water, and laughed aloud as the ducks and trout dived and leapt in competition to secure the prize. She gazed up at the clock tower on the roof of the Town Hall and, as usual, smiled at the weather vane which proudly sported a large trout. Startled, she flinched back as a small bird flitted past. Amused, her smile broadened as she recognized the black and white markings of a pied wagstaff. Realising it was almost time to meet at the White Hart, Madeleine, her mind still in a peaceful reverie, quickened her pace and walked smartly for a few minutes, finally reaching her destination. Opening the door of the White Hart, the chatter of the group of ladies brought her back to the anniversary celebrations.

"Hi, Madeleine. We started without you. What will you have to drink?" Red wine?" called out Lynn.

"Yea, that would be great."

"What kept you, what have you been buying?" Primrose wanted to know.

"Nothing, actually."

"Thought you might pick up a few cakes at Lillie Langtry's,"

"Not today. Maybe next week, I'll be buying armfuls of sweet things for Easter. Don't you just love that shop? It just tickles me that the Prince of Wales came to the races along with Lillie Langtry. I do love this town."

Lynn finished her glass of wine and whispered to Barbara, "She's always so positive. She makes me sick."

Barbara took up the conversation. "Oh, come on, Madeleine. We're in the middle of nowhere here. Nothing ever happens. You must miss London."

"Well, yes, I do. I also miss Belgium where I spent my youth. But I do love this place."

"I love it, too," commented Primrose. It's just so peaceful and so, well ... English, actually."

"But you must miss the sunshine, Primrose, coming from South Africa," insisted Barbara, as she refilled the glasses and gestured to the barmaid to bring another two bottles.

"You would think so, but I don't. I love the climate here. I miss the brightness of light from South Africa and I miss the people in Johannesburg, but I don't miss the sun." Primrose confessed, earnestly. "The air is so dry, your skin doesn't feel good. In winter the grass is yellow from lack of rain or burnt black from wild fires and it's really quite cold at night due to the high altitude ... six thousand feet above sea level. In summer, the rain falls around late afternoon each day and, often, you have hailstones the size of duck eggs. Here, you don't realize it, but the weather is poetry in motion. Your poets have written about spring and autumn ... all the seasons, really. You have the most wonderful variety of trees, plants, blossoms, birds. There is nothing to fear from insects or animals. Every day brings a fresh surprise. You know, I had never seen a daffodil until I came to live here. Or a primrose either, for that matter." She smiled now. "The English climate is one of the great joys of living here."

Murmurs and nods of agreement followed Primrose's appreciation of England.

"Happy Anniversary, Lynn," hailed Madeleine, as she raised her glass. "How many years?"

Lynn closed her eyes. "Twenty nine long years."

"Well, you have a fine son and daughter to show for it," said Alice.

"I don't know about that. My daughter seems to hang about pubs all the time. And my very clever son is proving to be a disaster at university."

"Oh, dear, I thought he was doing fine," commented Cathy, looking genuinely concerned.

"Well, he should be in his third year now, but he failed most of his exams in second year. He passed some re-sits before Christmas, but if he fails the remaining re-take this Easter, he's out on his ear. I just don't understand it. Everything was so easy for him before. But the worst bit is, he doesn't keep in contact. Barry used to phone him every day, but he doesn't answer the phone anymore. Now, Barry sends him text messages every day but he never responds. The only reason we know he's alive is that we can see his banking transactions online. It's almost as if he doesn't exist anymore."

"That's hard to take, Lynn," commented Madeleine."

"Yea, the stress doesn't help your marriage, either. I had a fight with Barry the day before his heart attack."

"Oh, you poor thing," Nancy sympathized.

"Yea, just stupid. Over the damn satellite navigation in the car. We were taking a trip to Bournemouth on Saturday. He never keys in the information before we take off. Always waits till we're on the motorway and swerves about, frightening the wits out of me. I shouted at him that I would key in the address. I put my hand towards the screen and he grabbed it and nearly broke my finger. We had a huge shouting match and I punched him on the face. It's a wonder he didn't kill us both."

"And he had the heart attack the next day," concluded Nancy.

"Yea, no wonder I spend my time shopping. There's just so much pressure in my life. I have to let off steam, somehow."

"Well, here's hoping Barry is better soon. You can have a belated anniversary celebration when he's out of hospital," said Madeleine, raising her glass and holding Lynn's gaze.

SPRING MEETING

The sky, like wet blotting paper with smudges of every shade of grey seeping together, wondered whether to collapse and cascade on the players below.

"The weather forecast is terrible," exclaimed Alice. "We're to get thunder, lightning and hailstones."

"She won't cancel unless it's actually raining," answered Primrose. "We just have to get on with it."

"I would rather be cleaning the kitchen floor, right now. It's awful playing in the rain," commented Madeleine.

"Need to get moving," said Nancy, her eyes on the first tee.

The foursome moved forward towards the starter, who gave a gesture of caution to stay back. Once the group in front had teed off, the starter called them forward to receive their score cards.

Primrose summarized the instructions. "So, the format is Foursomes. We have to decide, in our pair, who takes the drive on holes with odd numbers and who takes the ones with even numbers. Then it's alternate shots. And you're my partner, Madeleine."

"OK. Well, my long drives are generally good, but I have trouble getting on the green on the par threes. I can get the distance, but not the accuracy," confessed Madeleine.

"Well, my distance is not good, so I'm safer on the par threes. We've got three of those, one even and two odd. So, why don't I take the odd holes?" Primrose suggested.

"That's fine, answered Madeleine. "Odd hole to start, Primrose, although it's a par four, so your drive, my dear."

Primrose knew that all she had to do was stay slightly left. Veering right would bring all sorts of hazards into play – a ditch running along the side, a thick hedge and a dogleg which would need another shot to gain a view of the green. Tucking the head cover of her three wood into her golf bag, she daintily approached the tee. Her swing was neat and straight but lacked power, so the ball traveled only about 120 yards.

"That's fine. Nice and safe," encouraged Madeleine. "I just have to get it round the corner now."

Madeleine was quite proficient with her three wood and figured this was the right club to use, but she doubted her own accuracy and chose her seven wood, correctly assessing that this would stop short of the green, staying out of trouble in the bunkers.

"Do you spank your husband like you spank the ball?" joked Nancy. The others grinned.

Madeleine's shoulders shook, as she softly chuckled. Feeling satisfied with her shot, she commented to Primrose, "Give me a nice little chip onto the green, and then the pressure is on me to get it in the hole."

Primrose used her pitching wedge to reach the green, but scuffed the shot which stopped well short of the flag. A long putt by Madeleine, and a smart two foot putt into the hole by Primrose, gave them a score of five on the first hole.

"Hey, if we keep this up, we'll be doing alright," commented Madeleine in her usual positive manner.

Their opponents, Nancy and Alice, had fared less well. Nancy could give the ball a hefty whack, but her drive had taken the ball into the hedge on the right. After conferring, and rather than take a penalty drop, Alice decided to use her sand wedge to force the ball onto the fairway. Unfortunately, this strategy was risky. Alice did not muster enough skill for the shot, consequently the ball moved only a few feet. Nancy had to take another shot to position the ball back into play. Alice needed to follow up with a neat straight shot to position the ball at a decent angle to the green; this she accomplished easily but they had taken four shots already. A fifth shot took them close to the green. They needed to chip in but failed to beat their opponents on the par four.

"Oh, well, better luck on the next hole," commented Alice as they marched on, towards the second tee.

A flash of green and red erupted as a woodpecker flew, disturbed, from the ground to a treetop where he gave his loud, laughing call.

"Glad you're taking this next drive," said Primrose to Madeleine, with relief.

An army of gorse bushes, golden blooms on prickly spikes, guarded the ditch which was perfectly positioned to swallow the first bounce of a decent drive. Madeleine would have liked to use her driver for distance but knew, from experience, that the low trajectory would probably cause problems. Instead, she withdrew her three wood, concentrated on accelerating through the shot with a firm grip, and safely cleared the hazard gaining a fifty yard clearance on the other side of the ditch.

"Well done," said Alice, quaking that she had to take the drive on this hole.

Alice had a strategy of playing safe, so she used her five iron, guiding the ball to the left over a path, into a hazard free patch of rough. Startled by the disturbance, two buck deer raced across the fairway from left to right, limbs outstretched, keeping a wide invisible circle between humankind and their mysterious, secret world. The foursome stopped to gaze in wonder, feeling excluded from the magical existence of these woodland creatures.

Both pairs managed a bogey on the second hole and moved ahead to the third tee; this was a long par five with water in play. Both drives were quite decent but the second shot, if not kept on target, would bring the lake into play. Alice took the second shot with a six iron, but the ball bounced directly towards the banks of the lake. Surprised by their approach, a heron rose up with great effort, heaving himself reluctantly into the sky. Moving towards the bulrushes to search for the ball allowed time for a little conversation.

"Adam will be on TV tonight," said Madeleine. "On the news."

"Gosh, what has he done?" asked Primrose, playfully.

"He was interviewed about the oil situation. The problems are getting worse and oil prices are going up. He feels the interview went well but he's never had to deal with camera make-up before. He had two young men airbrushing his blemishes away. I asked him if he wore lipstick and mascara, but he's not sure. He just knew they did something with his eyes and mouth, as well as smearing and spraying stuff on his face. He didn't have a mirror so he had no idea what he looked like. A crew of eight people came to the office. Two make-up guys, a cameraman, an electrician, a sound technician, a production assistant, a director and a marketing executive. All for just five minutes on screen. Must have cost a fortune."

"Well, I'll be teasing him when I see him next."

"Found a ball!" exclaimed Nancy. "What are you playing?"

"A Nike," answered Alice.

"No, this is a Titleist," called back Nancy.

The group kept looking, thrashing the long grass with their clubs. "My daughter was burgled at the weekend," said Nancy. "They were obviously professional. They took both cars from the garage and all the paperwork from the study. But they suspect a woman was involved, too. Not just jewelry but some attractive porcelain figurines were taken, as well. She's really shaken up but her neighbors have been very kind. Brought her in and gave her a drink of champagne."

"Can't remember the last time I drank champagne," mused Primrose, wistfully remembering orange juice and champagne cocktails over weekend breakfasts with friends and family in South Africa.

"Burglaries are terribly disturbing," sighed Nancy. "Makes you feel so violated. And the inconvenience is incredibly time consuming. Think of the time they'll have to spend with insurance companies, not to mention replacing their possessions."

"Found it!" called back Madeleine. "A Nike Ball? It's here, right down the bank, just on the edge. Not sure what your best option is, Alice. You could take a penalty shot and move it out of the hazard, or attempt to play it as it lies."

"I'll take a penalty. Didn't have much luck with my fancy shot on the first hole," called back Alice, as she rushed towards the spot, slowing down warily towards the ball which perched two inches from the edge of the lake.

As if in slow motion, Alice reached out to grab the ball, lost her footing, attempted to regain her balance but landed on her back in the lake; her waterproof suit puffed out with the impact; her loud yell was suffocated as she submerged under the muddy water. As if jet propelled, she sprang back, hands outstretched. In an instant, Madeleine, Primrose and Robina were at the same spot, arms extended to meet Alice's grasp. Coordinating all their energy, while conscious of keeping their footing on the slippery bank, they hauled Alice out of the water. Gasping with shock, water flowing from her drenched body, Alice stood on the bank supported by the other three; she bowed her head with relief, her hands meeting her face to reinforce the emotion; exhaling deeply, her knees buckled under her.

"Steady girl," soothed Madeleine, as all three ladies renewed their grip on Alice, catching her under the arms to keep her upright.

"Move forward, Alice. Come off the bank. You'll be safer on level ground," Robina entreated.

Alice stumbled forward, the others moving their hands to support her back, while they pushed her wet body up the bank of the lake. Three small steps ahead, digging her toes into the mud, Alice allowed herself to fall onto her stomach where she felt safe.

"Come on, you gotta get up! You need to get onto the fairway. Up, up, Alice. Get up!" Madeleine's command forced Alice to bring her head and knees together into a crawl position; using her knees and elbows, she dragged herself up the banking. The others guarded her progress, ready to catch her round the waist if she faltered. Reaching the top of the bank, hunching into a more upright position, Alice now stood with her hands flat on the bank, her feet still on the slope. Nancy stood behind Alice, hands lightly supporting her back, while Primrose and

Madeleine clambered up the bank to clasp her hands, pulling her weight up. First one foot, then the other and Alice was safely standing upright, back on level ground. Now all four ladies stood on the fairway looking wildly at one another.

"You know, this is not a swimming club. It's a golf club, Alice," said Madeleine, breaking the tension.

"I've got my phone with me," said Primrose. "Switched off, of course, but I have the number of the club secretary keyed in. Let me ring for help."

Primrose reached into her golf bag and withdrew her slim Ericson, praying that the battery was powered up. Switching on, she was relieved to find she had a good signal. Pressing a few buttons, she was through to the clubhouse. "Hello, this is Primrose Pretorius. We have an emergency on the third hole. A lady has fallen in the water. No, she's OK. We got her out. Can you send transport to take her back to the clubhouse? Oh, and some nice clean, dry towels would be welcome. You'll be here in a few minutes? That's great. Thanks."

"I feel very strange," muttered Alice. "That was a weird experience. Just thinking of golf one second, then immersed in water the next. Almost as if I wanted to be there. Now, the last thing on my mind is golf … I feel quite bewildered." Alice started to shiver now, but there was nothing they could do to relieve her discomfort; she was dripping water from head to foot, her face streaked with mud, slimy weeds in various shades of green clinging to her navy and red windproof suit.

"Suggest you stay upright and let the water drain off you," said Madeleine. "Perhaps we can tell a joke to cheer you up. Anyone know a good joke?"

"Well, let's see," said Nancy looking up at the sky for inspiration. "Oh, yes … now, this should make you feel better … it's about good news and bad news."

"Oh, yes?" answered Alice, expectantly.

"Well, several centuries ago, the lord of the manor had been away on a long trip. On return, he was met by his faithful servant who sorrowfully explained that he had good news and bad news. The lord of the manor opted to hear the bad news first. 'Well, the bad news is that your favorite dog has died,' explained the servant. 'Not the white terrier!' the lord exclaimed. 'I'm afraid so, your lordship,' the servant answered. 'But how did this happen?' the lord questioned. 'Well, the grey mare kicked her,' was the reply. 'The grey mare kicked her? How did this come about?' the lord wanted to know. 'Well, it was when the stable caught fire. The grey mare was terrified, reared up and kicked the white terrier,' the servant replied. 'The stable caught fire?' repeated the lord. 'Well, yes, it was a spark from the big house which set it alight.' 'What do you mean it was a spark from the big house?' 'Well, it was the candles round the coffins which set it alight.' 'What coffins?' 'Well, your lordship, I'm sorry to report that your wife and children were lost to the black plague.' 'But, you said there was good news?' 'Oh, yes, with all that heat from the fire, the daffodils have come up early this year.'"

Roars of laughter from Madeleine and Primrose followed. Alice smiled wanly but looked more relaxed, having forgotten her plight for a few minutes. By now, the group behind had come into view. Cathy, Barbara, Robina and Lynn were heading towards them.

"Oh, dear. Now, we're holding up the field," exclaimed Alice.

"Don't worry about a thing. They can play through," answered Madeleine.

"Hey, what's happening?" called out Lynn.

"Alice fell in the lake," answered Nancy. "We phoned the clubhouse. They're sending transport to fetch her."

"Well, this is a first. No-one has ever managed to do this before. Any fish in there?" Lynn enquired.

"Gosh, look at you," commented Barbara. "Wish I had a camera."

"What about your game?" enquired Cathy. "You can't play without a partner, Nancy."

"Are you alright, Alice?" asked Robina, her earnest grey eyes assessing her condition. "Do you want to sit down? I wish there was something we could do for you. You'll soon be back in the clubhouse, nice and warm and dry."

"You ladies carry on," said Madeleine. "We don't want to hold up the field. We'll make sure Alice is OK."

"Yes, you're right. We'll move along and let you sort yourselves out," agreed Robina. "Here's your transport," she continued, as a heavy duty vehicle came into view.

Cathy, Barbara, Robina and Lynn moved off reluctantly, giving several backward glances, until each golf shot took them out of view of Alice and her dilemma.

Darren was driving the greenkeepers truck; he had locked up the pro shop to come to the rescue, since Anastasia would not allow any of her employees to perform the task. He approached the little group at high speed, turning the vehicle back round to face the direction of the clubhouse before stamping on the brake. Leaping out, his face wreathed in smiles, the young man called, "Well, ladies, what do we have here?"

"Alice decided to go swimming," answered Nancy. It was impossible not to notice the mischievous look which passed between them.

"You know what I think," said Madeleine. "You should strip off all those clothes here. You brought dry towels, Darren? We girls will shield you with the towels. Darren can look away. No-one else can see us. It means you can put all those wet things in the back of the vehicle. We can dry you off here. You can cover yourself up with those other dry towels until you get into the clubhouse."

"Actually, that's not a bad idea," said Primrose. "What do you think, Alice?"

"Well, I've not got any clothes to change into. How am I going to get home?"

"I'll fix you up with some dry clothes from the pro shop," offered Darren.

"Yea, that works," answered Nancy. "I'll come back with you. Make sure you're OK."

"But, what about your game?" Alice said, through chattering teeth.

"Oh, never mind that. Just get those clothes off and get yourself dried," Nancy instructed.

"I'll sit in the truck with my back to you," Darren said, as he moved away.

The three ladies helped Alice to remove her sodden clothing, rubbing her down with the dry towels in an attempt to get the circulation moving. Alice looked quite blue with cold, but revived considerably once she was dry and wrapped in several large white towels.

"Ready now," Nancy called to Darren. Alice took a few steps forward in bare feet while Darren turned the truck back round to fetch her.

"Actually, Nancy, I'll be fine," insisted Alice. "You carry on with Madeleine and Primrose. They need you to mark their score card. In any case, what are we thinking about? I've got clothes with me to change into for lunch."

"Gosh, that's right. By the time you've showered and changed, the players at the front of the field will be coming in, so you'll have company before too long," said Madeleine, adding, "Nancy, you don't need to mark our card. It's not important. Just do what suits you best."

Nancy answered, "Tell you what. I'll come in and keep Darren company in the pro-shop while you shower and change, Alice. Then we can have a coffee together in the clubhouse. How's that?"

Alice nodded, clambering aboard the truck, followed by Nancy. Darren stowed their golf clubs in the rear of the vehicle and, giving a wave, called out, "OK, ladies," as he drove off at high speed.

"Just you and me, now," Primrose said, looking despondently at Madeleine. "We're out of the competition with no-one to mark our card. I so want to win something. I thought we had a chance today."

"How about we carry on and use the rest of the round as practice?" suggested Madeleine.

"OK," answered Primrose, brightening up. "What shall we practice?"

"Dunno," Madeleine spluttered. "We'll think of something on the way round. Let's get moving. I'm really cold now. We don't need to play alternate shots. We can play our own balls."

Madeleine selected a ball from her bag. "I'm using a DDH," she informed Primrose. She moved from crouching position to fully upright and dropped the ball from shoulder height, arm fully outstretched. "Let's get going," she continued, using her five wood to take advantage of the clear fairway.

"Well, we've got the heavyweights in front now," commented Primrose.

"Heavyweights?"

"Captain, Past Captain, Immediate Past Captain, Silver Division Captain."

"True," acknowledged Madeleine.

"Would you like to be Captain, Madeleine?"

"Not desperately. It's not something I would seek to do, but if there was no-one else I would take responsibility. What about you, Primrose?"

"I would love to be Captain of this club."

"You would. Why?"

"Oh, the prestige. I'm not a very good golfer and I'm a foreigner, so no-one has much regard for me. If I was Captain, they would all have to sit up and take notice and I would have the influence of being a Past Captain for evermore."

Primrose had used her four iron to reach the green on the next hole. She knew that using a wood was a better choice for distance, but decided to use an iron to give more accuracy. Unfortunately, the fairly straight shot trickled into one of a series of bunkers, which were marked as 'Ground Under Repair'. "I can take a drop here, without penalty," she commented. "I'll bring it back over to the bunker on the left, so I can reach the green without having to get over a bunker."

"Primrose, you can't do that," responded Madeleine. "You have to take the nearest point of relief. You can't just choose where to go."

"Well, that's what the group of ladies were doing last week, so you're wrong," countered Primrose.

No, *they* are wrong," insisted Madeleine. "There is only *one* point of relief, which can be no nearer the hole. We'll double check with Darren, in the pro shop, when we get back in, but that's what you have to do. It's important to know all these things."

The pair finished the hole and walked in silence for some time, concentrating on their shots, but tension had grown between them; both struggled to gain control of their feelings of righteousness. They completed the fourth hole, avoiding eye contact, being coolly polite to each other with comments like, "Would you like the flag tended?" and "I wonder if you could mark your ball to the side."

Strolling down the fifth fairway, their feelings began to subside. "Look, bluebells!" said Madeleine.

"Oh, my goodness," gasped Primrose.

There they were. A carpet of freshness. Wild. Free. Roaming where they chose. Intense blue streaks coloring the landscape. A reminder to Madeleine of childhood, picking the fragile bells as a gift for her mother, remembering the snapping sound as the pressure of her little fingers broke the stems, feeling the sticky white sap on her palms, hearing the squeak of shiny green leaves under her feet, taking the woodland treasures home to be captured in a vase full of clear, cool water, seeing them adorn the kitchen windowsill, remembering her mother's peaceful smile.

The joy of the moment nourished Primrose and Madeleine; the tension between them evaporated; they approached the sixth tee in a dreamlike trance, both wordlessly taking their drives onto the fairway.

Breaking the spell, Madeleine continued their earlier conversation, "So you think being a foreigner is a disadvantage?"

"Well, they don't accept you," answered Primrose, wistfully. "I've tried to make friends here, but they're not interested."

"Yes, it is difficult."

"I've hosted dinner parties, but no-one invites you back. I suggest lunch dates which go on the calendar, and they cancel at the last minute, or they let you pay and don't reciprocate. And they actually ignore you without batting an eyelid. Have you noticed, in the clubhouse after golf, each week, they make social arrangements across the table while you're sitting there, as if you're invisible? Do you know, I think I could claim racial discrimination for the way I'm excluded."

"Do you really mean that, Primrose?"

"Absolutely. I feel emotionally dead here. The only time I feel wanted is when we're back in South Africa on vacation. You've no idea the number of people in this golf club who invited themselves out for a free holiday, once they realized we still own property over there. We're not accepted here. People either dismiss us, or else take advantage of us. I think their attitude is, if they ignore us long enough, we'll eventually go away. I feel like my bones have been picked clean here ... I daren't explore my feelings any further." Primrose bit her lip and blinked back the tears. "I can't explain any more."

"I *do* know what you mean, Primrose. Remember, I'm from Belgium."

"Yes, but you're accepted, Madeleine."

"I'm not sure that's true. Two situations in particular taught me a lesson. I issued a dinner invitation to one lady whose company I enjoyed – she shrank back as if I had leprosy. On another occasion, I asked someone I thought of as a friend if she would like to get together for lunch – she turned her head away as if I had slapped her, and made some excuse. I don't take the initiative anymore."

"But, you've been here a long time, Madeleine."

"I don't think it matters. I grew up and was educated somewhere else. I think unless you're born here, you'll always feel like an outsider."

"What about Adam?"

"Adam was born in Germany, but I don't think men want friends. Adam doesn't. He doesn't need other people. He can be very sociable, but he doesn't feel the need to be emotionally attached to other men. He would rather be with me than anyone else because we're best friends. I guess, also, he's an Alpha male."

"What do you mean, he's an Alpha male?"

"He's naturally the leader of the pack. He'll fight to hold and keep that position."

"So, you think of men in terms of the animal kingdom?"

"Well, not quite, but there are analogies."

"Suppose that might be happening in our household," acknowledged Primrose. "I have Marius, the old lion, fighting for dominance over the young lion ... his teenage son."

"Yes, and have you noticed that when men herd together, it's often as drinking buddies? Like jungle animals visiting the watering hole. Men compete with each other. They don't share their lives with each other. They either compete in the workplace, or want to win the chase for a woman, or be the champion at a sports tournament such as golf, or earn the highest academic awards. If success at these things eludes them, they compete at drinking. A night out with the boys, and they're boasting the next day about what a good time they had, and what a dreadful hangover they've got. Have you noticed how some of them boast about how many pints they drank, or how many bottles of wine they consumed? Eventually, they end up with a drinking problem, but they present it as a need to spend time with the boys. If alcohol wasn't involved, it would be a whole different scenario."

"You know, Madeleine, you've got a good point there. Marius always drinks huge amounts at the weekend and feels lousy all week. Mind you, it doesn't help that he drinks at home, too. Probably gets through a couple of bottles of scotch each week, not counting a bottle of wine with dinner each night."

"That's a lot, Primrose."

"Yes, I don't know what to do about it. Don't think there's anything I *can* do. I think Marius feels he has more mates here than I do because of his drinking buddies – almost as if there's collusion between them. He meets them at the pub and says they have such a good laugh together – it's a place to relax and forget the cares of the world. But if alcohol wasn't involved, I don't think he would be there. Actually, I think he uses alcohol as a means of escape. He thinks he's escaping his responsibilities for a while but, really, he's drinking to escape himself."

"You may be right."

"And it excludes his wife and family. I'm not sure, at times, if he's finding an excuse to get away from us, or if he has an alcohol dependency which he needs to feed."

"Yes, it can be difficult."

"It just doesn't help me feel I belong here."

"I think none of us feel we belong because, truly, our time on earth is short and we belong somewhere else. Don't you ever feel that your spirit longs to find its source, like tracing the source of a river?" enquired Madeleine, wistfully.

"You're right. But how?"

"We each have to find our own path."

Approaching the seventh tee, they became aware of a placard proclaiming a prize for the longest drive on this hole.

"Just look at the marker on the fairway," noted Madeleine. "Never in my wildest dreams would I be that far ahead."

"Probably Susan Trent. She plays every day, you know."

They reached the marker which confirmed that Susan had, indeed, won the longest drive, and passed on, without comment, shrugging their shoulders slightly indicating a resigned disinterest.

"Don't expect we'll be in the running, but even if we did have the longest drive, we're out of the competition, anyway," said Madeleine, mounting the steps to the tee box.

"Actually, we've caught up with the group in front now," observed Primrose, gazing ahead.

As they replaced their clubs in their bags, Primrose commented, "Did you know we're moving house?"

"You are?"

"Yes, moving out of our three bedroom townhouse."

"That's wonderful news, Primrose."

"Yes, we've been struggling since we came to this country, but now the business is established and doing really well, particularly since I got involved. We've saved relentlessly, and we're ready to move into something better."

"Tell me all about it."

"Well, it's half an acre of ground and five bedrooms."

"Gosh, you *are* making a big leap."

"Yes, indeed. Maybe they'll think me suitable for Captain if we have a big house."

Madeleine raised her eyebrows. "What stage are you at?"

"Well, I viewed it last Tuesday. Marius viewed it on Thursday, and we made an offer on Saturday which was accepted. We had the agent round on Monday to put our house on the market and now the 'For Sale' sign is up. The vendors have confirmed their acceptance of our offer in writing. We have to appoint a solicitor."

"I can give you the name of a friend," offered Madeleine.

"That would be great."

"Which estate agent are you using?" Madeleine wanted to know.

"Harvey & Peterson."

"Should be OK."

"Yea, I'm not sure. We had a few round. They all quoted similar values. We chose Harvey & Peterson because we thought the manager was a really nice guy. We liked dealing with him and thought potential buyers would too, but we've been disappointed, so far. He's got all the details wrong on the brochure, so we had to re-write the whole thing. And it's a week since we appointed him, but no-one has viewed yet."

"It won't happen overnight. It'll take time. Once he has advertised, you'll see a lot of interest," encouraged Madeleine.

"I expect you're right," answered Primrose, climbing the steps to the next tee. Watching her, Madeleine suddenly pointed a finger. Turning her head, Primrose was astonished to see two woodpeckers perched at the base of adjacent trees.

"They're 'Great Spotted' aren't they?" whispered Madeleine.

"Yes, black and white plumage, red crown," Primrose whispered back.

"But they're so small and I've never seen them at the base of a tree before. They're pecking but not making a noise."

"Maybe they're juveniles, just practicing."

"Could be, or they might be 'Lesser Spotted' – they're smaller. Look at them creep up the tree. Not seen them do that before, either."

They stood spellbound as the two woodpeckers made their way, in unison, up the tree trunk. The birds seemed unconcerned at their presence, occasionally looking towards them as if to say, 'Look what we can do.' Reaching the top of the trunk, they took a slow hesitant flight towards the top of another tree, disappearing from view.

"Gosh, what a privilege to see them today," said Primrose.

"Absolutely. Especially since their numbers have declined greatly in the last twenty years," endorsed Madeleine.

"I wonder why?" queried Primrose.

"Dutch elm disease has killed off their favorite nesting trees. You know, the impact of death in the world of nature is far reaching. But the impact of death in the human world only benefits the environment."

"Hmmmm," pondered Primrose. "Par three with those lovely bunkers next."

"Oh, yes, I can never get on that green. Always play short to avoid the bunkers. I'll experiment today and use a different club. Actually, there's a prize for nearest the pin on this hole."

Madeleine used a low tee with a five iron, got the distance right but veered to the left; holding her breath, she gave a sigh of relief as the ball stopped on the fringe, just inches from the bunker. Primrose was not so lucky; she landed well short of the green, probably needing to chip with a nine iron to get close to the flag.

Finishing the hole, Madeleine ventured, "Big celebrations in South Africa this week."

"Yes, ten years since the abolition of apartheid. Quite an achievement. Do you know, I'm beginning to realize I feel guilty about leaving," Primrose confessed.

"You do?"

"Oh, this long par five next. I always mess up this hole."

"Just think about your successes, Primrose. Think of all the good shots you've had on this hole and try to repeat them," coached Madeleine.

"Easier said than done."

"So, you feel guilty about leaving?" prompted Madeleine, as they walked between green and tee.

"Very mixed feelings, really. It's amazing how things have turned out in South Africa."

"True."

"What is so surprising is that South Africa is now a stable democracy. It's a big success story from a political point of view. I'm beginning to feel we abandoned it in a time of need."

Both parted company as they followed the direction of their balls to opposite sides of the fairway. A light drizzle descended briefly. They continued wordlessly, hoping the rain would stay away. Reaching the next tee, they donned waterproof hats and glumly took their drives, without enthusiasm.

"Wonder what's going to happen in Europe with these ten new countries coming into the European Union next week?" pondered Madeleine.

"Now, that's a hot potato."

"Well, if I can get someone from Eastern Europe to do the garden and clean the house, I'll be happy. If we do get people willing to work, rather than terrorists who claim benefits, it'll be a big success. Blair has his work cut out for him, that's for sure," asserted Madeleine.

Madeleine and Primrose reached the green. Primrose held the flag while Madeleine crouched down, assessing the incline and distance to sink her putt. A moving figure, hurrying towards them caught her eye. "Primrose!" called a voice, as the figure reached the edge of the green and, catching her attention, walked forward to where Primrose stood holding the flag. "Could you give me the recipe for that barbeque sauce? Make a copy and give it to me next week?" Primrose nodded agreement, and the figure hurried off.

"Well, I've seen it all now," uttered Madeleine, her shoulders heaving in a chuckle of amusement.

"You see what I mean!" spat out Primrose. "She was at my house for dinner two weeks ago. She and her husband arrived without any hostess gift ... no flowers, no chocolates, no wine ... nothing. Had a jolly old time drinking our booze. Thanked us in an offhand manner when they left, as if we were some sort of servants. Not a phone call or a note of appreciation. But now I have to run after her with a recipe. I'm afraid I'll be forgetting to do it."

"You know, Primrose, I wonder if you're just trying too hard. Maybe you're attempting to start relationships with the wrong people. Perhaps you might be happier just staying cool, keeping your distance and not bother with all this socializing."

"Do you think so, Madeleine?"

"Just be yourself. Believe in your own self worth. You may then find that you attract people with whom you have something in common."

Primrose stopped in her tracks. "You know, you may just be right."

"Look at that," said Madeleine, walking towards a ring of tiny mushrooms, red in color with an adornment of cream spots on the upper side. "I've never seen anything like it before."

"Nor have I," answered Primrose, as they gazed in amazement at the perfectly formed ring which stretched several feet in diameter.

"Do you think it's called a fairy ring?"

"I've heard the term but didn't know what it meant. The description seems to fit what we're seeing."

"I wonder if there's the stump of a dead tree underneath here. The mushrooms could be feeding off the decay," pondered Madeleine.

"That sounds like a possible explanation," nodded Primrose.

"Worth coming out today just to see that."

Madeleine took a decent drive on the next tee, but Primrose was not so fortunate. "Oh, fiddlesticks, I've gone in that bunker," she blurted out, her usual mask like expression weakening into a slight frown.

"Just remember your lesson with Darren," coached Madeleine. "Make sure your stance is wide enough and keep your weight on the left foot. Check that your ball is in a central position. Open your club face, take sand two inches behind the ball and accelerate through the shot."

"Easier said than done. Too much to remember all at once."

"Think positive and concentrate," advised Madeleine.

Primrose took her stance. Time stood still as she poised her club steadily behind the ball. Focusing her mind to control her coordination and picture the ball in play, she swung cleanly through the shot. The ball swooped out neatly, landing a good twenty yards ahead. "Whew, what a relief. Bunkers can kill a good score," she exclaimed, pulling the rake towards her as she walked backwards out of the hazard.

"Yes, and the rain's gone off again. Just heavy drizzle," said Madeleine, removing the waterproof hat which was pinching her forehead.

Primrose followed her lead, placing her hat on top of her wood covers, "Now, I'm really warm again inside this waterproof suit," she commented.

Putting out uneventfully, they completed the hole and walked towards the next tee in comfortable silence. Sighing, Madeleine ventured, "You know, I'm getting bored with golf. It's so time consuming. The whole scene is so structured." She looked into the distance, taking a casual swing which took the ball down the middle of the fairway.

"No!" responded Primrose. "You wouldn't want to give up golf, would you?"

"You know, I think I want golf just as a pastime," reflected Madeleine. "I don't want it to be a way of life."

"Hmmmm," voiced Primrose, as she took her drive. "Aaaaaahhhhh!" she exploded, as her ball hit a tree and ricocheted back towards her. "Goodness, now look where I've landed."

"Oooops," responded Madeleine, as they both walked towards the ball. "Horrible place in amongst that debris, with those branches above. You need to play off the back foot to keep the ball low. Anyway, we were supposed to be using this as a practice round, after Alice had her experience, so take your time."

Primrose selected a five iron to get under the ball and, as advised, positioned the ball in front of her back foot. The ball moved six inches into a nest of dry leaves. "Oh, dear," she muttered, bending down to remove all the surrounding obstacles including twigs and acorns. "I'll have another go," she called.

"You need more back swing," advised Madeleine, as Primrose positioned herself for another attempt.

"Hey presto," called Primrose cheerfully, as the ball sailed under the branches, and bounced a hundred yards along the fairway. As they met up again in the middle of the fairway, Primrose continued, "What I find tedious about golf is arranging a partner every week. I feel like a teenage boy at the school dance, asking people to play, knowing that those with better handicaps are reluctant and I'm loath to ask those who consider themselves to be on a higher social standing than me."

"Yes, and the worst bit is people being unreliable," agreed Madeleine. "You fix up to play months ahead, and then some people think nothing about cancelling out the day before just because they get a more interesting social engagement."

"Leaves you high and dry looking for another partner at short notice."

"I know. It's a real drag," Madeleine acknowledged.

"Hey, what a putt, partner," called Madeleine, as Primrose gently tapped her ball down a long, steep slope on the green. The ball kept a steady pace, stopping just two inches from the hole. "You judged that beautifully."

"Just lucky, but I feel good about it," answered Primrose.

"Only three more holes. This is when I feel tired, like I can't be bothered to continue," sighed Madeleine, as she wearily lifted out her driver, noting the yellow hazard markers ahead. The tempo of her next shot was fine, but she failed to keep her arm straight.

"Here, have a banana," offered Primrose, "Or, I have some protein bars, if you would prefer that. Give you some energy."

"Don't mind if I do," Madeleine said, gratefully accepting a strawberry flavored bar. "I think my ball has gone into the ditch."

"Well, I won't get that far," commented Primrose. Her gentle swing took the ball into the long grass a few yards in front of the hazard. "There, told you so."

Reaching the ditch, Madeleine decided to take a penalty shot, since the hazard was deep and narrow. "I should really try to play out of here for practice, but I think it would be dangerous to attempt it," she called. Dropping the ball in front of the hazard from shoulder height, she used a five wood to take the ball uphill towards the flag.

"I'm going to a Pilates class tonight," said Primrose, compressing her lips to conceal a smile.

"Why, that's great. I like Pilates," answered Madeleine. "Gentle exercise, really good."

"You've done it, then?"

"Just a few times."

"How does it compare to yoga?" wondered Primrose.

"Very similar, I think. Although Pilates seems to concentrate on the pelvic floor."

"What's that then?"

"Not sure, something to do with core muscles in the center of your body. I'm sure you'll enjoy it. Very relaxing." Madeleine smiled.

"That's just what I need. I'm on pills, you know," confided Primrose.

"What kind of pills?"

"Anti-depressants."

"No!"

After a shocked silence, Madeleine ventured, "You're struggling, then?"

"Yep." Primrose bit her lip.

"You poor dear," answered Madeleine. "Life gets us all down sometimes." After a pause, she continued, "I took them for a while."

"You did?"

"Yes, when our son was diagnosed with Asperger's syndrome."

"I hadn't realized."

"Well, he became more and more remote in his teens. It was only when he reached his third year at university that we realized his problems were serious." Madeleine's expression became tense and worried. "It took a long time to get a diagnosis."

"I'm so sorry."

"Well, I asked our doctor to help." Madeleine shook her head, shaking off the memory of difficult times. "I was an emotional wreck. He prescribed anti-depressants. I resent him for doing that. Counseling would have been a better option. Anyway, after a few months, I realized these pills were doing me more harm than good, so I flushed them down the toilet. Never looked back."

"Maybe I should think about counseling."

"If you know what's causing you to feel unhappy, it would be worth exploring."

"I'll think about it," Primrose contemplated.

They continued in silence, each lost in their own thoughts. Walking mechanically, looking straight ahead, the effort of holding back strong feelings contributed to a sharp focus on their golf shots.

"See, we should get emotional more often," said Madeleine. They both laughed to relieve the tension.

Reaching the eighteenth tee, Madeleine felt she wanted to return their conversation to safer ground. "I'm going to the Westwood exhibition tomorrow."

"You are?"

"Yes, at the Victoria and Albert Museum. It'll be fascinating to see her collection. I prefer her evening gowns to anything else. I think when she was influenced by McLaren she was finding herself. There's no doubt she could be criticized for producing facsimiles in some of her work during the nineties. I'm really looking forward to seeing the gold and silver wedding dress – that's my favorite."

"Gosh, you do get around," commented Primrose.

"Just look at those rhododendrons. I love this approach to the clubhouse." Madeleine changed the subject, as they reached the eighteenth tee. They both gazed at the rows of blossoms lining both sides of the fairway.

"Amazing at this time of year. Every color ... yellow, pink, purple, white, orange, red," responded Primrose.

"I believe this was actually the original driveway to the old manor house. Must have been stunning reaching here in your carriage, after driving out from London."

"They've done a great job making it a signature hole."

"Yea, takes your mind off that pond."

Madeleine stood on the tee and, unusually, took several practice swings. Each swing was a little faster in speed. She knew that she must accelerate through the shot to make the uphill approach over the water, with some chance of reaching the green.

"Bravo!" called Primrose as Madeleine's ball landed on the fringe, several yards from the green. The pair completed the round in good spirits, shaking hands and hugging each other before making their way to the clubhouse.

"We're not going to be picking up any prizes. We had to duck out of the competition," Primrose explained, as they handed in their score cards.

"Who cares?" added Madeleine, with a grin.

They changed into neat and simple clothing in the locker room, barely listening to the surrounding chatter; both were lost in reflections of their intimate conversations on the golf course; they occasionally glanced towards each other, checking that the progress in their toilette was keeping apace.

"Who won the longest drive?" Lynn's voice rose above the chatter.

"Susan Trent," called back a voice.

"Pooffff," exploded Barbara, muttering under her breath to Lynn, "These people who play every day, living miniscule lives in tiny houses, with the golf course as their garden."

Lynn stifled a snort of laughter, "Ssssshhhh."

"Well," said Barbara, raising herself up to full height and increasing the volume of her voice at the same time. She surveyed the locker room, taking note of who was there before continuing. "She's just a pot hunter, only turns up here when there's a prize to be won. I hope we don't have to listen to another one of her long acceptance speeches about how thrilled she is, and how much this means to her. It makes me sick." A volley of sniggers ricocheted around the room.

"Ready?" enquired Madeleine, as Primrose squirted a jet of perfume on her wrists.

"Yep, let's go," Primrose responded.

They made their way out of the locker room towards the prize table in the corridor outside. Stopping to glance at the array of prizes which included several plants, a basket of flowers, two large crystal vases, three golf umbrellas, a box of chocolates and several golf visors, they were amused at the comments floating around.

"... who needs more golf stuff ... all that crystal ... just dust collectors ... flowers are nice ... chocolates don't last long in our house ... houseplants are such a nuisance..."

Moving away towards the dining room, Madeleine enquired, "Glass of wine, Primrose?"

"For sure. Red would be fine. Thank you."

"What about Alice? Where is she?"

"Oh yes, over there. Shall I find out what she wants to drink?"

"Yes, and Nancy, too."

Primrose quickly returned. "They'll both have red wine."

Holding a glass of wine in each hand, Primrose and Madeleine approached the group who were swarming around Alice. "...we'll rename you lady of the lake ... must have been such a shock ... you look none the worse for your ordeal ... are you feeling OK?" were among the many comments buzzing around Alice's head.

"I need to have a tetanus jab. Going to the clinic at six this evening," informed Alice. "And, I'm coming down with a cold," she spluttered, catching a sneeze in her handkerchief. The sneeze scattered the group. Alice hunched further into her chair, as Madeleine and Primrose settled themselves on the sofa opposite.

Seconds later, Nancy joined them, sighing, "A glass of wine! Wonderful!" as she sank into a soft seat.

"You've got quite a rosy glow, already," Primrose commented to Nancy, giving her an enquiring look.

Barbara, Cathy, Robina and Lynn, unaware of the sneeze, seated themselves in the remaining empty chairs, all eyes taking in the discomfort of Alice, while failing to notice the tension focused on Nancy.

"So, you're the lady of the lake, now!" quipped Cathy, following this up with a hollow laugh.

"Only queen for a day," responded Alice, wishing to deflect the attention from herself. Putting on a brighter face, she changed the subject, "I notice lots of cars in the district are flying white flags with red crosses. What's that all about? Is there some religious significance that I've missed?"

"No," answered Primrose, knowledgeably. "It's the flag of St George. It represents England."

"Oh, it must be for the elections, then," Alice nodded.

"Darling, it's for the football," called out Barbara in a loud voice. "England plays France at the weekend in the first round of the European Championship."

As the laughter died down, Nancy interjected, "Have you heard about the new laws on bad driving?" All heads turned to hear the answer.

"Well, if you're a bad driver you have to fly one flag of St George out of your car window. And, if you're a really bad driver, you have to fly two flags."

"So, that's why all these flags are around." Alice looked blankly, while the others heaved with laughter. "It has nothing to do with St George."

"Do you think she's concussed?" queried Barbara.

"But in some ways it has a religious significance," Madeleine stated, as the laughter died down.

"How's that?" asked Alice, looking relieved that her humiliation was waning.

"Well, these sports personalities are the modern gods or idols of a large percentage of the population. Football is a religion to their followers. The churches in this country are empty, but the football stadiums are full of worshippers. And, it doesn't stop there ... the television screens are the altars to these idols, whether they be football players, pop singers or film stars. And, if you see these pop videos, they're close to being pornographic. I think the devil is hard at work in our society."

"Sport *is* like a religion to some people. It's something to belong to if they're supporters of a team," Cathy interjected, stridently.

"Well, perhaps that's so," accepted Madeleine. "I suppose a golf clubhouse is a place of worship instead of a church, and the ritual of the golf club calendar replaces the rituals of the church. I'm not judging, but perhaps there could be just the tiniest space in life to praise God."

An uncomfortable silence descended. "You're right," Robina said eventually, in a quiet voice. "When you're surrounded by the wonder of the countryside, you feel God's presence. You have to acknowledge that a powerful and joyful force has created our environment."

"Lunch is ready," the steward mingled among the tables, making the announcement discreetly.

"Let's eat," said Cathy.

"Yes, let's eat, drink and be merry," cheered Nancy, unaware of the troubles which lay ahead.

HAPPY BIRTHDAY

Damp. It was damp outside. Drizzle all morning. Bronze leaves curled up, sleepily resisting the next gust of wind, positioned in predictable pockets of space, varnished with wet, glistening, gloss. Teardrops, suspended from garden furniture, reluctant to release their existence. Intricate cobwebs encrusted with pearls of moisture, danced in tune to the flow of air, the unseen maestro protecting their place in the universe. Alice stared out of the window at the magnolias. A profusion of pink and white flesh provocatively displayed to the world. Bold, naked, vigorous and resilient. Tantalizing the elements with their defiant attitude. Looking in the mirror, she compared the fresh vitality of the blooms with her permed, brown, tinted hair, feeling disheartened at the weary, unsmiling expression gazing back, the fleshy upper lip emphasizing her sagging spirits.

"I'm sick of my life," muttered Alice to herself, as she wielded a duster to the dining room table. "There's going to be changes. That fall in the water has shocked me into thinking differently." She telephoned her daughter. "It's your Dad's sixtieth birthday next month. You must know that our relationship has been dutiful and not much more. I want to make changes. Life's too short. I want to buy him a Harley Davidson motorbike. He's always wanted one. Can you do some research?"

"With the greatest of pleasure, Mum. What a joy! I'll get right onto it."

The phone rang the following day. "OK, Mum. I've sussed it all out. You know, this is an inspired gift idea. Harley Davidson had their centenary last year, so there's lots of memorabilia other folks can buy for his birthday to link up with your plans. Harley Davidson supports the Muscular Dystrophy Association and they raised over seven million dollars last year with all the celebrations. Good, eh? I think he would like the 2004 Sporster, but it costs over five thousand pounds. You don't care about the cost? OK, do you want me to order one? Right, I'll keep you posted."

Alice pictured how Don might react when presented with the gift of his dreams; she saw the man she looked at every day; she saw the man with whom she had maintained only an appearance of an acceptable marriage; she saw the man to whom she spoke politely in public; she saw the man with whom she lived in almost total silence, the wordlessness broken only with fragmented exchanges of domestic details; she saw the stocky frame; she saw the weather beaten face underneath the perpetually untidy grey hair; she saw the strain behind the grey eyes; she saw the man he might have been if the love affair with the book-keeper had never happened; she saw the man who could relax and smile; she saw the man she had not seen for many years. Time was running out. Could a miracle make him smile at her again? Could a Harley Davidson motorbike spell forgiveness?

Don was tired. All these years, toiling in the garden center. Yes, he was a partner in the business and they did make a good living, but it was hard graft. Four brothers and their wives having to get along with each other and agree on business decisions was more than flesh and blood could stand, sometimes. Don was always the one to agree to everything rather than cause a fuss; usually, he took a back seat and let the others get their own way; occasionally, he would have a pertinent view or a good idea, which he would quietly put forward, but he would never fight for dominance; if no-one latched onto his views, he would allow matters to flow in another direction; he supposed he could be called passive, but was of the mind that this approach worked best for him; he didn't get involved in battles of will and, consequently, became the brother who soothed the waters behind the scenes; he used the same approach at home with Alice; he acquiesced to all the domestic arrangements, expressing a view only if required. Punishment for his affair with their book-keeper all those years ago? Probably yes, but at the same time, a passive approach suited Don's gentle spirit; he still wasn't sure how he got involved in a sexual relationship with another woman; he supposed he had just fallen prey to a needy and lonely woman who had been forced to seek employment when her marriage broke down; he did feel he loved her at the time but knew, soon after, that the affair was a hollow relationship; he had simply been flattered by her attentions; his protective instincts had been fuelled and his common sense had been knocked sideways by lust. Once he had been found out, the affair had to end. The fury from his brothers and their wives had been a more potent force than the bitter disappointment from Alice. The pressure had been immense, so Don retreated even further into his shell of self preservation. Slowly, the episode faded into the background leaving him, still, with an unsatiated sense of wickedness which he could never quite shake off. Don often dreamt of taking a job in London and leaving everything behind or emptying the bank account and disappearing to Greece, but he never translated any of his escape plans into action. Don was surprised how Alice had reacted to the crisis; their marriage had never been passionate and she had simply completely closed down emotionally and got on with the daily routine. Oddly, they still shared the same bedroom; they had never shared a bed because Alice had always suffered from back problems so, in their single beds, in the same bedroom, Don and Alice continued as before but without any physical relationship. It was as if they saw each other through glass, with sight but without touch.

Now, as he was approaching retirement, Don had discovered a situation which could affect the whole family. The land boundaries of the garden center were in jeopardy. Don and his brothers had co-existed peacefully for many years with their neighbors, a farmer and his wife with two sons; the sons had recently inherited the land after the death of their parents, and were now disputing the ownership of an adjoining acre of ground. A few days ago, while Don was inspecting some young rhododendron plants along the common boundary between the properties, he had experienced a verbally abusive attack from one of the sons. Don worried about whether to make his brothers aware of the incident or whether to ignore it and hope it would go away: by doing nothing, he hoped the situation would either resolve itself, or that a lawyer's letter would bring the matter to the attention of his brothers, without his intervention. Don sighed heavily; he reached for the telephone to place an order for terracotta pots from his supplier, wishing he could make a telephone call to start another life. Meanwhile, Alice was planning his surprise birthday party.

THE COMMITTEE MEETING

A cloudy summer's day. Temperatures had been rising steadily with constant sunshine for several weeks and rain seemed like a distant memory. Much cooler today. A short, sharp burst of heavy rain and the gardens groaned with relief. The deluge ceased suddenly, leaving the parched vegetation refreshed but with unquenched thirst.

The committee members were seated in the meeting room adjacent to the business suite. Lynn, in her capacity as Lady Captain, had chaired a discussion to review the Spring Meeting and was satisfied that favorable comments had been received. "OK. Any other business?" she asked.

"Yes," said Barbara. "I would like to lodge a complaint about standards of dress."

"Oh,yes?" answered Lynn. Everyone became more alert, raising themselves up in their chairs and stiffening their pose. Eyes were fixed on Barbara for the next installment of her statement.

"A number of members have raised this issue with me," Barbara continued. "Since I am now Silver Division Captain, I do get a lot of members approaching me with feedback. I think it's high time something was done about it."

"Can you be specific, Barbara?" asked Lynn.

"Yes. I've had a variety of comments about ladies *and* gents. The ladies are very unhappy about men wearing shorts on the course. None of them look smart. They should be wearing tailored shorts reaching to the knees, with long socks. Instead, they're going around in what looks like football shorts and short dark socks, instead of long white ones. And they're wearing their shirts hanging out of their waistband, instead of tucked in with a belt. Also, it has been noted that a number of ladies are wearing tops without collars and sleeves, some of which are too short to tuck into a waistband. And ladies, too, are wearing shorts which are rather skimpy."

"Well, they're selling those tops in pro shops, nowadays," commented Primrose.

"Not in *our* pro shop and it *is* really up to the pro shop to enforce the dress code. They can see people passing the window and could intercept them," answered Barbara.

"I say it's up to Anastasia to take responsibility. The pros are employees and have no authority over the members," chimed in Cathy, demanding the respect of her position as Immediate Past Captain.

"I agree that standards are poor." Alice supported the motion, enjoying her influence as Secretary. "I noticed a young man the other day in jeans which, as you know, are not allowed to be worn anywhere on the premises. He zoomed up in his car to collect a member of his family and ran towards the clubhouse, shouting to attract their attention."

"Should we approach Anastasia?" questioned Madeleine, taking a considered view, conscious of her new role as Bronze Division Captain.

"Yes, the pro shop can't be held accountable. Let Anastasia enforce the dress code," Nancy Ruff butted in, pushing her head forward with an aggressive air. As Vice Captain, Nancy felt she needed to add something to the discussion.

"All right then. I'll approach Anastasia," confirmed Lynn. "There being no other business," she paused, looking around enquiringly, "I declare the meeting closed." Lynn gathered her papers together, looked around the table, catching each person's eye to assess the mood. "Anyone for coffee?" she asked. Murmurs of approval circled the room.

Primrose, reveling in the importance of her new position as Handicap Secretary, felt she should have contributed more to the meeting; she compensated by offering to fetch the coffees, and returned to the meeting room with a laden tray. Lynn took charge of the proceedings by pouring coffee from the stainless steel pot into cups and saucers bearing the club logo. Turning her head towards Primrose, Lynn asked, "So, how's the house move going?"

"Uuuuuhhhhh," a soft sigh escaped from Primrose as she sank into her chair. "Well, we've had an offer to buy our house from people who are unable to proceed, so that's not much use. But we've discovered the house we want to buy doesn't have planning permission."

"But, it's on a new estate! It's a new house," answered Lynn.

"It's not an entirely new house. We're buying from a couple who have lived there for only one year, but his company are moving him to Birmingham. It seems that large developers *do* build on swathes of land without planning permission. They take out a professional indemnity policy and it's up to the owners to sue them if a problem emerges."

"I've never heard of such a thing." Cathy's brow wrinkled, as she spoke.

"Actually, there was an article in the Sunday Times a few weeks ago on this very subject," commented Barbara.

"Oh, really. You wouldn't still have it?" asked Primrose, hopefully.

"I'll check in the re-cycle bin. I don't think it's gone yet. I'll let you have it next time I see you," promised Barbara.

"That would be helpful. We're just not sure which way to turn, at the moment," a despondent Primrose replied.

"How much do we owe you for coffee?" asked Cathy.

"No, it's on me," answered Primrose, firmly.

"Actually, have you noticed she's put the price of coffee up by twenty pence?" commented Cathy. "And a sandwich has gone up by thirty pence. We're going to stop eating here. Rodney says we shouldn't encourage her. She makes enough money out of us already."

"Doesn't she just!" Barbara agreed. "But what can you expect from these foreigners. Beats me how she and her husband can come over here with all this money and buy our golf course. They're buying up everything in sight. Mansions in London, country estates, golf courses. Yet, we've lived and worked here all our lives and can just afford the mortgage. It's a mystery, I can tell you."

"I didn't notice the price increase," answered Robina, who had been silent during the meeting. As a recent Past Captain, trusted by the members, she had been drafted in, unofficially, as Assistant Handicap Secretary to give guidance to Primrose who welcomed the support. "But I was disappointed with the soup the other day," continued Robina, "It was such a tiny bowl, not very hot and with only two small slices of bread."

"Actually, I think they just pull everything out of the freezer. Nothing's fresh," added Alice.

"Hey, we arranged to go out for a meal this evening with husbands! We fixed the date last month," Lynn interjected, suddenly remembering.

"Yea, we could do with cheering up," Primrose answered.

"Where shall we go?" queried Alice.

"How about the Five Bells?" suggested Nancy.

"Yea, sounds good. Should we phone to make a reservation?"

"Actually, I've done that already," informed Lynn. "They're expecting us. We can have private use of that room at the back."

"Huh, speaking of telephones, I've had an obscene phone call," Nancy said.

"You have? What kind? What did he say?" Barbara was all agog.

"Well, he didn't say much. Just kept repeating himself."

"But what did he say?"

"You really don't need to know, Barbara," Nancy replied irritably. "It was quite upsetting."

"It must have been," soothed Robina.

"Did you report it to the police? When did this happen?" enquired Lynn.

"It was a few weeks ago and, yes, I did report it to the police but they can't do anything. Anyway, they're monitoring the line for six months, so if it happens again, they can trace it. But I know the voice. I kept him talking as long as possible because I thought that would help the police, but it didn't. But I do know the voice ... it keeps coming into my head. I keep trying to picture the face and match the voice, but I can't."

A ponderous silence ensued. Each of them was wondering how they would deal with an obscene phone call. Their minds were searching a database of male acquaintances to work out who might be driven to such a feeble act.

Breaking the silence, Lynn returned to the social arrangements. "Everybody OK for tonight with husbands?"

"Is it OK if I come on my own?" enquired Madeleine. "Adam's away."

"Sure thing. Where is he this time?" asked Lynn.

"Saudi Arabia, actually. He's a bit apprehensive about this trip. "

"Yes, traveling anywhere can be dangerous, these days." Robina shook her head slowly, as she spoke.

"I'll be very relieved to see him home," sighed Madeleine.

"Do you want us to pick you up?" asked Lynn

"No thanks. I can walk. It's a fair distance, but the exercise and fresh air will do me good."

"You bringing that silly dog with you? She's competing with Robina now. Did you know she's just got herself a Weimeramer?" Lynn spread her hands and hunched her shoulders in wordless comment.

"A what?" queried Barbara, her expression puckered into an incredulous frown.

"A Weimeramer. His name is Rex. He's a natural protector. Makes me feel more secure with Adam being away such a lot. He's a hound, originally bred as a hunter."

"What's it look like?" Barbara's eyebrows rose further.

"Grey, short hair, docked tail. Quite majestic, really. The breed dates back to eighteenth century Germany. He's quite fearless but, watch out, he likes to bark. He certainly lets me know if anything's amiss." Madeleine smiled. "But no, I won't bring him with me. I'll walk there and maybe someone can give me a lift back home."

"No problem," replied Lynn. "Come back with us."

Madeleine brightened up, mischief twinkling in her eyes. "Mind you, I could come on Adam's bicycle which he bought last month."

"Adam bought a bicycle? What for?" asked Barbara, eyebrows twitching.

"Dunno. He just took a notion. A foolish flutter. I expect we've got more flutterings to come at his age. I've no idea where to store the thing … it's in the garage at the moment, but the roof leaks." Madeleine shook her head. "On his first outing, he whizzed into the village for a newspaper, had an argument with a motorist on the way there and got caught in a thunderstorm on the way back." She shook her head again, and laughed. "I suppose it's better than a mistress."

"Right, I'm off," said Nancy, suddenly looking uncomfortable. "See you all tonight."

"OK, everyone. Five Bells at half past seven," confirmed Lynn.

Madeleine wondered what to wear; her mind was wandering through her wardrobe. Returning home to be greeted by a single bark of welcome from Rex, she went upstairs to the bedroom and drew out what she had pictured. She selected a long, sleeveless linen dress, slit to the knee on both sides, buttoned through from neck to hem, pale blue in color, lattice work on the collar and pockets. The dress would be comfortable; she pictured it billowing out while she walked. She would wear her navy Sebago sandals – they would cope with any slightly rough terrain. She would wear a little jewelry, maybe the matching gold necklace and ear-rings which Adam had brought home from his last visit to the gold souk in Saudi Arabia. Or, perhaps she would wear the more ethnic, Indian neckpiece along with dangling ear-rings which she had bought in Monsoon on a recent shopping trip to Southampton. Madeleine decided on the ethnic pieces, turquoise and copper colored, admiring her reflection in the mirror. She achieved the look she wanted – a simple, modest, loose flowing garment which would be quite suitable for the occasion, brightened up by inexpensive accessories. She draped a heavyweight cream colored cardigan over her shoulders, satisfied this would keep away the chill of a cool summer evening.

Madeleine enjoyed her walk down Church Hill and along Five Bells Lane. The rain had passed, easing the very hot temperatures of recent weeks, and given way to a fresh summer evening. The sky was clear blue without a single cloud. The cottages, en route, looked idyllic with their thatched roofs and whitewashed walls. Flowers blossomed everywhere in hanging baskets and in pots. Petunias wandered, geraniums trailed, lobelia whispered, impatiens commanded attention, begonias beckoned. An air of quiet contentment seeped out of every crevice.

Reaching the Five Bells Inn, Madeleine pushed open the door to see a few locals seated, at ease, around the bar. She smiled a greeting and made her way to the back room which emanated an excited chatter.

"Oh, they've moved the sofas," she exclaimed, giving a wave of acknowledgement to the group of familiar figures from the golf club, who were already assembled.

"Yes, they've moved all the furniture around and put the tables together for us, so that we can make up one big party," answered Lynn.

The husbands all came forward to give Madeleine an affectionate kiss on the cheek. The wives, from whom she had parted only a few hours before, smiled and waved. Once the greetings were over, Madeleine sank down in one of the sofas; the bright pink leather covering, so unexpected in this setting, always made her smile.

"We've chosen our menu from the chalk board," advised Lynn.

Reluctantly, Madeleine raised herself from her comfortable position, moving towards the blackboard. She made her choice, and rejoined the others who were now seated around the table. She positioned her elbows on the table, and tuned in to the surrounding conversations. The topics included the current Flower Festival at St Peter's Church in Stockbridge, Father's Day last weekend, mobile phone tariffs, water meters, house prices, summer sales and fishing.

During the buzz of discussion, Cathy and Rodney appeared. "Hope we're not too late to order," said Rodney, stooping to give Lynn a kiss on the cheek.

Nancy's head whipped round. She stared at Rodney in disbelief. Her eyes were wide with alarm. A message went to her brain, "... it's him ... it's him ..." She lowered her eyes to stare at the table. The brain messages continued, "... don't let him know ... don't let him know ... don't let him know." She stayed very still and quiet, not making eye contact with anyone. Recovering her composure, she watched him greet everyone, in turn. Rodney stretched out his arm to give her a hug and a kiss; she controlled herself sufficiently to allow the greeting. She watched him seat himself down, mercifully at right angles so that he was not directly opposite. Bottles of wine and glasses appeared; she felt as if she had drunk too much already; her hearing seemed to have changed dimension; conversations were taking place around her in an echo chamber with only Rodney's voice looming out of a tunnel to taunt her. She stared at her hands, her stomach was lurching; her brain seemed to freeze. She couldn't think how to handle the situation. "... he won't know I know ... he won't know I know ..." A mantra started in her head.

"Nancy?" Lynn was staring at her.

"Uh ..." She looked up, bewildered.

"What are you having?"

"Umm ... umm ...," she stammered, looking confused. Gathering her wits together, she blurted out, "Same as you."

Nancy stared down at her hands again; she wanted to escape. "Excuse me. Going to the ladies' room," she said, getting up and moving out of the room. As she walked purposefully towards the ladies room, she took the door on the right instead of the left, heaving a sigh of relief as she stood outside in the evening air. Nancy thought of her lover; Darren would be locking up the pro-shop right now; she wanted to tell him she recognized the mystery voice; Darren would console her; Darren would give her advice. The adrenalin running through her veins heightened Nancy's senses; she became aware of her body; she stumbled to her car and locked herself in; her head was throbbing now. She pictured Darren; he was like her son – tall, sinewy limbs, slim and dark haired with a brooding intensity. Desire raged through her. "... must get back ... what am I doing ... I've lost control ...," she whispered to herself. The ardor cooled. Embarrassment flooded Nancy's face; she looked around in the fading evening light; not a soul to be seen; she held her face in her hands. "... this is insane ... insane ..." she muttered. Nancy thought of her son; certainly she adored him; loved him like she had never loved her husband; loved him with such an intensity; she suddenly realized her love affair with Darren was a substitute for the loss of her son, who had died in a tragic climbing accident five years ago. "This is wrong!" she hissed into her hands. She shuddered. "What am I going to do?" She felt helpless. "I need to get back," she sighed. Smoothing down her clothes, Nancy got out of the car and locked the door. Looking around furtively, she checked that no-one was watching her; straightening herself and pushing back her shoulders, she walked purposefully back to the front of the building. Opening the door and peering round, she was satisfied that the coast was clear. She walked in front of the bar and round to where the others were seated.

"Hey, you alright?" called Lynn. "You look a little strange."

"Not feeling too good," Nancy answered quietly, slipping back into her chair.

"Can I get you some water?" enquired Madeleine.

"It's OK. I'll be fine. It'll pass." Nancy kept her eyes down. The pressure of being near Rodney made her feel sick; the nausea started in her chest and worked its way down to the pit of her stomach. "Tell you what," she said suddenly, "I'll have a brandy. That'll make me feel better. I think I need a double." She smiled weakly. The prospect of the alcohol made her feel braver. She felt the courage to look around the room now. An array of enquiring faces looked back at her.

"So, anyone going to Wimbledon?" Lynn swiftly diverted attention.

"Yes, we're going to stand in line for tickets some evening," Cathy responded. "You can get used tickets at the gate for a few quid, you know. As people leave, they return their tickets which are resold and those funds go to charity. Means you don't need to go if the weather is awful. You can choose a lovely summer's evening."

"Weren't you there this week, Madeleine?" enquired Alice.

"The day Venus was knocked out. Yes, we were there."

"What did you think?" Lynn wanted to know.

"Well, we were puzzled. We expected the point to be awarded to Venus, then wondered if there was a mistake on the board. But then we just assumed that our vision was faulty. We did have front row seats, just a little off center, so we had a good view. Yes, very puzzling. We saw Venus being interviewed afterwards. She was very philosophical. Gotta hand it to her. But I suppose, if she had argued, it would have put her off her game. Who knows?"

"Good game, though?" queried Barbara Blunt's husband, Percy.

"Gosh, yes." Madeleine flicked her eyes, taking in Percy's green cashmere sweater, the dark green designer logo catching her attention.

"So, how did you get tickets?" asked Colin Ruff, switching his gaze from the strange demeanor of his wife, Nancy.

"We were invited, actually."

"Oh, very nice. How did you manage that?" enquired Primrose's husband, Marius Pretorius, running a muscular hand through the luxurious waves of his thick, brown hair.

"It was a business event," replied Madeleine, noting that Marius was wearing his usual checked cotton shirt, tan corduroy trousers and dark brown, Timberland boots.

"Huh, very nice. So, you got treated wonderfully?" Marius continued in his heavy Afrikaans accent, his ample moustache moving awkwardly against his dusky skin as he spoke.

"We were most fortunate." Madeleine nodded.

"So, center court, obviously," commented Barry, leaning heavily on the table; he had lost a lot of weight since his heart attack and looked permanently troubled; he was seated at the opposite end of the table from Lynn; he seemed to spend a lot of time avoiding contact with his wife.

"Well, yes," confided Madeleine.

"And lunch after that?" enquired Rodney.

"Yes, a beautiful lunch."

"And champagne and everything?" Rodney continued.

"Yes."

"Come on, Madeleine, tell us all about it," entreated Primrose. "I wish I could lead your life."

"Well," Madeleine smiled, "it really was a wonderful occasion. Great tennis."

"Tell us about the lunch. All the nice bits," entreated Primrose.

"Well, the lunch was gorgeous. I don't know how they do it. The standard of catering was superb. We were in the Summer Marquee, which was quite splendid. Champagne and Pimms on arrival. Choice of wines and menu for lunch – the tastes were heavenly – must have been a top chef. Then you come back later for afternoon tea with sandwiches, cakes, scones, clotted cream and strawberries (*of course*!)."

"Hmmm," Robina and Hugo exhaled in unison.

Recovering from her appreciation of the menu, Robina asked, "What about the flowers?"

"You know, everything is pristine including the flowers which were all in Wimbledon colors – purple and cream agapanthus, purple and cream hydrangeas, lavender, purple and cream petunias, trailing ivy. And those yew hedges, clipped to perfection! It's a testament to civilization, really. The stewards are dressed so smartly and are relaxed and courteous. Personnel from various military backgrounds, in uniform, assist with security in such a polished and appropriate manner. The organization of dealing with the enormity of the event is awesome."

"How did you get there?" Primrose wondered.

"We have a driver," Madeleine admitted.

"Lucky you!" Percy interjected, his eyebrows shooting up in surprise.

"Well, it means that Adam can work during the journey. And, he's on the phone, all the time, as we're traveling. In fact, we got held up in traffic at Merton Park on the way. Much later and we would have missed lunch."

"And what did you wear?" Barbara showed an interest.

"Sensible shoes! You do a lot of walking."

"I wonder how many people actually attend?" queried Hugo, still savoring his vision of strawberries and cream at Wimbledon.

"I think I recall the highest attendance on any one day was over forty thousand people. Over the tournament, it's about ten times that. And the winner's prize money is over five hundred thousand pounds. But losers get prize money, too. The total payout of prize money is nearly ten million pounds."

"Wow," mouthed Primrose.

"Pity they can't control the weather, though," commented Lynn, who had been unusually silent.

"Well, they'll soon have more control over that. They've just decided to put a retractable roof over Center Court. It'll be ready in three years time." Madeleine was remembering information she read in the program.

"That'll cost plenty." Percy's face puckered, as if he were making mental calculations.

"The sum hasn't been disclosed, but it will be funded by debenture holders."

"What are debenture holders?" Primrose wanted to know.

"Well, loosely speaking, the people who hold business events," answered Madeleine.

"So, what goes around, comes around," Primrose ventured in summary.

"Oh, and guess what?" Madeleine chuckled. "They're making a movie called Wimbledon, being released in September. It's a love story. A romance between a coach and a player."

"Must watch out for that," commented Lynn, looking pointedly at Nancy.

"What's your next event, Madeleine? You're always doing something interesting," continued Primrose, wistfully.

"Well, the Voices Foundation Performance is next week. I'm quite involved with that."

"The voices Foundation?" echoed Primrose.

"It's been on the go for about ten years. It's really an education program to bring musical appreciation to children in schools, particularly through singing."

"So, what do you do?" asked Alice, who had shown little interest in Wimbledon.

"Simply help with the children on a voluntary basis. Singing has always been a love of mine. I had some training as a youngster and sang on stage."

"Hmmm," Lynn changed the subject, bringing the discussion of Madeleine's social life to a close. "Who wants coffee?"

Coffee and chocolate mints arrived swiftly. The staff, remaining pleasant and helpful, became brisk in their attentions, hoping to encourage a stir of energy to carry the revelers home. Lynn took charge of the administration. Aided by Cathy and Barbara, she worked out the cost per person and gave Alice the job of collecting cash from all the husbands.

"So, we're giving you a lift home." Lynn addressed Madeleine.

"You walked here, didn't you? Don't you want to walk back?" intervened Colin quickly. "You're not far from us. It's a lovely evening and I would like a walk. Tell you what. I'll run Nancy home now. I think she faded long ago. I'll leave the car at home, come back for you and walk you safely home. How's that?"

"Well ... OK," answered Madeleine, feeling a little uncomfortable.

Chairs were pushed back as everyone got to their feet in preparation for the journey home. Farewells were exchanged until, gradually, Madeleine was left with just the company of Alice and Don.

"We'll wait with you till Colin gets back," offered Alice, "but are you sure you want to walk? We can easily drive you home. It's not much out of our way."

"Well, it seems rude to decline his offer, so don't worry, I'm fine," assured Madeleine, suddenly feeling cold.

They stood outside the door, absorbing the change in atmosphere. A clear night. The full moon illuminated the surroundings. A cool light, bathed every detail. No stars visible. The sky was smooth, in the palest shade of blue tinged with yellow. The air was cool and still. An artist would have desired to capture such a moment. They stood quietly waiting, their hearing attuned to the smallest sounds.

"I think I hear footsteps now," uttered Don catching the sound of a rhythmical thud approaching.

Colin's silhouette advanced towards them. He walked purposefully, his arms hanging down by his side, his lean form intruding into the idyllic surroundings. He grinned as he approached them, displaying his small yellow teeth.

"Ah, there you are," Don greeted him, with relief.

Colin's grin widened. As he did so, his teeth seemed longer and narrower in the darkness, but he said nothing.

"Goodnight, then. We'll leave you to your walk," said Alice, giving Madeleine a concerned look, as she and Don walked towards their car at the rear of the Five Bells Inn.

Madeleine and Colin stood for a minute in silence, hearing the departing footsteps and the slamming car door, followed by the engine noise disappearing into the night.

"Up towards Church Hill?" Colin looked at her intently.

"Yes," Madeleine responded softly, without returning his gaze. Her arms crossed her body to pull her cardigan tightly at the waist with both hands. Her shoulders hunched forward as she prepared herself for walking uphill.

"Quite chilly," commented Colin.

"Yes, it is."

"Adam away then?"

"Uh huh."

"When's he back?"

"Not till after the weekend. He's in the Middle East. They work on Saturday and Sunday over there." She hastily added, "But I have a dog now, so I feel more secure when he's gone."

"Oh, right. He's gone a lot."

"Hmmmm."

"Don't you get lonely?"

Madeleine was feeling the effects of the uphill incline; her toes gripped the soles of her sandals; her lungs labored for breath. "No," she answered, emphatically.

They walked on in silence. Madeleine clenched her teeth as they continued to walk uphill. "I really don't like Colin," she thought, grimly, willing him to disappear. They continued to walk, without conversation, making their way towards the medieval church at the top of the hill.

"That church gives me the creeps," thought Madeleine as the eleventh century building came into view. The church was so attractive from the outside, but Madeleine remembered her last visit there, with a friend, during an afternoon walk on a hot summer's day; they had walked all around the outside, admiring the views and puzzling over the stone pyramid in memory of a Doctor of Physics whose particular details, on the stone plaque, had been mostly worn away by the weather of many centuries: they read the notices outside the church and decided to make their way inside: they turned the heavy iron ring to open the door but nothing happened. "It's locked," Madeleine had commented to her friend, noting the massive latch and wondering how the ring could ever make this leg of iron move; they had wandered back around the churchyard, going close, but not among, the gravestones. "I really would like to see inside that church," Madeleine recalled saying to her friend. "The notice says it is left unlocked. I don't understand why we can't get in." They had returned to the door on their way out of the churchyard, determined to see inside. "I'm going to try again." Madeleine remembered turning the heavy ring on the door for a second time. Miraculously, the door opened with no difficulty. "That's odd," she remembered commenting. She recalled pushing the door: the enormous weight resisted her efforts, at first, but suddenly changed its mind and swung open with a creaking defiance; they peered round the door to observe a dark and gloomy interior. Every part of the church was sheathed in polythene. "Must be doing restoration," she had whispered. "Creepy." She shivered, pulling a face at her friend, while letting go of the door handle. The door pushed back against them; the weight and speed and suddenness of the movement forced their footsteps backwards and they were returned to the outside world. The door slammed shut with an angry groan. Madeleine had tried to open the door again, but it wouldn't budge; the same force which allowed them to glimpse inside, was forbidding further passage. Madeleine remembered experiencing a feeling of fear and dread. She wondered if the forbidding presence was a figment of her imagination, or if there really was some unknown force controlling entry to the church.

The memory of that visit to the church made Madeleine's legs tremble. She stumbled on some uneven ground. Colin's arm reached out. One hand caught her shoulder. The other hand grabbed her buttock; his fingers dug into her flesh like the claws of a bird of prey. Madeleine shook herself free, trying to pretend the incident had not happened. They walked on uphill. They passed all the cottages in the village. They were now surrounded by unspoiled countryside, bewitching in the moonlight, and were crossing over the well worn footpaths in open fields.

Colin attempted conversation again. "Have you noticed how many bees are around this year?" he offered.

Madeleine thought, "Yea, there are plenty of b------- around," but answered instead with a hollow "Oh, really?"

"Our lime trees are buzzing with the little buggers. Hordes of them gathering pollen. The sound is amazing. Must be hundreds of them, if not thousands. They live in holes in the ground, you know," Colin stated, knowingly.

"Is that so?" she answered, her guard slipping now, her interest kindled.

Colin's hand reached out to stroke her hair. "You're very beautiful, you know," he murmured. Madeleine sighed, giving him no answer but shook herself free to give him no encouragement.

"Don't you miss some lovin' when Adam's away?" Colin's voice took on a mocking tone.

"No, I don't!" Madeleine spun round to face him now, spitting out the words in a fury.

"Aw, come on, Madeleine. Give us a kiss." Colin reached out with both arms to draw her towards him. She raised her elbows and clenched her fists, making a shield to keep him away. He grabbed her wrists, forcing her arms down by her sides. He bent his head, his mouth open and greedy, searching for her lips. She turned her face away. He forced one of her arms behind her back, still holding her wrist. He stretched her other arm wide. She balanced on her heels, to keep from falling. His knee came up between her legs. He pushed her backwards. She landed on her back, breath thudding out of her lungs. His hand still held one of her wrists. She couldn't get free of him. He bent over her. She writhed and kicked. He dragged her linen dress up to her throat. "Now, let's have a look at you," he roared, his eyes roaming over her body. "Very tasty," he announced. He laughed loudly. "Now, you're going to feel the full force of a real man," he called out as if to an audience. He threw the full weight of his body on top of her, unzipping his trousers with his free hand.

"Aaahhh!" At last, Madeleine found her voice. She moaned in pain and fear, the sound coming from deep inside her soul. "Don't! Please, don't. Please, please, please, don't," she begged.

"Hah," he retorted. "Little madam can't take the rough and tumble, eh?"

A headache started in Madeleine's forehead and worked its way down into her bowels. She squeezed her eyes shut. She couldn't bear to look at him. She was trapped. She couldn't kick anymore. He forced her knees apart. She felt him jabbing at her. He tore her flesh with an enormous thrust. She screamed and cried and yelled, hoping someone would hear. No one could hear, she knew, not in these open fields far away from anyone.

"You sound like a fox on heat," he chuckled. His jawbone was crushing her face. His breath was panting onto her. Her tears ran down to mingle with his saliva on her mouth, as he attempted to slobber her with kisses. She drew her lips inside her mouth, using her teeth to keep them safe, but his tongue was roving wildly over her face. One arm was still free, she realized. She punched at his face.

"I'm going to poke your eyes out!" she yelled at him. He laughed uproariously and bent his head so that only the top of his skull was within her reach. His thrusting into her body caused a numbness which she could feel rising up to her throat. She felt vomit gathering in the pit of her stomach. She reached her free arm out and flailed around on the ground. She felt a stone. She clutched the stone in her hand; it fitted perfectly inside her palm; her fingers clutched around it. She held the weapon, trying to think how she could use it. Her arm felt like lead. She had to summon up the will to inflict injury on him. She grunted loudly as she lifted the stone, smashing it against his head. He rolled over, leaving her body. She ran. She ran as fast as she could. The field was on a downhill slope. At the end of the field, she looked back. He was getting to his feet. She looked around wildly. He was pulling up his trousers with one hand, his other hand reaching to his head. He roared with laughter. He staggered forwards.

Madeleine kept running. The house was coming into view. She looked back. No sign of him. Where were her keys? She vomited. How was she going to get into the house? The vomit decorated her dress in a random pattern. She clutched her hair wildly, holding tufts between her fingers and clenching her fists. Where were her keys? She couldn't remember. How was she going to get into the house? Pockets in her dress. Nothing there. Panic swept through her. She stuffed her hands into the pockets of her cardigan. Her fingers touched a few bank notes in one pocket. Try the other pocket. Her hand grasped a wad of paper tissues. Her fingers reached further down and touched metal. Relief swirled round her head. She felt dizzy. She pulled the keys out with shaking hands. She looked back. No sign of him. Her legs were weak. She could barely walk now. She staggered towards the front door. Fumbling and shaking hands attached to a trembling body engaged the key in the lock. Shudders of relief lurched through her soul. Tears flowed. Breath came in irregular gasps. Whimpers of sorrow and loss tightened her chest. The door opened. She removed the keys and slammed the door shut. She clung to the handle on the inside of the door, slowly sliding down to the floor. Howls of anguish escaped.

A softness touched her hand, which lay limp on the polished wood floor of the hallway. Rex licked her fingers. Gasping and whimpering, she gazed into his beseeching eyes. Rex whimpered in sympathy. Touching his muzzle, with gratitude, her heart filled with love for her faithful companion. Moans of despair escaped from her throat. Rex raised his head and emitted low-pitched howls. Moving her hand to feel the silky fur on his neck, she gripped his collar. Rhythmic sobs accompanied her outward breaths. High pitched howls from Rex accompanied her enormous gasps for air. Knots of pressure gathered on her brow. Rex empathized with her grief, howling at full pitch now. A crescendo of howls cascaded from his lungs. Fury and revenge were promised in an unrelenting torrent. A kernel of concern implanted itself. She patted his neck. The howling continued. "Ssshhh, ssshhh, ssshhh," she whispered in his ear. The howling subsided. "Come on now, Rex," she entreated. The howling gradually decreased into whimpering. He needed permission to stop. "Come on now, Rex. Good boy. Good boy." The whimpering continued at a lower pitch and at less frequent intervals. He needed assurance. "Come on now, Rex. It's OK. It's OK. We're safe. We're safe. Good boy, Rex. Good boy, Rex." The assurance calmed them both. She leaned heavily on him and raised herself to her feet. Rex became quiet and alert, waiting for the next instruction.

Madeleine's tears flowed bitterly, as she kicked off her sandals in the hallway, leaving them lying on the floor. Still holding onto Rex's collar, they walked together into the kitchen. Rex's paws made a clicking noise on the polished wood floor; Madeleine's bare feet padded soundlessly beside him; the feel of the hard, smooth surface against the soles of her feet was comforting; her footprints on the dark wood left behind a ghostly image before melting away without a trace. "Tea. We need tea. I'll put the kettle on," she confided to Rex.

Leaning on the work surface, Madeleine waited for the water to boil. Rex crouched on his haunches, his head following her every move. Madeleine sipped the hot tea very carefully. The sipping motion helped to gather her thoughts. What had happened out there? Rape certainly? What to do? What to do? She continued to sip the tea, trying to focus her mind. She should contact the police. But what would that achieve? Articles in the newspapers, her name displaying shame. Did she encourage him? What was her reputation? What was her relationship with this man? How long had she known him? Why was she with him late at night? Wasn't she asking for trouble? So many questions. So much gossip. Too much intrusion. She would have to submit to a medical examination. She would have to put her life on hold while the criminal justice system dealt with her case. She pictured the police station in Stockbridge: a miniature wheelbarrow, painted in constabulary colors, brimming with colorful blossoms on one side of the door: a miniature police car, planted with summer flowers, on the other side of the door. So, what to do? What to do? The tea was cooler now: Madeleine gulped down the remaining liquid and banged the mug on the work surface. "Right, Rex. Upstairs," she announced.

Madeleine climbed the stairs, clutching the banister for support: she dragged her feet slowly and deliberately up to the first landing. Rex was already waiting for her to join him on the second ascent: he raced ahead, looking down expectantly as she heaved herself up each step. Reaching the top of the stairs, she paused to regain her strength before shuffling towards the master bedroom. Sighing heavily, she moved into the en-suite bathroom and washed her hands. Reaching into the linen cupboard, she pulled out a fluffy white bath towel. Sighing again, she risked a look in the mirror. Her stomach lurched. Lipstick was slobbered in wild directions where his tongue had been searching, her hair jutted out wildly at odd angles. A smear of dirt clung to her ear. The crispness of her linen dress was shattered into a thousand creases and covered with stains in a variety of grubby shades of abuse. She willed herself the strength to look into her eyes. She saw fear and resentment, anger and puzzlement, loathing and defilement, sorrow and grief. Staring at her reflection, she allowed each moment of her ordeal to imprint itself on her memory. She lowered her eyes, storing the data in a very private space; a space very separate from any other; a space only to be entered with extreme caution and a lot of preparation; a space locked away. She raised her eyes again to meet the mirror. Now she saw determination. She moved back into the bedroom. She opened the top drawer of the large oak chest; reaching into the drawer, she grasped the camera with one hand and placed it on top of the chest. She moved towards the wardrobe and opened the door; the full-length mirror on the inside of the door swung into view. She winced at her reflection. She placed the folded bath towel on the floor and stood on top of it. Somehow, the softness and whiteness below her feet made her feel cleaner. A coldness was seeping into her veins. An icy determination. She was thinking clearly now. Justice would be done. She moved back to the chest of drawers, fiddled with the camera and stood back several paces. Standing perfectly still, she allowed the automatic camera to record her appearance. She stood motionless for several minutes, lost in contemplation. She returned to the mirror and removed her dress, dropping it on the floor beside her. Disgust forced her lips into an ugly grimace. No bruises. Maybe tomorrow they would appear. She moved back to the chest of drawers. Lifting the camera, she fiddled again with the controls and stood back, allowing her naked image to be recorded for a second time. Returning to the chest, she switched off the camera and replaced it in the top drawer.

It was late. She was tired. She wanted to sleep. A plan was forming in Madeleine's mind. She wanted to sleep on it. She picked up her clothing from the bedroom floor and returned to the en-suite bathroom. She wrapped the clothing in a plastic bag and placed it in the laundry bin; her discarded blue dress, along with the photographs would be the evidence she needed. Opening the linen cupboard, she gathered up a bundle of white bath towels. Moving back to the bedroom, she made a pillow with one towel and placed it on the floor. She gathered the other towels round her so that she was wrapped tightly from head to foot in scented fabric, pure and pristine, warm and comfortable, safe and secure. Only her head was visible. She lay down on the floor, head resting on the makeshift pillow, knees bent towards her head. She closed her eyes and prayed for sleep. Rex lay down beside her. He stretched out, so that he took up more space than her crouched form. He strained to hear every sound, as he took up his protective pose.

WAITING FOR ADAM

The noise woke her. Rain battering down. The forecast had promised stormy weather. It had arrived. Madeleine raised herself up on one elbow. She looked at her watch. Four thirty in the morning. Just getting light. Rex was alert, his head resting on his paws, his eyes following every move. Madeleine used her other elbow to keep the toweling wrap in place, clutching the ends with one hand. She realized she hadn't closed the curtains last night. Staggering towards the window, encumbered by a sheath of white bath towels, she looked out. Sky the color of dark smoke. A solid smokescreen of water bursting onto the world. Trees swaying. Branches waving. Leaves rustling. Twigs and leaves littering the ground. A pause. A ray of sunshine. Another torrent. A jay twitching his head, hopping from branch to branch, his heavy form causing each branch to bend under his weight; branches springing back into place as his magnificent bulk traversed the tree, cackling as he patrolled his territory. It was morning. She had survived her ordeal. The nightmare was over. What to do? What to do? She couldn't stay like this till Adam got back. Three days till he got back.

Madeleine turned her back on the view from the eyebrow window and surveyed the bedroom. Her bones were aching from sleeping on the hard floor. Her eyes rested on the soft cream chair, no arms or legs, simply a square back and a square seat, skirted with a deep frill. She moved towards the chair, easing herself into the softness; her bones welcomed the comfort; she bent forward, elbows resting on her knees, thinking, thinking. Numerous faces floated before her eyes; she envisaged a room filled with those faces, an electronic device the focus of attention. Yes, that's what she would do.

Madeleine sprang from the chair, allowing the protective towels to fall loose; she strode into the en-suite bathroom and threw the towels in the linen basket. Returning to the bedroom, she opened the wardrobe door and surveyed her reflection in the mirror; her lips tight, she nodded with satisfaction. Bruises. Yes, they were there. She moved towards the chest of drawers, withdrew the camera, set the controls, stood back and repeated her photographic exercise of last night. She set the re-wind button, listening to the rhythmic response as the film noisily returned to its yellow canister. Opening the camera, she removed the canister, tossed it in the air and caught it in her hand with a firm grasp. She curled her bottom lip, intensifying the expression of satisfaction.

A shower. She had to have a shower now. Knowing she would wash away the evidence, Madeleine didn't care. She had her plan. Entering the cubicle, she doused herself in scented, creamy lotion. The sweet thrill of lilies entered her nostrils; she breathed in, filling her lungs with the heady perfume; she scrubbed; she massaged her scalp until it tingled; she rubbed her face until it felt numb; she smeared her body from top to toe in the white balm and caressed her limbs and torso with tender hands; she stayed under the drenching spray until the water began to run cold. Ah! She was renewed. She had nursed her misery, swirled it around in the innards of her soul, allowing the bile to corrode her raw emotions. A healing gel was forming now, soothing the ache into peaceful silence. The water of life had washed away the defilement. She had her plan. She began to sing, joyously traveling up and down the scales, "La la la la la la laaaaa. La la la la la la laaaaa. La la la la la la laaaaa," slowly at first, then reaching higher notes, until she laughed at her inability to reach the top of her range.

She dressed quickly. Business clothes – that's what she wanted to wear – that would make her feel able to cope. Madeleine donned the navy suit and made her way downstairs. Mrs Bunting, her housekeeper, would be here soon. How to pass the time until she arrived? She made coffee in the kitchen and moved into the study. Surf the net ... that's what she would do ... read the newspapers online ... that sort of stuff would keep her occupied for a few hours. Rex followed her around, getting more and more agitated. "You'll just have to wait until Mrs Bunting gets here, Rex. I'm not opening the door until then."

At last, the keys rattled in the lock, as Mrs Bunting let herself into the house. Rex raced to greet her, his nose catching the collection of scents from outside. "No, Rex. Stay. Stay," Mrs Bunting commanded, realizing that he was keen to venture outdoors.

Madeleine strode out to greet her. "Morning, Mrs Bunting," she said cheerily.

"Morning, dear," came the weary reply.

"Got a few errands for you this morning, Mrs Bunting." Madeleine smiled. You don't mind, do you? Not much cleaning needing done, but if you could take Rex out for a walk first and then take a trip into town for me, that would be good. I need some photographs developed."

"You all right, dear?" enquired Mrs Bunting.

"Oh, just a bit of a sore throat," replied Madeleine, knowing that all the howling and screaming from last night had strained her vocal chords.

"OK, then. I'll take Rex for a walk first. He looks desperate," Mrs Bunting agreed.

"That would be great. Actually, if you can take the photos to Andover rather than Stockbridge, that would be better. I need some groceries from Waitrose, as well as the photos developed. You could get the groceries while you wait. You can get photos developed somewhere in an hour, can't you?" Mrs Bunting nodded. "OK, here's the shopping list and the spool of film. I'll see you in a couple of hours. No need to hurry. Enjoy the trip." Madeleine smiled as she bundled Mrs Bunting and Rex out of the door. She had thought about it carefully. She could not risk having the photos developed in Stockbridge; someone might throw up an alert if they viewed the images. A bigger place like Andover was much more anonymous, much safer. Also, Mrs Bunting would receive the photos in a sealed package, so her natural curiosity could not encourage her to view the contents.

Madeleine wandered through all the rooms in the house, viewing but not seeing the surroundings. She looked at her watch. Just after eight o'clock. Better wait until nine o'clock before making the phone calls. No, maybe not, could catch some people before they started their day. No, on second thoughts, wait until husbands were out of the way. Research, that's what she could no in the meantime. Back into the study, rummaging around her files, her agitation grew.

Nine o'clock. First phone call. Madeleine was nervous. "Hello, Nancy? Glad I caught you. Just a quick call. I want to get a few social dates arranged. What Saturday nights do you have free in the next few weeks?"

"Oh, are you having a dinner party?" Nancy sounded pleased. "Let me just check. Give me a minute till I look at the calendar." Madeleine waited, hearing the sound of Nancy moving around and then the rustling of pages. "Well, we're free on the tenth of July and the seventeenth of July. Can't do the twenty fourth, because we have some friends coming down from Worcester. The whole of August is out. We've got our trip to Florida then. I know the weather will be very hot, but it's the only time we can take the grandchildren. Oh, and our great friends we've known since school days, the ones who live in Spain, I'm not sure when they'll be here over the summer, but we'll spend a Saturday with them. Now, let's see ..."

"Nancy," Madeleine interrupted, "You didn't mention the thirty first of July. Is that date OK?"

"Oh, yes, it is, actually. We were keeping it free in case Colin's brother was going to have a barbeque to celebrate his birthday which is on the Friday, but I'm not sure if he's going to have the barbeque on the Sunday, now. You see ..."

"Nancy, let's make it the seventeenth of July," Madeleine interrupted again. "You're definitely free then? No other possible clashes? OK, let's put it firmly on the calendar. I'm going to arrange a surprise event for the husbands. They mustn't know a thing about it. Only that they're going out for the night and it's a surprise. You can keep a secret from Colin, can't you? Knew you could. OK, you've got that date on your calendar, now? That's it, Saturday, the seventeenth of July. Don't tell Colin a thing. Don't tell him I'm organizing it. Nothing. Just a surprise evening with friends. OK. Good. I'll be in touch nearer the time with more details, for your ears only. See you at the golf club before then. OK, see you soon. 'Bye."

Madeleine slammed down the receiver in exasperation. "Hope the next call is not so exhausting," she muttered to herself, as she thumbed through the golf club list for the next number. "I just asked her if she was free. I don't want to know every activity in her life from now till Christmas."

Madeleine keyed in the next number. "Robina? Hello. Hope I'm not calling too early in the morning, but I thought you would probably be up and about."

"I'm feeding the birds."

"You are?"

"Yes, in my bath robe, with the phone in my pocket."

"Very good. I'm impressed. Listen, I want to arrange a surprise event for husbands. Are you free on Saturday, the seventeenth of July?"

A pause while Robina mentally checked off her calendar. "Yes, we're OK that evening."

"You are? That's great. Surprise evening with husbands. Don't tell Hugo a thing about it. Just a surprise evening with friends. OK. That's great. More details to follow. Won't keep you from your feathered friends. See you soon. 'Byeeee."

Feeling more cheerful, Madeleine rang the number for Alice and Don. "Alice, hi, it's Madeleine. Are you well?"

"Yes, I'm fine, thanks," Alice replied. "Well, apart from my shoulder. You know it always plays me up after every golf game."

"Oh, yes?"

"Well, I don't know what to do about it. The doctor says it's a frozen shoulder and it will take years to heal, but I think its bursitis. I'm sure

I've got it from all the gardening I do. You know, you do a lot of repetitive movements when you're gardening. And my back is ..."

"Alice, I'm just wondering if you and Don are free on Saturday, the seventeenth of July?"

"Saturday, the seventeenth of July? Sorry, we're not. That's Don's big birthday party. He'll be sixty, you know. We're just having family and very close friends. Just about twenty people. At home, here. I'll be doing the catering. Of course, my daughter will help me and ..."

"So, you're not free, Alice. That's a pity. Would have been nice to have you here. Have you recovered from your pond incident?"

"Yes, I'm OK, thanks, Madeleine. Quite a shock to the system that was."

"Well, I'm glad you're OK. Hope the shoulder improves. Sorry you can't join us that evening, but hope your party is a great success. See you at the golf club ... probably next week. OK. 'Bye."

Sighing, Madeleine keyed in the next number and got the answering machine in response. "You have reached the Cathy Crow School of Motoring. Sorry I can't take your call right now. I'm either away from my desk or instructing a pupil. Please leave a message and I'll get back to you as soon as possible."

"Cathy? Hi, it's Madeleine Minehead. Wonder if you can give me a call when you have a moment. Just a social matter. No great hurry. Thanks. 'Bye."

Madeleine replaced the receiver and thought about another cup of coffee. Who to ring next? No, forget the coffee. Just crack on. "Hello, Lynn. It's Madeleine. Hope I'm not disturbing you. I know your phone never stops ringing with golf club matters, but this is a social call."

"Oh. Hi, Madeleine. Yea, social calls are just fine."

"Well, I wondered if you and Barry were free on Saturday, the seventeenth of July."

"Let me check. Yes, we're OK for that date. What do you have in mind?"

"I want to arrange a surprise evening for husbands, so don't tell Barry a thing about it. Just tell him it's an evening with friends and all will be revealed later. Would you be happy with that?"

"Oh, yes, but I'm intrigued, Madeleine. What's this all about?"

"Well, I'd like it to be a surprise for you, too, Lynn. So, can I keep you guessing?"

"Well, if you must."

"But just don't mention it to Barry. It's really imperative that it's a surprise event, otherwise the whole evening won't work. But, OK, I'll let you in on some details once I get organized. How about if I tell you the guest list and the venue next time I see you?"

"OK, then."

"Right, so everything OK with you, Lynn?"

"Yes, fine. Just going shopping."

"Oh, anything special?"

"Well, I wanted a few more outfits for forthcoming events. Really, when you're Captain, you have to have quite an extensive wardrobe. I've told Barry that, so he needs to expect a lot of expense this year. Actually, I've bought quite a lot over the phone."

"You shop for clothing over the phone?"

"Well, if you watch the shopping channel on TV, there's lots of stuff. Mind you, a lot of it I end up not wearing, but then it's so much effort to send it back, so I push it to the back of the wardrobe and pass it on to charity shops later." Lynn sighed.

"Oh, well. Good luck with shopping today. I'll talk to you soon."

Who next? Primrose. Never know whether she's at the shop or at home. "Primrose? Hi, it's Madeleine. Where are you?"

"I'm in the car."

"Sorry, don't mean to make you break the law."

"No, that's OK. I have one of these blue tooth things now."

"What's that?"

"An earpiece thing, so I can talk while I'm driving."

"Well, I just wanted to check if you and Marius are free on Saturday, the seventeenth of July."

"Actually, my mother will be visiting from South Africa. I'm taking her to Wisley that day. She's crazy about English gardens, so it will be a real treat for her. You know, all the herbaceous borders and roses will be in full bloom ... and the water lilies, too."

"And she'll love all the cakes in the tearoom," added Madeleine, "but I'm thinking of a social gathering in the evening."

"Oh, yes. That should be OK. Mother will probably welcome an evening at home with the children."

"Speaking of home, how's the move going, Primrose?"

"Well, it's not. We were hoping to have moved in time for my mother's visit, but we pulled out of the estate house with no planning permission ... it will always be a problem to sell. We're now looking at one in Palestine, which is only a few miles further away, but we've discovered it's going to have a satellite mast erected outside. I guess that's why it's a bargain price. It's a nice house and the price is really tempting, but we have to think of the health factor. So ... we'll see," Primrose tailed off, wistfully.

"So, you think you can make it for the evening of the seventeenth of July?"

"Sure, Madeleine. What time?"

"Well, I need to work all that out. It's a surprise event for husbands, so don't tell Marius a thing. Just say it's a surprise, but I do need you to be on time. Probably seven thirty. Can you make that?"

"Oh, that's no problem. I expect we'll be home by six o'clock."

"Good stuff. I'll confirm further details nearer the time. Remember, it's a surprise. Don't mention it to anyone."

"No, I won't. Don't worry," promised Primrose, her voice broken by an electronic cackle.

"You're breaking up, Primrose. You must be losing the signal."

"I just came into a black spot."

"OK. See you soon. 'Bye."

What about that cup of coffee? OK. Take a little break. Put the kettle on. Madeleine's thoughts meandered with details of her plans for the surprise evening. Adam must be kept in the dark, too, along with everyone else.

The phone rang. "Hello?" she answered tentatively.

"Madeleine, I never could remember your last name," a male voice mocked her.

"Who is this?"

"It's Rodney Crow."

"Oh, you had me worried there. I didn't know who it was."

"It's only me. You left a message on the answering machine."

"Oh, yes, for Cathy."

"Anything I can do?"

"Eh ... well ... is Cathy around?"

"Not right now. Can I do something for you?"

"Ummm ... could you perhaps give her a message? Just say I called and could she get back to me whenever it's convenient."

"Sure, anything you want. Happy to oblige."

"OK. Thanks. 'Bye." Madeleine shuddered, as she replaced the receiver.

Now a cup of coffee was essential. Something creepy about that man. Those ghastly reptile eyes. She walked slowly into the kitchen, reflecting on her phone calls this morning. Probably only one more person to contact and that would be sufficient. Barbara was last on her list. What would she do for the rest of the day? She didn't want to face anyone until Adam was home. She just wanted her own company. Tears gathered in her eyes. She mustn't weaken. Stay strong. She trudged back into the study.

"Barbara? Hi, it's Madeleine Minehead."

"Oh hello, darling. How are you?"

"Yes, I'm fine, thanks. How are you?"

"Well, recovering from last night, really. What did you think of the evening?"

"Last night ... oh, yes at the Five Bells ... yes, it was fine."

"I thought Lynn was over the top."

"Oh."

"She just takes over everything. It's always me, me, me, with Lynn. She could have delegated someone else to organize the evening, don't you think? I mean it would have been far better to have a committee member make the arrangements. Then, we wouldn't have to listen to how busy she is, and how being Captain is taking over her life. She's not proving popular, you know. She seemed the obvious candidate, but she's upsetting a lot of people."

"Oh."

"Anyway, I don't like to talk about people. But the ladies are getting restless. I think they feel she's been the wrong choice." Barbara voiced her opinion readily.

"Well, we'll just have to support her as best we can," responded Madeleine, showing no interest.

"Yes, you're right. She needs us. But I was appalled to hear about her daughter traveling to work on a motorbike when she's pregnant. If I was her mother, I would step in there. One wrong move and that baby is in danger," Barbara criticized further.

"I didn't know there was a baby coming." Madeleine had not heard the news.

"Oh, well, it's not the best of circumstances. Bogus marriage to some foreigner. Britain is such a wonderful country, these illegal immigrants will do anything to stay here. And, now this baby. She won't say who the father is. Of course, Lynn doesn't want to face being a grandmother. Makes her look old. But, as for the motorbike, I would step in there and ..."

"Barbara, the reason I'm phoning is to see if you and Percy are free on Saturday, the seventeenth of July," Madeleine interjected.

"Oh, I don't know. We're just so busy. The social calendar gets so booked up. We're out most nights, actually. It just gets ridiculous. I don't know when we last had an evening at home. What date did you say, Madeleine?"

"Saturday, the seventeenth of July."

"Hmmm ... what did you have in mind?" Barbara queried.

"Well, I want to organize a surprise event for ladies on the golf club committee, along with husbands."

"What exactly do you mean?" enquired Barbara.

"I'll organize everything. Catering, venue, guest list. You won't need to do anything except turn up. You did say it would be nice if someone else on the committee got to organize something."

"Well, yes."

"But it has to be a surprise for the husbands," Madeleine emphasized.

"Sounds intriguing. What date did you say?"

"Saturday, the seventeenth of July."

"Actually, believe it or not, we could be available. We had the date earmarked for some friends visiting from Derbyshire, but we need to reschedule due to Percy's business commitments so, you're lucky, it's one of our few free Saturdays for months ahead."

"So, you can make it, Barbara? Good, that's excellent. I'll confirm details to you nearer the time, but it absolutely must be a secret from the husbands. Obviously, you'll need to tell Percy you have a social arrangement that evening, but don't give him any details."

"OK, darling. I'll put it on the calendar, but if something important comes up, we may have to call off," Barbara warned, to emphasize her busy schedule.

"Well, don't worry. If you can make it, that would be good. Remember, it's a secret. I'll see you soon at the golf club."

"OK, darling. 'Bye."

"Goodbye, Barbara."

Only Cathy to speak to now. What to do for the rest of the day? What to do until Adam came home? She had to look normal for Mrs Bunting's return. Stay in the business suit. She looked at her watch. She became agitated with nothing to focus her attention. What to do? Read a book? No ... difficult to concentrate. She opened a cupboard in the study. Photographs ... that would pass the time. She pulled out all the loose packets of photographs and piled them on the desk. She picked out one of the empty photograph albums and laid it alongside. She let the glossy images of the last few years of her life slide and sprawl over the desk. She stared at the younger versions of herself, Adam, her son and daughter and the many friends and acquaintances who had passed through their lives. What had they achieved in all that time? A myriad of relationships with people in different social settings. How could it be that her heart felt a sadness and loneliness and longed for something deeper? She jumped up, letting a photograph fall to the floor, as the ringing of the phone interrupted her reverie of how she might make changes in her life.

"Hello," she answered, tentatively.

"Hello, my darling. It's your loving husband."

"Ooooooohhh."

"You OK?"

"Oh ... eh ... yes ... just picking up a photo which fell to the floor when the phone rang."

"A photo?"

"Yes, just thought I would spend some time putting them in the album."

"That's a good thing to do."

"Yes. How are you, dear?"

"Yes, fine. Things are really tricky here. A lot of tension. The locals are very worried about their young people. Graduates with no jobs."

"That's a huge problem."

"Sure is. Seventy five percent of the population under the age of twenty five, and an unemployment rate of probably thirty percent."

"That's scary."

"Oil hit forty dollars a barrel today, so we have quite a situation."

"And your meetings? How are they going?"

"Well, we've made some headway, but it's a long haul negotiation."

"You'll be home in two days?"

"Yes. Can't wait to see you."

"I miss you. Shall I make one of your favorite dishes? How about lasagna?"

"Miss you too. Lasagna would be great, sweetheart. Must go. Next meeting starts in two minutes. Just called you between sessions."

"OK, dear. See you soon."

The tears flowed now. Madeleine just couldn't tell Adam she had been assaulted by Colin. If she told him, he would cut short his business trip and come home; she had already made her plan. Adam would find out soon enough. Madeleine brushed away the tears and felt all the loneliness and sadness seep out of her heart. Somehow, it felt better to meet this lost spirit, allowing it to emerge into the daylight; perhaps she could find a way of setting it free. She shook herself back to reality as a crunching sound on the gravel driveway announced the arrival of a car;

she wiped away the tears, rubbing color into her cheeks, as she opened the door to greet Mrs Bunting and Rex.

"Got everything, dear," called Mrs Bunting, as she slammed the car door. "Rex had a wonderful walk," she continued, making her way into the house, her hands clutching a bag of groceries; she waddled into the kitchen, dumping the bags of shopping on the table. "Do you need anything else doing?"

"No, that's fine, Mrs Bunting. That was great today. Shopping and dog walking is a bit of a change for you."

"I don't mind, dear. I'm happy to do anything. Oh, except gardening. Don't ask me to do that."

"No, I won't," smiled Madeleine. "So, I'll see you on Monday. Have a good weekend, Mrs Bunting."

"You too, dear. Look after that sore throat," Mrs Bunting called back as she returned through the open door to her car. Madeleine closed the door behind her. Rex followed and stood in the hallway, as she contemplated her next move. The phone rang again.

"Madeleine? Hi, it's Cathy Crow. You left a message for me."

"Oh, yes, Cathy," she had difficulty focusing now. The momentum seemed to have gone out of her plan. She could hardly remember what she wanted to say. Everything seemed to be slipping away. "You free on Saturday, the seventeenth of July?" She was tired of asking this question now.

"Let me check." Pages rustled. "Yes, we are," responded Cathy.

"I'm organizing a surprise event for the ladies on the golf club committee. With husbands."

"Oh, how much does it cost?" Cathy wanted to know.

"Well, nothing. I'm organizing it. I'll fix up the venue and the catering. You and Rodney just need to turn up."

"Well, that's OK then."

"This won't cost anything, Cathy. Just don't tell Rodney anything about it. Just tell him you're going out for the evening and it's a surprise. Can you do that?"

"Yes. Sure. I've made a note of the date."

"I better let you go. You must be busy with pupils."

"Yes, just phoned you between lessons."

"OK, thanks for phoning back. See you soon."

"OK. Cheers."

"Cheers."

Replacing the receiver with a sigh of weariness, Madeleine stood staring out of the window. Two whole days till Adam came home. How could she cope with this torment till then? Should she have told him on the phone? What was the point? He couldn't do anything. He couldn't make it go away. Madeleine always kept her problems to herself. A lifetime of being independent. Adam always had major business issues on his mind. She didn't want to worry him. When he came home would be time enough. She would tell Adam then. He would know immediately that something was wrong. She would tell him when he came home. She just had to wait. Two whole days.

Time was governed only by sunrise and sunset during those two days. Madeleine entered a primeval world; she ate frugally when hunger pangs gnawed at her insides, she drank water when her tongue was parched with thirst; her entire focus became the earth; she wandered around the garden, noting the areas which needed attention; she pruned and planted, she watered and fertilized. At dusk, she entered the house to sleep on the floor.

Today. Adam was due back today. Madeleine blinked, allowing the curtain of isolation to draw her back; her blood quickened. Must wash. She stood under the shower, allowing the warm water to wash away the dust and grime from the garden; she scrubbed under her finger nails until the earth disappeared. She dressed in white cotton jeans and a red shirt. She picked a simple bunch of daisies from the garden, and placed them in a vase on the kitchen table. She was ready.

Madeleine wasn't sure what time Adam's flight would arrive; she checked his itinerary. Only ninety minutes to wait now; she paced nervously round the house, tidying up everything which met her glance. In control, got to be in control. She jumped when she heard the car crunch on the driveway; the door slammed, a few words were exchanged and the car drove away. She heard Adam's footsteps approach the door and his key jingle in the lock; she stood in the hallway ready to greet him, biting her lip to keep control: the door opened to reveal his familiar shape silhouetted against the outside world.

"Wheew, glad to be back," Adam sighed, dropping his heavy briefcase on the polished floor. Turning to give her a smile and a kiss, his eyes engulfed her anxious presence. "You OK?"

"I forgot the lasagna," she whispered, her face crumbling. "I said I would make you lasagna."

"That doesn't matter. I'm home. Just feed me anything that's not surrounded in vine leaves," he grinned.

Madeleine turned away, walking towards the kitchen; tears flowed down her face, her chest trembling with the effort of holding back sobs of defeat; she had tried so hard to keep control; she was failing. "It's good to have you home," she called out over her shoulder.

THE AFTERMATH

A beautiful morning. Calm after the storm. Sky the color of Madeleine's blue eyes. Trees ripe with every shade of green, and painted with the shadows of sunshine. So still, not even a bird chirped. A day which would release energy. Flowers would be planted, shrubs would be pruned, lawns would be mowed, families would stroll, walkers would explore, cyclists would venture, shoppers would purchase, motorists would meander.

Breakfast was ready. Galia melon stuffed with fresh raspberries, brown bread and butter, a pot of tea. Madeleine sat staring at the table. Adam's firm footsteps entered the kitchen; he dragged at the wooden chair, positioning it as he sat down. "You OK, dear?" he ventured.

"Yes, fine." Madeleine glanced up, desolately.

"You're not quite yourself."

"I'm fine." She shook her head, irritably.

"What's bugging you?"

"Nothing."

"You've not been happy the last few days."

"I'm just fine," she answered tersely.

"You know, you've not been out much, lately."

"I guess not."

"It's not good to spend so much time on your own."

"I like it that way."

"It's not good for you, dear." He touched her hand.

"I'm bored."

"You need to see more people. You're isolating yourself. You're losing interest in your appearance."

Madeleine reflected on this comment. "You're right," she sighed. "It's hard to admit what you say." She rose from the table, clearing the plates. "Have a good day, dear. I'll keep myself busy."

Another dull day passed. Madeleine made an effort to look smart when Adam came home. She wore lipstick and mascara as a gesture towards Adam's concern. Over the evening meal, she raised the subject. "I've arranged a social gathering."

"You have? That's great."

"Yes. Saturday, the seventeenth of July. It's a surprise. I'll give you details on the day."

Adam was relieved; he worried about Madeleine; he worried about all the women in his life; his father had died when he was ten years old, so Adam had been catapulted into becoming the man of the house, feeling a huge responsibility towards his mother and his handicapped sister; he quickly matured beyond his years and retained this responsibility throughout his life, standing alone against the world.

Madeleine became purposeful that day, after Adam had gone to the office; she considered the catering and seating arrangements, she pondered the travel arrangements. Remembering she had promised to let Lynn know details prior to the event, she rang the number.

"Lynn. Hi. It's Madeleine."

"Oh, hello."

"I promised to give you some details of the surprise evening with husbands."

"Oh, yes, that's right. You did."

"OK. Well, the venue is my house. And, really, it's all the members on the ladies' committee with husbands. Apart from Alice, that is – she's having a party for Don's sixtieth birthday."

"Oh, yes, so she is. He's retiring, isn't he? I feel sorry for her. I don't know anyone whose husband is enjoying retirement. They all miss work and don't know what to do with themselves, apart from play golf and irritate their wives," sniggered Lynn.

"Well, not something we need to worry about for a while," Madeleine ventured.

"Thankfully. Anyway, so who's going to be there?" enquired Lynn.

"Well, like I said. The members on the ladies committee with husbands. Barbara, Cathy, Primrose, Robina, you, me ... and," she hesitated, "Nancy."

"Humph," answered Lynn, "You know about Nancy and Darren?"

"Well, I heard she's spending too much time alone with him."

"It's a disgrace. Cavorting around with a man half her age," Lynn spat out, angrily. "People are talking. I don't know how much is going on, but she's giving the club a bad name."

"Yes, rather surprising. Actually, I wondered, since they live near you ... if you could collect Nancy and Colin that evening. You would be passing their house in your car, so it would make sense."

Lynn hesitated. "Well, OK," she agreed, reluctantly. "Since you ask, I'll arrange that with her."

"Good. I like to think of everything."

"Well, here's something else for you to think about."

"Oh?" Madeleine wondered what was coming next.

"Seems like Rodney has been getting very friendly with Anastasia. She's vulnerable, you know, being a widow. Not sure if there's anything in it, but people are commenting. He's spending a lot of time in her office, after the staff have gone."

"Oh, dear," was all Madeleine could muster.

"Yes. Oh, dear. Anyway, must go. I see the delivery van outside." Lynn became agitated. "Got parcels arriving. Bought some great shoes on ebay. See you Saturday."

"Yes, remember, it's a surprise. Don't tell Barry where you're going. Just pick up Nancy and Colin and be at our house for seven thirty."

"OK, see you then." Lynn hurried to the door to accept her parcels.

Madeleine made similar calls to the others, emphasizing that the event must be kept as a surprise for their husbands.

LASAGNA

A glimmer of lightning followed by thunder. A few spots of rain. A crack of thunder shook the earth. Lime trees swayed in gusts of wind to welcome the storm, their seedlings scattering like ticker tape from a skyscraper building, their golden fingers curling round seedpods which fluttered to earth, adorning the grass in random pattern. A cloudburst emptied plumes of rain onto every surface. Rain, increasing in speed, thrashed the tender vegetation with punishing force. Lightning flicked a powerful sting. Thunder continued its angry path. Rain hissing in steady streams, accompanied by dripping tears.

The storm had eased by early afternoon when Madeleine and Adam were about to sit down to lunch in the kitchen. "OK, it's ready," she called out towards the study, standing by her chair, waiting for Adam to appear.

"What is it?" he asked, entering the kitchen.

"Vegetable crumble."

"Oh, nice. Want some apple juice?"

"No, thanks."

Adam moved towards the radio, tuning in to BBC 3 which emitted a jangling rendition of a classical piece. Irritated by the noisy intrusion, Madeleine walked out into the study. "Call me when you're sitting down," she shouted. Allowing a minute to elapse, she returned to the kitchen.

"All I wanted was to have some music while we eat," exploded Adam, angrily throwing spoonfuls of food onto his plate, some of it splashing onto the table.

"All I want is peace and quiet," answered Madeleine, softly.

Adam stood up, lifting the chair and throwing it to the ground. "All I find is you in a bad mood with the curtains closed, when I come home." He took his plate in one hand and stalked out into the study, slamming the door behind him.

"You can just go to hell," Madeleine yelled after him, as she slammed the kitchen door.

They didn't speak for the rest of the day. Madeleine made preparations for the evening – positioning furniture, setting out glassware, cutlery and serving dishes, checking the contents of the refrigerator to make sure nothing was forgotten. Adam spent the day in the study, watching sport on TV and catching up on paperwork.

An hour until the guests arrived. Catching sight of Adam in the kitchen, with his back to her as he was making himself a cup of coffee, Madeleine moved soundlessly behind him; she put her arms around his waist; he stiffened, holding the pose for a few seconds, then relaxed; he caught her hand and held it tightly.

"My heart is sore," Adam whispered. "Half of me is missing when we quarrel."

"You're the love of my life," Madeleine whispered back. They clung to each other in silence as their spirits merged into the embrace.

"We need to get ready for the evening," Madeleine broke the spell.

"Where are we going?" he asked.

"People are coming here ... from the golf club."

"Oh, right."

"Have your shower and change into something smart casual."

"Oh, alright," Adam sighed, wearily wishing for a quiet night in front of the television.

Madeleine wondered if she was doing the right thing; it had all been quite clear in her mind; the whole evening was planned in detail. Making up the quarrel had weakened her resolve, and she wondered if Adam would be very angry at what was about to enfold. Too late now. Everything was organized. Too late to turn back.

An hour later, cars crunched into the driveway. The doorbell rang. As the door opened, eight partygoers with eager faces were revealed. Barbara and Percy, Primrose and Marius, Robina and Hugo, Cathy and Rodney.

Barbara was first over the threshold and grabbed the conversation, as the others followed her. "London has come to a standstill with this thunderstorm," she announced, as she gave both Adam and Madeleine a kiss on the cheek.

"Yes, my sister was delayed on a train outside Waterloo for four hours," Robina added to the weather report.

"We were at Wisley and had to stay undercover for an hour," Primrose divulged. "Luckily, we were in the tearoom and not in the gardens, but so was everyone else. Mind you, we had a great view. Made me feel quite homesick. We used to get storms like that regularly in South Africa."

"We would love a holiday in South Africa, wouldn't we, Percy?" Barbara announced, meaningfully. "We'll come and stay with you. Lynn and Barry could come, too." Primrose and Marius remained silent during the pause which followed.

"Actually, the storm passed us by. We only had a short shower," Cathy pondered in a surprised tone.

"I just got back from France," smirked Rodney. "The roads on the way back were flooded." The others looked at him expectantly, wondering if he would reveal anything about his trip over the channel. "I was in a café in the Champs Elysees," he drawled, lazily. "Lots of continental atmosphere. One man was puffing smoke rings up in the air. Then, this tall young woman in high heels with a blonde pony tail came in, holding a cigarette in one hand and a miniature dog in the other. She ordered a bowl of steamed mussels, a bottle of water, a half bottle of wine and two glasses. She poured water into one glass and the dog drank out of it." The others looked at him in faint astonishment. It was unusual for Rodney to give away much information. Realizing he had dropped his guard, Rodney quickly concluded, "Great food in France."

"I think Anastasia is in France, right now," announced Barbara, loudly.

A look of confusion gathered on Cathy's brow. She blinked rapidly. Her shrill laugh shattered the air. The others turned towards her to assess the source of amusement, but were met with a blank response.

Rodney's gaze did not flicker. "Nice place you got here," he commented, his eyes roving the walls.

"Hey, man, where's the beer?" Marius complained. "I need a drink. Got my mother-in-law staying with us. A man needs some consolation." His brown eyes darted around.

"Of course," Adam stepped forward. "Where are we gathering, dear?" he posed the question to Madeleine.

"In the cellar," answered Madeleine. "Everybody make their way down. Third door on the left."

Hugo caught Madeleine's eye as the partygoers moved towards the cellar door; he stood in front of her, blocking her path, allowing time for the others to move out of earshot. "Madeleine, last time I saw you ... at the Valentines' dance ... well ... I was out of order."

Madeleine remembered the red wine spreading on the table cloth after Hugo's outburst that evening; she waited for the apology to come, but Hugo dropped his eyes. In the few seconds of awkwardness, she realized that nothing more would be forthcoming. Hugo raised his eyes again; she looked directly into his gaze, challenging him to look away. Hugo held firm, his gaze entreating her to accept his confession of guilt; she closed her eyes and nodded.

Overhearing Hugo, Adam moved back towards them, intending to seal the exchange. "Hey, Hugo, how ya doin'?"

"Yea, OK, mate. OK. How's business?"

"Tough," answered Adam.

"Doin' a lot of travelin'?"

"Yea, just got back from Saudi. Gotta go to Norway and then onto Moscow next week. How are things with you, Hugo?"

"Pretty bad," answered Hugo. "I've been under investigation at the bank."

Adam gave a sharp intake of breath. "Well, if you need to offload, give me a bell. We can have a drink in the study here."

"I may well take you up on that," Hugo answered.

Percy hung back, listening. "You two having problems?" he questioned, almost gleefully.

The doorbell rang. "Everything's just fine," Adam answered in a soothing tone, as he moved to open the door.

"Well, here we are," called Lynn giving Adam a cursory glance, as her eyes moved swiftly into the hallway. "Madeleine, we're here," she called in an excited tone. Madeleine turned to greet her and led her down to the cellar.

Feeling that Lynn had treated him like hired help, Adam raised his eyebrows to greet Barry, Nancy and Colin.

"How ya doin', mate?" Barry ventured.

"Pretty good. How are you feeling?"

"Never better. Never better," answered Barry, trying to push the memory of his heart attack into the background.

"Drinks are in the cellar. Third door on your left. Make your way down."

Adam's brow furrowed as he observed Nancy and Colin, both looking very uncomfortable. He heard Colin mutter, through clenched teeth, to Nancy. "What are we doing here?" She didn't answer, but looked very perplexed. "Get me home!" Colin hissed.

"Everything OK here?" Adam enquired. Colin shuffled his feet, his eyes sweeping the floor. Both Nancy and Adam stared at Colin. "Let me take you down to the cellar," Adam offered. "Third door on the left."

The footsteps of the three silent figures clattered on the stone steps, alerting the others that they had arrived. The partygoers looked up to greet them. Adam continued his hospitality role by taking on the job of bartender, ensuring all glasses were filled. Madeleine had done a fine job of creating the atmosphere of a continental wine vault. Candle effect sconces glowed on the stone walls which were painted cream in color.

Prints in simple black frames were a stark contrast, all showing scenes of vineyards or still life arrangements of wine bottles. The original stone floor had been restored and sealed. Tables and chairs were in black wrought iron. A heavy wooden trestle table was set up as the drinks counter. Plates, cutlery, napkins and earthenware dishes were set out on a long table, draped with a stiff white cloth.

"Help yourselves to food," announced Madeleine. "It's Italian. Hope you all like lasagna." She giggled a little, thinking that Adam would be served his favorite dish, at last.

Madeleine observed that everyone was engrossed in conversation, as they filled their plates and found seats in little groups at the small tables. She hung on the periphery of the party, ensuring that the catering arrangements were satisfactory. All the while, her eyes were pinned on Colin who was shuffling around following Nancy; he became more and more agitated, hopping from one foot to the other, until he looked like he had a wasp buzzing inside his trouser leg; he was attracting attention; heads were turning to note his odd behavior; he found a chair and sat on the edge of the seat, plate in hand, head hanging down, staring at the floor; his feet still shuffled and his knee was jiggling erratically.

Madeleine noted that conversation was stalling. Plates were empty. The time had come. "OK, everyone. We're going to play a party game. I'm going to pick someone to start the ball rolling. Afterwards you can all have a try, if you want to. Please have a seat over here." As the partygoers looked to seat themselves, it was now apparent that a group of chairs in another area of the cellar had been set out in classroom style, all facing one way. A table and chair faced the audience. "Colin, you look like you could start off the fun," Madeleine announced, without looking directly at him.

Colin jumped up in alarm, looking around wildly. "Yea, come on, Colin," encouraged a few voices. Hands pushed him into the center of the room.

"Nancy, I'd like you to help." Madeleine looked directly at her attacker's wife. Nancy was oblivious of what Colin had done, and could not have predicted what he was about to do; looking surprised, she stepped out in front of the audience. "Please ask your husband to sit here." Madeleine motioned to the single chair which faced the sea of expectant faces. Nancy pushed Colin onto the chair. "Now, please apply this." Madeleine handed a black eye mask to Nancy, gesturing that it should be placed over Colin's eyes. Nancy did as she was instructed. Colin was grimacing and biting his lip. He had stopped shuffling his feet, but his knee still jiggled; his body became rigid as the mask was applied.

"Now, folks, I'm going to unveil the party piece." With a flourish, Madeleine removed a green velvet cover from the table at her side; her audience craned their necks to identify the piece of equipment which was revealed.

"Now, Nancy, I need you to assist me in applying some connections." Madeleine, smiling mysteriously, produced two rubber tubes; she placed one around Colin's upper chest, the other around his abdomen.

Colin's torso became rigid as he held his breath and swayed sideways. "What's going on?" he mouthed, exhaling loudly.

"It's a party game, Colin. Stay still," instructed Nancy. "You're usually game for a bit of fun. Stay still." Madeleine smiled smugly at this unexpected enforcement.

"Take his right hand," Madeleine instructed. "We will now apply these." She placed a small metal plate across his ring finger; once in position, she placed another metal plate on his index finger.

"Now, Nancy, I'm going to hand you four cards. I want you to read each card aloud. Can you do that?" Madeleine savored the anticipation on the faces turned in her direction.

"Sure," answered Nancy, eagerly.

Madeleine handed her the first card. Nancy blinked as she looked at the card; she looked up at the audience and shrugged. In a firm voice, she read, "Is your name Colin Ruff?" Colin twitched and shifted in the chair, but did not answer.

Madeleine nodded encouragement to Nancy. "Come on, Colin, answer the question," demanded Nancy. "It's just a bit of fun." She repeated the question. "Is your name Colin Ruff?"

"Yes," he answered, gruffly.

Madeleine handed over another card. "Do you live in Hampshire?" Nancy read aloud, her attention wavering from Colin as she surveyed the puzzled expressions turned in her direction.

"Yes," he responded.

Madeleine handed Nancy a third card. "Are you a member of Middle Wallop Golf Club?" Nancy's voice lilted, as she became more comfortable with the questions.

"Yes." Colin relaxed a little now, beginning to believe this might be fun.

Madeleine handed Nancy the fourth card. As Nancy read the words, her head jerked forward, a sick feeling gathered in the pit of her stomach. Looking shocked and shaking her head, she turned to Madeleine. Madeleine nodded her head several times; her expression had become gravely serious. Madeleine held Nancy's gaze and, stretching out her arm with open palm, gestured that she should continue. Nancy cleared her throat and swallowed. In a slow, trembling voice, she read aloud the writing on the fourth card. "Did you rape Madeleine?"

Colin leapt up from the chair, breaking the fastenings around his chest and abdomen. He ripped off the black eye mask and pulled the connections away from his fingers. Looking round wildly, scattering everything in his path, he sprang towards the stone steps of the cellar; his sinewy form disappeared in seconds; the partygoers could hear his footsteps, upstairs, thudding on the polished wooden floor of the hallway as he made his way to the front door and fled out into the humid night air.

Some of the men stood up, unsure whether to follow him. The women were transfixed at the scene they had witnessed; their bodies became statues; their faces held expressions of astonishment. Adam stood motionless, his arms straight by his side, his fists clenched.

"Let him go," instructed Madeleine.

All eyes turned to Madeleine. "Is this true?" Adam's voice strained to control his emotions.

"Here is the evidence." Madeleine gestured towards the equipment on the table. "This is a polygraph, otherwise known as a lie detector. I have just applied a test which is often used in criminal cases. The results are ninety percent accurate."

"How does it work?" Barbara was fascinated.

"By tracing changes in breathing and movement. Also changes in blood pressure, pulse rate and skin resistance." Madeleine's demeanor was brisk.

"So, what now?" continued Barbara, while Adam stared at her intently, pondering the same question.

"Well, I could analyze the charts, but I don't think that's necessary. You all saw his reaction." Madeleine's gaze traversed the room as she spoke.

Nancy stood by Madeleine's side. "Do you still need me? Can I go now?" she whispered; tears were rolling down her cheeks; she felt humiliated and ashamed; she felt somehow responsible; she felt like a schoolgirl who had been caught in the act of some misdemeanor and been punished in front of the class.

"Go." Madeleine didn't spare her a glance.

Shielding her face with one hand, Nancy moved heavily up the steps; realizing she would have to walk home, she turned halfway. Lynn looked up and called softly, "We'll take you home." She pulled Barry by the sleeve, drawing his attention to Nancy. "We'll need to take her home. She came in the car with us." Barry nodded; they both got up from their seats. Barry lifted his hand in a mournful farewell. Moving towards the steps, their footsteps echoed against the stone as they made their ascent to join Nancy. "In fact, come home with us, Nancy. Stay overnight," Lynn soothed, looking to Barry for approval. Raising his eyebrows, Barry nodded agreement.

The sound of wrought iron chairs scraping the stone floor jarred the ears, as the partygoers moved to release themselves from the classroom formation, grouping themselves in the center of the room.

Hugo looked back at Madeleine and Adam who were standing apart. "I think, perhaps, we should all leave now," he stated.

"I think we should lynch him," called out Percy.

Rodney sniggered. "Yea," he voiced, looking down at the floor; he would willingly become a spectator.

Marius exploded, "Where I come from, he would never be seen again. Let's go after him."

Adam had not moved; he was still standing, arms by his side, fists clenched. "We cannot have a vigilante society." He spoke slowly and deliberately. "I can understand the temptation to name and shame, but a vigilante society metes out different punishments between factions. A vigilante society is a corrosive force. Crime needs an intellectual response. The law is dispassionate and objective and applies common standards. We can only fight crime within the law."

The partygoers were silent as they digested Adam's statement; their emotions in response to the evening's event were wide ranging. The women felt anguish at how they might deal with being raped; Primrose was in awe of Madeleine's dramatic public display; Barbara felt jealous of her professional control; Lynn felt she must have given Colin some encouragement; Cathy felt disgust at being an unwilling participant in the drama; Robina swallowed a feeling of diminished respect for Madeleine. All were astonished that Madeleine, whose career had been in the legal profession, had operated outside the law. Everyone wondered how they would react in similar circumstances. The men were split into two camps – those who agreed with Adam and those who would relish the opportunity to unleash a violent response; Hugo felt anger that such a crime should be perpetrated within their community; Rodney felt entertained and was curious for more details; Barry was uncomfortable at being an unwilling witness, and felt uneasy at projecting himself into possible police interviews; Percy was formulating a few bawdy comments to be used for momentary attention.

Barbara broke the silence. "Hey, girl, you did well!" That bastard needs whipping. Us girls should take revenge." Her dark eyes danced with mischief; she became agitated, throwing her hands around, heavy bracelets making a clunking sound. "You're one of us, girl. We'll sort the bastard out." She looked around at the other women for support; their eyes, which had been transfixed by her melodramatic display, wavered and looked away.

Somehow, Barbara's outburst cracked Madeleine's resolve; her control crumbled; her knees buckled; tears gathered in her eyes; a sob escaped. Adam moved towards her, putting his arm round her shoulders; she turned her face into his chest and cried like a baby.

Hugo called softly, "We'll go now." Adam nodded, his expression gravely serious.

OVERNIGHT

Barry drove home in silence. Lynn and Nancy, slumped in the back seat, murmured softly, but he could not hear the words. The windscreen wipers hypnotized him; he had to force his mind to concentrate. Occasionally, he screwed up his eyes to blot out the dazzling yellow spikes of light from the headlights of passing cars. He felt numbed by what he had witnessed; he forced himself not to consider how he might react if his wife had been the victim. He focused on the possible impact of having Nancy under his roof, feeling uncomfortable at the prospect of playing the role of overnight protector.

Nosing the car into the narrow driveway, wing mirrors just clearing the laurel hedge on either side, Barry applied the brake and turned off the ignition. Eyes glancing in the rear view mirror, he twisted his neck round to address Lynn and Nancy. "We're here." His voice broke into their private world.

"Oh, right," Lynn answered in a weary fashion; she felt exhausted and desperately wanted to put her head on her soft pillow, letting her mind drift away from the evening's events; she half regretted offering overnight accommodation to Nancy who, suddenly, felt like a lead burden next to her on the seat. "Straight to bed or a nightcap?" she asked, putting her arm round Nancy's shoulders as they entered the house, her feet enjoying the thick cream carpet after the hard, echoing surface of Madeleine's cellar.

"Bed sounds wonderful," Nancy sighed. Lynn and Barry exchanged glances of relief.

"OK, I'll take you upstairs and settle you in," Lynn agreed.

Three pairs of feet climbed the stairs. Barry softly called, "Goodnight, Nancy," as if he were blowing a wish into the air; he watched the two women turn towards the guest bedroom. As he undressed next door, he heard the muffled sounds of conversation followed by the familiar sounds of the curtains being drawn.

A few minutes later, Lynn appeared. "Oh, I'm so tired. Let's get to sleep and talk about this in the morning," she sighed. Barry shrugged and wordlessly settled himself under the covers; without desire, he watched Lynn throw off her summer dress, showing her thickened body encased in expensive embroidered underwear. Lynn switched off the bedside light. They both lay awake in the darkness, contemplating the events which had brought them an unwelcome guest.

Lynn woke in the morning: yawning, she stretched out, enjoying the freedom of being alone in bed: Barry must already be dressed and downstairs. Listening to squawking geese fly overhead, she realized the morning must be well advanced. Rolling her legs onto the floor, she raised herself out of bed and reached for a cotton wrap; she made her way downstairs, but Barry was nowhere to be seen. Entering the kitchen, she found a scrawled note by the kettle: Barry had gone to the office. Lumbering back upstairs, Lynn tapped gently on the door of the guest bedroom.

"Nancy," she called softly. No response. "Nancy, would you like some tea?"

A soft moan escaped from the other side of the door. "Nancy, are you awake? Would you like some tea?"

After a pause, "Oh, yea, thanks," from the other side of the door, followed by another soft moan.

"OK, I'm putting on the kettle. See you downstairs."

Lynn wanted to rid herself of the responsibility of her guest; she had enough problems under her own roof, dealing with her daughter; she had felt obliged last night to offer support but, this morning, felt unwilling to become further involved in the situation. She had just finished making two mugs of tea when Nancy entered the kitchen; handing one of the mugs to Nancy, Lynn smiled and pointed to the green wording on the white stoneware which read 'Golfers don't need to diet ... they live on greens'. Nancy smiled weakly back.

"Let's make ourselves comfy in a soft seat." Lynn led the way into the sitting room and dropped into the sofa. Nancy followed and sat next to her noting, with surprise, that the fine beige fabric was a little threadbare. They sat in silence for some time, their ears noting the sounds of their environment – the refrigerator quietly shuddering in the kitchen, an occasional car swishing past, church bells in the distance.

Summoning all her emotional energy, Lynn broached the subject. "Quite a shock last night."

Nancy looked down into the reflections on the mug of tea; a sharp puff of air escaped from her nostrils as her lungs emptied in disgust; she made no answer, her mind a rabbit warren of jumbled thoughts, all leading nowhere.

"What will you do?" enquired Lynn.

Nancy's eyebrows raised. "Do? What can I do? It's all been done. I suppose Adam will have contacted the police."

"I mean, will you divorce him?" questioned Lynn.

"That's a few jumps ahead. I can't think straight." Nancy's face screwed up with annoyance.

"Well, you need to start thinking. Your life has taken quite a turn. You need to sort yourself out," advised Lynn.

"I suppose that's right," answered Nancy, feeling pressurized.

"Do you love him?"

Nancy snorted "Love? You must be joking. I never loved him."

"You didn't?" But you've been married a long time. You married young. You must have loved him then," insisted Lynn.

"I was pregnant. I had no choice. It would be different nowadays. I just went along with it. I couldn't support a baby on my own. The only man I've ever really loved is my son ... from the moment he was born, the tenderness, the intimacy between us ... made everything else worthwhile." Nancy's voice shook.

"So, you've been unhappy."

"You could say that." Nancy paused. "He's a brute, actually." A cold cloud narrowed her eyes.

"A brute?"

"Never gave me any peace. Makes me wonder if he's done this sort of thing before."

Lynn's jaw dropped; she had not considered this possibility. "Why didn't you leave him?" she asked.

"Where would I go? How would I live? I'm tied to him with the caravan site. How else could I earn a living? I've lived in this area all my life. My relatives are all around ... judging. He was never mean with money. I could spend what I wanted. I could go where I wanted. It would be hard to leave ... but now ... everything's changed ... now I have a reason." Nancy's mouth compressed into a firm line of determination.

"What about Darren?"

Shaken, Nancy swallowed. Her voice wavered. "Darren?"

"Yes, Darren. Everyone knows about it."

Nancy felt as if she had been nailed to the sofa; her legs felt heavy; she wanted to run away but couldn't summon the willpower to escape Lynn's questioning; her eyes moved to follow the black and white flash of a magpie gliding past the window. "Darren," she repeated, unlocking that door in her brain. "So, people know. What are they saying?"

"It really doesn't matter what they're saying. He's part of this equation. What are you going to do about him?" Lynn demanded.

"I don't know."

"Well, do you love him?"

"Do I love him? I feel a tenderness towards him. The intimacy ... is a consolation to me ... I know I'm satisfying a young man's desires ... and my own. I'm an experience for him. I know that. I know it probably won't last ... but it might."

"So, will you end it or let it run out of steam?" Lynn wanted to know.

"I haven't had happiness in the past. I won't end it," admitted Nancy.

"You know it will end in tears," counseled Lynn.

"I'll take my chances." Nancy puckered her brow, pondering her whole situation.

Lynn sighed and patted Nancy's knee. "Better get you home. Take your time. Once we've showered and dressed, I'll make breakfast and drive you home."

An hour later, they were ready to leave. Lynn stood in the hallway, keys in hand. "Got everything?"

Nancy nodded. "Thanks." She was deeply grateful for the security of Lynn's home last night; their discussion this morning, although uncomfortable, had helped her see things a little more clearly.

Lynn reversed the car out of the narrow driveway onto the road, her eyes rippling over the grass verge in search of hazards. Skeletons of foxgloves stared back at her; their purple bells had suckled bees but now they stood dry and withered, like elderly ladies waiting for death. Anchored alongside, yellow trumpets of evening primrose swayed in the breeze, promising eternal youth.

"She was certainly the center of attention last night," Lynn commented, as they drove past Madeleine's house.

"You could say that," Nancy agreed.

"Little Miss Perfect. Well, she's not top of the class anymore. Don't you think she must have led him on?"

Nancy's brow furrowed as she considered this possibility. Lynn continued, "Well, we offered her a lift home that night at the Five Bells. You might not remember. You weren't feeling so good. But why didn't she come home with us? She was the one who chose to be with him, walking alone at night in the dark across the fields. What did she expect? She was asking for trouble. Either that or she was looking for some action. What do you think?"

Nancy was confused. A moment ago her mind had accepted the fact that Colin would be jailed and she would be free. Now, she was forced to think about the possibility that he may have a defense and might not be convicted. Head spinning, the jumble of thoughts became a ball of pressure bursting inside her skull.

As they reached the caravan site, Lynn's curiosity was awakened. "I wonder what you'll find here. I better come in with you," she offered.

"Are you sure? Don't you have a busy day?" Nancy felt relieved at Lynn's offer but was, at the same time, reluctant to have her witness a confrontation with Colin.

"No, nothing much on today. Doing the laundry and then I'll catch the shopping channel on TV," replied Lynn, her face brightening up.

What they would find was a broken pane of glass. Colin had run across the fields last night. No-one knew this area like he did; he ran like the wind, until his chest was pounding and he was forced to stop. He estimated he had covered two miles; he clutched his knees with his hands, gasping for air. Once he could breathe more easily, he looked around to find his bearings; he worked out a safe route back to the caravan site. Plodding along now, sweat running down his back, he made his way at a walking pace. Reaching the site, he crouched in the undergrowth, watching; his legs ached, his windpipe burned, his bones absorbed the dampness from his clothing. As he recovered his breath in the quiet of the night, a closed part of his mind creaked open; he was ten years old again, hiding from his father; terror flashed through every pore; his innards recoiled; he flinched, as the plastic cable whipped into his shoulders; later would come the punches and the bruises, the slaps and the cigarette burns on his buttocks. Again, he was crouching, hiding, cowering, filled with shame and humiliation; if only he had the courage to run away from home, but his boyish mind could not form a plan. An hour passed; drops of rain heralded a cloudburst; no-one had appeared; he would risk it. Nancy had the keys; he would have to break in. He checked the kitchen door; sure enough, the keys were dangling inside the lock. He threw a stone; the musical sound of glass tinkling, as the pane shattered, was followed by the thud of the stone skidding across the floor; he picked away the hanging shards to give himself a clean entry. Reaching his hand through, he turned the key and let himself inside. As soon as he opened the door, the alarm beeped; he raced to the hallway to enter the security code. No time to lose. He grabbed a backpack from the cupboard under the stairs and raced up to the bedroom, tearing off his clothing as he moved. Stuffing items into the backpack, he changed into dry clothing at the same time. Clattering downstairs in heavy shoes, he threw open the door of the office. Sliding back a wall panel, his fingers reached for the keypad on the safe.

Turning the handle of the fireproof door, he lifted out his passport and slid it into his back pocket; he estimated the bundle of banknotes neatly stacked on the middle shelf of the safe amounted to around three thousand pounds; he stuffed the bundle into the backpack. No time to lose; he had everything he needed. At last, after all these years of entrapment, he could run away from home. He listened carefully; not a sound; only the breeze rustling the trees outside. He let himself out of the front door, stopping to listen again on the doorstep. All clear. He walked briskly into the roadway; with the backpack and heavy shoes, he now looked like one of the many holidaymakers who hiked around the area; he donned a knitted hat to complete the picture and walked out into the night. Relief. He felt relief; the past few weeks had been torture, not knowing if the police would come knocking at the door. Madeleine occupied most of his waking hours; after the alcohol had worn off that night, guilt crept into his guts; he felt dirty and ashamed; remorse nagged at him each day. But it was too late, too late for anything now except to run away. He would make for the coast. Once over the channel, he would disappear. Madeleine ... if only she could know how sorry he was ... if only he could turn back the clock.

BOURNEMOUTH

Madeleine cried. Adam held her gently, allowing her grief to seep into his soul. Steadying himself, he lifted her in his arms and carried her to the steps of the cellar, his back straining to bear the weight; he dropped her slowly to her feet at the bottom of the stone steps, knowing that it would be impossible to carry her up the narrow stairway. Questions without answers shot between them as their eyes met. Adam moved up the steps; taking Madeleine's hand, his energy pulled them both up to the door at the top. Reaching the hallway, he slipped one hand around her waist, the other around her shoulders; together they climbed slowly up the main staircase to the confines of their bedroom. Madeleine's expression was blank as Adam turned her round to face him; her tears flowed freely, without sobs, a simple weeping oozing from her soul.

"Do you want to talk?" Adam's words didn't seem to mean anything to her; her eyes felt puffed up; she wanted sleep to banish the torment.

"OK," she sighed.

"I think it's important. I know you probably don't feel like it, Madeleine, but we need to talk. You need to tell me what happened."

"OK." She drew a deep breath. "There was an evening at the Five Bells for the ladies on the golf club committee. Husbands were also invited. You were away in the Middle East." Madeleine stopped, wondering how much detail to divulge.

"Yes?" Adam encouraged.

"I walked there. It was a beautiful summer's evening. I didn't think much about getting home. I knew someone would give me a lift. He offered to walk home with me. I wasn't too comfortable but just went along with it. Halfway there, he pushed me to the ground and attacked me. I couldn't stop him. I hit him with a stone and managed to run away."

"But did he rape you?" Adam needed clarification.

"Yes."

"You didn't report it to the police?"

"What's the point?" Madeleine exploded. "Can you imagine what that would bring? I would have to be examined, have to give interviews. It would be in the newspapers. I would have to give evidence, have to go to court. My reputation would be put into question."

A heavy silence hung between them. Adam didn't trust himself to speak. In the cellar, he had used all his powers of self control; he had wanted to tear that guy apart. Only knowing that he was no physical match for his opponent had prevented him from launching an attack. Anger and a thirst for revenge curdled his blood; he felt as if his body would burst out of his clothing with the power of his emotions. A range of options swam in front of his eyes; he could take a shotgun and go after Madeleine's attacker; he could shoot him at the caravan site some dark night, he could find some way to damage his family; he could affect his finances by messing up his business. Determination that no-one would get away with violating his wife, invading his territory, was a primeval force galvanizing Adam's energy; common sense dragged him back from the brink. No point in being imprisoned for murder when his wife needed looking after; she came first, she would take a bit of nursing, she would need treatment. Intelligence was his best weapon; he would have to defend his territory by thinking his way out of the problem; he would have to come up with a sophisticated method of revenge. Doubt crept into Adam's thoughts; what on earth was Madeleine thinking about wandering the fields at night with another woman's husband; he tried hard not to imagine the scene but images of her chatting and laughing with this man burrowed into his brain like a worm; perhaps she had been familiar with him ... perhaps she had led him on ... he banished the thoughts; she hadn't told him about it, she had kept it from him ... he couldn't understand why.

Madeleine slumped over the bedroom chair; her legs were giving way; she leaned over to grasp Adam's arm, and eased herself into a weary slouching position.

"Why didn't you tell me?"

"You were away. It was difficult to talk. You just can't say something like that on the phone. I just couldn't ... couldn't find the words. And what were you going to do? Come home? Inform the police? I needed time to think, to work out a plan."

"Well, that was certainly some plan. Are you ... in need of medical attention?"

"I'm fine. I'll live. I've survived so far." Madeleine was feeling disappointed and defiant.

"You're too independent, sweetheart. I'm lost for words that you handled this alone. You shut me out. I could have helped you," Adam entreated.

"Yes, well, there you go. You weren't here."

"Well, I'm here now." Adam felt the stab of accusation in her statement. "I won't leave your side until you're over this." He slid the phone out of his trouser pocket; the pip, pip, pip told him he had a signal and was able to leave a message for his secretary. "Hello, it's Adam. I have some personal business to take care of at home. Can you clear my commitments for next week, please. I don't plan to come into the office, but I will listen to voice messages regularly. Cheers."

Madeleine let out a moan of anguish. Now, she could allow her feelings out; she wasn't alone, anymore. Sobs racked her body. Adam moved across the room and held her gently in his arms. "You won't want to be with me anymore," she wailed. "Our intimacy together is gone."

"Nonsense," Adam blurted out. "Nothing can take that away from us. But won't you see a doctor? I would feel much happier if you were checked out."

"I don't need that," Madeleine yelled.

"Please, for me. For peace of mind. For both of us. I think we could both do with counseling; this is not the kind of thing we're equipped to handle without support."

"OK, OK. Whatever you say."

"And I must contact the police," added Adam.

"OK, OK, OK," Madeleine shouted, letting a thin stream of anger escape.

"Madeleine, I love you. You're the most precious person in the world to me. You're the center of my universe. You must allow me to look after you," pleaded Adam.

Madeleine slumped back into the chair, feeling defeated; she had fought this thing, now she had to let go; she knew she had to accept help now; she couldn't carry on alone. Adam bent over her, enfolding her in his arms; a flood of emotions pumped through his chest; an overwhelming sense of duty that he must protect his wife and do everything in his power to bring her back to contented wellbeing surged through his veins; a cloud of doubt that he was able to erase this misery circled his brain; a cloak of tenderness spun out of his heart to envelope her in safety; a thirsting rage pulsed in the back of his neck; a nagging fear that his grip on the business would weaken while he took time out gnawed at his stomach. He took Madeleine's hand and gently raised her to her feet: as he did so, a determined strength forged itself into his legs; he lifted Madeleine up and carried her over to the bed; taking off her shoes, he swung her into a comfortable position; he sat on the edge of the bed, kicking his own shoes away; he stroked her hair with gentle caresses. Tears cascaded down Madeleine's face; her skin was bathed in a salty dampness; her heart emptied out all the unhappiness, not just from the rough, coarse abuse she had recently suffered, but every little hurt of recent years surfaced from the depths of her spirit; each sob released another clutch of sorrow. They lay motionless together; the sense of loss was overpowering; the physical tension was immense; the shared grief filled the room. Time passed in silence. Adam held her gently as if she were an injured bird suffering intense pain; a bird, summoning strength to fly to freedom.

At last Madeleine spoke. "I'm cold," she uttered.

"Get under the covers," Adam instructed. "We'll cuddle up together."

The morning found them both weary and exhausted; eventually they had gained a few hours of sleep. Before switching off the light, they had changed out of their evening finery. Madeleine's dress was now hanging drunkenly from a hanger on the door. Adam's smart jacket and trousers lay collapsed in a crumpled heap on the floor. It was Sunday. The sky was grey; the air was still, the absence of birdsong left a mournful silence.

Moving slightly, Adam whispered, "Rex must be desperate for a walk."

"Yes," Madeleine whispered back, weakly. After a pause, she murmured, "Don't leave me."

"Come to the kitchen with me. We'll make some tea," entreated Adam; he took her hand and gently pulled her towards him. Madeleine sighed heavily and raised herself up with one elbow. Putting her blue velvet dressing gown into her hand, Adam commanded, "Come on. Downstairs." Obeying his instruction, Madeleine swung herself out of bed wrapping the robe around her, as her feet touched the floor. Holding hands, they shuffled downstairs together.

Rex was, indeed, desperate for a walk; he ran up and down the kitchen in agitation, whining impatiently. Moving out to the back porch, Adam slipped his feet into outdoor shoes and opened the door. Rex didn't need a second invitation; he raced outside, waiting for Adam.

"Keep the back door open. We'll be back in a minute," called Adam.

Madeleine felt a huge void as he left, as if she had fallen down a well with darkness enveloping her, and her only hope of survival was for Adam's face to appear from the bright light at the top; she stood immobilized, waiting: minutes passed: panic was starting to set in, but subsided as she heard them return.

"Whew, that was a quick sprint. I'm quite out of breath," laughed

Adam, kicking off his shoes. Turning back into the kitchen, he added, "I just had a thought. How about a day at the seaside?" Madeleine's mouth puckered, as she considered the suggestion. Adam continued, "We could take Rex, let him run along the beach. We can just wear our jeans, grab a casual snack somewhere, walk on the esplanade, watch the sunset, see everyone pass by and no-one will know us. How does that sound?"

"Sounds good," agreed Madeleine. "Bournemouth?"

"Nowhere better. Pop up and have your shower, once you've finished breakfast. We can be out the door in half an hour." Adam sounded cheerful now.

The phone rang. Madeleine looked startled. Adam advised, "No need to answer. They can leave a message. You don't need to talk to anyone until you're ready."

The message recorded, "Madeleine, it's Alice. I just wanted to say hello. If you feel like it, call me back. Otherwise, I'll try again."

Madeleine closed her eyes until the message stooped. "OK. Bournemouth," she stated, making her way upstairs.

"Just one thing." Adam stopped her progress. "We need to inform the police."

"If you say so." She looked at the ground, pondering, and then offered, "I have evidence. Photos and clothing."

"That's my girl."

"Tomorrow. We'll do it tomorrow. Let's have a day of freedom today."

FOLLOW THROUGH

Monday. A day to face the world. Madeleine heard a noise outside; looking out of the window, she saw two squirrels chasing each other, playfully, round the girth of a pine tree, the grip of their claws making a scratching sound as they performed an intermittent dance on the rough bark. Phone calls. Lots of them. Adam had already phoned the local police. She would respond to some of the messages on the answering machine. Alice was first on the list.

"Hello, Alice. It's Madeleine."

"Madeleine!" Alice's voice expressed surprise and relief. "It's you. How are you?"

"I'm OK." Making it easy for Alice, she followed up with, "You heard?"

"I did."

"Adam has been in touch with the police this morning. So, we'll go from there."

"You know he's done a runner?" questioned Alice.

"He has?"

"Broke into the house that night. Took his passport and a wad of money and not been seen since."

"Oh ... suppose it's what you would expect, really. Might save me a lot of angst if he never turns up," responded Madeleine. A silence followed, neither of them knowing quite what to say next. Madeleine changed the subject. "How was the birthday party, Alice?"

"Oh, just wonderful. My daughter made the cake, it looked gorgeous. I made up for lost time and sent him six birthday cards."

"Six birthday cards?"

"Yes, one for each decade ... and party poppers everywhere. I had birthday balloons pinned all over the place." Alice paused for effect. "And ... I bought him a motorbike."

"You did?"

"He's always wanted one," confirmed Alice. A Harley Davidson. You know, we've been married a long time. Things have not been as they should for many years. Another woman. I couldn't forgive him. But time heals. We're not getting any younger, you know. A sixtieth birthday. What's the point of a miserable old age? He might have left me, now that he's retiring. So ... a new life ... a new beginning. I hope, anyway."

"Alice, that's marvelous. How did Don react?"

"He was astonished. He wasn't expecting anything lavish. He was over the moon with the motorbike ... like a young man again. He says if he lives to be a hundred, this will be a birthday to remember."

"That's just wonderful." Madeleine's spirits lifted.

"Madeleine, can I do anything for you? I know Adam travels a lot. Do you need company?"

"I'm OK. Adam's taking time out to stay with me this week. Feels I shouldn't be left alone. We went to Bournemouth yesterday. Took Rex to the beach. It was *so* good to escape." Madeleine laughed, self consciously.

"Well, you know I'm here if you need me at any time."

"I do. Thanks for getting in touch, Alice ... and I'm thrilled about the birthday party. Good luck to both of you."

"Thanks. Talk to you soon."

"Bye."

The doorbell rang. Standing in the hallway, Madeleine wondered whether to answer. Adam walked smartly out of the study to open the front door. "Flowers for Mrs Minehead," the caller announced, pushing a large bouquet into Adam's hands.

"Oh, thank you," Adam answered, accepting the bundle, while looking quizzically at the little envelope peeping from between the blooms. Closing the door, he handed the delivery to Madeleine who moved slowly into the kitchen, her eyes willing the envelope to divulge its secret. Placing the cellophane covered gift on the countertop, she plucked the envelope from its perky position and tore it open with her forefinger. "It's from Robina and Hugo," she called out to Adam who was now standing behind her. "Thinking of you. Love from Robina and Hugo," she read out the message.

"Well, that's very nice," commented Adam, with heartfelt appreciation.

"Very nice, indeed," Madeleine cast her eyes over the bouquet, assessing which vase would be most suitable to display them to best advantage; her initial appreciation of the gesture was now overtaken by practical considerations. "I must phone her." She ran the cold water and plunged the grateful stems into the sink. "I'll sort them later. Best to phone her now."

Lifting the receiver, she dialed Robina's number hoping that she, rather than Hugo, would answer. Adam waited until Madeleine spoke, moving back to the study once she was engaged in conversation.

"Robina? It's Madeleine."

"Oh, hi, Madeleine," Robina responded, with surprise.

"Thank you for the flowers. That was very thoughtful of you."

"Well, it's difficult to know what to say."

"I know."

"You didn't need to phone. You don't need to talk."

"I just wanted to say thank you, Robina."

"How are you?"

"OK, OK. Adam is taking this week off to be with me. Arranging lots of treats. He's just about to go on the internet to book tickets for Romeo and Juliet."

"Oh, what a nice idea. Where's it showing?"

"At the globe. Shakespeare's Globe."

"Do you know, we've never been there."

"Oh, it's easy. You can walk there from Waterloo station, so we'll take the train. We're hoping to catch an afternoon performance this week, then we'll walk over Millennium Bridge to the City and grab a steak in Davy's Wine Bar ... that'll be down memory lane for me ... one of my favorite haunts ... used to go there with my colleagues from the law firm." Changing the focus of attention away from herself, Madeleine enquired politely, "How's Hugo?"

"Not so good."

"Oh?"

"Things are really bad at work. He's at home ... on leave while under investigation."

"Oh, dear," Madeleine moved towards the study, as she spoke.

"It's a terrible strain."

"Does he want to talk it over with Adam? I heard it mentioned between them," Madeleine asked in a louder voice. She had reached the study by now and could make eye contact with Adam; she mouthed Hugo's name to him while pointing to the phone and raised her eyebrows in silent question.

"Well, maybe ... I don't know." Robina's voice trailed off.

Adam took hold of the receiver. "Robina, it's Adam. Your old man needs some company. Put him on the phone."

"Oh, OK," Robina acquiesced. "Hugo?" she called out in a loud voice, with her hand over the mouthpiece. Removing her hand again, she continued, "I'll just go and find him."

Moments later, Hugo's voice cut the brief silence. "Adam. How ya doin'?"

"Just fine. You need some company. I'm home this week to look after Madeleine. Come over."

"Yea, that would be good."

"This afternoon suit you? Bring Robina ... if she wants to come."

"OK, I'm sure she'll want to. Let me check." A pause while he yelled Robina's name. Another pause while he waited for a response. "I'll just go and find her. Don't know where she's disappeared to," he added tersely; he was short of patience these days. In a quieter voice, "Robina, I'm going over to see Adam today. Do you want to come and see Madeleine?"

"Well, of course, but does she want company?"

Hugo started to relay the message, but Adam continued, "A visit from Robina would do her good. How about three o'clock?"

"Sounds good to me," answered Hugo. Placing his hand over the mouthpiece to shield the increased volume of his voice, he enquired, "Three o'clock, Robina?" A brief nod of her head and a look into her earnest grey eyes told him she was happy to accompany him, although her expression was clouded with anxiety.

"Yea, that's fine. We'll both come over."

"Look forward to seeing you."

Just after three o'clock, Hugo's car crunched into the driveway. Seeing them from the study, Adam opened the front door and was standing to greet them. "Come on in," his voice rang out, his welcoming tone accompanied by clamping a hand on Hugo's shoulder and a brief kiss on the cheek for Robina.

"I made a chocolate cake," announced Robina, holding up a huge container; moist whirls of tantalizing chocolate fudge icing beckoned.

"Robina made a chocolate cake," Adam called out cheerfully to Madeleine.

"A chocolate cake. Oh, wow!" Madeleine came racing out of the kitchen, her face brightening with delight. "Come on in." She lowered her eyes quickly, having only briefly forgotten the reasons for their visit. Adam and Hugo immediately turned into the study, quietly closing the door behind them. "I expect tea will appear before too long," Adam smiled as he gestured to a leather sofa. As they seated themselves, he offered, "So things are not going too well, Hugo?"

"You could say that. I'm on leave ... under investigation for fraud."

"Is it something you can tell me about? Might help to clear your mind," offered Adam.

"I can't divulge too much at the moment ... but there are moves afoot to extradite me to the United States for questioning," Hugo sighed.

"Gee, that sounds really serious."

"Yep."

"Forgive me, but if it's gone that far, there must be evidence linking you to this," commented Adam.

"I've been stabbed in the back by a junior member of staff," explained Hugo. "Someone I tried to help in the past. He now has bad relationships throughout the bank. He messed up a transaction and tried to pin it on me, claiming I instructed him. Since I'm ultimately responsible for the portfolio of clients, I come under scrutiny."

"Nowadays, Hugo, with all this focus on corporate governance, one tends to be guilty until proved innocent so we need to be very forensic about the facts and, hopefully, establish enough evidence to support your position."

"Yes, I took your advice. I now have a top notch lawyer to represent me in court."

"Well, that's an important step in the right direction, so try to relax and let the guy do his job," encouraged Adam.

"Gee, that's easier said than done, but thanks for taking an interest and I'll keep you posted. But, actually, today is quite a good opportunity to tell you something which concerns you, Adam. It's nothing to do with the bank or work or Madeleine, but it's a nasty business and I'm not sure if you're in the right frame of mind to hear it. You have enough on your plate looking after Madeleine."

"Come on, Hugo, don't stop there. Spill."

"Well, the last time we played golf together, Percy was in our group. He is saying around the club that you cheated that day."

"Whoa, say that again." Adam's voice rose.

"Well, what he's saying is that you miscounted your score, making it less. Also, that you tried to play a ball which wasn't yours, and that you deliberately tried to distract other players to put them off their game." Hugo spoke plainly.

"You know, Hugo, the opposite is the case. I was marking that shithead's card and turned a blind eye rather than make a scene. I had to correct his score at every hole; he was conveniently forgetting shots each time. He also tried to play a ball out of the rough which didn't belong to him. In the end, he was playing so badly that his score didn't matter, so I gave up correcting him. He's a nightmare. Also, I don't know if you recall, but what he does is jingle coins on the putting green to distract everyone else." Adam was conscious of how trivial all this sounded in comparison with Hugo's problems.

"I haven't been concentrating on anything apart from my own problems, so I wasn't taking note," admitted Hugo.

"What I'm hearing is guilt rearing its ugly head, but I won't be a patsy for that idiot. Let's get him on the phone." Adam reached across the desk.

"Wow, that's confrontational, but perhaps it's the only way to handle it. Head on," agreed Hugo.

"You've got it. All we have in life is our personal integrity and I'm not letting somebody like Percy impugn mine." Adam's voice rose louder.

"So, we're kinda in the same boat, pal," Hugo smiled.

"Well, I ain't going to jail for this, so I think there's a question of degree; but you're right, the principle is the same," agreed Adam.

"So, you're going to phone him?"

"Right now." Adam lifted the receiver from his desk, at the same time looking up the number on the golf club list. Dialing the number, he had the instant gratification of a male voice answering.

"Percy, this is Adam Minehead here."

"Oh, hello, Adam."

"Percy, I've heard something that I don't want to believe and I need to ask you to clarify things for me."

"Oh."

"It concerns the golf club."

"Oh."

"I've heard an allegation that you claim I cheated during the Saturday competition," challenged Adam.

"Eh, eh ... who's telling you that?" stammered Percy.

"Well ... I don't know if we need to get to that. Just clarify to me, Percy, please, have you ever made this allegation to anyone?"

"I don't know what you're talking about."

"Well, I'm mighty relieved to hear you've never made that allegation. Just as a matter of record, I have another golf club member standing in the room with me, Percy. You're on the speaker phone. So, if you or anybody else makes these false allegations against me again, the third party will be able to clarify things on my behalf. Enjoy the rest of your day."

Adam firmly replaced the receiver and turned to Hugo. "OK, buddy, I would appreciate if you would feed back this conversation to whatever sources have been circulating false allegations. I'm not going to raise the issue that Percy Blunt was the one who was cheating. I simply won't be marking his card again. Let's hope that's the end of the matter. Thank you for the decency of telling me this, despite your own personal problems. Let's now focus on any help I can give you."

Outside in the garden, Robina and Madeleine strolled, viewing the development of new shrubs which had been planted earlier in the year. Robina was valiantly keeping up a light hearted chatter. "You know, I was in the village store the other day. I wanted to buy stuff for false teeth because I heard it's brilliant for cleaning flower vases. As I pulled the tube from the shelf the top came loose and the contents emptied onto the floor. The whole shop took notice. Now, everyone in the district will think I have false teeth." Robina chuckled, hoping to make Madeleine smile. "And the grandchildren, they make you feel foolish at times," Robina sputtered on. "My little grandson said to me the other day, 'Nana, you've got old person's arms. Does that mean you're going to die soon?' I thought it might be a good opportunity to discuss the facts of life, so I said to him, 'We all have to die at some time.' Then he said, 'They'll take you away in a car with big windows, you know.'" A little laugh escaped from Madeleine; for just a few moments, she escaped her inner torment. Delighted at Madeleine's amusement, Robina burbled on, "Just wait till you have grandchildren. I was looking after the youngest the other day and decided we could make little cakes for the church fete. I thought he could smear on the icing and fix the decorations. Unfortunately, he sneezed all over the cakes and put the decorations in his mouth, so we had to start all over again. Our efforts raised ten pounds towards a new roof for the church, but if we hadn't started afresh we would have cost the National Health Service vast sums by infecting parishioners with germs from snot and saliva."

Madeleine laughed aloud; her eyes twinkled with amusement. "It's so good to have you here, Robina. You're a tonic." They strolled further, admiring the garden; the light hearted moments had relaxed them both. A comfortable silence ensued between them; both were lost in their own thoughts, allowing the little anecdotes to lift their spirits. Several minutes passed as they savored the sweetness of their companionship.

Eventually, Madeleine felt compelled to break the silence in order to acknowledge their personal difficulties. "So, what are they saying about me?"

"Huh! Whatever they say is not worth hearing. If nothing else, you'll find out who your friends are, Madeleine, through this experience. There will be those who give you support and those you never hear from."

"I'm sure that's right." After a pause of reflection, Madeleine ventured, "You sound as if you speak from experience."

"Not really. It's just that my parents were in the military. We traveled a lot. New environment every few years ... until I went to boarding school. You see a lot of relationships come and go."

"Yes, I understand. Adam traveled a lot too with his parents, but ... you've lived in this area a long time. You're settled here."

"A long time, yes, but not as long as some. I don't have a home town because we moved so much. You get used to making and losing friends. You learn to become self possessed. But, you do get to see a lot of life. And you get to learn not everyone will support you when you're down ... which is why I say that you'll find out who your friends are."

Madeleine's eyes fixed on the ground as she paused to reflect on the truth of this statement. After a while, she lifted her eyes and enquired softly, "How is Hugo?"

"He's bearing up. You get an inner strength from somewhere when faced with adversity. But, we're having to review our finances. We really stretched ourselves to buy that house a few years ago, so there's no spare cash. We expected to make large repayments in the next few years, and then build up a cash reserve for our retirement with Hugo's annual bonuses from the bank, but we're strapped now with the possibility of legal fees and our assets being seized. So ... what we've done is sell the house to the children; they've re-mortgaged their houses so they can make the repayments between the four of them and we get to stay in the house. The repayments will be tough for my oldest daughter; her husband is quite resentful of the situation and I hope he doesn't cause trouble but, if anything happens to us, the children have the capital investment and we have the liquid cash to be able to cope with any situation. We had planned that the kids would inherit from us, but we now have the humiliation of asking them to do this."

Madeleine frowned, working out the sense and potential pitfalls in this arrangement, while considering different approaches to the problem. "Hopefully, Hugo will find it useful talking to Adam."

"I'm sure he will. Although, Hugo won't divulge any of our personal finances. I'm just telling you privately. Men don't share too much. They just acknowledge each other's difficulties and make allowances, but perhaps Adam can help Hugo have a different perspective on his problems with the bank. It'll be in the newspapers soon, anyway."

"Just like my little experience, I expect," sighed Madeleine, the weary strain returning. She heaved a deep sigh, thinking that if Colin never re-appeared she would be spared the intrusion of a court case and publicity in the newspapers. After a few moments, she brightened up and, forcing a cheerful note into her voice, suggested, "How about some tea and getting stuck into that chocolate cake?"

"Sounds good."

"OK, let's summon the boys." Madeleine led the way, through the garden, towards the study window. Tapping on the glass and peering in, she called out, "Tea in ten minutes." Adam looked out and gave her the thumbs up sign.

Returning to the kitchen, Madeleine and Robina busied themselves setting out afternoon tea. Pretty china tea cups and saucers tinkled against silver spoons, as Madeleine carried the loaded tray into the hallway. Robina followed behind, proudly bearing the chocolate cake on a large platter in one hand, while grasping the teapot with the other. Hearing the imminent arrival of their wives, Hugo quickly concluded their discussion. "So you can see how serious it is, Adam. A fellow banker on Wall Street has just been sentenced to eighteen months in prison for obstruction of justice in connection with an email message."

"Open up," Madeleine called through the study door. Swiftly, Adam threw open the door and stood aside to allow the little procession to enter. "Come in, ladies. This looks wonderful. What a treat." His eyes brightened with appreciation. Hugo's eyes widened as he imagined a huge slice of cake comforting him in just a few moments.

Once they had settled down to enjoy the convivial refreshments, Robina continued with her little anecdotes. Social chit-chat did not come easily to her, but they all understood that she was making the effort to cover what might otherwise be uncomfortable silences. "I visited Aunt Mavis in Oxford last week," she announced. "She had a nasty experience while out shopping. She's ninety three years old, you know, and still going strong. A young man on a bicycle crashed into her and she ended up with a broken arm and shoulder. Poor thing. But you know what she said to me? 'I'm very lucky,' she said, 'if I was an elderly person, I would have been killed.'" Aunt Mavis's positive attitude fostered wide smiles all round.

Seizing the moment, Adam's face took on a jovial expression. "Did you hear about the old guy of seventy who married a young girl of twenty?" He paused, waiting for his little audience to catch up with his mood. "Well, his doctor advised him that sex could be fatal. "I understand, doctor,' the old man replied, 'but I'll just have to take that risk. If she dies, she dies.'"

Hearty laughter followed, interrupted by the phone ringing. Adam swiftly answered, "Oh, hello, Primrose." Madeleine shook her head.

"Primrose, Madeleine's just busy at the moment. Can she call you back? You're OK? And Marius? Yes, we're fine, thanks. Good to hear from you. Madeleine will call you back later." He replaced the receiver, noting with satisfaction that everyone's eyes were still twinkling with amusement.

"We best be off," Hugo ventured once they had all done justice to the tea and cake. "Really good to see you both. Thanks for the chat, Adam. Glad to see he's looking after you, Madeleine."

Somehow, there was little more to say. The respite of light-hearted moments had lifted their spirits and strengthened their resolve to deal with the difficulties ahead. Brief farewells were exchanged on the doorstep. Disturbed by their movements, a kestrel's rapid wing beats, interspersed with glides, focused their attention, his shrill cry a distraction away from the nest.

In silence, Adam returned to the study. Madeleine made her way back to the kitchen, muttering, "Must phone Primrose." Late afternoon. Where would Primrose be? At work, in the car or at home? Madeleine dialed the number and was pleased to hear Primrose's distinctive accent on the other end of the line.

"Primrose, thanks for phoning earlier. Good of you to call."

"Well, I just wondered how you were coping."

"I'm OK. Adam has taken this week off to be at home with me. He's arranged lots of treats, so it will be good to spend time together. Quality time, as they say."

"We were so shocked by what has happened to you."

"It's been the most unhappy time of my life. To be attacked by a man you knew and thought you could trust is difficult to come to terms with … the physical trauma … and the emotions … not what you ever expect to have to deal with … it happens to other people … you never think it can happen to you."

"Not in this country, anyway … in a quiet backwater like this. Madeleine, are you getting professional help? Counseling … that sort of thing …you really should, you know," advised Primrose.

"I'm sure you're right. I have to give interviews to the police tomorrow, so I expect I'll think about it after that." Wanting to shift the focus away from herself, she continued, "How's your mother's visit going, Primrose?"

"Oh, I just love having her here. She adores England. It's just not easy in our cramped living conditions when she's used to lots of space and not doing any housework."

"I can imagine."

"She's hopeless, really. She thought she would be helpful and hang the washing outside on the line, which I don't think she's ever done before. What she actually did was hang out the dirty washing which I had put in the machine, ready to switch on later. You would think it would occur to her the clothes weren't wet or didn't look clean."

"Oh, dear."

"Oh, and the cooking. Well, like I say, she tries to help. We were having roast beef yesterday. I should have known better. Marius and I were out working in the garden; he was mowing the lawn and I was doing the weeding. Mother asked if she could help. Well, she's never done gardening in her life so, to make her feel useful, we asked her to tidy up the kitchen and put the roast in the oven at a hundred and eighty degrees. It was only, later, when the fumes and smoke were pouring out of the kitchen that we realized she had set the oven temperature to the maximum of two hundred and eighty degrees and the meat was burnt to a cinder."

"Oh, my! You do have your hands full. What about the house move? Any luck?" enquired Madeleine.

"Not really. We were quite interested in a newly renovated three story place in the center of Andover, but then we discovered it was classified for multiple occupation, and couldn't legally be converted back to a single family dwelling. The agent didn't tell us this ... we only found out once we had incurred legal costs ... but maybe he was unaware. Who knows?"

"Well, the right thing will come along, eventually," Madeleine encouraged.

"Well, you just wonder if it's worth all the hassle. We're getting quite despondent. Anyway, enough of my domestic woes. How can we get you back to being yourself again?"

"Time. I guess it will take time."

"I guess so. Listen, I'll phone you each day and see how you're feeling. Would that be all right?"

"That would make me feel very good."

"OK. Will do. I'll let you get back to Adam now."

"Thanks, Primrose. 'Bye for now." Madeleine replaced the receiver. Dreamily, she stood gazing out of the kitchen window, her reverie only halted by a soft thump as an apple fell to the ground.

BACK TO BUSINESS

September brought dazzling days of fine English weather. Cars in driveways held a sheath of moisture overnight; windows gathered condensation by the dawn of morning; cloudless blue skies lifted spirits over breakfast; soft breezes fluttered gently through the day; early darkness heralded the end of summer.

Madeleine's life dragged on. Interviews with the police had been conducted. An arrest warrant had been issued. Adam's week at home had pulled her back from the brink; the heaviness in her heart had melted away. However, she had not orientated herself back into society; her days were spent reading, gardening, cooking and watching television. Eight weeks had passed and she had still not left the confines of her own home; the quiet cocoon of familiar and safe surroundings was a comfort she had no desire to shed. The phone calls and visits from friends and relatives lessened as they dealt with important issues in their own lives. The attack was becoming a past event in the minds of others, and Madeleine allowed herself to drift into a solitary lifestyle which left her undisturbed.

Adam returned home late one evening after a particularly tense business meeting. Madeleine had prepared a meager supper and had not bothered much with her appearance. Adam's mood was one of churning resentment; he had tolerated Madeleine's recuperation with great patience but his anger at her attacker had nowhere to go, since appeals for news of his whereabouts had been to no avail. Madeleine's lethargic existence worried him and her disinterest in attempting to return to a normal life frustrated his action orientated character. Settling down in the family room after supper, his features were tense and drawn as he poured coffee from a stoneware pot into matching cups; he watched, with annoyance, as huge drops splurged out onto the pale blue carpet, the dark stains penetrating the fibers. As Madeleine entered to join him in time to watch the nine o'clock news, Adam wearily stated, "There's something wrong with that coffee pot."

"What do you mean there's something wrong with it?" Madeleine's voice rose, as her brow furrowed.

"Well, there's coffee on the floor."

"How did that happen?"

"I don't know. I poured the coffee. It came out all over the floor."

"Get up," Madeleine instructed, as she inspected the area around his feet. "This is really serious," she announced, taken aback by the darkness of the stains.

"What do you mean, this is really serious? It's only a few drops of coffee."

"I'll have to use tons of water to get rid of this. You have no idea how difficult it is to remove coffee stains."

"Oh, shut your face," answered Adam, reverting to a childlike response.

"Shut your own it's uglier," retorted Madeleine. "I'm trying to help you and this is the way you treat me," she exploded.

"I don't want your help. You're just obnoxious and have been for weeks."

"OK, that's fine," yelled Madeleine. "You won't get it again. No help from me. In anything in life. Ever. Ever. In fact, why don't you just get out of my life?"

"I might just do that."

"Good. Do it tonight. Tonight. Tonight," she screamed.

Adam stormed out of the room and strode into the study, slamming the door behind him; he threw himself onto the leather sofa and switched on the television, the pressure around his skull mounting as he pushed away images of himself packing his bags and driving off into the night. Madeleine's heart was beating wildly with fury, as she used water to swab down the stricken carpet; she marched up and down the hallway into the family room with fresh bowls of water until her frantic efforts had removed the stains. The coffee cups stared back, the black untouched liquid an accusing statement. Slamming the stoneware crockery and coffee pot back onto the tray, she marched into the kitchen and threw the door shut with determined fury. Viewing the disarray in the kitchen from recent neglect, her energy focused on bringing order to the chaos; she grabbed all the homeless objects and threw them into their customary drawers and cupboards, slamming doors with as much vengeance as possible; she filled the sink with warm, soapy water and washed all the cooking implements which had been mounting up on the draining board for several days. Viewing the clean, tidy surfaces with satisfaction, she wondered how to vent the whirlwind which was swirling in her veins. Opening the refrigerator, she had an idea for creating further noise and grabbed every vegetable from the bottom shelves; she hauled out the food processor; she thrilled to the response of the pulse, as the chopper violated the air with a vicious whine. Crouching down to the bottom shelf of a corner cupboard, she hauled out a huge saucepan and emptied the finely chopped vegetables into its cavernous depths. An hour later an enormous pot of vegetable soup was born. Somehow, Madeleine's anger had completely disappeared as the soup had bubbled into existence, and a bubble of laughter had been injected into her heart. Striding back into the hallway, she softly opened the study door and, with an impish look, asked, "I've made a pot of soup. Do you want some?"

Somehow, the coffee and soup were milestones in Madeleine's recovery. As the next few days passed, her voice took on a more cheerful note and she walked with a little more spring in her step; she began to think of facing the outside world again. Only once she felt more optimistic, did she realize what a strain the attack had inflicted on her relationship with Adam; she resolved to get involved with the golf club again and to follow up on her intention to visit a professional counselor. Entering the study, she looked up the telephone number of the counselor but her courage dissipated as she was rewarded with an answering machine; refusing to falter, she left a message. "Hello, my name is Madeleine Minehead. I'm leaving a message for Martha Donovan. I need to arrange a few counseling sessions to discuss a criminal attack. My telephone number is 553264. I look forward to hearing from you. Thanks. 'Bye." How would she spend the day, waiting for the phone to ring? Well, she needed to make a bonfire to deal with all the garden rubbish and she could do with a haircut. Donning her grubby jeans, windproof jacket and sensible shoes, she strode into the garden, tucking the phone into her pocket so that she wouldn't miss any calls. On her way to the bottom of the garden, she dialed the number of her hairdresser.

"Hello, it's Madeleine Minehead. Could I have an appointment with Helen today? She's fully booked? Oh, I just need a quick trim. Couldn't she just squeeze me in? Yes, I'll hold on. Oh, she'll do me in her lunch hour? I do appreciate that, but she does need a break. I don't want to put her under pressure. Oh, she's very happy to see me? Terrific. Please thank her very much. See you at one thirty. Many thanks."

What to burn? There was a huge pile of debris from the inner sanctum of the pampas grass which begged to be reduced to ash, allowing new plumes space to flourish. The north wind had swept heaps of autumn leaves into convenient corners, waiting to be collected. Standing back, several hours later, with aching muscles, having watched the dry skeletons of nature flare up into yet another cycle of

swift footsteps; she could see her former life returning, beckoning her to take part. "...what will I wear ... gotta find something suitable for the weather ... looks like rain ... how about a golf shirt with lightweight trousers ... could wear the waterproof suit on top without being too warm ... what to change into for lunch ... maybe that pale blue suit ... probably the last chance to wear summer clothes before the clocks change ..."

As Madeleine's thoughts turned to the mixed competition on Sunday, she bounded upstairs ready to search through her wardrobe for suitable outfits for the occasion. The phone rang; she stopped halfway on the stairs, wondering whether to walk down or up. Down was quicker, she decided, her footsteps taking her into the hallway. "Maybe it's that counselor phoning me back," she thought.

"Hello," she answered eagerly.

"I hear you fought back."

Stunned by the voice, she was unable to answer. Panic swept her breast, but then she listened, shutting out all other sounds. Silence. Tension stiffened her body as fear entered her gut. "Who is this?" she demanded; at the same time, a voice inside her head told her she knew this man. A dim outline of his silhouette etched itself on her mind.

"Will you fight back with the other boys at the golf club?"

A demeanor entered her consciousness. The voice was slow. Slow, deliberate movements began to give bulk to the silhouette. "...keep him talking ... keep him talking ...," her brain told her, " ... you know this man ... you know this man ..."

"Who the hell are you?" she yelled. "How dare you!" He laughed. A feeble, weak laugh. " ... who is it ... who is it ...," her brain was racing, trying to fit all the faces of the men she knew to the voice.

"I'm free tonight. Would you like me to visit you tonight?"

Madeleine laughed. Hysterical laughter. She knew who it was; her natural ear for music picked up the intonation on the last syllable. " ... should I let him know ... should I let him know ... I know his identity ... I know his identity ..." Instinctively, she realized that blowing his cover would weaken her accusation. "Don't phone here again!" she challenged, as she slammed down the phone, hoping he would be unable to resist another attempt. Another attempt would catch him, once she could arrange for the phone line to be monitored by the police.

SMILE PLEASE

October rolled in on a wave of dry days. Autumn, which had gripped the nation in earlier weeks, loosened its hold. Lynn's fuscia pink outfit was much admired at her daughter's wedding celebration; her hat was a masterpiece crowned with fluffy pink ostrich feathers. The bride looked self-conscious in her magnificent, pearl encrusted, white gown as she led the procession of five bridesmaids, clad in yellow velvet, into the reception room. The groom stood, impassively, facing the procession making its way towards him; he read out a prepared welcome to the assembled guests who wondered at his accent and pondered who might have written his lines. No-one asked any questions about the wedding ceremony, although tidbits of information were slipped into conversations. Bright smiles, although a little forced, shone around the room. Gay laughter, although somewhat loud, filled the air. A collection of foreign looking persons silently watched the proceedings. Holding a glass of champagne and sporting a beaming smile, Lynn commented to Barry during a few brief seconds while they were not mingling with the guests, "Well, the Royals have been doing it for centuries. Arranged marriages are a mark of the upper classes."

"This is all a pretence and it turns my stomach," Barry replied in an uncontrolled, loud voice, his eyes roving round the room. A few heads turned as his words reached their ears.

"Anastasia introduced them, so you could say she was the matchmaker." Lynn's voice became louder for the benefit of onlookers.

"And who introduced Anastasia to Rodney?" Barry queried, with a smirk. He moved towards the bar. "I need another drink."

Lynn's ostrich feathered hat twitched vigorously as she looked around the room, hoping that no-one would hear; her taut nerves relaxed a little, remembering that she had invited nobody from the golf club, the guest list being limited to close family and her daughter's friends. A fading smile re-emerged as she imagined herself passing round photographs of the wedding party. Following in Barry's wake towards the bar, keeping her bright smile in place she hissed at him, "The taxi will be here in two hours. Try and stay sober till then." Barry winced at her words; he knew he shouldn't be drinking so much after his recent heart attack, but felt the alcohol helped ease the shock and strain of his daughter's situation. Unaware that forthcoming news would bring a bigger shock and change his life forever, Barry gulped at his glass of red wine.

The weekend passed. The wedding party and guests had dispersed. Barry was relieved that Monday morning had dawned, bringing with it freedom from family and domestic affairs. Breakfast was tea and toast, alone in the chaotic kitchen, before driving off to work. He delighted at taking the narrow twisting bends of the Hampshire countryside at top speed, hammering through the gears while the engine power invigorated his latest acquisition. "Well," he thought, "she spends plenty on all those daft outfits ... why shouldn't I spend money on things I enjoy ... I work damn hard ... work gives me a buzz ... hope we get that contract ... so, our daughter is married ... load of bollocks that reception ... just to keep up appearances ... wish I could feel content ... she's not found a good husband ... nothing but trouble ahead there ..." He nosed the Boxer into the yard surrounding the printing sheds, giving a grin and a wave to a passing Land Rover.

Lynn woke much later and realized, with a shock, that the photographer would be here soon; her mind whirled into gear, as she relished the anticipation of his visit. "... wonder what to order ... suppose he'll give us time to choose ... need to pass them around to everyone ... relatives first, probably ... can't wait to show them round the golf club ... I'm Captain ... need to stay on top ... can't let these women look down on me ... like when I was young ... nothing to be proud of there ... I'll show them ... photos should be wonderful ... really pleased with my outfit ... wedding party looked classy ... wish that guy spoke better English ... makes me feel uncomfortable ... anyway, grandchild on the way ... that'll make me feel old ... until then, live for today."

THE MIXED COMPETITION

The week passed. Mornings were duller. Evenings were darker. Wet and windy weather returned. Sunday morning. The day of the mixed competition. Torrential rain. Adam and Madeleine looked desolately out of the window. "It'll be cancelled," Madeleine announced, confidently.

"I hope so," Adam replied. "It would be madness to play in this weather."

"We don't have to play if our partners agree to pull out," soothed Madeleine.

"Phone and persuade them. Who are we playing with?"

"Well, it's not chosen partners. It's a draw," Madeleine's voice faltered.

Adam sensed he was not going to like the answer to his question. "So ... who?"

"Percy and Barbara ... there was nothing I could do about it."

"Pull out!" Adam shouted, angrily. "Phone them. Of all people, I need to be teamed up with that cheat like I need a hole in the head. I've got better ways to spend my Sunday."

Madeleine rang the number. "Barbara, it's Madeleine. Have you seen the weather?"

"Yes, pretty wet, but good news."

"Oh, yes?"

"The course is open. We can play," Barbara announced, enthusiastically.

"In this weather?"

"The only reason for not playing is if the course is closed."

"Oh, I see."

"So, our tee time is nine forty six."

"Eh ... right," responded Madeleine, stuck for words.

"So, we'll see you there."

"I'm hoping the course is closed, Barbara."

"You can't be Bronze Captain, Madeleine, and be a fair weather golfer."

"Apparently not. OK, see you there."

The mood over breakfast was sullen. Neither Madeleine nor Adam wished to be in the company of the Blunts. Driving towards the golf course, the monotonous mourning of the windscreen wipers soured Adam's mood increasingly, with each mile the car devoured. Removing their golf clubs from the car in silence, Madeleine observed her attacker's wife walking towards the pro shop. "I'll be back in a minute," she said to Adam, making her way towards Nancy Ruff. Seeing Madeleine's purposeful stride in her direction, Nancy's face flushed with confusion. "Nancy, could I have a word?" Madeleine spoke briskly. Nancy did not respond but waited for her to continue. "I'm not going to mention your husband. It's something else I need to talk to you about. You had a nasty phone call some months ago." Nancy straightened her posture. Madeleine continued, "Do you think you know who it was?"

"I have my suspicions." Nancy's eyes narrowed, as she spoke.

"I had a horrible phone call recently and I wonder if it might be the same person." Nancy's eyes widened. "I'm going to write a name down on a piece of paper. You can do the same. If we have the same name, perhaps we need to talk. Do you have something to write on?" Nancy wordlessly rummaged in her golf bag and took out a blank score card and short pencil; she tore the card in two, giving one piece to Madeleine. After writing a name on the card, she handed the pencil to Madeleine who followed suit; they exchanged cards, which had now become damp with rain, and were not surprised to see they had both written down the name of Rodney Crow. Madeleine nodded, "I thought so. We'll talk later."

Joining Adam back at the car, he looked at her searchingly. "What was all that about?"

"Obscene phone calls. She had one, too. We know who it was. Rodney Crow."

Adam froze. "How do you know?" Madeleine explained the exchange which had just taken place.

"Well, we'll see about this," was Adam's response.

"One problem at a time. First, we have to cope with four hours on the golf course with the Blunts," Madeleine sighed and added, wearily, "In the rain."

"I don't need this. I would rather stick needles in my eyes."

"Be a gentleman. Rise above it," coaxed Madeleine.

A cheerful group congregated on the first tee. "Hey, it's the Mineheads," called one voice. "Welcome back, you two," called another. Adam gravitated towards a group of men to discuss the latest sports results. Madeleine held back, not feeling in the mood for conversation;

she smiled wanly at the group but stood apart. Taking out her driver, ready for a practice swing, her eyes met a carpet of pine needles at her feet; she moved further away to a patch of rough, the spikes of her shoes crunching on fallen acorns. Scatterings of sweet chestnuts met her gaze, some still in bunches in their protective, spiky, green shells; others were cracked open with shiny centers exposed to the elements, ready to ripen in the forthcoming weeks. After a few swings with the driver, the attention of the others moved away from her, and Madeleine felt able to raise her gaze. Holly trees waved at her in the wind, their branches laden with red berries, ready to provide a winter feast for the bird population.

"Hey, the rain's easing off," a voice sounded. Madeleine looked up. Lynn Harper, standing close to Madeleine, had just spoken.

Moving over, Madeleine spoke softly to Lynn, "Unfortunate pairing in the draw for today."

Lynn looked at her expectantly, with a glint of mischief in her eyes. "Oh, yes, who have you got?"

"The Blunts. You know he was spreading lies about my husband. They're the last people on earth we want to spend time with," answered Madeleine.

"Would you like me to change it?" Lynn spoke with exaggerated innocence.

"And make a fuss? No, thanks." Madeleine moved away to join Adam.

"What's the format?" Adam asked.

"Texas scramble, I think."

"How does that go, again?" Adam asked for clarification.

"We all drive, choose the best shot, mark the spot, then we all play a shot from there, take the best one ... and continue like that until you reach the pin."

"Oh, how jolly. A team effort," Adam snorted.

"Let me check. I'll collect our card." Madeleine moved towards the starter, an elderly former captain who looked serene under his huge red umbrella. Greeting him with a cheery good morning and exchanging comments about the rain, Madeleine returned with the card tucked safe and dry in the pocket of her waterproof jacket. "The format is foursomes," she informed Adam.

"That's a relief." Adam gave a terse smile.

"So, we're actually playing against them. We have to decide who's taking which drives. Do you want odd or even holes?"

"Odd." Adam staked his claim.

"So, you take the first drive. Make it a good one," encouraged Madeleine.

The foursomes format was fortunate. In some ways, the rain was fortunate, too; it matched the mood of the Mineheads and the Blunts. The cold atmosphere between them competed with the ambient air temperature; their waterproof suits became darker in color as the rain took hold. The only conversation during the round was the affirmation of the day's format and confirmation of the score at the end of each hole.

Gradually, the rain eased off, and some patches of blue sky emerged. Moving off from the eleventh tee, after Adam hit a remarkable drive, Madeleine felt she had to be civil to Barbara, if not to Percy. "So, any holidays planned?" she enquired, addressing Barbara.

"Not till after Christmas."

"Spain again?" enquired Madeleine.

"Probably."

"Lynn and Cathy went to Spain together, didn't they? What part did they go to?"

Barbara snorted "Not any more."

"No? They don't like Spain now?"

"They don't holiday together now."

"Oh?"

"Well, you've been out of circulation. You probably haven't heard. They're not on the best of terms after that holiday."

"I suppose spending too much time together is stressful," ventured Madeleine.

"Well, Rodney's so tight with his money. He made them split the bill down to the last penny every time. He was even calculating who had what to drink and whose meal cost more. Then, Cathy was trying to take control about how much to tip the waiter; and if anyone was a minute late for anything, she gave them the sharp end of her tongue. She also tried to organize everybody all the time into doing what she wanted. So ... how to spend your time and how to spend your money ... sure fire ways to ruin a friendship."

Madeleine said nothing further on the subject. However, she was feeling assertive, particularly as she and Adam were winning the game, so far. She pondered for some time whether to raise the subject. Winning the twelfth hole, she decided to part the curtain of pretence. "You know your husband was spreading lies about Adam?" she ventured.

Consternation flooded into Barbara's face. "What are you talking about?"

"Percy was going round telling members that Adam is a cheat. Well, you should know that your husband is the cheat. Adam confronted Percy about it in the presence of another member of the club."

Barbara could feel her legs shaking; she didn't know how to respond to this statement. "I'm sure you've got that wrong," she answered.

"I certainly have not. He didn't deny it," countered Madeleine. "I'm not going to say any more about it, but you should know what's going on. You need to know how your husband is behaving."

Barbara recovered her composure, answering smugly, "Well, since I'm going to be Vice Captain, it's useful to know what's being said around the club."

Madeleine smiled, her eyebrows lifting at the news that Barbara was imparting. Shrugging off the information to the back of her mind, she assessed the next shot, decided to use her three wood off the fairway and, without a practice swing, landed the ball on the fringe of the green; an unkind bounce took the ball off to the right, but it was still a great shot and gave them the opportunity to sink the hole with a chip and a putt. The game continued without further conversation. The Mineheads were clear winners by the fourteenth hole, being five up with four to go; it was unlikely they would be winners in the clubhouse, but Madeleine felt satisfied that her two month layoff had little adverse impact on her game; perhaps her short game could be sharper, but she hadn't forgotten how to use her woods or irons.

Two heavy rain showers accompanied the four on their way towards the eighteenth hole. The first shower could be anticipated since heavy black clouds were looming in the distance; however, the speed of arrival and the severity of the second downpour came as a shock. There was no alternative but to hoist up the umbrellas and shelter under trees until the storm passed. Sleet was a contributing factor in the onslaught, melting as it touched the earth. The cloudburst passed, leaving a rainbow spanning the fairway ahead. Sunshine bathed the world in a flattering light. Long shadows accentuated the approach of winter. A gentle shower bade them a wistful farewell as the four made their way towards the eighteenth green. After signing and exchanging cards under the canopy at the pro shop, the four were liberated from the shackles of protocol which bound them together on the course.

"Who are we sitting with?" asked Adam, once the Blunts moved away.

"Well, them, obviously. We have to be at the same table, but we don't need to sit right next to them. Nancy and Darren were in front ... now, that's an interesting pairing ... so, they could be at our table, and they were playing with Alice and Don. Behind us were Hugo and Robina along with Marius and Primrose ... so, it could be that four. Tables of eight, so it just depends how it works out." Madeleine shrugged.

"I just want to get back home to the fireside and read the Sunday newspaper," Adam sighed, wearily.

"Isn't it nice that we beat them? You played really well. I didn't do too badly, either," ventured Madeleine.

"I don't care that we beat them. I just wasn't going to let them beat us."

"Anyway, I'll leave you to get changed. See you in the members' lounge."

Madeleine entered the ladies' locker room; the atmosphere was sullen; no-one had enjoyed playing in the rain. The usual vibrant chatter was missing while wet clothing was removed. Mutterings of complaint were escaping, "... my socks are soaking ... I'll need to get new shoes ... my gloves are both sodden ... my waterproof trousers are covered in mud ... my umbrella got ruined in a blast of wind ..."

Unpeeling her jacket, Madeleine looked up to see someone advancing towards her. "I told Darren about Rodney Crow's phone calls," said Nancy, under her breath. "He's furious," she added, with meaningful emphasis, as she moved towards the shower cubicles.

Primroses' locker was next to Madeleine's so they were able to exchange a few quiet words, as they swiftly removed wet garments. "I'm not going to bother with a shower, are you?" asked Primrose.

"Had enough showers out there," answered Madeleine, grimly. "You know, we were paired with the Blunts?"

Primrose gave a sharp intake of breath. "How was it?"

"We beat them." Madeleine couldn't prevent a little smug smile from appearing. "How was your game?"

"We won, too. Marius was hitting some lovely shots. Hugo was playing very badly, didn't seem able to concentrate. Wasn't much fun in that rain."

"You could say that. Can't wait to get stuck into some roast beef and a glass of wine." Madeleine zipped up her skirt. "Hey, Barbara tells me she's going to be Vice Captain," she confided to Primrose in a soft voice.

"Bit early in the year for that kind of announcement. It's only October. The changeover of office bearers is not until January. Lynn and Nancy must have asked her already." Primrose's voice tailed off.

"I guess so. Bit of a surprise she's let the cat out of the bag so early," commented Madeleine.

"That's Barbara for you. So, that puts me out of the running," sighed Primrose. I did have a tiny bit of hope that I might be asked. After all, I've done all the handicapping which is very time consuming. So ... I'll just have to swallow the disappointment. Maybe next year." Primrose's expression conveyed none of her feelings; her stomach was churning with resentment, but she managed to keep her features in their customary immobile mask.

"So, how's the house hunting going?" Madeleine changed the subject. "Did you like the one you saw the other evening?"

"Not really ... it needed such a lot done to it. Think we might wait until after Christmas to see how things are in the spring. There's very little on the market right now. Anyway, business picks up at this time of year, so we can't really spend any more time viewing houses at the moment." Primrose slipped on her Ferragamo shoes, admiring how neatly they encased her feet. The shoes were a farewell gift from her mother during their last shopping trip together in Winchester; the gift gave her a little pang of nostalgia every time she wore them, as she pictured her mother who had now settled back in South Africa after her recent vacation.

"I'm ready," said Madeleine. "How about you?"

"Ya, I'll come out with you," responded Primrose, her South African accent stronger as she still thought of her mother. Together, they walked out of the locker room into the corridor and along to the members' lounge. "It's good to have you here," said Primrose, squeezing Madeleine's arm. Madeleine felt a little glow of warmth touch her heart, giving her the confidence to meet the sea of faces in the members' lounge.

"Just look at that." Madeleine gazed, in wonder, out of the picture window. "A perfect autumn scene. Who would believe that we've just spent almost four hours in that awful weather." After the rain, it was a miracle. Sky bright blue, a gentle breeze sent sunlight dancing to whisper in the trees. The faint glimmer of gold promised greater glory to follow.

"Hey, Madeleine. Welcome back," a voice, close by, greeted her. A kiss was planted on her cheek. Others came towards her, making her shrink into a self-conscious withdrawal. Keeping her head down, but raising her eyes briefly as she passed each group to wave a hand in greeting, Madeleine followed Primrose as they made their way towards Adam and Marius who were already seated in soft armchairs.

Standing up to greet them, their husbands settled the wine order and passed the menu to Primrose and Madeleine. "What are you having?" enquired Marius, keen to send the orders into the kitchen.

"Roast beef," answered Madeleine. "I don't need to look at the menu."

"What about a starter?"

"Anything with fish?"

"Salmon terrine."

"Fine for me," nodded Madeleine.

"Primrose?"

"The beef, of course. Smoked chicken salad to start. What are you guys having?"

"We're both having beef. Adam's having duck pate to start. I'm having the soup. I think it's minestrone."

"OK, that's that taken care of." Madeleine settled back into the chair, grasping the glass of red wine with relish.

"Cheers," said Adam, raising his glass towards the ladies; he was rewarded with satisfied smiles and responses of, "Yes, cheers. Good health."

"You still looking to move house?" Adam enquired.

"Well, I was just telling Madeleine," Primrose replied, "we're going to wait till after Christmas. Prices are coming down and there's not much on the market, so we'll hold off and look again next year."

"Sounds sensible," Adam agreed.

"What do you think of Tony Blair's new house?" Madeleine threw out the question. Without waiting for an answer, she continued, "I read in the newspapers that he's bought that place for three million and they've put down one million as a deposit. He's got a tenant, already, who is paying a hundred and fifty thousand a year in rent. That's almost a million paid off, if you look ahead five years, taking account of rent increases. He intends to stay in office for another five years, and that looks like a fair bet. Even so, if he bows out of the top job, he'll earn a fortune in speaking engagements. It's a great investment. In five years time, it'll have soared in value. In the meantime, the rental income will have paid the mortgage and he can sell for a handsome profit."

"Interesting scenario," agreed Marius.

"Good luck to him, I say," continued Madeleine. "He must be one of the few people in the country not to have benefited from the property boom. Look at that Russian oligarch, whatever his name is. He waltzes into this country with his roubles and buys up prime property in London, as well as a bunch of major corporations. Tony Blair has given years of public service, but an unknown foreigner has more of a financial stake in this country than our Prime Minister. Just doesn't seem fair."

"Yes, and Adam couldn't afford to buy a major corporation," Primrose teased.

"No, but I'd like to," acknowledged Adam.

Hugo and Robina approached. "We're at your table," Robina stated. We've ordered our meal already."

"Great to see you." Adam stood up to give Robina a hug of welcome. Marius pulled over another two chairs before giving a handshake of welcome to Hugo and a kiss on the cheek to Robina. The others completed their greetings and the group sat in comfort, each with wine glass in hand.

Adam looked across at Madeleine; his heart leapt at seeing her in this environment. It was intensely gratifying to see her back in circulation. She looked so well; her skin glowed from the hours spent outdoors; she had become animated in her passionate outburst on the Prime Ministers' house purchase; she looked smart in her cream skirt and brown checked jacket; her slender legs were alluring in pale, shimmering stockings. The nightmare of her attack seemed to be over.

"How's business, Hugo?" boomed out Marius.

"Just great. Might be making a trip to the States very soon," Hugo replied, with a wry smile, looking around to see who might overhear.

"Oh, a quick trip for one of your meetings?" Marius was familiar with Hugo's frequent transatlantic flights.

"Not quite. I might be gone for a long time. Bit of an investigation at the bank." After a pause, Hugo continued, "Might be extradited."

"Extradited!" Marius's voice became louder. Heads turned towards their table.

"It'll be in the papers any day now, I expect," acknowledged Hugo.

"But ... that sounds a bit far fetched. Surely, it's only terrorists or drug runners who get extradited?" Marius looked shocked.

"Eh, no, Marius," Hugo continued. "The laws changed last year. The new Extradition Act is a treaty whereby the British government is required to hand over citizens to the United States, if the American government wishes to question those persons. The treaty is not reciprocal. The American government is not required to hand over anyone to the United Kingdom. I am not a criminal. No evidence has been provided to link me with any criminal activities. However, I may be charged with a criminal offence in connection with a transaction for one of our clients." Hugo spoke very firmly and in a steady tone; his face now reddened as he almost choked on his words and raised his voice. "Without any evidence," he emphasized loudly, his gaze scanning the room.

"Hey, man. How can that be?"

"Beats me, Marius." Hugo resumed his usual firm, businesslike manner. "The law is difficult to comprehend, at times." He lost his composure again, as he raised his voice, his face now reddening with the strength of emotion. "I am not a criminal."

Robina turned to Madeleine. "Do you pray, Madeleine?" she asked, almost in a whisper.

Taken aback by the question, Madeleine answered, "Well, no, not really. Other than to say 'God help me' and that kind of thing."

"I'm praying now. All the time," Robina stated. "This situation could ruin us. If Hugo is extradited, he could be imprisoned over there for ... up to two years before his case gets to court ... he would not be allowed bail. The legal costs of fighting the case could amount to a million pounds ... that money would be lost forever, even assuming the courts find him innocent."

Madeleine was aghast. "Dear God. I'm speechless."

"Pray for us, Madeleine. If you only say 'God help Hugo' every day, that's a prayer." Gripping the arms of the chair, tears filled Robina's eyes; she looked down at her feet, biting her lip to keep her emotions in check.

Madeleine put her hand over Robina's. "Yes, I will pray for Hugo. Every day."

"So, are you all having roast beef, then?" Alice queried, as she approached their table.

Facing Alice and Don, Primrose answered, "Of course. What else. You too?"

"I am, certainly," Alice replied. Turning to her husband, she enquired, "Don ... what did you order ... chicken in white wine, wasn't it?" Don nodded agreement. "You know, in some ways, I miss cooking roast beef at home on a Sunday. We used to have it cold the next day with potato salad. Actually, in our mother's day, they had roast beef on Sunday, ate it cold on Monday and made cottage pie with the leftover meat and vegetables on Tuesday."

"What did they eat on Wednesday?" teased Primrose.

"Probably nothing very much," answered Alice. "My folks were honest and hard working, but there was very little money." Catching her thoughts, she continued, "Oh ... and, if it was chicken, the carcass was used to make soup which lasted several days."

"So, how are you enjoying retirement, Don?" Primrose enquired, changing the subject.

"Yes. Good," answered Don, smiling benignly, but without saying anything further.

"I was quite worried about it." Alice took over the conversation again. "I know a lot of women who are struggling with their husbands once they retire. My neighbor's husband does nothing but play golf every day. He eats breakfast and lunch at the golf club, so it's a greasy fry up in the morning followed by sandwiches for lunch. It's such a bad diet." The others looked at Alice, indulgently, hoping someone would stop her hogging the conversation before she got into full flow. "And he used to do all the maintenance at home," Alice continued. "Now, he does nothing, and the house is falling apart. She thinks he's missing work. He's gone from being someone important to being nothing. She thinks he's depressed." The men looked at Alice, grimly, willing her to stop but she continued, "You see, the problem with men retiring is they have nothing to talk about. Another friend of mine, all her husband does is walk the dog. I told her he should get a little job, maybe two days a week. Nothing stressful. Just something to get him out among other people."

Mistaking all eyes riveted on her as fascination with her conversation, Alice continued unabated, "I'm hoping Don will start up a little business. Something we can do together. After all, we've both been working in the garden center all these years, so we do know a little. Nothing too demanding. Maybe something to keep us occupied a few days a week. That would be nice, wouldn't it Don?" She turned to look at her husband, who continued smiling, but said nothing. "But not at the moment. We're having too much fun with the motorbike."

"Motorbike?" Marius repeated, with great interest.

"Yes, got him a Harley Davidson for his birthday. A retirement present, really. We're getting all the gear now. Got our buckskin leathers. I sit on the back. It's great fun, isn't it Don?"

Don continued smiling, putting his arm round Alice to give her a big hug. "Best present I ever had," he acknowledged in his strong Hampshire accent, his face glowing with satisfaction.

"Has anyone not seen the photos?" Lynn approached the table now, beaming with pride. "My daughter's wedding," she continued.

"Oh, do let's see," Primrose encouraged. Marius rolled his eyes to the ceiling; he was ravenous and impatient to move into the dining room.

"Oh, my! Very posh!" Primrose commented. "Five bridesmaids, too.

Are those all her friends or some relatives?"

"All friends," Lynn answered. "They all wanted to dress up for the occasion."

"The groom looks quite handsome. Did I hear he's Turkish?" asked Robina.

"No, Russian, actually," replied Lynn.

"Oh, same as Anastasia," Robina recalled.

"That's how they met ... through Anastasia," confirmed Lynn. The group looked puzzled, wondering how Anastasia could become involved.

"Russia's not in the European Union, is it?" asked Alice.

"No, dear. Too exotic for that," Lynn smiled thinly. "Anyway, what do you think of my outfit?" she continued, deflecting comments away from the groom's immigration status, as she turned over another page in the photograph album.

All the men rolled their eyes, as the ladies continued to show an avid interest "Gosh, your hat is fantastic ... that color really suits you ... where did you get your shoes ... you decided against a handbag ... I hear Alresford has some really nice shops." were some of the many comments.

"Shall we eat?" Hugo suggested, seeing the steward gesture that their table was ready.

"Sure thing," responded Marius, jumping up from his seat. "I want to hear more about the motorbike, after lunch, Don."

The group moved into the dining room, taking their places at the table indicated by the steward. Madeleine made sure that she and Adam were seated between the other two couples, so that the Blunts would not be sitting next to them. Barbara and Percy joined the table just as the starter was served. Conversation over lunch was subdued, mainly focusing on the catering, the weather and the condition of the golf course. After the competition winners were announced, there was a general scramble to get back home. It had been a long day and everyone wanted to relax in front of the television. As they left the table, Barbara caught Madeleine's attention. "Could I have a word?" she asked with uncharacteristic meekness. Madeleine didn't answer but waited for her to continue. "About Percy."

"Oh, yes?" Madeleine looked surprised.

"Percy has recently been diagnosed with an illness. He's got Alzheimer's."

Madeleine froze. After a long pause, she stammered, "I ... don't know what to say."

"What can you say? I'll just have to cope," Barbara shrugged. "But I think it might explain the problem with scoring. I'm sure Percy genuinely believed Adam was cheating last time they played together."

"What devastating news."

"It's getting worse very quickly. So, like I say, I'll just have to cope. Anyway, I thought it was worth explaining to you, Madeleine."

"I'm glad you mentioned it, Barbara. Is it confidential?"

"I'm not making a secret of it. How can I? People will notice odd behavior."

"I expect you're going to have quite a challenge ahead of you. If there's anything we can do, please let us know."

"Thanks," Barbara acknowledged. "Anyway, better get home." Casting her eyes downward, she moved away towards the exit sign.

Madeleine felt a surge of pity for Barbara, as she watched her retreating from view. Having heard Alzheimer's described as the relatives' disease, it was impossible to comprehend the difficulties ahead. Barbara would need a lot of support. Sighing, Madeleine caught the attention of Adam who was with a group of men at an adjacent table, discussing the possible control of Manchester United by billionaire businessman, Malcolm Glazer. Surrounding the table were a group of ladies, chatting and laughing at some speculative gossip surrounding Anastasia and Rodney's affair. Silently, Madeleine mouthed the question, "Home?"

Adam nodded in agreement, imparted a few farewell comments and moved across to join her. "OK, let's go!" he urged, adding, out of earshot, "Get me away from that shower of cackling whores."

Madeleine chuckled. "You really are a shocker."

Darren was one of the few people left in the dining room; he excused himself during lunch to make some phone calls, and was now engaged in conversation with Rodney Crow. "So, Rodney, how's your game these days?" Darren enquired, with a sociable air; the lean, young frame and relaxed stance of the professional golfer contrasted with Rodney's jaded body and weary posture.

"Oh, alright, could be better," replied Rodney, his bulging eyes widening.

"Short game or long game? Where would you like to improve?"

"Can't seem to get the rhythm with my irons. Woods are OK, but approach shots to the green are letting me down," answered Rodney, despondently.

"Want a five minute refresher? I'm happy to take a quick look at your swing. Why don't we spend a minute or two on the driving range before you go home?" Observing Rodney's uncertain expression, Darren continued, "Oh, no charge. Courtesy golf lesson. Compliments of the house."

Rodney smiled greedily, his tongue slipping out to move from side to side. "Oh, that would be great," he replied.

Darren offered, "If you've got time, I can spend a bit longer with you. I was only going home to watch BBC television ... Michael Palin crossing the Himalayas ... but that's not on till later, anyway. Why don't you let your wife go ahead and I'll drop you off when we've finished?" Unable to believe his good fortune, Rodney eagerly agreed to the arrangement.

"OK, let's go across, now," suggested Darren, after Rodney had given his car keys to Cathy. They ambled slowly towards the covered driving range. As Darren opened the door, Rodney was surprised to see a number of young golfers practicing their game so late in the afternoon, as daylight was fading. "Let's use this bay here." Darren indicated the last bay on the right. "OK, grip this iron for me. Let's have a look." Darren studied Rodney's grasp of the club. "Why don't you have a couple of swings and I'll record you on the video." Darren moved beyond the bay in the direction of the video controls.

Rodney doubled over from the blow to the back of his neck; the golf club slid from his hands. Gasping for air, a kick to the back of his legs brought him onto his knees. A hand grasped his collar, pulling him upright. A fist connected with his chin, sending his neck snapping backwards. Another blow to his cheek; he bunched his fists, attempting to reach a protective crouching position. Blows rained on his head; he was powerless. He fell to the ground in a kneeling position, moving his hands to protect his face. Another kick to his thigh sent him on his side. Several kicks to his ribs clouded the world into a blackening fog; he was unable to focus on the sea of faces flitting in and out of his vision. A hand grasped his collar, twisting his silk tie, dragging him off the ground. A guttural voice split his consciousness, "One more phone call and your bollocks will feel the spikes from these golf shoes." The hand released its grasp, letting his head thud onto the concrete.

It was almost dark when Rodney regained consciousness, surprised to find that he was still alive. "Those guys on the driving range ... wonder if they're members of the club ... or local thugs ... what did they take ... my wallet ... my phone." Rodney's hands moved to his pockets to check the contents; numbness had entered his body; he found it difficult to move. Finding his possessions intact, his mind wandered again. "So, they didn't take anything ... wonder why they jumped me ...

where's Darren ... he brought me here ..." His mind was a blank; he couldn't think. Suddenly, the guttural voice echoed in his brain. "... the phone calls ... they know about the phone calls ..." Alarm spread through his head, adrenalin rushing into his veins as he recalled the rough voice giving him a warning. "... they know about the phone calls ... how could they possibly know ... doesn't matter how they know ... I'm a marked man ... everyone will know ... they must be mates of Darren's ... why should he care ..." Panic gripped him now. "... how am I going to get home ... Cathy ... what will I tell Cathy ... better phone her ..." Removing the phone from his pocket, he activated the signal and croaked "Home" into the voice recognition system; the call did not connect; the hoarseness of his voice did not register; he tried again to no avail. "... have to dial the number ... what's the number ...can't remember ... can't remember ..." Suddenly, clarity returned. "... check the menu ... must be on the list of last numbers dialed ..." He scrolled through the list. "... yes ... that's it ... that's it ..." He pressed the green button and watched the number connect on the screen. "Cathy? Cathy, it's me. Yes, I know it's late. No, I'm not drunk. I can't walk home. Cathy, please. I've been attacked. Come and get me. Please!" Relief flooded through, once he knew that Cathy was on her way. He realized he was cold now. "... why should Darren do this ... did people know about him and Anastasia ... why should Darren care ... the phone calls ... Nancy ... ah ... yes ... Nancy ... one of his ladies ... bored ladies who were glad of a bit of excitement ... could tell their friends ... give them a bit of attention ... bet they enjoyed it ... just as much as he did ..." He got to his knees now. Pain surged through him. Every inch of his body was in pain; sharp stabbing pains in his joints as he moved; dull, spreading aches in his guts; throbbing in his head; his vision clouded. The world spun round as he tried to get up. He crawled towards the wall of the driving bay, using the edge to claw his way to a more upright position. The effort of moving left him gasping for breath. Clarity sharpened his wits as he wondered what to tell Cathy. "... have to tell her I was mugged ... tell her they took my wallet ... she'll wonder about Darren ... have to tell her he tried to fight them off ..." He staggered out of the driving range towards some soft earth at the base of a tree. He dug a space with his hands and buried the black leather wallet containing all his credit cards and a wad of cash. "... come back and get it tomorrow ... come back and get it tomorrow ... yes, that'll work ... that'll work ..." He regained an upright position, keeping his knees bent; somehow, he didn't have the strength to stand straight. "... have to make a note ... this tree ... which one ... OK ... looks like a sycamore ..." He was guessing in the darkness. "... right ... count the trees ... five from the edge of the driving range ... should be able to find it ... come back tomorrow ... get it tomorrow ..." A car engine, droning in the distance, gave him hope. Holding his breath, listening. "... yes ... getting closer ..." Headlights entered the darkness, lighting up the entrance to the club house. "... must be Cathy ... must be her ... hope it's her ... need to get out of here ... out of here ..." He staggered back towards the door of the driving range, letting himself out onto the pebble drive. The headlights of Cathy's car dazzled his vision. He held up his hand, as if hailing a stranger.

PARCEL FOR YOU

"Parcel for you, Mrs Harper," the deliveryman announced cheerfully, as Lynn answered his knock at the door.

"Oooooh, thanks." Lynn signed the acceptance form, while scrutinizing the package. "Wonder what's in here?" She spoke to herself, dreamily imagining which of the many items she ordered might be inside the sturdy cardboard box. Closing the door and moving into the kitchen, she laid the parcel on the nearest countertop and switched on the kettle.

"Aaaahh! Cup of coffee. Put the wet clothes in the dryer and then sit back and open the box." She continued thinking aloud as she carried out her tasks. Filling a kitchen mug with instant coffee, she poured boiling water on the granules, added milk and sugar and moved into the family room holding the hot drink in one hand and gripping the parcel tightly with the other. She pressed the remote control on the TV and settled down to watch the personal crises of the British public on daytime television.

Barry had been in the office for several hours. Business had not been good for some years. Making profits in the printing business had become increasingly difficult; the sector had shrunk, as individuals became more computer literate. Every day, as he drove to work, he considered his options; whether to speculate in another direction, whether to downsize his operation by laying off staff or whether to sell out to a competitor. Each day, he viewed the difficulties from a different perspective. As yet, he had not come up with an attractive scenario. Each month, he lost ground by not tackling the issues. He was lost in thought when his intercom buzzed.

"It's the police," his secretary announced, anxiously. "They want to speak to you, Barry. Shall I send them through?"

"Oh, hell, what's this?" he answered, irritably.

"They didn't say. Shall I send them through?"

"You mean they're here in person? Well, I suppose so. What do they want?"

"They didn't say."

"I'll come out." Barry strode out of the office, still thinking about another possible course of action. Perhaps he could merge with another printing company. Perhaps he could approach the bank for a loan to secure a buyout. More time. He needed more time to consider his options. Two uniforms invaded the space in the outer reception area; politely introducing themselves, they suggested a private meeting. Barry ushered them into his office and offered them a seat.

"Mr Harper, we have some very bad news." Scanning their faces, Barry froze. The silence was endless. Curiosity and dread focused his hearing; his shoulders sagged; he exhaled slowly. "It's your wife," the officer continued. Barry's stomach churned. "There's been an accident." The last few words echoed in his ears. He blinked rapidly. "A fire ... at your home." Gauging his reactions, the voice continued, "I'm afraid your wife did not survive." Stunned, Barry could feel his scalp react as the words penetrated. Staring at the police officers, his world had suddenly become a hollow place. Words would not come. Numbness hardened his facial muscles to form a thick, protective mask. Tremors of terror shredded his guts. Sounds became muffled as his hearing rebelled against the news. "Would you like a cup of tea, Mr Harper?" the officer enquired, gently. Barry nodded slowly. The officer quietly left the room; his colleague waited silently.

The activity of tea being served by his secretary scratched at the shock. Barry made no attempt to lift the teacup. Questions were forming in his mind. "How ...?" he faltered.

"An electrical fault. Seems to have been in the utility room, possibly the tumble dryer. The fire department are there now."

"And my wife?"

The officer did not answer immediately, allowing a respectful silence. "The body needs to be identified. And there will be a post mortem, sir. I'm sorry."

"Can I ... should I ... go home?"

"Best not, sir. Are there any family members who need to be contacted?"

"My daughter." Recent memories of the wedding reception flooded back.

"Would you like us to contact your daughter?"

"No, I'll do that." Piercing his vision were recent items ... the wedding photographs ... Lynn's fluffy pink hat. Closing off his emotions, Barry took control. "If I can't go home, I'll have to find somewhere to stay. How long ...?"

The news spread fast. Words he never expected to hear floated around. Widowed. Life insurance. Death certificate. Mortuary. Funeral.

Living alone. He was the center of attention for several weeks with letters of condolence, sympathy cards, floral tributes and telephone calls raising him to a different spiritual plane. Once the attention tailed off, he was left with a void. Business didn't seem to matter, anymore; the golf club seemed an alien place; he was tired of staying in a hotel. Consolation came from a closer relationship with his daughter, although her situation worried him more each day. Gradually, the jumble of feelings settled down. He was left with one nagging feeling which would not go away. Guilt. He felt guilty about all the things he should have done, as well as all the things he wished he hadn't said; most of all, he felt guilty at all the secret thoughts he had harbored. Sleep was difficult. He closed his eyes, but sleep did not come. Only a light veil covered his eyes; he tossed and turned as tormented dreams darkened his world. Shunning friends and relatives, he spent his days shut in the office poring over paperwork; he spent his nights shut in the hotel room, hopping channels on television.

MARSHMALLOW

Bereavement counseling ... these were the latest words floating around; his daughter suggested it several times, but he had scoffed at the notion. As time passed, with each night becoming harder to face and each day becoming duller and more pointless, Barry considered the possibility. Next time his daughter mentioned it, he agreed to give it a try. Apparently, there was a Martha Donovan who was highly recommended; this afternoon was his first appointment.

Anticipation of a change of scene made Barry feel better, as he nosed the car along the narrow street of Victorian terraced houses. Number nineteen came into view, but there were no parking spaces on that side of the street; slowly, he moved on until he found a place to turn and was relieved to find a spot almost opposite the house. Crossing the street, he noted a bicycle claiming possession of the doorway. Dry leaves blown into a corner of the dusty black and white patterned tiles on a doorstep made him wonder about the occupant. Raising his arm to ring the bell, he felt rather vulnerable and was tempted to drop his hand. Surprisingly, before he could change his mind, his finger pressed the white button, making an urgent ring; he heard footsteps on a wooden floor.

"Hello, I'm Martha Donovan." She held the door open.

"Barry Harper. Three o'clock appointment." His features were tense; his feet thudded on the floorboards as he entered.

"Marshmallow," Barry thought afterwards, as he recalled his first impressions. A little over average height, and a lot over average weight. Martha's body bounced; he was sure, if he touched her, the flesh would yield and spring back into place. Loose fitting, flowing garments in shades of black and grey matched her random patterned hair in similar shades of grey and black; a little pink mouth, spread into a whimsical smile encouraged him; bright hazel eyes, lit with humor, beckoned him.

"Just follow me downstairs." Martha's broad back blocked his vision.

Clattering down the wooden stairs, he followed her into a basement room; a window, below ground level, looked out into a weed-infested courtyard. The room was sparsely furnished; polished wood floors, a coat stand, an electric clock on top of a battered antique bureau, two shabby but comfortable chairs and a small glass coffee table. Scented candles burned on the coffee table and on the bureau.

"Make yourself comfortable." Martha gestured to a chair, as she wriggled herself into position opposite him. "I hope you're OK with candles. I like candles." She smiled into his eyes.

"Yes, fine." He slowly eased himself into the strange chair; he liked the environment; it felt safe; he relaxed.

"So, just to follow on from when we spoke on the phone, Barry, you're here because you want bereavement counseling." Martha settled further back into her chair.

Barry wasn't sure what to say. He gazed into the flame of the candle. Martha waited. "Yes, my wife." He saw Lynn's silhouette in the flame. As the flame danced, he saw her dance. He felt numb. He didn't know why he was here. He didn't know what to say. He hesitated, before going on, "She would laugh in my face if she could see me now." He blurted out the words, lifting up his eyes to meet Martha's gaze; she narrowed her eyes in puzzlement. "This is the last thing she would expect me to do ... go for bereavement counseling." He spat out a laugh.

"You weren't close, Barry. You and your wife." Martha nodded, slowly.

"You could say that." After a lengthy silence, he volunteered, "My daughter sent me here."

"And you agreed to come."

"I agreed to come," he acknowledged, exhaling slowly.

"So, you need permission."

"No," he denied immediately, his brow furrowing at the statement. "I just wouldn't have considered it."

"But someone else suggesting it, makes it OK."

Barry's face puckered in thought. "Maybe. I'm not sure why that is."

"I wonder if things didn't happen without your wife's permission."

Barry laughed, bowing his head, resentment and a feeling of shame creeping out from behind a stone. He stared at his knees. He wanted to run away. His feet and legs ached to jump up and leave. He thought of all those people at the golf club and wondered, "...is that what they think ... that Lynn called the shots ... but she did ... let's be honest ... this isn't what I expected ... why am I here ... I expected sympathy ... what's this got to do with bereavement counseling ... but she's got a point ... it's true ..." He swallowed hard.

"Well, she liked to get her own way." He blew out a deep breath; he wanted a cigarette, even though he gave up ten years ago. He watched his feet twitch.

"Avoiding conflict is often the easiest way to deal with difficult people," Martha acknowledged. He looked up, grateful to feel the pressure ease. "I expect you found her quite demanding."

"You could say. It had to be all her way. Anything I had to say just brought on the tears. I couldn't stand the tears. She made me feel like a callous brute. Convinced me that everything she wanted was just little things."

"So, now you don't have all the demands. It's just you now, Barry. Just you, alone. No more demands."

Barry nodded. "You'd think I'd feel relieved, wouldn't you?" Martha gazed into his eyes, sharing his grief.

Barry threw himself back in the chair, his arms outstretched. "So, where do I go from here?"

"Where do you want to go, Barry?"

"I just don't know. I don't know. I can't go back home. She died in a fire. The place is being rebuilt. The insurance company are pestering the life out of me. I'm stuck in a hotel at night. I'm stuck in the office during the day. I feel like I'm in a prison. I'm free to do anything I want. I'm free to go anywhere I want. But, I feel trapped."

"Trapped. And you should be free."

"She's there. Accusing me." Martha looked worried, so he continued, "Like it's *my* fault this happened."

"Somehow, you feel guilty."

"Everything was always *my* fault."

"Perhaps she felt you didn't care about her."

"Maybe," he sighed; his shoulders sagged.

"Perhaps you didn't love her."

"I think I hated her, actually."

"And she knew."

Barry nodded, straightening himself up now, into a defensive pose.

"It's good to acknowledge these things. It's good to unlock those feelings." Martha's voice was soothing, comforting.

"She changed. We were young, it was fun, we got married. But then she changed."

"People do change. Circumstances change."

"The business became successful. I was working longer and longer hours. I neglected maintenance at the house. She didn't seem to understand. I was doing it for the family. She started being silly. Spending money on stupid stuff. Never at home. Always at that damn golf club. Always whining about something. Maintenance needing done in the house. People upsetting her. And the tears. When things didn't please her. She threw things. Anything. Plates. Anything that was near at hand. I couldn't stand it. I would just get out of the house and come back when she had calmed down." Barry's face was contorted with distress.

"A bit of a handful." Martha nodded.

"Nothing seemed to please her."

"You didn't always hate her. Sometimes you loved her."

A huge sense of loss welled up in Barry. Tension spread across his shoulders, rising up his neck. Tears pricked his eyes; he smiled, remembering times when she was happy ... at a golf club dance, wearing a new outfit, laughing and dancing ... when they first met ... the wind blowing in her hair.

"Sometimes, she was the girl I once knew."

"Carefree," stated Madeleine.

"Carefree. That's how we used to be. We used to do things together. We used to have fun."

"Before you had responsibilities."

"Before I had to do everything she wanted. I had to mix with her friends. People at the golf club. I had to do what she wanted at weekends. Always at that damn golf club. She was the Captain this year. Every day was taken up with golf. Not just this year." He shook his head. "Many years."

"I can see it made you angry." Martha nodded.

"She didn't seem to care. We always had to do what she wanted."

"And she wanted to spend all her time at the golf club."

"Trying to impress people," Barry snorted.

"You had arguments," pondered Martha.

"Lots." Barry grimaced at the memory of all the disagreements.

"And you said things."

Barry didn't answer. He stared at his hands. Quietly, he answered, "I said lots of things." He watched the candle flicker. "Things I wish I hadn't said."

"We all say things we wish we hadn't."

"But they don't come true, do they? I ...", his voice trailed off. "One thing, in particular, I wish I hadn't said." He paused, a slight rocking movement took hold of his body. "The last argument we had. It was bad. I told her ... I told her she could burn in hell, for all I cared. If I hadn't said that. If I had looked after the maintenance in the house ..."

"You're blaming yourself for her death."

"If I hadn't said that ... maybe ... maybe ..."

"Maybe the fire wouldn't have happened." Martha finished the sentence for him. "You didn't start the fire, Barry. You're not responsible."

"But I *am* responsible. I wished it on her."

Martha sighed. "Perhaps you want to believe that you *are* responsible for the fire."

"Why would I do that?"

"Power? Regaining power in the relationship?" Martha suggested.

Barry's eyes wavered as he considered this possibility. Somehow, a space opened in the wall of guilt. He stared ahead, looking at the avenue created by the space. He sank back into his chair. Martha watched carefully as his expression changed from one of distress to a calmer, reflective look. He moved one arm and swallowed.

"You want to be able to move on from this, Barry. You don't need permission from anyone else. You have the power."

Barry watched the clock on the bureau, silently ticking away the rest of his life. Leaning on the arms of the chair, he smiled. "This isn't what I thought it would be." He shook his head. "Bereavement counseling. I thought you would sympathize with me ... tell me what to do."

Martha smiled back. "You'll get plenty of advice and sympathy from friends and relatives. Counseling is something different, altogether. This is a difficult time in your life."

"That's true."

"You have a lot to think about. You need time. So, speaking of time, our time is up for this session, Barry."

Barry looked a little bewildered, as if he was waking from a dream. Martha continued, "You can come back and talk again ... or not. Whatever you want to do."

"I'd like to come back." Barry nodded vigorously.

"OK. Let's do that. Let's talk again." Martha leaned forward in the chair, at the same time raising herself slightly. Barry mirrored her movements and stood up. Martha led the way back up the wooden stairs to the narrow hallway; she opened the door, smiling as Barry stepped back out into the real world. He crossed the street to his car; he spent some time sitting in the driver's seat to orientate himself back into his own world, before driving off slowly to the end of the street and into the mainstream of traffic.

CATHY AND RODNEY

"What happened?" was Cathy's first question, as Rodney opened the car door. He staggered towards her and slumped against the side of the car; she was about to go out to help him, but he managed to ease open the door and drop himself into the passenger seat.

"Attacked!" His words were slurred.

"Let me see." The dim courtesy light in the car showed blood on his mouth; his clothes looked disheveled.

"Who attacked you?" Cathy wanted to know.

"Dunno. Been mugged. Took my wallet." He gasped out the words.

"I should get you to the hospital."

"No, no. Just get me home."

"How badly are you hurt?"

"Dunno. Just get me home."

Cathy clamped up, saying no more; she drove at a steady pace along the familiar route. It was eerie, driving around the country lanes at night; no streetlights, nothing moved, the headlights collided with high hedges, vision was limited to the next twisting bend. She kept her wits about her, concentrating on keeping the car within the white lines, knowing that the headlights of another car would be seen for miles around, but that she had to be alert for sudden hazards. The silence in the car was loaded; he had told her nothing and yet there were many questions forming in her head.

Automatic reaction forced Cathy's foot onto the brake pedal; something caught her vision ahead. A blur, a few yards in front, blocked the road, swiftly disappearing into the night. "What was that?" she called aloud. Getting no answer from Rodney, she answered her own question. "Probably a fox. Tawny color. About the right size. Just caught a last look at the tail, as he crossed the road." She realized she was talking to herself; looking across at Rodney, she saw that his eyes were closed, his body slumped against the door, his head resting against the window. Cathy felt really fearful now, wondering if he was alive or dead. Tension kept her staring ahead for further hazards, her stomach knotted into spasms of dread. A few more minutes would get them home. She stretched out her hand, prodding his stomach to see if he would respond. A deep moan escaped him; his head moved slightly; no further reaction. "Well ... he's still alive," she thought, "... have to see to him when we get home ... medicine cupboard ... everything in there I need." After what seemed like hours, but was only minutes, she nosed the car into the driveway onto the yellow brick paving. "Forget the garage ... leave the car out tonight ... need to get him indoors." She switched off the lights and the engine, thankful for the streetlights illuminating the surroundings. Getting hold of Rodney's jacket, she pulled him away from leaning on the window and allowed his head to slump forward onto the dashboard. Moving round to the passenger door, she gently eased the door until it was wide open.

"Rodney, you're going to have to wake up now. We're home."

"Whaaaat?" he moaned.

"Pull yourself together," Cathy said in a loud voice. "If you can't wake up, I'm going to have to get the neighbors to pull you out of the car. You got into the car. You can get yourself out again." He moved one foot onto the driveway. "That's it. Come on. The other foot now," she encouraged. "Right, I'm here to catch you. Just lift yourself up into a standing position." He did as he was told. "Right, drape your arm over my shoulders and we'll walk to the door." They staggered together to the doorway. She leaned him against the wall of the threshold, making sure he was going to stay upright, before inserting her key into the lock. She ran inside to turn off the alarm and returned to find him, thankfully, in the same position. "OK, my boy, into the house." He obeyed her instruction; she steered him into the kitchen and sat him on a hard chair; he slumped over, resting his head on the table. She retraced her steps into the hallway and closed the front door. Returning to the kitchen, Cathy announced, "Right, my boy, I'm going to make some tea and get you cleaned up. Then, you're going to tell me what happened."

A few minutes later, with a mug of tea in his hand, resting his head on his elbow, Rodney came under scrutiny. "Right, tell me what happened," Cathy demanded.

"Good job you used to be a nurse," he muttered cynically, fingering the bandaging she had administered.

"Yes. Lucky for you, and lucky you appear to have nothing broken. A visit to the hospital tomorrow is probably in order. Now, tell me what happened."

Rodney gave her his version of events; he told her that Darren had given him the lesson, that a gang had attacked him and he woke up with his wallet missing; he didn't know what happened to Darren.

"I'll phone Darren and find out what happened." Cathy rose from her chair, purposefully.

"No. Leave it. It's late. I'll phone him in the morning," Rodney insisted.

Giving him a hard look, her eyes glittering with suspicion, Cathy shrugged. "Suit yourself. In the meantime, you need to get into bed. You'll be very sore in the morning. I'll use the spare room." She offered him her shoulder to lean on. Together, they climbed the stairs. She settled him in the main bedroom, collected her nightdress from under the pillow and padded, barefoot, into the spare room.

Morning light, filtering through the thin curtains of the spare room, caused Cathy to wake; opening her eyes, she stared into the blankness of the cream colored wall; she recalled the events of last night. Swinging her legs onto the floor, she moved quietly to the next room to check on Rodney; he looked peaceful but she wanted to check his condition.

"Good morning, Mr Crow. How are we this morning?" she called in a loud voice from beside the bed. Rodney's eyes opened. "How are you?" Are you feeling sore?" He nodded. "Would you like some breakfast?" He shook his head. "How about some tea?" He nodded slowly. "Where are you most sore?" She wanted to get him to talk.

"Here and here," Rodney answered in a feeble voice, pointing to his ribs and his leg.

"Well, you might just live." She smiled. "We'll have another look when I bring the tea. In the meantime, I'll get some clothes on quickly." Cathy opened the wardrobe, taking out a pair of jeans and a purple polo neck sweater. Moving back to the spare room, she pulled on her clothes, made the bed and went downstairs to the kitchen.

As the kettle boiled, the doorbell rang. Checking her watch, Cathy saw that it was just after nine o'clock. Looking out of the sitting room window, she was alarmed to see a police car in the driveway.

"Sorry to disturb you, Madam, but we're looking for a Mr Crow. Does he live here?" the constable enquired, when she opened the door.

"Well, yes. Is there something wrong?"

"We would like to talk to him."

"You would? Why?"

"His wallet has been handed in to the police station. Found by an honest gentleman walking his dog, this morning. The dog unearthed it under a tree."

Cathy's brow furrowed, while she considered this piece of news. "Well, actually, he's in bed at the moment."

"Perhaps you would tell him we called. We can come back later when it's more convenient," the police constable smiled, politely.

"Yes, that might be better," Cathy agreed.

"We'll be passing this way around lunch time. Would that be suitable?"

"Yes, fine, I think."

Rodney looked very surprised when Cathy gave him the news. By lunchtime, he had managed to get dressed; he was in the sitting room, waiting anxiously, when the constable returned. Moving to the door with difficulty, he signed for the return of his property, shrugging off the questions about his injuries. Removing the wallet from the clear plastic bag, he noted that everything seemed to be intact although particles of earth were invading every compartment. He smiled thinly to himself, his bulbous eyes narrowing in the process. He removed the cash and credit cards and walked towards the video cabinet. Opening a drawer holding dozens of videos, he quickly dispersed the cash and credit cards among the cardboard covers. "Cash and credit cards are missing," he called out to Cathy as he walked into the hallway, towards the kitchen. "You won't be able to use the cards. I'll have to phone and report them stolen."

"What about Darren? Aren't you going to phone him? Why didn't you tell the police you were attacked, Rodney?" Cathy questioned him.

"Who needs all the questions? Forget it. It's over," he answered curtly. "Are you making some food? I fancy bacon and eggs."

Rodney made short work of the late breakfast, scraping the plate with his knife and fork. The screeching sound never ceased to irritate Cathy, but his slight deafness seemed to eliminate this pitch from Rodney's hearing; she watched him carefully as he ate greedily, a faint feeling of nausea permeating her senses as he ate without any refinement; somehow, she couldn't take her eyes away. After noisily chewing the last scrap of bacon, he clattered the knife and fork onto the plate.

"Right, I'm going back to bed," he announced, heaving himself up to a standing position. "Oooooh, that hurts," he groaned.

"I'll help you upstairs, but you need to get to the hospital," Cathy urged.

"I'm fine. I'll manage." He slouched out of the kitchen; she heard him make his way slowly upstairs, puffing and moaning.

Cathy made her way into the sitting room. Earlier, she heard Rodney open the drawer of the video cabinet and wondered what could have prompted this action; she decided to investigate. Trawling around the drawer, she could see nothing that attracted her attention. Still puzzled, she decided to take each video out of the cover. The fifth tape revealed its secret, then the seventh and several more after that. Once she had searched every video, Cathy recovered all the credit cards and cash. Twisting her mouth in deliberation, she pondered the possible reasons for this odd behavior. Concussion would hardly explain it. She heard him snoring upstairs and decided to look for his wallet. Climbing upstairs, she entered the bedroom and saw the wallet in a plastic bag at the side of the bed. Moving towards the bed, she dared to take the chance. She lifted up the bag containing the wallet, turned around and quietly slipped into the spare bedroom. She eagerly took out the wallet, watching particles of earth fall onto the carpet. Opening every compartment, while listening intently to the volume and frequency of Rodney's snores, she carefully examined the contents of his wallet. Lottery tickets at the back, a bunch of business cards tucked into the next compartment, credit card receipts at the front. Two compartments were empty, presumably where he normally kept his cash and credit cards. Cathy checked the business cards, first of all. A huge cloud of worry descended on her world. Each business card was printed with the name of Rodney Crow, all with their home telephone number, but each card represented different companies, the names of which she had never heard; some of the cards were actually printed in languages she could not understand and in lettering she did not recognize. Cathy's stomach flipped over; her fingers trembled as she removed the credit card receipts of which there were only three; the first was for a winter coat he had purchased in Harrods, the second was for a lawnmower, the last was for a hotel room in Paris. Nothing too sinister in any of that, except she was unaware the coat had been bought in Harrods; she had assumed he made the purchase in Winchester since he hadn't mentioned being in London recently. The lawnmower ... that was sitting outside in the garden shed. The hotel in Paris ... well, the odd thing was he never stayed overnight when he went to France; he always hired the white van and came back within twenty-four hours, there was no need to stay overnight. The snoring stopped; Cathy froze; the sound of her racing heartbeats was all she could hear. She listened, heard him turn over in bed. She heaved a sigh of relief. She tiptoed downstairs, grabbed a pen, wrote down the name and telephone number of the Paris hotel on a scrap of paper and crept back upstairs. Sitting on the edge of the bed in the spare room, she carefully returned everything the way she had found it; she picked up the particles of earth from the carpet and tucked them back inside the wallet. Stealthily now, she made her way towards the main bedroom. The snoring was steady. She moved slowly and silently until she reached his bedside, placing the plastic bag containing the wallet back in its original position. She stood staring at him for some minutes; the urge to place a pillow over his face was strong; it would be easy to stop him breathing; her head pounded at the thought of removing him from her life. Suddenly, his eyes flew open in alarm.

"What is it?" he demanded.

Cathy felt cool and in control. "What do you mean?" she answered coldly.

"Why are you standing there?"

"Just making sure you're alright."

"Well, I am. You gave me the creeps standing there like that." Rodney raised himself on his elbows and turned over. "I'm getting up now."

"OK. I'll leave you to it." She turned out of the room and downstairs into the study.

Cathy sat at the desk in the study, staring into space, her mind in a dream; she heard him moving about upstairs; she thought about what she had just discovered. All her suspicions were aroused. Rodney was not quite what he seemed; she had turned a blind eye to that for a long time, but now needed to face reality. "... should I just let it continue ... say nothing ... ask no questions ... after all, nothing has really changed ... he still lives in this house ... he will still pay the bills ... we would still share the same bed ... we would still lead different lives ... only golf is a shared interest ... stirring things up would just make it difficult for me ... just let it continue ... wonder who attacked him ... wonder what that's all about ... must be shady business dealings ... wish I could talk to someone ... that hotel bill in Paris ... really curious ... think I'll phone and check up on that ... wouldn't change anything ... just satisfy my curiosity ... where would I go if I left him ... a woman on her own ... not an easy way of life ... would have to find a house ... would have to pay the bills ... don't think I could manage from my earnings ... wish I could talk to someone ..." Rodney's footsteps on the stairs brought an abrupt end to her musings.

PRIMROSE AND MARIUS

November slipped into the calendar. British Summer Time ended with clocks moving back one hour. Store windows displayed skeletons and witches, pumpkins and broomsticks. Newsreaders sported poppies in their lapels. The morning air was disturbed by the blasting snorts from domestic blowers chasing autumn leaves into mounds for mulch. The night air was split with the whine, boom, bang, crack, spurt and fizzle of fireworks. Colored stars in fleeting bursts of wonderment claimed the blackness of the skies. The population concentrated on their daily lives; hiring fancy dress costumes; making toffee apples; buying poppies from war veterans. Mothers woke households on misty mornings. Children returned to school after half-term. The work force traveled on pavements, buses, trains, bicycles, and cars to reach their place of employment.

"I hate this weather," Marius complained.

"You don't notice the autumn colors or the holly berries, do you?" answered Primrose.

"I notice them. I appreciate them, but I hate this time of year."

"You don't notice when it's a beautiful autumn day, when the sun is shining, the sky is blue, it's not cold and you can enjoy a pub lunch outdoors even in November."

"I notice grey skies, rain, darkness, and people who don't smile."

Primrose sighed. Time was running out. Marius was restless, his vision more and more focusing on the country he had left behind. Truthfully, Primrose felt the same, but she tended to balance aspects of England and South Africa, whenever Marius lapsed into a negative viewpoint. If they were both totally honest, the reasons for living in England had changed. At the same time, the reasons for not living in South Africa had also changed. They had arrived in England with trepidation. Looking on the pessimistic side they had envisaged making no friends, not being able to afford a decent house and finding it impossible to set up business. Instead, they had generated a wide social circle, they could afford a larger property but were yet to buy one, and the business had developed so well they might think of expanding. Concerns about education had been a big factor, too, but the children had adjusted well to their new environment, although their streetwise awareness of sex, drugs and other adult issues was a surprising aspect of the youth culture in England.

Primrose sighed again; South Africa would never let go of their hearts. The humor, the way of life, the ease of welcome into each other's homes and family ties had never released their magnetic hold. Relationships with Marius's brothers were becoming a little tense; they felt that his father, approaching the age of seventy and in good health, should be allowed to retire from the business or, at least, take life a little easier. The two brothers were struggling to keep the business going. Marius had been the driving force in starting up and expanding the dry cleaning shops around Johannesburg; without his energy and vision, the business was not doing well; his brothers had recently suggested the partnership should be dissolved so that they could all liquidate their assets. Marius was loath to cut his ties with his homeland and was feeling increasingly restless; he wasn't sleeping well at night, tossing and turning as he agonized over the situation; he spent more and more time at the pub, dulling his anxieties with beer. Primrose was feeling stressed with their circumstances. Marius was becoming aggressive, shouting and swearing whenever she tried to discuss their future. Tears filled her eyes at the memory of their recent argument; he had become violent, grabbing her by the shoulders and shaking her before pushing her to the ground; she lay sobbing on the floor, but he had drunk too many beers to care about her distress. On the following morning, he had taken her breakfast in bed, his way of saying sorry but the memory lingered on; she still felt humiliated and angry.

Reflecting on how life might develop in England, Primrose fervently hoped that moving house would give them all a new lease of life; with increased living space, she hoped that Marius would not feel the need to spend his evenings in the pub; the children would have more peace to do homework and a bigger garden to play with friends. Primrose longed for more time at home; once they had moved house and became accustomed to paying a bigger mortgage, she hoped that she could cut down on her hours in the shop; surely her dreams would turn into reality soon. Looking further ahead, she hoped that her commitment to the golf club would produce her nomination for Captain; she longed for the esteem and recognition, which would seal her endeavors in the community.

Agonizing over their situation, Primrose considered all the angles as she made breakfast on a chill November morning. "... what would I gain by going back to South Africa ... well, sunshine and family ... how much do family count ... Marius's father and brothers matter a lot to him ... I miss my mother ... but she could come and live with us here ... that would be best for mother ... healthcare ... she would get better healthcare here ... no brothers and sisters on my side ... no-one else to look after mother but me ... no family for me to miss apart from my mother ... although, I do miss Marius's family ... the wives and children ... we're not connected here ... no family ties ... it does make a difference ... but I don't want to give up our chances here ... just when we're on the brink of achieving our ambitions ... a new house ... more space for the kids ... more time for me ... maybe Captain at the golf club in a few years ... that would mean a lot ... but Marius ... I don't like the drinking ... he wouldn't be doing that in South Africa ... no pubs there ... he would have to drink at home ... he never used to drink every night ... only when there was company ... too easy to find drinking companions here ... strangers ... don't know who he's mixing with ... same with the kids ... the street culture here worries me ... they can walk anywhere ... walk to school ... walk to shopping centers ... too much freedom ... don't know who they're with ... or the dangers they face ... freedom for them ... but worry for me ... in South Africa they need me more ... need me to drive them everywhere ... more control over the children there ... what about me ... what's best for me ... probably I would stay here ... at least a bit longer ... achieve our ambitions ... bigger house ... expand the business ... become Captain at the golf club ... but I could do all that in South Africa ... just don't want to give up here, before we get to the end of the journey ... but the pressures have increased ... from Marius's brothers ... life has moved on ... didn't plan to go back to South Africa ... determined to make a go of it here ... and we have ... just don't want to look back with regret ... the children have a better future here ... wish we could persuade Marius's family to live in England ... but Marius ... our marriage ... our life here has put a strain on him ... he depends on me in the business ... better to depend on his brothers ... short term gain to go back ... look further ahead ... maybe we need to go back for a few years ... sort things out over there ...we could let a manager run the business here ... or Marius could go back on his own for a while ... that would be no good for our marriage ... some woman would get her claws into him ... a man alone ... not a good scene ... he wouldn't look after himself properly ... could stay with his brothers ... but that would only work for a little while ... maybe we should just sell everything up in South Africa ... the house and the business ... cut our ties ..."

"Mum, where's my football socks?" called her son from the top of the stairs; his voice brought her back to the day's activities.

"Down here. In the laundry basket," she called back. Her musings continued, "... that's another thing ... have to do all my own housework here ... all my own laundry ... Marius has to do the garden ... wouldn't have to do that in South Africa ... easy to get people to help there ... easier life ... driving is easier ... parking is easier ... everything is easier ... cost of living is cheaper ... but the children ... they have a better future in England ... better career prospects ... but Marius ... the drinking ... his brothers ... the business ..."

"I've got orchestra practice after school today," her daughter announced, as she propped her violin case on the kitchen counter.

"... orchestra ..." Primrose continued to swirl thoughts around in her head like tea-leaves in a cup, hoping for an answer "... that trip to Leeds Castle ... when we first came to England ... we went to an open air concert ... we were enchanted ... the castle ... everywhere so green ... everywhere so lush ... everyone so posh ... picnics everywhere ... white table cloths ... dining tables ... people had brought dining tables ... and silver candelabras ... they lit candles as dusk fell ... enchanting music ... fireworks at the end ... a wonderful summer evening ... enchanting ... but we were new here ... tourists really ... that's how it still feels ... as if we're tourists ... we'll never fit in ... not really ... we'll never feel English ... perhaps the kids will feel English ... eventually ... but not me ... Marius ... oh, I don't know ..."

"That's the postman," her younger son yelled, his feet thudding loudly on the stairs as he raced towards the door: picking up the envelopes on the mat, he brought them into the kitchen, sifting through the mail for clues. "One from South Africa," he shouted with excitement.

"Will you stop yelling!" Marius chastised the boy. "Give it here." He stretched out his hand for the letter. "Who's it from?"

"Pretorius. To Mr & Mrs Pretorius. From Mr & Mrs Pretorius," the boy answered, smugly, handing over the blue airmail letter.

Marius slit open the envelope, quickly scanning the contents for the latest news. Looking thoughtful, he held the letter in his outstretched hand. "Who wants to read it next?"

As the letter passed round the eager hands of his family, Marius pictured his father "... not getting any younger ... that's what they said in the letter ... can't stand it any longer ... have to do something about this ... ten years since we left ... a long time ... passed so quickly ... things have got a lot better in South Africa ... hard to believe what's happened ... gotta hand it to Mandela ... a stable democracy now ... three elections ... Mbeki voted in again ... economy restructured ... inflation down ...

we, Afrikaaners ... believed the country was ours ... Ordinances of Creation ... hard to swallow our beliefs."

"Look at the condensation on these windows. This dampness isn't good for us. We need a house with double glazing." Primrose's voice, airing a concern, reached his ears with a complaining edge.

Marius gave no answer, but continued to muse "... maybe we could set up shop in Cape Town ... yes, that would be exciting ... not return to the old life in Johannesburg ... keep that in the past ... move to Cape Town ... keep the shops around Jo'burg ... Rosebank ... Sandton ... Germiston ... Boxburg ... Pretoria ... Roodepoort ... split them into districts ... brothers could manage them ... give them a district each ... let father retire ... he could come to Cape town with us ... the Waterfront ... cosmopolitan area now, they say ... Table Mountain ... my country ... so many changes ... self employed ... that's the only answer ... keep the business going for my children ..."

"Eat your cereal, my angel," Primrose cajoled their teenage daughter.

Marius took no notice, but wondered "... will she want to go back ... I don't think so ... she's become ambitious here ... for herself ... for the kids ... only got her mother back in South Africa ... how can I tell her ... have to persuade her ... what if she won't agree ... the other evening ... lost my temper ... pushed her around ... feel ashamed ... don't know what came over me ..."

"OK, kids, collect all your stuff. I'll drive you to school today." Primrose was tidying up the breakfast table, as she spoke.

Marius was lost in thought "... more than anything I miss my language ... have to speak English here ... even the kids speak English at home ... me and Primrose ... the only time I can speak Afrikaans now ... what would make me really happy ... sitting on the stoop of my own house ... my father and brothers around me ... talking about the rugby ... can of Castle in my hand ... barbeque sizzling away ... did I even *think* the word barbeque ... man, I'm losing my identity."

BARBARA AND PERCY

"It's a beautiful day. Let's go for a walk." Barbara's voice roused Percy from his scrutiny of the Sunday Times. Lowering the newspaper, he gazed at her while considering the suggestion.

Letting his eyes wander to the window, Percy admired the bright blue sky and dazzling sunshine; he really had no inclination to venture outside. In the past, he would have resisted Barbara, but now he acquiesced. "OK," he answered meekly, dropping the newspaper to his knees. Barbara watched him closely; his responses were slower, less spirited.

Wrapping up warmly in fleece jackets, they made their way along a familiar route; the first frost of winter was beginning to thaw. Reaching Lillie Langtry's Supper Rooms, they turned into the lane to follow the flow of the River Test, passing a field of sleepy sheep and confronting a herd of beefy cattle before climbing over a stile to reach open terrain. On days like this, they would normally have been seen at the golf club, smartly dressed, bright smiles, keen to play, chatting with great enthusiasm, looking forward to lunch. Life had changed; Alzheimer's had entered their world. The bright smiles had gone, replaced by anxious expressions; the clothes were still smart but the accessories were lacking; they were mostly absent from golf competitions; their witty conversation had disappeared, replaced by somber discussions; their appetites for fine dining had dulled, replaced by concoctions of alternative medicines. Rather than face enquiring looks and countless questions, they had withdrawn into a more solitary existence. Today was a good day; Percy looked quite alert. Today, Barbara wanted to have a serious discussion.

Returning from their joyless walk, Barbara prepared afternoon tea. "Percy, I need to talk to you," she ventured, as she laid down the tray. He stared and nodded in response. "We need to make some plans." He nodded again. "You need to get all your paperwork in order. You're going on a journey and I can't come with you." Tears filled her eyes. After a deep breath, she continued. "We need to get everything in order. I want you to listen carefully." He nodded again. "Best if we don't do any more traveling, so you won't be needing your passport." She smiled at him. "And driving. Probably best if you avoid that, don't you agree?"

"I'm not sure about that." Percy's face clouded.

"Well, we can talk about that later. I've got your driver's license here. Perhaps we ought to discuss it with the doctor." Without waiting for his reply, she continued, "Your will was made a year ago which is fortunate. I don't see any reason to make changes. Do you agree?"

"It's not complicated, so yes, leave it be," Percy responded, wearily.

"There will come a time, Percy, when I won't be able to cope. You will need more care than I can give you. I'll need to look at suitable establishments in readiness. I know it's a hard thing to face, but it would mean a lot if we could look at places together ... then I know it has your approval."

"Well, this really is a fun conversation," he quipped.

"Let's get it over with all at once. It has to be done." Barbara was firm.

"OK, so you want me to tour the funny farms with you."

"Please be serious, Percy."

"Yea, OK, fine. Line them up," Percy agreed.

"And the business. What's going to happen to the business?" Before he could answer, Barbara carried on, "I've been thinking about it. I have some background in the jewelry trade. I've met a lot of your contacts socially. I hear you talk to dealers and clients all the time. I think I could pick it up. I think I should accompany you now. Act as your personal assistant. Listen and learn. Gradually take on responsibilities. But most of all, I'll be there to safeguard you. Watch over you. Step in if I see anything that seems amiss. You'd like a bit of company now and then, wouldn't you, my love?"

An expression of surprise held Percy's features, as if Barbara had planned a birthday party without his knowledge. The passport and the driver's license he could understand; no traveling, no driving; but business transactions with his wife at his side made him feel very uncomfortable; he couldn't quite pinpoint why it didn't feel right, but he didn't seem to have the words to counteract her suggestion; his mind felt like an appliance in need of repair, an old house in need of re-wiring; sometimes, he had full power, sometimes the lights flickered; sometimes there was a power surge, sometimes there was a power failure. If only, he could fix the lights ... if only.

"So, we'll take a look at your calendar," Barbara suggested. "Let's see when I should come with you. Perhaps not immediately. Maybe it's something we can build in gradually. Perhaps we may even think of getting a driver for you. We'll see how things go."

Relieved that she had sown the seeds and thankful that Percy had not resisted her suggestions, Barbara looked fondly at the man with whom she had shared her life; he was fading. Dashing was how she always thought of Percy; that first time she saw him in Bond Street; his dark hair, luxurious and wavy; his suntanned skin, smooth and fine; mischief in his eyes; dazzling white teeth; his smile caught her heart. The carefully chosen designer clothes, the expensive accessories; everything about him danced to her tune. Flash, some people would call him; she knew that. After all these years, he still looked dashing, she believed; the luxurious hair had turned to a distinguished white; the eyes had developed fine lines; he looked successful, she thought. Not today. Today, he looked faded; his hair, normally without a strand out of place, was untidy today; his clothes, normally pristine, were crumpled today; but his eyes, which lately were dull and lifeless, were bright and alert today.

Today, Percy dozed off rather a lot on the sofa. The walk in the sunlight was one of the many recommendations; as much daylight as possible, they advised; she was going to have to cope with sleeping disorders; daytime dozing was not a difficult situation but night-time wakening and disorientated wandering would be a challenge.

Live for today; that's how they had always lived; never stinting, always the best of everything, living to the limits of their means. Now, she was going to have to live for tomorrow. She would have to plan, anticipate the stages of farewell. Thinking of farewells, Barbara thought of her daughter in Canada, "... how can I tell her ... just not the kind of thing you want to say on the phone ... would be good to have her support ... but she's gone ... searching for another life ... don't want to mention it on the phone ... not the diagnosis ... she's coming home for Christmas ... can tell her then ... she'll see that he's different ... lost his sparkle ... no energy ... she'll notice little things ... she'll show concern ... best to wait till she's home ... make the most of this Christmas ... what would be best ... big party with all his friends ... quiet time to spend with the family .... maybe we need both ... before he's gone ... it's going to be a long haul ... don't know if I can face it ... all the caring ... no life for me ... what an existence ... living with a man who won't recognize me ... and for how long ... could be years and years ... not sure I can cope ... not used to being independent ... dealing with everything ... going to be a heavy burden ... not used to illness ... he's starting to do silly things ... found his cufflinks in the refrigerator ... his car keys in the bathroom cabinet ... you have to laugh sometimes ... what about the golf club ... Vice Captain ... it has to be me ... he can't deprive me of that ... that would keep me sane ... a focus out of the house ... female company ... all the chatter ... all the gossip ... couldn't live without that ... the social life ... dinner dances ... he can come to those ... surely."

"I wouldn't be here if my father had worn his boots." Percy had a faraway look in his eyes, as he spoke.

"What?"

"The sergeant detailed some men to clear mines. My father wasn't ready. Needed to put on his boots. The sergeant took someone else who was blown up. I would never be born if my father had kept his boots on."

Barbara looked at him strangely. "... wish she wouldn't look at me like that ..." Percy thought, "... as if I'm crazy ... quite insulting ... I've just got a condition ... like millions of other people ... what I said just now was very sensible ... sometimes she's impatient with me ... makes me sad ... very hurtful when she's sharp with me ... don't deserve it ... haven't done anything wrong ... must try not to be difficult ... just agree to everything ... then she won't get angry ... how do I look today ... not going anywhere important ... like to look my best ... don't know if she's going to cope ... she's never been good with illness ... she's always hated hospitals ... she looks cross today ... wonder what I've done wrong ... wish I could think better ... hard to work things out ... what's wrong with me ... am I sick ... have I got flu ... feels like flu ... can't think straight ... what's that noise ... wonder what's for breakfast ... wish she wouldn't look at me like that ... upsets me ... sunny day ... maybe we could go for a walk ... that might cheer her up ... the business ... she mentioned it ... what did she say ... need to get into London ... can't sit around here reading the newspaper ..."

"Going upstairs," Percy called out. "Need to get into London. Can't waste time chatting."

"Darling, it's Sunday. No work today. Just relax by the fire."

Percy looked puzzled, but gave up his struggle to rise from the sofa: falling back against the cushions, he gazed out of the window. "... so, where was I ... before she interrupted me ... so rude ... sometimes she's so rude ... she's trying to steal my things ... stuff not where I left it ... she's trying to annoy me ... she's bossing me around ... telling me what to do ... need to stand up to her ... that's it ... don't stand any nonsense ... this is nice and cozy ... sitting here by the fire ... taking tea ... reading the newspaper ... need to spend more time reading ... keep yourself informed ... need to keep up with world affairs ... have to keep the mind active ... yes, that's what they said ... keep the mind active ..."

Percy straightened up on the sofa, folding the newspaper neatly with brisk movements. "Barbara," he announced in a loud voice, "I'm going to learn French."

"What?"

"Really useful in wartime. Barter with the natives. Trade cigarettes for coffee."

A log sparked in the grate; Percy looked into the hearth: the glow oozed a comforting warmth; the ash gathered as powder; the dust floated on the beams of sunlight.

NANCY AND DARREN

"Christmas is going to be a problem," sighed Nancy, as she folded clothes ready for ironing.

"Suppose so," Darren responded.

"Well, where do we go? I'm sure your family don't want me around," Nancy stated, without rancor, "But, go to your folks. I don't mind."

"Well, it might be simpler."

"You could spend the twenty fourth here with my lot," Nancy offered. "My daughter will be here with her husband and the kids."

"Yea, maybe. Let's see. It's a bit far ahead."

"It's just over a month. Only a few weeks away."

"Hmmm." Darren was non committal.

"I've never liked Christmas," Nancy continued.

"Really?" Darren's gaze drifted to the television.

"Well, it's so pressurized. If you have it at your house, you have the problem of who else is there. Do you ask your brothers and sisters with their family, or not? If someone else offers to do it, do you go to them? Lots of people are going away, now, to escape the hassle. It's just so commercialized. Just a way for stores to keep boosting their profits. Do you know, I have about thirty gifts to buy. If I spend forty or fifty pounds on each, which is what you need to spend to get something decent, that adds up to a whole lot of money. I mean, it's nice to give presents, but when we were young you didn't get the mountain of stuff these kids have got today. And, anyway, who needs more stuff? I told my daughter not to get me anything. I'd rather she spent the money on the kids."

Darren held the TV remote control, gazing in rapt attention at Jeremy Clarkson on Top Gear, extolling the virtues of the latest roadsters. "Gee, look at that one," he called out.

"I love the decorations, though, don't you?" Winchester looks wonderful this year. Darren, you're not paying attention. Don't you like Christmas?"

"Yea, it's OK."

"Well, thankfully, the father of my children is nowhere to be seen. So, we don't need to worry about where he spends Christmas Day.

Wonder where he is? What do you reckon? Took his passport and a wad of money, but the police can't trace him. I bet he headed for Spain. They say criminals make for familiar territory when they're hiding out." Nancy pondered that Colin had been missing for almost six months and that Darren had been living with her ever since his disappearance; she often wondered what would happen if Colin did turn up; she knew perpetrators often returned to the scene of a crime; she worried that, if Colin ran out of money, he might appear at the caravan site to seize cash; she wondered if Darren would arrange for him to get a beating, the way he had done with Rodney – rough justice, but it was one way of punishing misdemeanors.

"Could be in Spain," Darren agreed, as he continued to focus on the television, holding the remote control like a weapon, ready to be fired; sounds of engines revving filled the room as Jeremy Clarkson concluded the program. Darren stretched out his arm to kill the sound on the adverts; his attention wandered to the newspapers and magazines on the coffee table.

Nancy stood watching him. The only sounds were the clock ticking, occasionally masked by the crackle of glossy paper as Darren leafed his way through the pages of a golf magazine. Wanting to keep the conversation going, but struggling for topics, Nancy searched around in her head for tidbits of news that might hold his attention. "Hey, you know Percy's got Alzheimer's. Apparently, he's declined quite quickly," she confided.

"Poor guy. How old is he?" Darren showed only mild interest.

"Oh … older than me. You know, they start forgetting things when they get that disease." To catch Darren's attention Nancy changed the subject. "What do you want for dinner?" she asked with a grin.

"Something fried."

"You need to watch your fat content, young man. The government is giving out health warnings about the amount of fat and sugar in our diets."

"Who cares!" was Darren's response.

"Yes, who cares! Let me rustle something up." Nancy sauntered out into the kitchen. Rummaging through the freezer, her eyes roved around the contents. Picking out a carton, she leaned against the doorframe and enquired, "How about chicken pie, with broccoli on the side?"

"Sounds good. Forget the broccoli."

Nancy turned on the oven to reach the required temperature and returned to the living room. Darren was reading the latest edition of

Club Golfer. "This is not good news," he said, showing her the front page. "Ninety percent of golf clubs across the country are stuck for members."

"Yea, it's a bit puzzling," commented Nancy. Our ladies section used to have a long waiting list, but you can get in immediately, now. Wonder what's changed. Whether too many new golf clubs have sprung up, or whether golf doesn't seem attractive anymore ... or people are working so hard, they just don't have the time."

"Says here that junior sections are thriving, but that doesn't help my livelihood; kids haven't got the money to spend. My basic income depends on members needing lessons and spending money in the pro shop. OK, I might make some money winning tournaments, but that has to be a bonus. Really, there's not much spare cash jingling around in my pockets right now."

"You don't need to worry about money when you're with me. You keep everything you earn. Household bills are all organized. Just enjoy yourself." Nancy smiled fondly. Darren settled back onto the sofa. "How about having the lads round?" Nancy continued, "Some night when I'm at choir practice, I could organize takeaways for you ... pizza, curry, fish and chips ... just let me know what you want. I'll get some beers in for you. You could watch the sport and have a laugh." Nancy knew Darren was restless; she was desperately trying to keep him content.

"Sounds great," answered Darren, putting his feet up on the coffee table.

Forty minutes later, the oven timer signaled that the chicken pie was ready. "We'll just eat in front of the TV," suggested Nancy, as she brought a tray in to the living room.

"Hmmm, smells good," answered Darren straightening up his pose while taking his feet off the table. They ate in silence, the TV blaring out the news that Yasser Arafat had died in Paris, his battle for the Palestinian cause still unresolved. Once they had satisfied their hunger, Darren settled back to channel hopping on the television.

Nancy ran her fingers through her hair. Breaking the silence, she offered, "You now, I asked Barbara to be my Vice Captain. Won't be long till I'm Captain, only a few months, but I wonder how she's going to cope if she's got him to look after."

"The committee could ask me for my views, you know," Darren dropped the remote control, taking an interest in the discussion.

"Oh, really?"

"Well, they have in the past. Informally, of course, but they like to get soundings from various sections of the club," informed Darren.

"Hmmm, what do you think? Do you think she can do the job well if she's got to be running after Percy? I know it's her duty and everything, but I've got to think how it affects me. I need someone who can support me, someone who's able to give the time."

"Speaking of time, I said I'd drop in to the pub tonight. Catch up with the lads. Nine thirty already. I'll walk down and grab a pint."

Darren roused himself from the sofa, standing to full height, automatically stretching himself into the warm up exercises of a professional golfer. "Oh, next week, you won't see much of me."

"Oh, what's happening?" Nancy felt alarmed.

"Well, you know Anastasia has been advertising these golfing holidays. Off peak. Winter rates. Stay at the Grosvenor Hotel, all meals included. Full use of Middle Wallop golf course, with group and private lessons from the resident professional ... that's me, of course." Darren smiled proudly. "Well, I'm expected to have dinner with them each night. Butter them up so they want to book private lessons with me. You know, she's flying these punters in to Popham airport. They expect to leave after a week with a handicap. Most of them'll be hopeless, but I'll give them a handicap, anyway. Keep them happy," he grinned.

"Oh, right. Well, business comes first, of course," answered Nancy, with a worried frown. "I'll have to start thinking about the caravan site soon. Rather neglected it the last few months. Takings were good in the summer, but we're not busy now the clocks have changed. Cold weather doesn't bring fishermen to the Test Valley. Fish won't come up for bait in these temperatures."

"Yea, it's a bit chilly these days," Darren acknowledged.

"Once it's near freezing and they're desperate, the fish will take the bait, but business is dead right now. What I have to think about is maintenance ... not something I had to worry about in the past ... he ... Colin used to take care of it. Things need looked at now. The flat roof on the store worries me. I think it needs renewed. Everywhere needs painted, but that'll have to wait till the spring. I need to get the hedges cut back. The caravans all need inspected. Wear and tear. Everything needs to be taken care of, for next season. I need someone to deal with all the maintenance. If I have to pay a handyman, it eats into the profits."

"Right, well, I'll leave you to think about that. I'm off to the pub. See you later." Darren rose from the sofa.

"You don't need to go so soon." Nancy stretched out her arms towards him. "Come to Momma. The pub can wait."

"Right, they'll be wondering what's keeping me," grinned Darren, some time later.

"You can tell them you've been a lucky boy," Nancy retorted, tossing her head, as she gathered her discarded clothes from the sofa.

"Well, I'll see you later then." Darren pulled his sweater over his head. Making his way out of the room, he gave Nancy's buttock a gentle slap. Chuckling, he strode to the front door and let himself out into the night; he walked briskly towards the pub, looking forward to a pint with his mates.

Nancy's fears always leapt to the surface when Darren went to the pub "... what does he talk about when he's with his mates ... do they laugh at my expense ... how many women have thrown themselves at him ... attractive young man ... available ... what do people say about me ..." Shivering, she pulled on her clothes. Feeling a need to keep busy, she tidied up the living room; plates lying on the coffee table; mugs resting on the floor; newspapers and magazines scattered on the sofa. Gathering items onto a tray, she carried the burden into the kitchen. Stacking the dishwasher, she returned to her earlier self doubts, "... what do they say about me ... old slapper ... a disgrace ... woman of her age ... throwing herself at a young man ... should know better ... bringing shame on her family ... they don't know how hard it's been for me ... living here on my own ... scary ... lonely ... embarrassed at his crime ... worrying about him turning up ... in the middle of the night ... no telling what he might do ... need to keep money here ... in case he turns up ... demanding money ... give it to him ... let him disappear again ... that's the best policy ... Darren ... he'd sort him out ... threaten him ... make him leave ... Darren ... keep him here ... the maintenance ... that was a mistake ... scared him off ... can't mention that again ... hoped he might offer to help ... need to find a handyman ... need to ask around ... need to advertize ... they don't work for nothing ... eat into the profits ... meager living this place ... lots of land ... lots of work ... hard graft ... not easy ... Darren ... keep him here ... give him what he can't get elsewhere ... young women aren't available like me ... they work ... they go out ... do other things ... I'm always around ... available ... woman of my age ..." Nancy laughed aloud at her own foolishness, as she slammed shut the door of the dishwasher; the appliance took over the task, humming as the electronics responded to the cycle. Looking towards the utility room, a shiver of fear ran down her spine, as her eyes rested on the pane of glass; the pane of glass Colin broke the night he ran away; her life shattered the night he smashed that pane of glass.

The pane of glass was mended, but her life continued to fracture into a thousand fragments.

Darren walked down the cart track from the Old Dairy, enjoying the feel of uneven ground playing on his leg muscles. As he made his way towards the main road, he considered his relationship with Nancy "...well, she's keen ... always up for it ... always ready ... mature woman ... eager to please ... no confessions of undying love ... no tears ... no tantrums ... no demands ... no commitment ... except that mention of maintenance ... made me feel uncomfortable ... she better not be looking for me to do that ... no way ... forget it ... that's a commitment ... that's pressure ... she can solve her own problems ... move out ... that's what's coming down the tracks ... if she hints at that again ... can do without that ... maybe a mistake moving in ... never done it before ... happened gradually ... stay overnight ... her invitations ... come back once you close the shop ... stay overnight ... come back for dinner ... my folks are getting difficult ... you're having an affair with that woman ... well, you're a grown man ... make your own mistakes ... people are talking ... who cares ... you should be dating women your own age ... you should be settling down ... who cares ... oh, I need a pint ..."

No stars tonight. An overcast sky. The moon slipping in and out between pillows of threatening clouds. Shapes of trees standing out in the darkness. Fine damp drizzle shrouding every surface with moisture. Darren reached the main road; his feet adjusted to a steady march on the even surface as his thoughts continued "... wonder if Marius will be there ... he's there a lot ... must spend a fortune in the pub ... married man ... kids ... not for me ... keep that life ... single life for me ... footloose and fancy free ... might win a big competition ... then let the good times roll ... young women ... flash car ... really fancied that one on TV tonight ... MG ... zero to sixty miles an hour in four point nine seconds ... what a mover ... five liter engine ... SVR ... yea, that's what it's called ... costs a fortune ... eighty three grand ... you know you've made it if you're driving that ... now, that would make me happy ..."

Darren felt cheerful as he reached the pub. Lots of cars parked outside, none of them special. Lights glowing in the windows. Anticipation flowed through his fingertips, as he pushed open the door. A variety of sounds reached his ears; roars of masculine laughter, the intermittent thud of darts, a constant clink of glasses, a velvet curtain of voices. Mixed odors reached his nostrils; welcoming beer fumes, tantalizing cooking aromas, curling cigarette smoke, enervating perfume tones. The perfume alerted him; he looked around; a new barmaid, blonde, smiling, young, lots of cleavage. Pushing his way through the forest of bodies to the bar, he stood watching her; he noted the denim jeans slung on the hips, a metal studded belt pressing into her belly, a band of bare flesh showing below the tight tee-shirt, a lightweight silver chain round her neck dangling between her breasts; his senses tingled. Catching her eyes, with a glint of interest, he ordered, "Pint o' Pride, love."

MADELEINE AND ADAM

"I hope your next wife is a vegetarian, anorexic, lousy cook with no brains," Madeleine giggled uncontrollably.

Adam had been complaining for a long time about Madeleine's eating habits, irritated by her plowing slowly through the contents of her plate long after he had finished eating, weary that she chattered animatedly during the meal, impatient when she asked for another glass of wine. Madeleine decided to win the battle this evening; rather than allow Adam to serve himself first, she helped herself from the serving dishes; immediately, she focused on the contents of her plate, keeping a watchful eye on Adam's progress, never speaking until her meal was finished. Laying down her knife and fork, she stared at Adam until he finished his meal. Suddenly, what had started out as cold determination turned into a mischievous prank. Covering her face with her hands to hide her glee, cascades of giggles shook her frame.

"There's a lot of bile there," Adam responded, coolly.

Adam was tired, really tired. Tired of all the political intrigue in the company; tired of senior executives who despised each other and could bring the company down with their inability to work together; each of them used every opportunity to show each other in a bad light, scoring points in meetings by highlighting weaknesses in the other camp. Lots of issues remained unresolved; senior executives who had proved to be lightweight needed to move on; geographical areas which were unprofitable needed to control costs; sniffs of corruption rising from executives, who seemed able to pull off unlikely deals, needed investigation.

"I'm going to send you to Conversational English classes. You never spoke once during that meal," Madeleine answered.

"That'll be right next door to the Active Listening class you'll be attending," Adam retorted.

"Cheeky monkey." Giggles continued to wave through Madeleine. "You made no attempt to start a conversation. There was nothing to listen to."

"Well, last night I had to listen to you attempting to analyze the Ukrainian election, and the night before you were going on about

Captain Cook's discovery of Tahiti. Why can't you just comment on the weather?" Adam wore a long-suffering expression.

Madeleine retorted, "You know, I make you a full roast dinner and sit down to enjoy it over polite conversation in a candlelit dining room. I really wish I hadn't bothered."

"You don't understand me."

"Oh, oh, warning bells. Next you'll be taking a lover, telling her your wife doesn't understand you."

"Hey, I'm the straightest guy in the universe."

"So you tell me."

"That's right."

"What's happening with all the cash you're using these days?" Madeleine had been wondering about this for some time.

"What?" Adam looked alarmed.

"Well, you're taking a lot of cash out of the bank. It doesn't seem to last long."

"You're using it as well," he answered.

"Actually, I'm not. I've been getting cash back when I buy groceries, so all the cash out of the bank has been withdrawn by you," Madeleine insisted.

Adam looked shaken. "Well, I bought lottery tickets."

"How many?"

"I don't know. Go and look. They're in a drawer in the kitchen."

Madeleine ignored the suggestion. "You can't have spent all of it on lottery tickets," she challenged.

"Well, I gave a donation to charity. Someone at the office needed sponsorship. That was forty pounds. What are you trying to say?"

"Well, I'm just concerned. The government is saying that gambling is becoming an epidemic. I just wonder if your lottery tickets are getting out of control. Aren't you in a syndicate in the office, as well?"

"That's a tenner a month. So, I do the lottery. Is that a crime?"

"No, it's a vice."

"Oh, gimme a break." Adam was getting angry now.

"Look, we have to talk," Madeleine suggested, a more serious mood descending on her. "We're not happy, are we? We need to look at what's making us unhappy."

"Yea, OK."

"Let's have a brain storming session, with brain storming rules. Only suggestions. No evaluation or problem solving. We can use the flip chart."

"OK," agreed Adam.

Madeleine cleared away the remnants of the meal from the dining room. The vegetable dishes were empty; nothing left of the cabbage stewed in butter; only hints of the carrot and parsnip mash adhering to the serving spoon. The roast beef, she carefully stored in the refrigerator to be eaten tomorrow along with a potato salad she would make from the leftovers. Cleaning the table and fixing the chairs back into position, she turned her attention to the study. Opening a tall cupboard, she unveiled the flip chart, which awaited the latest flow of ideas to emanate from the Minehead household. Making two mugs of coffee, she settled herself into one of the tan leather swivel chairs.

"OK, Adam it's all set up," she called out.

"Be with you in a minute."

"Coffee's sitting waiting for you."

"Yea, just coming."

Several minutes later, Adam appeared looking weary, to find Madeleine perched on the edge of her seat looking bright and alert.

"All set up," repeated Madeleine, gazing eagerly at the blank paper. "Do you want to do the writing?"

"OK."

"Or, I can do it, if you like."

"Whatever you want."

"OK, why don't you do it?" Madeleine offered. "You'll feel more in control if you're doing the writing." Adam sighed.

"Right, several headings will probably emerge, but let's put up 'Not Happy' to start with," Madeleine continued.

Adam wrote the words at the top of the chart. "So, what things are we not happy with?" questioned Madeleine.

"House," Adam answered, without hesitation, writing the word in neat letters with the black felt tip pen.

Madeleine's eyebrows rose. "Work," she suggested. Scrutinizing the back of Adam's head as he wrote the word, she noticed that his hair was beginning to thin at the crown.

"Family," Madeleine continued, watching the word appear in Adam's neat handwriting. "Social life," she added, just as Adam's head was turning towards her. He wrote the word below the others.

"Weather," Adam stated firmly, adding the word to the list.

"Eating," Madeleine spat out the word. After a pause, she added "Culture," and watched while Adam continued writing.

"Spirituality," Adam spoke quietly, writing the word slowly and deliberately.

"Hmmm. We've got lots of stuff there," commented Madeleine.

After a few minutes of staring at the chart while no further suggestions emerged, she asked, "Should we break these headings down, now?"

"OK"

"Oh, and add 'Clothes'." Adam followed instructions.

"And 'Golf'." Adam wrote the word on the chart, at the same time as he uttered the two syllables.

"Enough. Enough," laughed Madeleine. "We'll never get through all this. First item is 'House'. What factors do we want to consider here?"

"Well, location, really," answered Adam, "and style."

"Can you clarify?"

"This is a gorgeous house, but it's not my style. I miss living in London and I would prefer something more contemporary. I want glass, lots of light, hard edged, and a view."

"Right, next is 'Work'." Madeleine was keen to tackle this one. "I want to go back to the legal profession. I want to specialize in rape cases."

"And, I've just about had a belly full. I'm into a situation of diminishing returns. The money just doesn't compensate for the constant traveling, constant pressure and constantly feeling exhausted, just to meet shareholders expectations. I don't know what else I'll do, but it's time for a serious re-think."

Madeleine showed no surprise. "Next is 'Family'".

"Well, we can't do anything about that."

"Unfortunately, that's true. A son with Asperger's syndrome and a daughter we rarely see. We just have to cope with the Asperger's and hope that our daughter turns back to us, once she's finished university. As for your mother ... well." Madeleine rolled her eyes to the ceiling.

"I know. I know. Yours isn't much better," Adam replied, gesturing an open hand in Madeleine's direction to emphasize his feelings.

"Social life," Madeleine added. "We're dying out here in the country. I know we can get to London fairly easily, but it's more than that. I just need more stimulation. I want a cosmopolitan environment."

"I think I do, too," Adam agreed.

"Weather." Adam was firm on this subject. "I can't stand this greyness."

"It doesn't bother me too much, but I know what you're saying. Maybe we should have a place in the sun," acknowledged Madeleine.

"You've just evaluated and problem solved."

"OK, scrub that."

Madeleine smiled. "Eating," she said emphatically. "Meal times are a trial in this house. You're always so uptight about something. I just don't enjoy sitting across a table from you."

Adam was shocked. "It's not as bad as that."

"Believe me, it is."

"Culture," Madeleine sighed. "I don't feel I fit in here. I'm not sure if I mean being outside London or in general. But I would miss the English culture of theater, art, concerts, architecture, history. I would miss the countryside, too. All that stuff, which I know you're not bothered about."

Adam showed no interest. "Spirituality," he pondered, "We just don't have that in our lives."

"I agree. We need to do something about that. There's a missing dimension." Madeleine looked wistful, but then brought her attention back to the next word on the board. "Clothes," she announced.

"Yes?" questioned Adam. "Don't you have enough of them?"

"I mean *your* clothes. At weekends, you always ask me what you should wear. Then you argue with any suggestions I make. I don't want you to ask me for advice, anymore. It causes too much agro."

Adam blinked and looked at the floor, hiding his hurt. Looking up again, he sighed, "Golf."

"You know, it's great to be a member of a golf club, but I just wonder how much more of my life I want to devote to it," Madeleine pondered.

"We're on the same wavelength here," agreed Adam. "It's a wonderful facility, but there are lots of golf courses all over the world. We don't need to be tied to this one. In fact, we don't need to actually belong to a golf club. We can just pay green fees and avoid all the hassle."

"Now, *you're* problem solving," Madeleine scolded, looking annoyed. After a pause, while studying the flipchart, she added, "Hmmm, let's review. You're not happy with the house, which I love, but I admit to being bored with the location. I want to go back to work and the winds of change are blowing through you, too."

"Are we into problem solving, now?"

"Seems like it."

"OK, let's aim to move house. Back to London." Adam was looking enthusiastic.

"Definitely," Madeleine agreed, adding, "And buy a place in the sun. Maybe Spain."

"Or France or Italy," countered Adam.

"Fine by me," confirmed Madeleine. "Work. I guess I'll have to wait to see where we're located before I sort something out."

"I guess so. And, now you know how I'm feeling don't be surprised by any work changes I make. Do you have any views on this?"

"I've always adapted to your career. Make your decisions and I'll work around them. I think I do a damn good job of coping with all of that." Madeleine got no answer from Adam.

"Family. We'll just have to go with the flow there." Adam changed the subject. Pausing, he continued, "Social life?" and proceeded to answer his own question. "That will change as we move house." Gaining momentum, he continued, "Weather will be taken care of, in large part, by buying a second home. And we'll be encountering a different attitude by moving house, too."

"Eating," Madeleine continued. "I'm going to serve myself first, in future. Also, I insist you talk to me over dinner. As well as that, you ought to replenish my wine glass, not wait for me to ask and then get annoyed."

"OK, OK. We'll try those tactics." Adam clenched his fists. "Culture," he continued. "Well, that will improve by moving back to the city. But, spirituality, now that's something we have to consider. We don't attend a church. I'm feeling that I want to search for a greater understanding of why we're here on this earth."

"I'll go along with that. Do you want to go along to a Sunday service at the Parish Church? Maybe try a few other churches, too. See what feels right?" Madeleine suggested.

"Yea, why don't you check that out?" Adam agreed. "Establish the times of services at the various churches in the district," Adam confirmed, before continuing, "Clothes. Well, you've made your point there. We don't need to revisit that. As for golf, what I said earlier is valid. How would you feel about not renewing our membership, but just paying green fees when we feel like playing?"

"Well, I'm on the committee, so it would come as a bit of a surprise to everyone, I suppose, especially since I'm Bronze Captain." Madeleine shrugged. "But, if we're planning to move out of the area, it won't matter, really."

"So, lots of action points," Adam summarized. "Start looking for a house in the city and a house in the sun. Change our work situations. Find a church."

"And talk, darling. Talk over dinner."

"Yea, well, I'm just so tired when I get home."

"Doesn't matter. If I were a client, you would put in the effort. You need to give me the same courtesy."

"OK, it's a deal." Adam grinned. "Are we finished?"

"I guess so." Madeleine looked uncomfortable.

"Anything else?" Adam enquired.

"Well, there's something else I have to tell you. It's not very pleasant, but it does concern you. I wish I didn't have to say this, but there's no way of avoiding it." Madeleine looked embarrassed; her eyes fell to the ground.

"Well?" Adam looked anxious.

"I've got athlete's foot."

"You what? How on earth did this come about?" Adam wanted to know.

"Probably from using the showers at the golf club," admitted Madeleine.

"That damn golf club!"

ROBINA AND HUGO

"It's disappointing." Robina bit her lip, tears in her eyes.

"We'll just have to accept it."

"I was sure they would name the date soon. Our youngest daughter. It would be the last wedding in the family."

"Lots of people do it, nowadays," Hugo soothed.

"I suppose so."

"Look, they're getting married, they're happy. Does it really matter that they're doing it in the Caribbean?"

"Yes, but they don't want anyone there. The whole family are disappointed."

Hugo shrugged. "He has no close family, it's difficult for him. Try to understand." Sobs broke out from Robina. Hugo put his arm round her shoulder. "Just accept it. We could throw a surprise party for them when they get back."

"Suppose so," Robina choked back.

"Now, what about this other party we're going to have? Let's not have anything spoil that. We really do have lots to celebrate. How about combining the party with Uncle Leonard's eightieth birthday party?" Hugo encouraged.

"Should we do that?" wondered Robina.

"I certainly think so. Now, who are we going to invite?"

I've got a list in my head. I'll have to start writing it down." Robina looked more cheerful.

"It's such a relief. I can't believe it's over. You know, the maintenance department has actually removed pictures from my office. I don't know what role I'm going to play at the bank now."

"It's like a huge black cloud has disappeared. The last few months have felt like swimming underwater, with a concrete block round your neck. I think this has been the most unhappy time of our lives," sighed Robina.

"But, you know, mud sticks. Even though I've been exonerated, this whole episode has damaged me. I don't know if I'll ever recover my reputation at the bank. I think I want to move on. I had my supporters, but there were many who stood on the sidelines to watch me sink."

"I know, love."

"I think I'm going to make it known that I'm open to offers. You never know what might turn up."

Robina looked anxiously at Hugo. Something outside the window caught her eye; she stood very still, observing. "Hugo," she called. "Come and see." Hugo moved to stand at her side. "What do you think?" she asked.

"Can't see properly," Hugo answered.

"Too big for a robin, although the breast is red. The tail is longer and dark. Seems like dark tips to the wings, black cap on the head. Oh, and look when he moves, a white rump. He's pecking at that fir tree. Short black beak." Robina paused to consider. "I think it's a bullfinch. You don't see them very often. They're quite secretive, but it's early morning and it's quiet. What do you think?"

"I'm sure you're right, dear."

"If we can time Uncle Leonard's party to coincide with the New Zealand visitors, as well as the honeymooners, wouldn't that be fantastic?" Robina enthused, with sudden inspiration. "We could have the most wonderful family gathering."

"I wish you wouldn't call them the New Zealand visitors. I'm sure your daughter wouldn't like it." Hugo smiled through his disapproval.

"Oh, well, then everyone knows who I mean. I don't need to explain. You know, I can't wait to see that little grandchild again. I didn't think I would love them like my own, but my heart just leaps towards her. She came running to me with arms outstretched. Those tiny little teeth – so perfect. That wonderful smile. Her eyes full of delight, full of trust, full of innocence, full of love."

"I know. There's nothing you wouldn't do for them. They just steal your heart."

"The first time I saw her come running towards me, it was like looking at myself in a mirror. As if I could see through a time tunnel, almost like a re-incarnation. Of course, that's nonsense. I'm still here. You can't be reincarnated if you're still alive."

"You certainly are very much alive, dear. Large as life," joked Hugo.

Robina's face dimpled in mock offence. "I know you shouldn't have favorites," she continued, "but that little girl is my favorite grandchild. I can't wait to see her. You know, a friend of mine tells all her grandchildren they're her favorite. I'm not sure I could do that."

"So, when are you having this party?"

"Yes, we need to work that out. Let me talk to the girls and chat to Uncle Leonard and see what date we can come up with. Do you have any ideas about venue or anything?"

"Oh, I think we need to have it here. The house is plenty big enough and it's good to use all this space."

"What about invitations? Who should we invite?" Robina wondered.

"I think we should keep it just within the family," Hugo responded.

"Yes, I'm sure that's best. After all, the kids do own the house now," agreed Robina.

"Yes, I need to reconsider the financial arrangements. We've got this huge lump sum, which I thought I would need for legal fees and living expenses. I'm not sure how to play the finances now. The kids have the mortgage on this house. Maybe we need to take another look at our wills. If we split the lump sum between us now, Robina, that might make matters simple. So, if one of us dies it would only be half the lump sum which gets clobbered for inheritance tax. Rather than make our wills in favor of each other, all our monies could go straight to the kids in the event of either of us dying. It's unlikely that we would both die together, so it would spread the inheritance tax."

"Right, and they could pay off their mortgages. That would be a relief, especially for Felicity and George. The others are OK, but I know they're finding it a particular strain to make the payments each month."

"I've never taken to that husband of hers." Hugo's bottom lip jutted out. "I know he resents these financial arrangements with the house. I'm sure he thinks we should have sold the place."

"I think he probably feels the others pushed him into it. Hard for him to stand up and be the lone voice complaining when the rest of the family are rallying round." Robina defended her son-in-law.

"A good time for me to talk to everyone would be at the party. Not that night, of course, but assuming they all stay the weekend. I can have a private chat with each of them." Hugo liked the thought of fatherly chats; he envisaged himself engaged in earnest conversation, perhaps over a coffee or a glass of port.

"Yes, that's a good opportunity. But what are we going to do with all this money?" An idea was forming in Robina's mind.

"Well, first thing, my love, we're going on a cruise. Get the brochures and decide where you want to go."

"Yes, that will be lovely, but what about all the rest of the money?"

"Well, it would be yours, to do as you please. You'll have half and I'll have half."

"Ooohh, this is very exciting. I know exactly what I'll do with mine," breathed Robina.

"You do? Well, it didn't take you long to work that out."

"I'm going to use it for the family. Anything they want, they just have to ask. I'll be like a bank, except I'll just pay out. It wouldn't be a loan. Just a fund they can use for luxuries." Robina was thrilled at the notion.

"Well, I'm still a banker. I'll be looking for the best investments. If you want any financial advice, you know who to ask. Of course, if we gift the money to the family now, perhaps by setting up a trust, inheritance tax wouldn't be an issue after seven years."

"Yes, lots to consider. The party would be a good time for discussions. I wonder when would be the best date." Robina had a faraway look. "Either January or February would be fine. The New Zealand visitors will be here, the honeymooners will be back from Barbados, and I'll be free of responsibility at the golf club."

"They're very lucky you agreed to take that on again," asserted Hugo.

"Well, someone had to do it. Bringing in a Past Captain until the end of the year was the best option. Such a shock, losing Lynn. That awful fire. It's a good job we don't know what's in front of us." Robina shuddered.

"So, when's the Annual Meeting?"

"I'll need to check the calendar. Yes, I'd like to get that over with before the party. It's not going to be easy sorting out a new committee. Captain and Vice Captain should be obvious. Nancy is Vice Captain at the moment, as you know but, really, I'm not sure that she should step up to Captain. That horrible business with Colin seems to have destabilized her. Rushing into having an affair with young Darren in the pro shop. It's just so … so, unseemly, really. Unsavory, somehow. It makes the members feel very uncomfortable. It just doesn't feel right having your Lady Captain carrying on like that. People feel it brings down the reputation of the club."

"I think the members are right to feel like that. Our golf club is very prestigious," Hugo agreed. "How can she command respect in the club, or in the whole district for that matter, when she's carrying on that way? I know they're both unattached, but it's inappropriate behavior."

"That's the general feeling. Mind you, look at the current antics from both sides of the House of Commons."

"Different situations, really," answered Hugo.

"I know. It's difficult. Perhaps I shouldn't compare the situations."

"You see, the thing is with politicians," Hugo explained, "a lot of people feel if they cheat on their wife, they'll cheat on the voters, too. If their wife can't trust them, why should we?"

"I agree with that. But then, it's not a matter of trust with Nancy for the Captaincy, is it? It's a matter of decorum, really, and respect and dignity." Robina chewed her lip, as she mulled over the situation, before continuing. "I'm also worried about Barbara. She expects to become Vice Captain, but there's Percy to consider. He will need a lot of looking after and she's going to be under a lot of strain. Alzheimer's is called the relatives' disease. I'm just not sure she can cope with such a huge problem, as well as being Vice Captain *and* being Captain the following year, with Percy getting steadily worse."

"Who else would be right for the job?" asked Hugo.

"That's the big question. I'll have to start discussing all this with the other Past Captains."

"How about some tea, dear?" entreated Hugo.

"What would you like with it?"

"What have you got?"

"Hmmm. Wonderful carrot cake, if I say so myself. I was really pleased with the texture, this time. Or I've got gingerbread, you like that. Or, lemon drizzle cake, there's just two slices left."

"But, we haven't had breakfast yet, Robina."

"Oh ... no, we haven't, have we? I was just so pleased with that carrot cake. When you mentioned tea ... all I could think about was cake."

"Oh, we're celebrating. Bring out the lot. What the hell."

As Robina busied herself in the kitchen, Hugo looked out of the window, admiring the changing colors on the trees; red, orange, gold; his eyes caught a spread of tawny beech leaves, desperately clinging to their life support system, afraid to fall to their death.

ANASTASIA AND RODNEY

Oak trees, always the last to let go, saying a sad goodbye to their cherished leaves, as they floated in the air to join crisp cousins on the funereal carpet below. Early December. Frost most mornings. Naked trees allowing low wattage light to filter lazily into forbidden places; places where the dazzling energy of the summer sun never reached. Winter gradually building up a command culture, stealthily injecting acquiescence, taking control, forcing earthly subjects to follow.

"You must stop coming here."

"Why, what's up?"

"People are noticing."

"What people?"

"The staff in the office say you are here very often." Anastasia's Russian accent conjured up images of sleigh bells in the snow, shapely fir trees, shots of vodka, fur collars and extravagant architecture.

Rodney sniffed in defiance, with the air of a dodgy builder. "So what?"

"Your wallet. That man took it to the police."

"Oh, yea?"

"The police came here."

Rodney's expression froze; his pale eyes slid from side to side, the red veins hoping to hypnotize his prey.

Anastasia continued. "They ask me to look in the wallet. They ask me do I know this man. They say the wallet is found on this land. Of course, I say you are a member. But I see all the cards. With your name. All different companies. But the same name. They ask me do I know these companies. I shake my head. You must stop coming here."

"So, where we gonna meet, Princess?"

"I tell you later. You don't come to this office again."

"What about Lynn? Nasty business, that fire."

"What about her?

"Who's gonna replace her? She was taking the deliveries. Shopping online was a good cover story. We need someone else to keep this scheme working."

"That is not your business."

"But the deliveries. We need another collection point." Rodney looked perplexed as he slouched, one arm draped over a filing cabinet.

"You will get your instructions." Anastasia moved away towards the desk. Turning to face Rodney, she asked, "You can ride a motorbike?"

"Sure thing."

"Buy one. Not new. Pay cash."

"OK. What about the daughter? What happened to her motorbike?"

"Stupid girl. She is pregnant. You know that? Kasim, he will get the British passport. Then, who knows about the daughter."

"Smart move, marrying her off to your cousin, Anastasia."

"She is so stupid. Give her some drinks. Send her some flowers. She do what you want."

Anastasia lifted her head, hearing footsteps in the corridor. Waiting, she listened, but the footsteps faded away. "Now listen. Get a motorbike. Get everything. All leather to wear. Get a helmet. No-one can see your face. They don't know you are a man or a woman. Get a box in the back. Like a delivery person. You pay cash for everything. You understand? A sign. You need a sign. Get some printed. The same names as the companies on your cards. You keep the signs in the box. You change the signs each time. Your contact will know you from the sign on the back." A smile played around her mouth. "Maybe I be your contact some time. A woman can be lonely."

"You ride a motorbike, Princess?"

"I do what I need to do."

"What about your old man?"

"What old man?"

"Your husband. What's the deal there?"

Anastasia looked at him quizzically. "He is not an old man. His age is like me."

"You know, they all think you're a widow, Princess."

"Of course, that is what I tell them. Where we live, no-one can see what goes on. You think all my money is in this place? You have to be mad. I follow instructions." She shrugged. "I have a good life. I know many people. I make contacts. We make money. Anyway, it is not your business." She looked away. Changing her posture to full height, drawing in her breath, she continued in a lighter tone of voice, "This ... ah ... beating you get. When they take your wallet. What is this about?"

"Well, who knows? Lots of nasty people about, eh Princess?"

"A lot of stupid people about. You be very careful. I do not want to see you disappear."

"You know they call you 'The Turtle'?"

"What are you saying?"

"A turtle. Swims in the water."

"What are you talking about?"

"A turtle." Rodney used a breaststroke swimming action with his arms, as he waded across the room. Anastasia blinked rapidly, without comprehension. Rodney laughed aloud. "Here, I'll show you." He took a pen out of the stand on the desk, spun the blank telephone pad towards him, drew a child's image of a turtle on the paper and held it up for her to see.

"So, what is this? You playing some game?"

"No, Princess. It's your nickname." He laughed louder, enjoying being in control. Handing her the paper, he whispered confidentially, "You keep this. A little souvenir." He sniggered. Intoxicated by his feeling of power, he wagged his finger. "You watch you don't get overturned, Princess." He chortled like a drunken sailor. Stretching out his arm, he held his hand flat, flipping it over as he repeated, "Overturned. You watch you don't get overturned, my turtle friend." Repeating the hand flipping action several times, wheezing with helpless laughter, Rodney's knees bent as the source of his amusement fixated his wits.

Watching him coldly, Anastasia warned, "You don't play games with me, my friend."

ALICE AND DON

"That was just wonderful," breathed Don, laying his helmet on the back of the Harley.

"I know." Alice echoed his sentiments.

"Now, I understand why dogs stick their head out of the window when they're in a car," Don laughed.

Alice giggled. "I know. I know. It's like a library of scents as you zoom along."

"Can't believe it. Grass, trees, earth, heather, ponies. No idea that all these scents were so strong, or that they could assail your senses so vividly," enthused Don.

"If someone had said to me, just a few weeks ago, that I would be sleeping in a tent with a lot of bikers around, I would have said they were mad. It's all such a change from my usual world of routine." Alice giggled again.

"It's certainly made me forget all the problems with the garden center. Puts everything into perspective." Don looked unusually relaxed, as he spoke.

"So, you'll just give those two fellows next door a bunch of money to forget the boundary problems?"

"It's only money. It solves the problem. I'll firm up the legal details and then I'll tell the others. It won't cost them a penny. I'll pay for it from our retirement savings. I should have let them know when this all blew up, in the beginning." Don imagined he would be a hero in the eyes of his brothers; his gesture would turn back time; his brothers would forgive him for the foolish affair with the book-keeper all those years ago.

"Well, I just hope they'll agree with what you're doing. Shouldn't you let them know about it?"

"It's the best way," asserted Don.

"Whatever you think, then."

"But what a weekend." Don returned to reminiscing about the rally. "I was really tempted to have a tattoo."

"You silly billy."

"Well, I'm retired now. I can do what I want. I don't need to care about keeping up appearances. Anyway, I wasn't going to have it on my forehead."

"Where would you have it?"

"I would let you choose." Don's eyes, full of mischief, met Alice's grave expression. A burst of laughter escaped him. "Oh, don't worry. I'm not going to do it."

"You could have some artwork painted on your leather jacket," Alice suggested. "That airbrush artist was doing a fabulous job."

"Yea, could do that. We could both have something done. Then, we'd really look cool and sexy." Don laughed again. "Wasn't the Motorcycle World at Beaulieu just amazing," he continued.

"I'm just amazed at the people," replied Alice.

"You're right. I would have thought they would be a bunch of rockers, but they're all different kinds of people. It's like being part of an international family."

"I know," Alice breathed. "People just seem to leave their background at home. It doesn't seem to matter who you are, or what you've got, or where you came from."

"You're right. You're simply accepted and welcomed for being yourself." In a louder voice, while throwing his arms wide, Don added, "It's exhilarating."

Alice watched him with amusement. Feeling hunger pains gather, she suggested, "Let's get inside and have something to eat. I'm starving."

"Good idea. Burgers and dogs were fine at the rally, but now I need some proper food," Don agreed. "I'll put the bike away while you start on the meal."

Alice unlocked the front door and, passing through the hallway, switched on the radio tucked away in the space they used as a study. The headlines boomed out, "Motorbike death was not an accident. Dollar slides to new low against the pound. Black Watch regiment to be disbanded."

Alice's footsteps echoed on the kitchen floor; her leather gear lay in a bundle in the hallway to be carefully put away after supper; she now wore flat house shoes. All sorts of noises competed with the radio waves; her feet pattered on the floor as she busied herself preparing a meal; cupboard doors slammed as she chose suitable dishes; stoneware crockery clanked onto the kitchen table; the refrigerator door squeaked as she removed several items; the chopping board thumped onto the countertop; a drawer breathed back and forth as she removed knives and forks, a rhythmic clacking erupted as she chopped vegetables. Don opened the kitchen door. Without turning round, she said, "I'm making a salad nicoise."

"What's that again? I always forget."

"Hard boiled eggs, green beans, and tuna on a bed of lettuce. Oh, and olives, too."

"Salads in winter. I think I prefer them in the summer time."

"Well, it's quick and easy. All very healthy to counteract the fat content of the dogs and burgers," Alice giggled.

"Well, does it really matter what we eat when we're over sixty? Mind you, we could get mad cow disease from the burgers," Don teased.

Alice smiled. "Mad motorbike disease, more like. Do you think the New Forest Region would be the one for us to join?"

"Well, it seems sensible. We have the New Forest on our doorstep. Region 19 it's called."

"They're having a Christmas Event on the tenth of December, meeting at the Forester's Arms in Bishopstoke. Do you want to go to that?" asked Alice.

"Certainly do. Should be great fun."

"OK. All ready," Alice announced, as she placed the bowls of salad on the kitchen table. Do you want any dressing?"

"How about some un-dressing?"

"Finish your salad and then we'll see."

They ate in silence, glancing at each other with anticipation, the sound of their teeth crunching on lettuce and green beans, somehow, out of tune with their anticipated activities.

Sitting on the sofa in the curve of his arm, Alice felt sure she was unable to meet Don's expectations of a celebratory physical feast after all these years of famine. Springing back in alarm, she spontaneously uttered, "You know, you really must cut your nose hairs."

BARRY AND MARTHA

"Come on in, Barry," Martha encouraged, as she opened the door.

"Hi," he responded, brushing his feet vigorously on the doormat, while unbuttoning his coat.

"We're not downstairs today. We're upstairs," Martha advised, as she led him into a front sitting room. Barry looked around uncertainly, taking in the atmosphere of a different environment.

Dark colors everywhere gave the room a peaceful Victorian aura. Somehow, there was a glow of light and warmth. "Take a seat," Martha offered. Barry looked around uncertainly. "Over here," Martha suggested, leading the way to an enormous sofa. The fabric felt rough to Barry's hands, as he seated himself in the soft depths of feathers.

"So, how have you been? We haven't seen each other for quite a while," asked Martha, settling herself on the other end of the sofa.

"I've been pretty good. Talking about Lynn was good for me. Just what I needed. But I want to talk to you about my daughter."

"Okay, tell me about her."

"Well, she married this guy. Not too long ago. Thankfully, Lynn was around. She got to enjoy arranging a wedding celebration party. Photos, cake, dresses. All that stuff. The problem is that it *was* arranged. I mean the guy is an immigrant of some kind. Don't ask me about him. I know almost nothing of his background. Anyway, like I say, it was an arranged marriage. She agreed to the ceremony so that he could claim a British passport. In return, she got a sum of money." Barry spoke in agitation, the words tumbling out. He paused to look at Martha, gauging her response. He took in her quizzical expression. "It was done before I could do anything about it," he added. Martha's expression did not change. "Anyway, I'm worried about her. The way she's living. It doesn't seem right." Again, he looked at Martha; her expression of concern encouraged him to continue. "I don't know where the money's coming from. I mean, I don't know what he does for a living, and she's stopped working because she's pregnant. So, where do they get an income? I just don't know. He doesn't work anywhere, but they just spend, spend, spend. The house is full of fresh flowers, they eat out all the time, they buy tons of food at the supermarket and throw most of it away, the heating is on all the time, so the bills must be enormous. I just don't understand it. She can buy clothes in the most expensive shops. And, he's not there most of the time. Where does he go? Who does he spend his time with? It worries me and I don't know what to do about it." Barry leaned forward, resting his arms on his knees, his head bowed hoping for an answer.

"What options have you considered?" asked Martha.

"What *can* I do about it? If I ask either of them, I'm not going to get a proper answer, am I? I mean, people who have money to spend with no obvious source of income are not going to tell you the truth. And if I ask them, they're going to be defensive and maybe they'll shut me out of their life. It has to be something illegal that brings in the money. I mean, they're renting a house, and it's small but there's no mention of buying a place or moving to somewhere bigger."

"I can see it's a great cause of anxiety for you," soothed Martha.

"Yea, and I can't do anything about it. But that's not the worst thing. She's talking about being left on her own all the time. How she's going to feel abandoned when the baby comes, because she's got no mother to support her. And, with a husband who's gone all the time, maybe she shouldn't have the baby. I'm just terrified she'll have an abortion."

"Oooh, that's scary." Martha looked worried now.

"I know. I mean, she could just take off, and do that without telling anyone. I'm not sure he would care. Like I say, he's gone a lot of the time. On business, she says. If you ask her what line of business, she just shrugs and says he works for his father and acts as his representative. The guy is very polite and respectful to me, but it feels like just a front. He never attempts a conversation, just replies very courteously. But there's no warmth in him. It's like dealing with a stranger. You don't get to know him. He just gives vague answers to any questions. So, like I say, I get more and more worried about the baby. She could have an abortion without telling him or anyone, for that matter. She must know this guy doesn't care about her, really. I don't know what she was thinking about getting herself pregnant."

"What do her friends think?"

"I haven't talked to her friends. I don't really know them. To be honest, she went a bit off the rails in the last few years. Out late, drinking. She dropped her old friends and took up with new ones she met in pubs. Lynn was too involved with the golf club to … to have any influence over her. So … I don't know what her friends think."

"It might be useful to find out."

"I suppose that's true. I could drop in to see her, unannounced. Do that a couple of times. See who's there when she's not expecting me. Get them to talk to me. See what they think about the baby coming. Whether it's just me who's paranoid or if they think she could do anything she might regret."

"How do you think she'll react about you dropping in unexpectedly?"

"Oh, she won't get angry. She'll just be a bit surprised. She's not a girl who gets angry. She's more inclined to be moody and sulk. But, of course, the hormones are working differently right now, so she may react differently."

Martha smiled. "A new baby would make you a grandfather."

"Well, that's right. It would. It would make me feel anchored. A new life. Someone to love. Someone to care for. Someone who needs me."

"You're lonely, Barry."

Barry breathed deeply, acknowledging his feelings. He closed his eyes. "You're right."

"That's a hard thing to fix." added Martha.

Barry sighed. "You're right. You're at the mercy of other people. I'm vulnerable. I could fall into situations that are not ideal, just because I need some company."

"It's good to be aware."

"I *am* lonely," continued Barry. I get invited to friends' houses for dinner, but it all feels so stiff and uncomfortable, like my situation is top of the agenda, but nobody mentions it. They all take a turn to invite me, but it doesn't happen a second time because it has nowhere to go. I'm not part of a couple. I don't fit in, anymore. If I go to the golf club with just the lads, it's OK at the time, but they go back to their wives and families and I have no-one."

"You have your daughter."

"I do, but that's different. It's not the same, is it?"

Martha made no answer, but her hazel eyes looked into his soul, soothing the ache, understanding and caring, making no judgment. Barry held her gaze for some time; feeling the consolation, he blinked and looked away. Silence followed. Barry sighed several times. Agitation crept back in; he moved his feet, his legs, his arms. Looking at the ground, he ventured, "Martha, I wonder if you ... would consider ... um I mean ..." He swallowed. "It would be a great honor ... if you would have dinner with me," he blurted out in a rush of words. "I mean, you're the most wonderful woman I've ever met. You make me feel so good. You just accept me for myself. You make no demands on me. I just feel we could have such a wonderful relationship."

Martha sighed, letting her sad expression relay her response, before answering. "Barry, we do have a wonderful relationship. It's a professional relationship. I'm your counselor. You pay a fee to come and see me. I will always be your counselor. I will always be here for you. I want the best for you. You *will* find someone to share your life. Be patient. It will happen when you least expect it. In the meantime, we might think whether you want to make another appointment."

CHRISTMAS COMPETITION

"Oh, look at her hat."

"It all lights up. Oh, how funny. Reindeer horns all glowing in different colors."

"Wonder where she got it?"

"Probably from her daughter. She lives in Canada. You get all that flashy stuff over there." All eyes focused on Barbara, who, along with three other ladies, was midway down the fairway of the first hole.

The Christmas competition was well underway. Sixty eight ladies, trickling towards the first tee in groups of four, had turned out to support Robina in her last event as Temporary Captain.

"Is Barbara going to be Vice Captain?" the question was directed towards Robina, by an elderly lady in a red woolen hat.

"Ginger wine, girls?" Robina responded, ignoring the question, as she held out tiny plastic wine glasses. The fiery liquid swirled in dizzy festive mood, hoping to tempt the ladies into its seductive world.

"Ohhh, can't resist. You do think up the most wonderful enticements, Robina," a chubby new member commented.

"I've got shortbread, too. Made it this morning. My special recipe with almonds. Goes really well with ginger wine. Do have some," Robina encouraged, as she lifted a laden plate from the makeshift table; the festive tablecloth flapped in the wind.

"Don't mind if I do." Primrose stretched out her hand in a delicate motion, pursing her lips in anticipation of a wicked mid morning treat. "Well, it *is* Christmas time."

"Where did you get those earrings?" asked Cathy, with a mesmerized gaze.

"Oh, at Compton Acres Garden Center. They have the most amazing stuff. Do you like them?" Primrose touched both ears to draw further attention to the plastic Christmas trees flashing on either side of her head. Cathy's mouth gaped open to reply, but the attention of the group was diverted by the arrival of Madeleine and Alice.

"We're next out, aren't we?" Alice enquired.

"That's right, girls. You can tee off any time now. They've cleared the green in front. Remember, the competition is three clubs and a putter. Record the best two scores on each hole."

Conversation stopped as the foursome turned their attention to the nine hole competition. The winners would each receive a fresh turkey from John Peterson's High Class Family Butchers, complete with chestnut stuffing and chipolata sausages.

"Have a good game, girls," Robina encouraged, as the group strode out cheerfully. "Lunch will be served at one thirty," she reminded them. "So, you'll have plenty of time to change."

"Thanks for the treats, Robina," Madeleine responded. A chorus of thankyous added to Madeleine's offering. The question of Vice Captain remained unanswered.

Several hours later, the dining room was filled with girlish laughter. Smoked salmon had been generally well received as a starter; the chef was now carving a massive turkey while his staff delivered dishes of vegetables to each table.

"My first turkey dinner of the season." Madeleine held her knife and fork in her fists, with great anticipation, her gaze taking in the rest of the committee who shared the large round table.

"You look as if you'll do it justice," joked Primrose.

"*I* certainly will," chimed in Robina.

"I think we should have had a hot starter," commented Barbara. "In this weather, I think all the courses should be warming. To me, smoked salmon is better in the summer."

"It's very good for you," answered Cathy. "You need to eat oily fish twice a week."

"Hark at her," interjected Nancy. "When did you become the club dietician?"

"I used to be a nurse, so I do know a little of what I'm talking about," Cathy answered, haughtily.

"Yes," agreed Alice. "Especially if you're on HRT, you do need to watch your diet."

"I'm coming off it," Robina answered. "Especially after this last scare. You shouldn't stay on it for any longer than five years."

"You'll get all your symptoms back again," commented Cathy.

"Well, I'll just have to cope," Robina smiled back.

"Hey, did anyone watch the 'X factor' on Sunday night?" asked Madeleine, changing the subject.

"No, we were out on the Harley," Alice responded.

"We've recorded it, but haven't watched it yet," said Barbara. "How was it?"

"G4 and Steve were the two finalists. Guess who won?" Madeleine pressed her lips together.

"Has to be G4. Their voices are fantastic. Those guys are so cute, especially the blond one. I could just take him home with me," fantasized Barbara, looking dreamily into the distance.

"No. G4 didn't win. It was Steve. G4 were outstanding and should have won." Madeleine was passionate in her views.

"Of course, you should know what you're talking about," acknowledged Nancy. "You're involved with the Voices Foundation."

"And, you know that guy, Tabby, who was knocked out the week before?" Alice commented. "Guess what? He's been signed up for a record contract. The bikers really liked Tabby. He's a great rock 'n roller."

"We recorded Strictly Come Dancing on Saturday. We're hooked on that." Primrose announced. "We'll watch it tonight."

"Oh, it's wonderful. Takes me back to my youth." Barbara looked wistfully into the distance. "We wore fabulous dresses. I hope ballroom dancing comes back into fashion. Young people have nowhere to meet these days. They have no opportunity to dress up and look their best."

"So, do we have to pay for the wine, Robina?" enquired Madeleine, breaking off Barbara's reminiscing.

"No, it's included," Robina nodded.

"I think that turkey was very dry," Barbara commented. "And the portions were much too large. How can they expect us to eat all that?"

"Well, you can always leave it on your plate. Better too much than too little," Nancy answered.

"So, how's Hugo?" Madeleine diverted attention away from discussion of the menu.

"He's in good spirits. It's such a relief to have his name cleared. We're planning a family party after Christmas, when my New Zealand visitors are here."

"And the rest of the family?" continued Madeleine.

"Oh, they're well, thanks. Just our son-in-law, George. He's a bit of a difficult one. We have a financial arrangement with him, and the rest of the family, which is not a great success, so we'll have to get our heads round that." Robina's expression clouded with worry and a sense of foreboding, but cleared as she added, "But, I'm so looking forward to seeing my little granddaughter again." Turning to Barbara, Robina enquired, "How's Percy? I haven't seen him for some time."

"Oh, he's doing OK. It's called the relatives' disease, you know, but I'm dealing with it as best I can," Barbara answered, with a long suffering expression.

"And how's business, Primrose? You and Marius keeping busy?" Robina continued the social enquiries.

"Yes, we're busy alright. We've just got some issues brewing with Marius's brothers in South Africa. They really need him over there to sort things out. It's a very difficult time for us, at the moment."

"What about the house move?" Barbara was keen to know.

"Oh, I don't know about that. It's not a good time to sell right now, and there's nothing much to look at on the market. It depends on the South African situation. Whether Marius goes over there, on his own, to sort it out ... or what. Oh, I don't know. It's really difficult. It's quite a strain actually." Tears brimmed in Primrose's eyes.

"How are the bikers?" Madeleine enquired, looking at Alice.

"Oh, we're having a great time. The motorbike has given us a new lease of life. We just have to sort out insurance, and we can't do that until Don passes his test. I didn't realize you had to pass a test. I really thought your driver's license was okay for a motorbike. But, he drives very carefully, so we should be fine. We're going to a Christmas thing at Bishopstoke with all the bikers. So, we're looking forward to that. What a bunch of people they are, all different kinds of people," Alice enthused, hiding her anxiety about Don spending yet another day without insurance for the motorbike; since he retired, he seemed to have thrown caution to the winds.

"And you don't miss the garden center?" Barbara enquired.

"No, not really. Perhaps Don does, just a little, but he has the most marvelous Christmas present organized for his brothers. It's to do with the garden center. We hope they'll be thrilled."

"Sounds intriguing," responded Barbara.

"I haven't seen Rodney for ages." Alice turned to Cathy. "Thought I saw him on a motorbike yesterday, but I must have been mistaken."

"No, he's been busy ... and he doesn't have a motorbike," Cathy answered, tersely, as she looked away. Turning back to the others on the table, she asked, "So, what are we all doing for Christmas?"

"Oh, we've got our daughter coming over from Canada," chimed in Barbara. "It will be so nice to have all the family together." Abruptly, she followed her answer with, "Nancy, what are you doing for Christmas? I hope you won't be on your own."

Nancy's face flushed as she answered, quietly, "My daughter and the kids are coming over."

"Oh, as long as you're not on your own," Barbara repeated, pointedly.

"Here comes dessert." Madeleine looked up, with anticipation, as a rich, dark, Christmas pudding, decorated with a sprig of holly, was delivered to the table along with a jug of thick brandy sauce. "Oh, it's worth having Christmas just for the pudding," she sighed, in appreciation.

"I would much rather have a fruit salad than all these calories," Barbara commented.

"And, what about Adam?" How is he?" Primrose enquired.

"Oh, struggling on. Always problems to solve," answered Madeleine, looking troubled.

"And, how's the oil price?" Primrose enjoyed hearing about business issues.

"Well, it depends if you're talking about sweet or sour, light or crude."

"Eh?" Primrose looked uncomprehending.

"Well, in general, the oil price is coming down. I really think the whole world economy is manipulated by some very powerful people."

"You do?" Primrose wanted to hear more about Madeleine's view of the world.

"Well, think about it. All of a sudden, the price of oil shoots up to a record high, apparently due to lack of supply, although the newspapers were commenting that speculators were pushing the price up. Anyway, it raises big concerns about the global economy In the meantime, investors have made billions of dollars while the price was high. Now, after these few months of panic, suddenly, the oil price has dropped almost twenty five percent since the record price in October. And what's happened to the dollar now? It's sliding down a greasy pole. I do believe all of this is orchestrated to line the pockets of those who are already mega rich and powerful."

"What does Adam think?" asked Primrose.

"Oh, he thinks it's impossible. He doesn't believe any group of people is powerful enough to manipulate the world economy. He gets quite worked up about it. He's warned me never to express these views in the company of his business associates." Silence descended on the table as Madeleine's comments were digested.

"So, when can we open the Christmas presents?" Primrose chirped, with a bright smile, wondering whether she should have started the discussion with Madeleine.

"Now, this is one thing I do agree with," Barbara commented. "It's much better to bring the present unwrapped. When we used to bring them all wrapped up, some people brought the most amazing rubbish." There was a general rolling of eyes around the table. "So, that's one good change you've brought in, Robina. And, I'm pleased to see the budget has been kept to five pounds. Of course, some people don't spend that much. You find you've trailed round the shops looking for something really nice and you've gone over budget, and someone else has thrown in something they had in a cupboard, which obviously cost much less than five pounds." Barbara gave a scowl of disapproval.

Alice's eyes narrowed, flickering over the gift she had contributed, wishing that anyone but Barbara was the recipient of the basket of bath oils she had agonized over. "So, don't you like your gift, Barbara?" Alice enquired.

"Well!" Barbara wore an expression of disdain; she said nothing further, but passed her hand dismissively over the items, as if she were a magician, hoping for the offering to turn into something else entirely.

Robina stood up, tapping her coffee spoon against her wine glass; the tinkling sound waves sent the golden liquid shivering into a silent seesaw of anticipation. "Ladies!" Robina caught the attention of the festive gathering. "Before I pass you over to Anastasia, the proprietor of our club who will announce today's winners, I want to extend our thanks to Anastasia for kindly donating the prizes. You will be amused to hear that no-one on your committee will be collecting a prize today. We all played fairly well, but couldn't notch up a winning score." Robina's cheerful face took on a more somber expression, as she continued, "I know you'll want to join me in remembering Lynn in your prayers over Christmas. The loss of our Lady Captain in such tragic circumstances, a person with such vitality, is keenly felt by all the members and we honor her memory. Our prayers also go to Lynn's family who will feel such an emptiness this Christmas." Heads bowed around the room, a stillness descending as each member paid their silent respects, remembering the fire at Lynn's home. Allowing a brief pause, Robina continued, "It remains for me to wish all of you a peaceful and joyful Christmas. Today is my last social gathering as your Temporary Captain. I thank you all for your support in recent months. We will be holding discussions, after our next committee meeting, and will be able to formally make announcements regarding your new Captain and the committee at the Annual Meeting." Eyebrows rose, since members were accustomed to hearing the announcement of their new Captain and Vice Captain at the Christmas competition. "So, take time to enjoy your coffee. Today, is a good opportunity to start off next year's calendar by arranging playing partners for upcoming competitions. So, again, I wish you all a wonderful Christmas and look forward to seeing you in the New Year."

NEXT IN LINE

Christmas arrived in a haze of excitement. Christmas cards were received with delight or cast carelessly aside. Grocery shopping took on gigantic proportions, as shoppers stockpiled delicacies from stores brimming with gargantuan quantities of produce from all over the world. Telephone lines burned with chatter as relatives and friends organized social gatherings.

Stress and tension levels soared as travelers braved motorways and airlines to spend time with loved ones. The despairing hunt for presents had come to an end, recipients either squealing with delight or politely setting gifts aside. Grumblings that Christmas was just a commercial enterprise were forgotten, as shafts of joy speared the winter darkness.

Boxing Day, the day after Christmas and the more relaxed time of the winter festivities, received a seismic shock as the word 'tsunami' numbed the senses of the world. Aid agencies and rescue workers were overwhelmed with the scale of the disaster in Asia. New Year's Eve celebrations were muted, as those alive and well in the western world, shared their good fortune with those in desperate need, on the other side of the globe.

January rolled slowly forward. Looking back on the year gone by, all across the United Kingdom, thoughts of how to make the year ahead better than the year before were taking root. Looking forward, members of Middle Wallop Golf Club considered how their lives might change in the forthcoming months.

Robina, still as Temporary Captain until the Annual Meeting, had set a date for chairing her last committee meeting. In discussion with Past Captains, the decision had been made about who would take the ladies' section forward in 2005 as Captain and Vice Captain of Middle Wallop Golf Club. Robina was uncomfortable with the task ahead, but believed the right decisions had been made.

Friday, the twenty first of January, was the date for the committee meeting. A glorious winter morning. Mild temperatures. Not a breath of wind. The countryside displaying a contemporary appearance. Minimalist branches and twigs silhouetted against the pale sunlight, illuminating the clear blue sky. Birdsong, high in the trees, giving a feel of spring to the air.

Unlike the atmosphere of previous committee meetings, where spirits and energy levels were high, on this occasion faces were drawn, mirroring feelings of tension and apprehension. Everyone knew that Nancy would be Captain, since she was already Vice Captain, but who would be nominated to take her place as Captain for the following year? There was not a more closely kept secret. Only those who were Past Captains knew the answer, guarding their knowledge with a common shield, never making reference to the loaded question, or alluding to the merits or demerits of any possible candidate. Names had been bandied around the clubhouse by members in conversations over coffee cups; other names had been whispered around dinner tables, while husbands discussed sport and business. Who would it be? Today would reveal the answer.

"Well, ladies, we've covered everything on the agenda," stated Robina, biting her lip, as she thought of the task ahead. "I just need a private word with each of you, now. After each individual session, I would appreciate if you could make your way home. It would be helpful if our private discussion remained confidential, and I know that will be difficult if you stay on the premises. This is merely a request, with a view to respecting your feelings and avoiding embarrassment. It's inevitable that some disappointment will follow, and I'm sure you'll join me in wanting to maintain a civilized appearance." All eyes stared at Robina. "Nancy, how would you like to be first?" Robina smiled encouragingly. "We can use the accounts office today." Robina stood up, waiting for Nancy to accept her invitation. Nancy copied Robina's body language, standing up slowly and following her into the small office.

Both Robina and Nancy held their breath as they entered the office, making no eye contact as they seated themselves on either side of the small wooden desk in the cramped surroundings. Robina exhaled deeply, placing her hands on the desk in front of her. "Nancy," she started, while looking at her hands. Raising her eyes to meet Nancy's gaze, she continued, "How are you?"

"Oh ... eh ... fine," answered Nancy, rather thrown by the question.

"It's been a difficult year for you," Robina continued.

"Well, yes it has."

"You've had that nasty business with Colin, such a shock, and you've been left to live alone."

"Well ... yes." Nancy wondered that Robina made no mention of her hasty living arrangements with Darren after Colin disappeared.

"But we're not here to talk about that," Robina continued. "We're here to talk about the Past Captain's nominations for the year ahead."

"Right." Nancy exhaled a sigh of relief.

"Nancy, this is not easy for me. I would prefer not to have to broach this subject, and it may not be a total surprise to hear what I have to say." Robina fixed Nancy with a meaningful stare. Nancy stared back. "Nancy, it's common knowledge that you're having an affair with Darren, who is not a stranger to this club. He's the resident professional golfer and there are reputations to uphold, all round." Nancy blushed and looked away. Robina continued, "I know you must be feeling uncomfortable that I've raised this matter, but later you'll understand that it had to be taken into consideration. Nancy, the club just can't have this kind of situation. I know you could argue that you're both effectively single, but we can't have the position of Captain scandalized. The view is that your relationship with Darren is in conflict with the needs of the club. The feeling is that every time you represent the club, there will be whisperings and this is a situation we would prefer not to have." Robina observed tears filling Nancy's eyes. "Now, this is not to say that we never want you as Captain. It's been a really difficult year for you, and you have a lot of sorting out to do in the time ahead. We just don't feel the time is right. Do you understand?"

Nancy nodded. As she did so, tears spilled down her cheeks. She tried to speak, but her voice was hoarse; a sob caught in her breath. Tensing every muscle, she asked, "What am I going to tell people? I mean, I'm Vice Captain. Everyone expects me to be Captain."

"Well, I can't tell you what to say, but if you state that it's been a really difficult year for you, and you want to defer being Captain until your personal life is more settled, I think everyone would accept that. I think the members would be relieved at your decision, and I think it really would give you time to stabilize your life. You'll enjoy being Captain much more if you leave it until another year."

Nancy trembled, tears brimming over her eyelids. "OK, I suppose that's the way to handle it. I expect they'll swallow that. I wanted to be Captain so much, Robina," her eyes pleaded, hoping she might melt a fraction of Robina's resolve.

"I know. I know. Perhaps next year," Robina soothed. "Now, let's get you home," she added, injecting action into her words by standing up.

Looking bewildered, Nancy stood up without meeting Robina's eyes again. "Yes, I do need to get my house in order," she muttered, her head bowed as she picked up her multi-colored patchwork handbag. Without a word of farewell, she walked slowly out of the room.

"Safe home," called Robina to Nancy's retreating back.

Robina sat down with a sigh; she remained motionless for several minutes, staring ahead at the blank wall. Eventually, she shuffled her feet, bringing herself back to the task at hand. Walking slowly back to the outer area, a group of expectant eyes fixed on her returning bulk. "Barbara, are you ready?" Robina produced a bright smile of encouragement to cover her anxiety. Barbara jumped to her feet, picking up her Burberry handbag, arriving to face Robina with surprising speed. Stepping back to gain some personal space, Robina turned back into the small office.

Sitting down at the desk, Robina found Barbara's eager countenance quite disconcerting. Robina's confidence ebbed as Barbara's energy filled the room. "Barbara, this is not easy for me. It's not going to be easy for you, either." Barbara's eager looks turned to an accusing scowl. "I know you were expecting to be Vice Captain this year." Barbara's features became rigid as she stared at Robina. "Well, a lot has happened this year. Nancy has had a difficult year and you have too, for very different reasons." A red glow appeared on Barbara's neck. "The feeling is that taking on being Vice Captain this year, and being Captain the following year, is too much to expect. You have a husband who needs you. We feel the demands of the club and the pressures of life at home would be too much of a strain for anyone in your circumstances. Therefore, we are allowing you to defer the responsibility, until such time as you might be more free to enjoy the role."

The red glow flooded from Barbara's neck to color her face; the chords on her neck stood out as she stood up. "You can't be serious," she hissed. Robina made no answer. "Are you telling me," Barbara's voice rose, as she spoke slowly and deliberately, "that after Nancy asking me to be her Vice Captain, you're saying you don't want that to happen?"

"Well, it's not that I don't want it to happen. It's just that the Past Captains feel it would be better if you take a break to deal with Percy. Spend time with him. You'll need to get him settled into a situation where he has constant care. We're allowing you time out of your commitment to the club, so that you can get your personal life stabilized."

"How dare you!" spat out Barbara. "How dare you, or anyone else, prescribe how I should handle my personal life!"

"Barbara, please see that we're looking after your best interests."

"My best interests? You've got to be joking. Quite clearly, you prefer someone else. And, if you think I'm going to take this lying down, you can think again. I've given more than anybody to this club. I've given my time and support to every event, not just last year, but over many years. This is just a kick in the teeth." Barbara's face contorted with rage.

"It's not like that, Barbara, really," Robina protested, her grey eyes earnestly beseeching.

"Well, what is it like, then? Explain it. Just exactly what is it like, if it's not a kick in the teeth? I've told people that I'll be Vice Captain. Just what are they going to think when that doesn't happen? Don't you see? I'll never get any respect from the members if you do this to me!" Barbara's voice became gradually louder with each word she uttered, as the pain of rejection pricked every pore of her skin.

"Barbara, it's not a good idea to give out information, which has not been ratified by the Past Captains. You must know that."

"I tell you what I do know. This stinks! You can just shove your golf club. Do you think I need you lot? I need you like a hole in the head. I'm going to take over Percy's business. And, you see if I don't make a big success of it. I resign from this club." Barbara stalked out of the room, slamming the door behind her. The energy of her anger filled the small office. The walls seemed to reverberate with the force of Barbara's feelings: the room felt as if it must explode with the power of her rage.

Realizing that she was shaking slightly from the effort of dealing with Barbara, Robina remained motionless allowing the beginning of calmness to return. After a few minutes, she sighed deeply and slowly made her way to the outer area. "I need a cup of tea," she stated simply. Moving across to the drinks machine, she slid a pound coin into the slot and placed a cup under the spout. The hot liquid squirted into the white earthenware cup, steam creating condensation on the saucer. Turning away from the machine, her flow of energy easing back, Robina forced a tiny smile towards Madeleine who remained seated at the table among the remaining committee members. "Madeleine, I would like to speak to you next." Robina looked down at the cup with its promise of revival. "Give me a minute or two."

Allowing Robina time to enjoy her cup of tea, Madeleine remained silent at the table, while the others speculated about what had caused Barbara to storm out of the building. "Suppose I better go in now," Madeleine muttered, after what seemed a decent interval. Looking anxious, she made her way into the narrow corridor towards the accounts office. Reaching the open door, she inclined her head while asking, "Would you like more time to finish your tea, Robina?"

"No, no. Finished already. Come in. Come in," Robina enthused. "Sit down, Madeleine."

Madeleine made herself comfortable in the chair opposite Robina, and looked expectantly across the desk. Robina's expression was now one of delight, as she anticipated the news she was about to impart. "Madeleine, you've not been a member of the club as long as some of the other ladies." Madeleine blinked, wondering what was about to follow. "But, we feel you have represented us extremely well." Madeleine smiled at the compliment. "You've been Bronze Division Captain this year, your first year as an office bearer, and you've shown yourself to be very committed to your responsibilities. You can be relied on to handle an assignment with great flair and you supported other committee members with their responsibilities. You've reduced your handicap which is another feather in your cap. You overcame great difficulties, and put them behind you when you had that dreadful business with Nancy's husband. Some might say, mind you, that you were a little too smart in the way you handled that but, never mind, others think you did a brilliant job to name and shame. In summary, Madeleine, the Past Captains believe you are very capable and would like you to represent the club as Captain."

Madeleine gaped at Robina with astonishment. "But I don't have enough experience. There must be many other people who want to do this; people who are expecting this appointment."

"Yes, that's true. We were all looking forward to Nancy being Captain, but she feels she needs time to sort her life out, now that her circumstances have changed."

"Really?" Madeleine looked dubious. "And Barbara?" she questioned. "It's common knowledge that Barbara expects to be Vice Captain. She told me herself. She's Silver Division Captain. She should step up to be Captain."

"Well, you see, Barbara has Percy to consider. He's going downhill quite rapidly and has to be her first priority. In fact, I'm not sure she'll want to play much golf, while she's dealing with all the changes in her life."

"Oh." Madeleine looked down at the floor, blinking rapidly, "Robina, I ..."

"It's such an honor, Madeleine, and I will give you all the help and support you could ever need. Really. I've got a lot of experience under my belt, and I know the members very well, so I would be delighted to give you any advice and guidance. Not that you'd need it," Robina rushed on, "but I'm here whenever you want to call on me for anything at all."

"Robina, really, I'm not the right person."

"Of course you are. All the Past Captains have supported your nomination, Madeleine. You should be proud."

"Well, I am very honored but, really, I can't accept."

"Why ever not?" Robina answered sharply.

"Well, it's just not something I want to do. You have to be really dedicated to be Captain. You have to devote yourself entirely to the position. I just don't feel I have that kind of commitment."

"Well, yes, you do have to be dedicated, Madeleine, but you won't be doing the job alone. You'll have tremendous support from your committee and you can look to any of the Past Captains for advice and guidance."

"Robina, I just can't. I don't feel I want to embrace this. I think, to take on the position of Captain, you have to feel excited and enthusiastic about the prospect. I don't feel like that. I have other interests and commitments and I feel they would suffer."

"Oh, come on, Madeleine. Surely, you can make other things a low priority, just for one year?" entreated Robina.

"Well, of course, I could. Other people have done so. It's just not something I want to take on."

"You really disappoint me, Madeleine." Robina's brow furrowed and her lips pursed.

"I'm sorry, Robina."

"You know, Madeleine, I really stuck my neck out to get you this nomination."

Madeleine looked down at the floor, her eyes fixing on the gold buckles of her black Russell & Bromley shoes, but she made no answer. A few seconds of uncomfortable silence followed. "It's not just that, Robina. Things are changing in my life. Adam and I have been thinking that we want to move back to London. We also want to buy a place in the sun, probably Spain."

"Oh … but what about his job?"

"Well, he does so much traveling, it doesn't matter where he's based."

"Oh."

"In any case, he's thinking of giving up his job." Madeleine sighed.

"What?"

"Well, he's just sick of it, really. Trying to please demanding shareholders and board members is a battle he no longer wants to fight. So … we are, in fact, waiting to hear from a charity whether they will take us both on in Asia."

"You are?"

"Well, yes. At Christmas time, we were just so overwhelmed with the scale of the tsunami disaster, we both felt our lives were worthless if we sat back in luxury, while people on the other side of the world needed our help. So, all being well, that's what we'll do."

"Oh, my word."

Madeleine sucked her breath through her teeth. "Don't think we're not apprehensive and they may not want us, anyway, but we've applied and will just see how it all works out."

Robina sighed, "And, I've just told Nancy she can't be Captain and Barbara has resigned from the club."

"What?"

"Well, I never imagined you wouldn't want to be Captain."

"But you said ..."

"I know what I said, but you have to be diplomatic, don't you?" Robina shook her head and sighed again in an agitated way. "And now I've lost it. I've blurted this out to you. You have to keep this under your hat, Madeleine. Please respect my confidence on this."

"Of course."

So, as far as you, and everyone else, is concerned, Nancy wants to stabilize her personal life and Barbara is focusing on looking after Percy. Right? That's the story." Robina nodded to emphasize her request. "But, honestly, we can't have Nancy as our Captain when she's carrying on with young Darren. She has to choose where she wants to focus her energies. It would be bad enough a lady member having a fling with the young professional, but the Captain ... well, it's just not on. As for Barbara ... well, she's just so negative all the time, and very opinionated, and she's not got a good word to say for anyone ... although, Percy having Alzheimer's is a serious issue. So ... we thought we would grab you while we can. But, I guess, we weren't quick enough." Robina spoke rapidly as the words spilled out. Looking uncomfortable, the pace of Robina's words slowed as she continued, "But, Madeleine, what I've just said now is totally confidential, between you and me. It's just for your information, under these special circumstances. I trust you to keep this private and not to mention it to anyone."

"Of course."

"So, like I say, Nancy wants to stabilize her personal life, and Barbara is spending less time on golf now that she's looking after Percy. Right?"

"Got it," Madeleine confirmed.

"Well, Madeleine, I wish you success in your endeavors. I really admire you. It's such a brave thing to do ... throwing everything up to help others in distress. You will keep me posted on developments, won't you?"

"Sure will." Madeleine stood up, bending over to give Robina a kiss on the cheek. "And good luck on sorting out your Captain problems."

Robina smiled weakly. "Thanks, I think I'm going to need good luck."

Madeleine seemed to simply disappear from the room, but suddenly reappeared, looking alarmed. "Oh, Robina, our plans about the charity work in Asia are confidential. That goes without saying. Don't mention it to anyone until we've got it confirmed. I'll let you know when we hear," her clear voice rang out an alert.

"Yes, OK," Robina assented. Madeleine disappeared again, leaving a trail of agitation behind. Suddenly, Robina jumped up from the chair to follow Madeleine down the corridor. "What about the dog?" Robina called out. Madeleine turned round and looked blankly. "What about Rex? If you go away what's going to happen to him, Madeleine? We could take him, if you want."

Madeleine's features registered surprise. "Oh, thanks, Robina. We haven't got to thinking that far." Looking a little bewildered, and hoping no-one had overheard, Madeleine turned back towards the exit door.

Robina returned to the accounts office, noticing for the first time the calendar on the wall showing a scene of the Cotswolds in the snow. Dropping herself into the brown leather chair, she leaned her elbows on the desk, bringing her face to meet her hands. Dragging her fingers through her hair, holding it in place behind her ears, her palms touched the roughness of her silver earrings. Gathering her thoughts, she wondered, "... I think Hugo would be happy to take Rex ... he would be company for Spindle ... what am I going to do ... I really thought Madeleine would be thrilled ... what am I going to do ... we have no Captain ... no Vice Captain ... can't think what to do next ... the Past Captains ... what are they going to say ... I've messed this up ... no, they've messed this up ... we should have considered all possibilities ... why didn't we consider that Madeleine would turn us down ... what am I going to do next ... can't run round phoning everyone ... would take weeks to sort this out ... perhaps I ought to plow on ... just use my own judgment ... which committee members are sitting out there ... it's got to be one of them ... perhaps if I just prioritize ... call them in order of preference ... see how it all works out ... that's all I can do ... the Past Captains will just have to accept that I had no alternative ..." Robina's hair was slightly mussed up where she had run her hands through again. She moved objects around the desk, a pen, a notepad, her car keys. Picking up her well worn navy handbag, she rummaged around inside, pulling out a small packet of tissues. Drawing a tissue from the packet, she crumpled the softness in her hand before rubbing it briskly across her forehead; a deep pink glow from the rough treatment emblazoned her brow. Letting her breath out in deep puffs, Robina regained her composure. "… so what next … who next … let's see … Alice … how about Alice … yes, don't see why not … she's been a member a long time … don't think anyone would object … maybe she's a bit dull … and talks too much … but she's reliable … what does it matter … she'll be competent enough … don't see why she can't … under the circumstances … whew … that's a relief … Alice … yes, Alice would be fine … no real objections there … she'd be OK … yes, that's what I'll do …" Robina straightened her clothes, using the palms of her hands to smooth down her sides, tugging the bottom of her navy woolen sweater until the wrinkles disappeared, leaving the garment hanging obediently in shape. Standing up, she held her head high and adjusted her posture to shrug off the slouch which had manifested itself during the morning sessions. Taking two steps towards the door, she stood for a moment. After a deep breath, she confidently said aloud, "Right. Alice. Here we go." Walking smartly into the outer area, Robina made eye contact with Alice. "Alice, are you ready?"

Alice carried on talking as she stood up, "… the chip into the shop and they develop them. You just choose on the screen the pictures you want, so you don't end up with rubbish photos." She gathered her belongings, dropping items into her handbag as she continued, "… I really like it, and it fits into the handbag no problem, lightweight too, perfect for holidays. I was so thrilled with it. A perfect present, but my daughter is so thoughtful, she always comes up with good ideas for gifts." Robina stood, patiently waiting. "Be right with you, Robina," assured Alice, glancing up from fiddling with her handbag. Pushing her chair back into position, Alice turned towards Robina. "I was just telling them about the digital camera my daughter got me for Christmas. I never thought I wanted one." Robina turned round to walk towards the accounts office, politely inclining her head to indicate that she was listening, as Alice followed her footsteps. Robina reached the office and sat down heavily. Alice stood, holding the back of the chair opposite. "Have you got a digital camera, Robina? With all your grandchildren, it would be a wonderful thing to have. You can print them from your computer, as well." Alice placed her handbag at the side of the chair.

"There might even be really good bargains in the sales. I must get to the sales, you know. I would like to get new curtains for the bedroom." Alice sat down neatly, shuffling the chair until it was parallel to the desk. "Have you been to the sales yet, Robina?"

Robina smiled. "Alice, I need to talk to you about the golf club."

"Oh, yes, that's what you're talking to everyone about. We were just wondering who's going to be Vice Captain. We normally know by this time. It's awfully ..."

"It's you," Robina cut in.

Alice shook her head. "... late in the year," she continued, "I think we always know around November time. I can't think why we don't know already. I mean it's the middle of January, already. In the ..."

"Alice," Robina cut in again. "I'm asking you to be Captain of the club this year."

"Oh, that can't be right. It's Nancy who's going to be Captain. Everyone knows that." Alice frowned.

"Well, no. Things have changed." Robina had Alice's full attention now.

"Changed. Why, what's happened?"

"Well, Nancy has had a difficult time this year, as you know, so she has deferred being Captain until she has her life sorted out."

"Yes, but Barbara is Vice Captain, so she would slot in, surely?" Alice looked perplexed.

"Well, she's going through a difficult period. Percy needs a lot of looking after, so Barbara is giving golf a back seat for a while."

Robina and Alice became frozen in a moment of time, as both tried to reach each others frame of reference across the desk. Robina's eyes held a beseeching gaze, while Alice frowned in concentration, trying to make sense of this new information. Robina felt her body temperature drop a few degrees, as she observed Alice's reactions; she moved her arms and shoulders as cold air seemed to settle onto her skin.

The ground seemed to shift underneath Alice, as her fondness for routine and order were shaken. She shook her head. "This isn't right," she whispered, shaking her head again.

"How do you mean?" Robina asked.

"Well, it just isn't right. Nancy was appointed as Vice Captain. She should be Captain. It doesn't matter that she's had a difficult year. There's nothing she can't deal with. She should be Captain."

"Yes, I know, Alice. In an ideal world, you're absolutely right. But we're not in an ideal world."

"Even so, Barbara is expecting to be Vice Captain. She told me so.

Nancy asked her. So, Barbara should be next in line as Captain."

"Yes, well, things don't always work out to plan, Alice. You must know that." A look of frustration gathered on Robina's features. Alice gazed at Robina, in a dumfounded way. Robina continued, "Look, Alice. What happens at the garden center? You plant seeds, don't you? They don't always take root. Or you have plants that become diseased. You don't sell them, do you? You throw them away and use the healthy plants."

"What's that got to do with the golf club?"

Robina sighed. "Well, I'm just trying to show you that, if things don't turn out, you have to make changes. Just like at the garden center."

"But that's plants. Not people. You can't treat people like plants."

A huge gasp of air escaped from Robina, as she drew her arms into her sides in a defensive pose. "Things haven't worked out as we expected, Alice."

"At the garden center, we've all worked together for years. Through thick and thin. No matter what happened, we just kept on going. There were difficulties between us, but we soldiered on. Steady business, that's what we had. Always."

"I know, I know, Alice. And that was great. But we need you. We need you to step in as Captain. You've been Secretary. You've been on the committee a number of years. You've proved yourself. You're steady. You're reliable. That's what we need. A steady pair of hands."

Alice shook her head, obstinately. "This just isn't right, Robina. I don't want to step in, under these circumstances."

"I thought you would be thrilled, Alice. You would do such a good job. You know you would. You're so reliable. We wouldn't have any disasters if you were Captain."

"What kind of disasters?"

"The kind we've got at the moment." Robina's voice was raised now, as her composure slipped.

"Oh?"

"Well, here's the truth of it, Alice. Nancy's having an affair with young Darren. The members feel it's entirely inappropriate for the Lady Captain to be acting in such a fashion. We've made our views known to Nancy and she has deferred being Captain, until such times as her life is back in order. As for Barbara, well, the members have made strong representation that they don't want to see her being Captain of this club."

"Why ever not?"

"Oh, Alice, please don't make this any more difficult for me," pleaded Robina.

"What's wrong with Barbara that she can't be Captain?" Alice insisted.

"Oh, you must know, yourself, that Barbara has shown herself to be a somewhat different personality, more recently. Initially, she was popular because she was full of life and gave a lot of time to the club, but she's become overconfident, she's become rather negative, outspoken and complaining, and it's not what people want."

"Well, people are just too fussy. They should be pleased that people like Barbara and Nancy are willing to give up their time for the sake of the club," Alice stated, stoutly.

"Alice. This is an opportunity for you. Don't you want to be Captain? Surely, you must. You wouldn't be on the committee, otherwise."

"At some point, yes. But I'm not prepared for this, Robina. I might consider being Vice Captain. I'd have to talk it over with Don. It's out of the question for me to be Captain. Don has just retired. We're having great fun with the motorbike. Our marriage hasn't been this good for a long time. I'm not prepared to put that at risk. I'm not the kind of person who likes to be thrown in at the deep end. I like to be prepared. Perhaps, if you find someone else to be Captain, I would consider being Vice Captain. But I would have to think it over, and I would have to talk to Don. Give me time."

"Well, okay, Alice. I understand," Robina acknowledged. "I know it's thrown you, asking you to consider this out of the blue. Give it some thought and come back to me in your own time."

Alice looked hard at Robina. "It's just that ..."

"I know. I know. Alice, think it over."

"Robina, you surprise me."

"I do?"

"Yes. You're not acting like yourself. All this changing about. It's not like you."

"Well, I don't act alone. I have to carry out the wishes of the club."

"It all seems a bit desperate."

"Well, desperate times require desperate measures."

"I don't envy you." Alice's face tightened with disapproval. "Anyway, I'll leave you to it."

"Thanks, Alice."

Alice gathered up her belongings in neat little movements, predetermining every action. She stood up straight, her back stiff, her fingers wrapping round the straps of her new Jane Shulton handbag.

Reaching the door, she turned to face Robina's profile. "Good luck," she offered before making her way outside.

"Wheeeew," Robina exhaled deeply, dropping her head on the desk, her arms outstretched before her. "...what next ... what on earth do I do now ... who's left out there ... can't finish today without ... without a Captain ... no Captain ... no Vice Captain ... oh, I know ... Primrose ... she's still here ... she's Handicap Secretary ... that would be OK ... she's done a good job ... learned all there is to know ... it's a difficult job ... probably the most difficult on the committee ... takes a lot of time ... under the circumstances ... if she agreed ... that would be fine ... can't think people would object ... they might be surprised ... but they wouldn't object ... the Past Captains would understand ... desperate times ... desperate measures ... shouldn't be like this ... we shouldn't be desperate ... members should feel honored to take this on ... oh, well ... better pull myself together ... better get on with it ... Alice was a pain in the neck, just now ... preaching to me ... just let her try dealing with this ... see how she would get on ... all very well ... making judgments from the sidelines ... her time will come ... then maybe she'll understand ... mind you, she's got a point ... anyway ... don't think about that ... get on with the task in hand ... Primrose ... Primrose ... yes ... she's next in line ... next in line to the throne ... huh ... all the privilege ... all the pressure ... all the isolation ... all the complaints ... is it worth it ... hmmm ... don't think about that ... get on with the job in hand ... Primrose ... right ... need a cuppa ... let's get a proper one ..." Robina heaved herself out of the chair, almost staggering with her first few steps out of the office. Reaching the outer area, she noted that only Primrose and Cathy were left seated at the round table; both looked up expectantly. "Going to get a coffee," Robina announced. "A proper one."

Sauntering, at a deliberately slow pace in an effort to stay calm, Robina reached the black granite counter; her eyes roved over all the cakes and pastries; muffins in plastic wrappers, flapjacks neatly piled together, a few Danish pastries left from the morning, fresh cakes ready for the afternoon. Giving a little groan of appreciation, she asked, "What's that one?" pointing to a moist, round temptation.

"Apple and ginger," was the reply from the shy looking, young waitress.

"Oooooh, sure it's not too heavy?" The girl looked at her, without answering. "Why don't you cut me a piece? Let's see how it looks in the middle." The girl obliged. "Hmmm, looks a bit stodgy." Robina eyed the two other cakes. "What are the other two? Can't tell from the topping."

The girl answered, "This one is cherry and coconut. The other one is date and walnut with coffee butter icing."

"Oh, yes, that's the one for me," Robina declared, emphatically. "And a cappuccino, please."

Walking at a considerably slow pace, one hand balancing the plate which proudly displayed the wedge of cake, the other hand keeping the frothy drink steady, Robina made her way back towards the accounts office. For the first time, she noticed that the carpet was a mottled mixture of blues and purples, a flat, hard wearing, covering suitable for withstanding the pounding of many feet over a long period of time. Arriving back at the table where Cathy and Primrose were seated, she commented, "You still here, Cathy?"

"Well, yes, I am the Immediate Past Captain, so I'm still a committee member, ex officio."

"Well, so you are. So nice of you to stay behind with the others." Robina's voice held a faint air of surprise. Cathy gave a tight little smile which showed no trace of humor.

"Do you want me to come in now, Robina?" Primrose enquired.

Robina would really have liked just five minutes of luxury time to allow the solace of the cake to seep into the hollow aches of her soul. "Eh ... yes, OK," she answered in a distracted, airy fashion. As the waitress had sliced the knife through the moist confection, she had visions of holding the wedge up to her mouth, had anticipated the sensation of the butter icing, feeling the smooth texture consoling her inadequacies while the bitter sweet coffee flavor alerted her taste buds. A cloud of disappointment descended on her spirit. Inspiration quickly kicked in. "Oh, I've forgotten a cake fork. You wouldn't do me a favor and bring me one, would you?" she entreated.

"Yes, OK." Primrose stood up to respond to her request.

"Thanks." Robina turned her back on Cathy to avoid any more conversation or further obstacles to the secret enjoyment ahead. Reaching the accounts office, she lowered the cup and saucer onto the table. Without sitting down, she took hold of the cake, held it up in the air and slowly brought the wedge towards her mouth; she allowed the soothing mixture to melt on her tongue. Swallowing gently, she closed her eyes as the comforting moment revived her spirit.

Primrose appeared at her side, holding out a fork. "Oh, thanks." Robina laid the cake down on the desk, putting the fork on the plate. "I'll finish it later," she explained. "Just have the coffee now. Don't you want a coffee, Primrose?"

"Just had one, thanks."

"Oh, right." Robina moved the cup and saucer closer to her, running a finger along the thin blue line which decorated the edge of the china. "So ... Primrose, sorry you've been kept waiting, but obviously I do need to talk to everyone on the committee about what's happening next year." Primrose smiled and nodded. Robina moved her elbows across the desk to bridge the distance between herself and Primrose, who was sitting bolt upright, waiting to drink in what Robina was about to say. "Primrose, you've been Handicap Secretary this year and you've done a fantastic job."

"Thank you." Primrose brightened with pleasure at the compliment.

"Have you enjoyed it?"

"Oh, yes, I really did. It's been a great learning experience and I've enjoyed being part of the committee."

"Yes, you've had a good year. So much so, that the club ... that is the Past Captains, want you to become Captain next year."

Primrose closed her eyes and moved her head from side to side. Opening her eyes again, she exclaimed, "I must be dreaming."

A little chuckle escaped from Robina. A light hearted feeling of relief flooded the muscles on her neck and shoulders, which had become taut during the afternoon's discussions. "Surprised?" she beamed a huge smile at Primrose.

"Well, astounded, really. I understood that Nancy would be Captain."

"Well, that hasn't worked out. Problems at home ... you know."

Primrose raised her eyebrows and blinked rapidly. "I'm having difficulty taking this in. This is the last thing I expected you to say."

"Great news, isn't it?" Robina was smiling broadly now.

Primrose looked troubled. "But Barbara is next in line. Surely, she should be Captain if Nancy can't take it on?"

"Barbara has to look after Percy. You know he's got Alzheimer's. It's getting much worse." Robina was tired of repeating the same story, and wary of giving the true reasons to Primrose whom she knew less well than any of the others. "So, it's over to you, my dear. You've won the popularity contest."

"Hah," an involuntary laugh escaped from Primrose. Having allowed her mirth to show, she couldn't help letting out several peals of laughter, throwing her head back with apparent amusement.

"You're happy, Primrose?" Robina needed confirmation.

"Well, I'm happy that you've asked me. It's what I've wanted ever since I joined this club. But, it's not going to work." Primrose threw her chin out and looked up at the ceiling. "Why does everything come right for me when it's too late?"

Robina looked puzzled. "How do you mean too late?"

"I'm not going to be here."

"You're not going to be here?" Robina repeated, her voice intoning a question.

"'Fraid not."

"Wh ... where are you going to be?"

"Hopefully, Australia."

"Australia?"

"Well, you know we've been trying to move house. Right? And everything we looked at turned to dust. And we couldn't get a buyer for our house." Primrose sighed. "And, then things became difficult in South Africa. Marius's father doesn't want to continue in the business much longer, and his brothers haven't got his commitment ... they want Marius back to sort things out. So, Marius has decided to go back for, probably six months, to deal with that. I'll carry on here. In the meantime, we'll put the business here up for sale. It seems the economy is going well this year. With the election coming up, the government will want to keep it what way. If we drop the price on our house and take the best offer we can get for the business, we can be up and away, before the end of the year, with enough money to start again." Primrose ran out of breath, but quickly continued. "Now, while we're still young enough."

"Why would you want to go to Australia?"

"There's no class structure. If you work hard, you can only be successful. Health care is free. Nobody judges you by your background. Australians are open and welcoming. We've given ten years to this country and we're still outsiders, Robina. It's time to move on."

Robina slumped back in her chair. "What am I going to do?"

"Do?" Primrose repeated the question.

"And Madeleine, too." Robina stared at the ceiling with her mouth slightly open.

"Madeleine?" queried Primrose.

"Oh, never mind." Robina regained her composure. "I certainly wish you well, Primrose. We'll miss you."

"That's nice to hear," Primrose answered, wishing it were true.

"So, thanks for waiting around." Robina smiled, her statement indicating that their session was concluded. Primrose didn't quite smile, her mouth moved into the beginnings of a pleasant expression but she pressed her lips together, holding back her emotions. Without another word, she picked up her crocodile skin handbag, a Christmas gift from her mother in South Africa, and moved quietly out into the corridor towards the exit door and the welcome relief of fresh air.

Robina felt tears prick her eyes; she had been charged with the responsibility of positioning the office bearers for the year ahead but was now faced with the daunting task of reporting back to the Past Captains that each approach had met with failure. "...what could I have done differently ...," she wondered, "...I did my best ... it's not my fault that three people turned down the Captaincy ... who could have predicted that ... what on earth are we going to do ... we must have a Captain ... someone has to do it ... not me ... I stepped in when we lost Lynn ... it'll have to be someone else ... perhaps we were foolish not to have Nancy and Barbara ... in fact, in hindsight ... yes ... hindsight's a wonderful thing ... we were just too fussy ... if we had just stuck with Nancy and Barbara ... we wouldn't have a problem ..." Robina's eyes wandered over the desk, locking on to the vision of the date and walnut cake. A thrill of delight surged through her; she put forward her hand to bring the plate closer; her fingers shook slightly as she grasped the cake tenderly; she smiled as she observed her teeth marks on the butter icing, still there from her earlier first bite; opening her jaws wide, she coaxed a large portion into her mouth. "Mmmmmmm," she groaned with pleasure. Within sixty seconds, only crumbs remained. "Oh, that was good," she whispered to herself.

Sitting motionless, staring at the snow scene on the calendar on the wall, a dark shape emerged into the corner of her eye. Startled, Robina looked to her right to find Cathy standing there. "Oh, it's you, Cathy. You startled me. I forgot you were still here."

Cathy glided in to sit on the chair opposite Robina. "So, how did it go?" The strangulated quality of her voice was evident, although her voice was soft and low.

Glad she had finished the cake without being disturbed, after a few seconds pause, Robina answered, "Dreadful." The word escaped from her with a huge mournful sigh.

"Oh?" Cathy enquired.

Robina noticed that Cathy was wearing a dark business suit. The material looked like polyester, but was well tailored with a nipped waist and a zip front. "...she must be cold in that ... looks such a thin fabric ... perhaps she's got a warm coat ... even so...," her thoughts were wandering.

"Robina?" Cathy's voice penetrated.

"Oh, Cathy, what a disaster," she confessed.

"Why, what have you done?" Cathy's eyes glittered accusingly.

"Well, it's not my fault. I can't help it if everyone refuses."

"Everyone? What are you talking about?"

"Madeleine. She was our choice at the meeting, remember? She can't do it because ... because of Adam's work. Alice won't do it because Don has just retired. Primrose can't do it because they're moving away. We can't fall back on Nancy or Barbara ... that would be such a humiliation. Anyway, I think Barbara will leave the club and ..."

"That's no loss, in my opinion," Cathy cut in.

"So, Cathy, what do I do now?"

"What you should have done at the outset. You should have consulted. I was out there. You could have called me in to discuss it." Cathy spoke briskly.

"I ... I forgot you were there."

"You couldn't even have phoned one of the Past Captains?"

"Whheeww ... I did think about it, but I felt I had to plow on. After all, who else is there?"

"We'll have to fall back on one of the Past Captains. The way we did with you when Lynn died."

"Yes, of course." Robina brightened up, her shoulders relaxing. "You ... Cathy, you were a very efficient Captain. You're the Immediate Past Captain. It's obvious. This is a crisis. We need you to step in."

"No thanks."

"Just like that." Anger kindled in Robina's heart. "You can't just abandon this problem. It's as much yours as mine. We all have a duty to keep the Ladies' Section going. All the Past Captains have a responsibility."

Cathy looked down at the floor. Keeping her face impassive, she murmured, "You see, my life is changing. I've made some decisions."

Silence filled the room. Cathy waited for Robina to speak. Robina wondered whether to say anything. Eventually, Cathy was forced to continue. "I'm going back to nursing."

Robina said nothing at first, her head was buzzing with the confusion of the day. After a few moments, she reacted. "Nursing? Why ever would you do that? I thought your driving school was doing well."

"It is, actually ... but going back to nursing gives me a roof over my head at the hospital."

"What? Which hospital? Why can't you travel there every day?"

"Because I'm leaving my marriage. It was a mistake. I never loved him. Anyway, he's such a louse. The police are investigating him and I don't want to be around."

"Rodney under investigation by the police? Whatever for?"

"Who knows? I don't know what he gets up to. But I don't want to be there when he's arrested. If I get out now, with any luck, I'll have no ties to him when the time comes."

"Goodness, Cathy, this is quite a shock. You must have been through a really difficult time, recently."

Cathy sighed, "Yes, well, you just cope as best you can." Her voice, shrill and sharp, held back the mountain of sobs she needed to release.

"If there's anything I can do ..." Robina's voice trailed off, knowing how feeble her offer of help must sound. They sat in silence, both lost in drifting thoughts. Eventually, Robina offered, "Do you want to talk about it?"

"No ... no ... just let me sort myself out." Cathy struggled with the packet of tissues on the desk. She blew her nose gently. Her muffled voice continued, "I must go ... things to do."

Robina moved across to the other side of the desk. Putting an arm round the dejected figure, she offered, "Can I walk you to your car?"

"I'll be fine." Cathy's bent figure moved towards the door, her hand still holding the tissue to her face.

"Are you sure you're OK to drive?"

"I'm fine, Robina. Just fine." Impatient to get away, Cathy's voice flattened. Blowing her nose loudly, she walked uncertainly along the corridor in search of the exit door.

Standing watching her, Robina felt worried. "... goodness, what a situation ... leaving Rodney ... you don't think about other people's marriages ... whether there's love or not ... you just assume ... police investigation ... wonder what on earth he's done ... she must have some suspicions ... can't imagine what she's going through ... mind you, she'll cope ... she's a survivor ... she should be OK." As Cathy disappeared from view, a huge swell of heat enveloped Robina, bursting at the base of her throat, flashing to the back of her neck, traveling down her shoulders, settling in the middle of her back. "... that damn HRT ... problems with it ... problems without it ... time to go home ... what a relief today is over ... don't know what we're going to do about this situation ... have to phone everyone ... all the Past Captains ... what a chore ... we should all be in email contact ... must suggest that ... don't know why we haven't done that before ... what a powwow we're going to have ... expect there'll be disapproval of how I handled things ... no-one will say outright ... there'll just be tiny comments ... much worse ... won't get the chance to explain ... have to insist that I get some time on the agenda ... outline how things came about ... whheeww ... time to go home ..." A headache started low in her forehead, the pain moving quickly to settle behind her eyes.

As Robina turned back towards the accounts office, Anastasia came into view. Robina froze in her tracks, unable to take in all the detail of her appearance, as daylight was beginning to fade; her eyes, however were attracted to Anastasia's shoulder over which hung a handbag; snakeskin, burgundy in color, soft contours forming an ample pouch, dangling from double silver chains, a motif of intertwined snakes with jeweled eyes adorning the clasp. "Oh, Anastasia. It's you," she uttered lamely. Receiving no answer, she commented, "What a fascinating handbag. I've never seen anything like it."

"Oh, some designer thing." Anastasia's monotone reply was accompanied by a dismissive wave of her hand. Robina's eyes were glued to the handbag, as she wondered who the designer was and how much it cost. "How was your day?" Anastasia's accent was alluring, but always managed to put Robina on alert.

Tearing her attention away from the intertwined snakes, Robina answered, "Yes, OK."

"You have been here a very long time. It is almost dark, already."

"Yes. We've been appointing the new Captain."

"And?"

"And, it's been difficult."

"Difficult?"

"Well, we don't have anyone."

"How can this be?"

"Well, as you know, we don't feel the time is right for Nancy and Barbara. We wanted Madeleine, but she turned us down. I asked Alice, but she won't do it. I tried Primrose, and she can't accept. And Cathy won't step in like I did."

"What is all this about?"

"Well, you know that Colin has disappeared and you're aware of Percy's Alzheimer's. Adam's job makes things difficult, Don has just retired, Marius has to go to South Africa to sort out some business and … Rodney is … well, that's another story."

"So, really, men are the problem." An expression of contempt settled on Anastasia's features.

THE ANNOUNCEMENT

January proved to be a surprisingly dry month in Hampshire. Each morning, the sky was streaked with pink and yellow as dawn greeted another day. Each evening, orange tints glowed as the sun slid slowly to its resting place. Birdsong demanded attention morning and evening, as increased daylight filled tree dwellers with excitement at the prospect of spring. Each day, the clouds managed to squeeze only a few drops of drizzle during the afternoon. Today, however, was different. Perhaps we would get winter, after all. Today, the north wind was blowing. Specks of icy drizzle stung the skin early in the morning. By afternoon, gigantic splashes of sleet were spattering down, leaving slush on every surface.

Car doors slammed. Ladies ran from their cars, clothes flapping as gusts of wind challenged their meticulous appearance. Judging by so many parked cars it looked like being a record turnout for the Annual Meeting. The high attendance could be attributed to a significant level of curiosity regarding the question of Captain for the year ahead.

As the ladies gathered in the coffee lounge of Middle Wallop Golf Club, lots of comments could be overheard. "...I'm going to bring this up under any other business ... it's ridiculous we don't know ... who can it possibly be ... it's not right that we have all this secrecy ... why don't they just come out and tell us ... it wasn't like this in my day ... things have gone to the dogs ..."

Empty coffee cups gave evidence that the Annual Meting was about to start. Ladies looked at their watches, noting to each other that the appointed hour was due. Groups of bodies drifted from the carpeted lounge onto the polished wood floor of the meeting room. Gradually, the knots of seated ladies spread out to fill the rows of chairs. Latecomers herded together at the back, turning their heads each time the double doors opened, pulling a grimace of kinship with the latest arrivals.

A glass chinked at the top table to signal that the meeting was about to start. Members gave their complete attention to the proceedings. Before long, a restlessness rustled through the room. Little attention was paid to the minutes of last year's meeting or the list of prize-winners throughout the year. Whispered conversations started to break out, suppressed by a skinny new member hissing, "Sssshhh ... she's going to announce the committee ... wonder who'll be Captain."

Alert now to the proceedings at the top table, all ears strained to hear every syllable, "... and it gives me great pleasure to announce your committee for the year ahead. We're sorry that family considerations prevent Nancy and Barbara from taking up their posts and our thoughts are with them at this difficult time. The Past Captains are acutely aware that we need a Captain who can command respect, not only within the club but to represent us at other clubs throughout the district. It gives me great pleasure to announce who will lead you forward in the year ahead. This lady has been a member of the club for many years. She has been a prize winner on numerous occasions. She has served on the committee and has our full support. We know that you will also give your full support to your new Captain. Your Captain for the year is Stella Hudson. Stella, would you like to join me at the top table. I'm delighted to perform the duty of investing you with the badge of Lady Captain." A figure rose from the front row to stand facing the membership.

Agitation gripped the room. Questions with few answers buzzed around. "... who ... Stella who ... never heard of her ... where did she come from ... never seen her before ... she looks OK ... what age do you think she is ... maybe it's a good thing ... she used to play a lot ... went back to work ... normally only plays on Saturdays ... that's why few people know her ... really surprised about Nancy and Barbara ... how's this Stella person going to be Captain if she works ... oh, she's working part time now ... oh well ... that's the excitement over ... better go over and congratulate her ... there must be a few noses out of joint ..."

The hum of voices could be heard outside the meeting room. Well groomed heads gathered in little groups to comment on the news. No-one wanted to leave. Everyone wanted to learn more about Stella Hudson and to speculate how she might handle being Captain. Gradually, the little groups ran out of steam. Eyes roved the room. The excited tone of voices dropped to a softer level. Necks craned to look for familiar faces with whom to spend a pleasant hour, eager to sit in the comfort of the coffee lounge.

"Ladies!" A male voice boomed out. The chatter ceased immediately. A uniformed police officer stepped into the meeting room and closed the door behind him. "Ladies, could I have your attention, please." The room became completely silent. "We are investigating an incident and believe that many ladies here could help us with our enquiries. We have a team of investigating officers located in the coffee lounge. We expect we may delay your departure by perhaps one hour. If anyone has a pressing engagement, please come and see me now."

A bewildered muttering gained momentum, until a voice rang out from the middle of the room. "Officer, could you tell us what kind of incident delays our departure. I mean, if someone's car has been broken into, I don't see why we all have to be questioned."

"I regret, Madam, that a body has been found on the golf course."

INVESTIGATION

"So, let's summarize," commented Detective Inspector Norton. "You've done good work collecting information on members of Middle Wallop Golf club. Let's see if it leads anywhere," he continued, while moving towards the white board on the wall of his office. Two junior officers looked on, with rapt attention. "It's not clear if a crime has been committed until the cause of death has been established, but we have …," the inspector started writing names on the board, as he spoke, "… Madeleine Minehead, born in Belgium, an experienced lawyer, victim of rape by Colin Ruff. Adam Minehead, born in Germany, chairman of an oil company, travels constantly, hot tempered reputation. Next … Nancy Ruff, husband absconded and wanted for rape … she's having an affair … correction … got a two-timing boyfriend living with her … young Darren Swift, the golf pro, who keeps company with young thugs in the area, and is reputed to have given a kicking to Rodney Crow. Rodney Crow, source of income unknown, takes regular trips to France, accusations of obscene phone calls. Cathy Crow, driving instructor, walked out on her marriage and returned to nursing. Anastasia Mironov, proprietor of the golf club, originally from Russia, assumed to be widowed in recent years, reputed to be having some kind of relationship with Rodney Crow. Barry Harper, also widowed, wife died in a fire last year, business not doing well. Hugo Restler, another one with business problems, just had his name cleared after an investigation at his bank, hasn't returned to work, recently changed his will. Robina Restler, also changed her will recently, a sudden drop in popularity in connection with appointing a new captain at the golf club. Hey … there's a lot of names here. Help me out, lads, who else have we got?"

"Well, there's Primrose. Pretty little thing," volunteered the young detective sergeant, conscious of a shaving rash prickling his sallow skin.

"This is not a beauty pageant," responded Detective Inspector Norton, although he couldn't help smiling. "What's her last name?" he wanted to know.

"Pretoris … no Pretorius … that's it … from South Africa. British passport, husband Marius has a South African passport and he's a heavy drinker. They have three young kids. In the process of selling up to go back to South Africa."

"Who else?"

"Alice and Don Tolkein. Wife recently bought him a motorbike as a retirement gift ... he's been driving without a license. Funnily enough, she thinks she saw Rodney Crow on a motorbike, recently."

"Wonder if ...," interjected the junior detective constable, a rosy glow showing on his smooth, pale complexion.

"And the Blunts," interrupted the detective sergeant, jostling for position with his boss. "He's in the diamond trade, first name Percy, recently diagnosed with Alzheimer's, wife's name Barbara ... she took over the business, daughter emigrated to Canada."

"Is there a common thread?" Detective Inspector Norton whirled round to face his two assistants.

The junior officer started, "Well ... there's the golf club, of course. They're all members. But more than that. I discovered from Alice Tolkein that there's been a bit of trouble over appointing a new captain. Lots of noses out of joint. Some who thought they should be captain. Others turned it down. It seems to me ..."

"Of course, I didn't interview her," interrupted his superior officer, the prickle on his shaving rash intensifying, as he blotted out the competition for Detective Inspector Norton's attention, "but she does seem to talk a lot, so no difficulty in getting information out of her, is there?"

"If you say so, sir." The junior officer backed off.

"So cause of death unknown, at this stage." Detective Inspector Norton turned back to face the board which was now scrawled with a list of names. "We await the results of the autopsy from the coroner."

"And the body, yet to be identified," the newest recruit added, trying to regain some authority.

"Didn't you know?" Detective Inspector Norton's brow furrowed, as his eyes moved across the two faces, resting with a faint air of surprise on the newly promoted detective sergeant.

"Oh, yes, just came in," was the reaction from the object of Inspector Norton's gaze. "Discovered on the golf course, as you know, on the day of the Annual Meeting. The body has been identified as that of Barbara Blunt."

VERDICT

Hampshire coroner, David Caldwell, gulped a last mouthful of lukewarm coffee, gathered his papers together, and slowly made his way into the courtroom; his left knee, damaged by a fall many years ago, was stiff and painful this afternoon; he realized he was almost limping, and struggled to keep his balance as he took his seat. Glancing up, he noted two police officers, one newspaper reporter and a few members of the public eyeing him with mild interest.

Summing up the evidence, which had been presented in the morning session, the coroner lost no time. "I am satisfied that the deceased, Barbara Blunt, did not intend to kill herself. The deceased took actions under the influence of drugs and alcohol. There is no doubt in my mind that drugs and alcohol were likely to have affected her mood and judgment. The post mortem examination has found the cause of death to be exposure to adverse weather conditions when her state of mind was affected by alcohol, prescription drugs and confusion due to her personal situation. I would not declare this death as a suicide because of the influence of alcohol and drugs. There is not enough evidence to show that the deceased killed herself or had an accident through misadventure. The verdict is that the deceased died of exposure, under the influence of drugs and alcohol."

Clearing his throat, the coroner continued, "It is a tragedy that this woman ended her life in this way. It has become apparent that she was suffering great strain in dealing with her husband's illness which also caused her to take on considerable business responsibilities. The tragic consequences will be her husband's battle with a debilitating illness, without the love and support of his wife, and her daughter's dilemma of whether to dramatically change her circumstances in order to care for her father. It is particularly tragic that the deceased, who was well known in her community, seems to have received no support or understanding in dealing with her difficulties. It is a sad indictment of our society that a respectable woman, with many acquaintances and associations in the district, died alone and friendless in her time of great need."

EPILOGUE

Four years later, the effects of the worldwide financial crisis during 2008 were felt in every corner of the globe. Retirement portfolios plummeted and home values sank. The banking sector crashed and retailers went bankrupt. Golf clubs were affected by a drop in membership and an increase in maintenance costs. Relationships and circumstances at Middle Wallop Golf Club had moved on. Madeleine and Adam Minehead were fortunate to sell their country cottage at the top of the market; they moved back to London with their dog, Rex, and no longer play golf; their plan to do voluntary work in Asia did not succeed because Adam was diagnosed with diabetes; they joined a church and are now active in Habitat for Humanity, a charity which deals with homelessness throughout the world. Hugo Restler accepted early retirement from the bank, departing with a significant payout; he now operates a successful business as an independent financial advisor. Robina's life is unchanged, apart from more regular visits from her family who rely on her generosity to fund school fees and vacations. Cathy Crow's return to nursing was welcomed by the community; she divorced Rodney and, two years later, married a heart specialist. Rodney Crow was convicted and sentenced to ten years in prison for possession of cocaine, with intent to supply and import drugs. Anastasia Mironov surprised the neighborhood by selling the golf club to an adjacent hotel, prior to Rodney's arrest; she disappeared from Hampshire, and is reputed to be living somewhere in Eastern Europe. Colin Ruff has never been traced, although there are occasional reported sightings. Nancy Ruff became Captain of Middle Wallop Golf Club in 2006 and, in the following year, increased the revenue of the caravan site through referrals from Darren Swift, the golf professional, who matured considerably after his marriage to the young barmaid at the local pub. Percy Blunt lives in an assisted living community dedicated to Alzheimer's patients; his condition has stabilized and there is hope of new drugs on the horizon; his daughter continues to live in Canada. Primrose and Marius Pretorius returned to South Africa for three years and recently moved, with their extended family, to Australia. Barry Harper sold his printing business and is currently living with Martha Donovan, who relinquished her role as his counselor. Don and Alice Tolkein retired from the garden center and opened a motorbike store; within a year, Barry Harper became a partner and expanded the business into the supply of parts for classic cars. Barbara Blunt's ashes were scattered around the azaleas at the entrance to Middle Wallop Golf Club.

ABOUT THE AUTHOR

The author was born, educated and married in Scotland where she spent half her life; she now lives, with her husband, in Europe and the United States.

9 780982 454107